CIRCLE DANCE

Library of Congress Control Number 2004101987

I.S.B.N. 1-932455-07-8

First published in 2004 by:
Cosmos Publishing Co., Inc.
P.O. Box 2252
River Vale, NJ 07675
Phone: 201-664-3494
Fax: 201-664-3402
E-mail: info@greeceinprint.com
Website: www.greeceinprint.com

Printed in Greece

LYNNE CONSTANTINE
VALERIE CONSTANTINE

CIRCLE DANCE

Anne Constantine

Valerie Constantine

COSMOS PUBLISHING

Acknowledgements

If it were possible to achieve one's goals alone, it would be a lonely journey indeed. During the long days and hours we spent on this project, we were assisted and supported by so many incredible friends and colleagues.

First to our wonderful publisher. It has been a pleasure working with Cosmos' excellent team of editors and staff. Their guidance, insights, and advice have been invaluable.

To our mother, Ginny, and our aunt, Ann Graff, thank you for your surpassing generosity in the cheerful willingness to read, re-read and read again a work in progress.

To our brother, Michael Constantine. Your knowledge and expertise as a builder allowed us to authenticate the plot. Thank you for putting everything aside to help us.

To our good friend, Dr. Peter Sitaras, thanks for your patience and graciousness in simplifying for us the complex world of science and medicine. Any technical blunders are solely our doing.

Our appreciation to our attorney Nina Graybill for her sound counsel, advice and friendship.

We are forever grateful to an entire cheering section of family and friends who rooted for us along the way: Adam, David, Christopher, Drew, Stanley and Lynn, Honey and Valerie, Dorothy and Richard, Terry, Sean, Trevor and Becky, Lisa, Traci, Lizzie and Jennifer.

And of course a most special thanks to our husbands, Colin and Rick, whose faith and belief in our abilities have been constant and enduring.

And finally, gratitude to the Supreme author, without whom, nothing would be possible.

To Gus and Ginny, who taught us to treasure and cherish family.

PROLOGUE

BALTIMORE - AUGUST

The three women seated in the front pew of the Annunciation Cathedral were dressed in black. They sat in silence as the chanter's hypnotic singing droned on. From the huge pipe organ came the somber strains of a Byzantine melody that sounded vaguely familiar.

"*Kyrie Eleison, Kyrie Eleison*," the toneless chanting continued. In automatic response, the women crossed themselves.

The air was heavily mingled with the sweet scent of carnations and the burning sting of incense. Rays of sunlight, muted by the tall stained glass windows, cast uneven shadows on the walls of the church.

Ushers in dark suits quietly led the mourners to their seats as the church continued to fill. Theodora sat next to her mother Eleni and her sister Nicole. The air was making her sick. She found her mother's and sister's hands and squeezed them gently, as much to steady herself as to comfort them. The three continued to stare straight ahead at the altar, upon which sat a shiny black casket.

The Greek Orthodox priest appeared from behind the lattice-carved wooden screen dressed in his vestments, and, carrying a large gold-encrusted Bible, turned to face the congregation. Theodora closed her eyes and took a deep breath, willing herself to remain composed. She still couldn't believe he was dead. So much had happened in one short year. She closed her eyes and thought back to that perfect last summer in Ikaria.

ONE YEAR EARLIER

Chapter 1

IKARIA, GREECE - JUNE

*T*he morning sun ascended the sky over the dazzling blue Aegean Sea. The gaily-painted fishing boats had gone out hours ago before dawn, while the rest of the island was still asleep. Now the beach was crowded, echoing with laughter and animated conversations in rapid fire Greek.

Theodora raised herself on one elbow and surveyed the scene. It was her last day on the island, and even mundane details seemed precious. She smiled, listening to some grandmothers clucking their tongues disapprovingly as they watched their children's children display their bare bodies. The self-consciousness and poor body image so common in America were strikingly absent here. She turned to make a remark to her sister, but Nicole had just vacated her beach towel to plunge into the water.

Theo watched her sister swim out into the cobalt sea. The small dot that was her head moved steadily away, then disappeared. Suddenly Theodora rose in alarm. What was Nicole thinking? She was too far out. In rising panic Theo ran over to a group of young men and grabbed Stavros' hand.

"Look!" She pointed toward the raft bobbing up and down about a hundred yards off shore. "You've got to go get her. Hurry!"

By now several of the boys had come over to see what the commotion was about. Stavros shrugged his shoulders lazily and smiled at the distraught young woman with undisguised admiration. She was a real beauty, he thought. That long chestnut hair, brown eyes, generous smile - and a round figure that would give a guy something to hold on to. "Don't worry pretty girl," he said in Greek, "Nicole's all right. She's a swimmer."

"Yeah, don't worry," piped in another. "Your sister's a little dare-devil."

It was true, Theodora thought, calming down a bit. Nicole was a risk-taker who thrived on adventure. Her fierce independence was something Theodora both envied and admired.

Stavros pointed. "Here she comes now."

Theodora turned toward the water to see the tall, slender figure emerge and thought for the thousandth time how she would love to have those narrow hips instead of her hourglass figure.

"Water's magnificent!" Nicole grabbed a towel and blotted the dripping water from her shiny black hair, and an admiring whistle rang out from somewhere.

"What?" she said, taking the towel away from her head, and gave the little group surrounding her a puzzled look.

Stavros yanked the towel from her hand playfully. "Your little sister here was worried about you. Thought you might drown," he said.

Theodora, relieved, sat down on the rocky beach. "You scared me half to death. You know how rough the water can get here. It's risky to go out so far."

"Seems pretty minor next to the chance you're getting ready to take," she laughed, only half joking. Theodora was to be married in the fall.

"Only you," Theodora said with good humor, "would consider marriage to be a dangerous undertaking."

Theodora's words were truer than Nicole wanted to admit, and she turned quickly to Stavros to avoid the serious turn the conversation might take. Putting on a Greek accent, she said, "Stavros, Theo's getting married when we get back to the States. Why don't you and I run off and elope, and then I can stay here forever."

Stavros' hearty laughter rose over the squeals of children prancing in the surf. They had played together as children every summer on this very beach, and he remembered the young Nicole, always mischievous and as elusive as the island's lacy white butterflies that alight just a brief and beautiful moment on their chosen flower.

"Sure, we'll have lots of babies and you'll grow to be big and fat. But I'll still love you when you're my little plumpling." He spread his arms wide and laughed, dodging the towel that Nicole snapped in the direction of his backside. In mock terror, he ran to the water and jumped in.

Nicole lay down on the beach next to her sister, happy to have a chance to collect her thoughts. Her teasing exchange with Theo about the impending wedding had interrupted her mood. Nicole's ordinarily clear and logical thoughts became disordered when she contemplated Theodora's fiancé, Stewart Elliot. He was a complicated mixture, all right. There was no question that the suave man Theodora was about to marry could be charming, but there was something about him that nagged forebodingly at Nicole, something unsettling that she could neither explain nor identify with certainty. Sometimes she even questioned this feeling, attributing it to her innate sense of drama and intrigue.

He had utterly ingratiated himself with Nick, their father, and had been comfortably ensconced in the family contracting business for several years. She hadn't heard any complaints at the office, but then, she was, up to this point, just a part-time employee, a graduate student and the boss's daughter. When she returned to the U.S. at the end of the month, she would assume a full time position at Parsenis Contracting, and then she would be working with Stewart every day. She hoped her reservations would be quashed and the control Stuart sometimes seemed to exert over her sister was merely because he was ten years older than Theodora. Nicole glanced at her sister lying beside her.

Theodora's beautiful face was serene, eyes closed. She was listening to the sound of the sea lapping against the shore. It was their last day on the island, she thought, this glorious place they visited for a month each summer with their grandparents. This ancient land of her ancestors was a part of her soul. It was here, summer after summer, she had indulged in childish romances and heard the melancholy chords of a lone mandolin dancing across the warm night air. It was here that she had tasted life with a sweetness that exploded in her mouth like uncorked champagne, here that she felt at one with herself. And now her marriage next month would mark the end of this era in her life. But there would be other things, good things, she thought. Life was fluid, always moving away from one thing and toward another. It was right that this chapter come to a close. A whirlwind of activity awaited her return, but for now, things were simple and she relished the lazy days which required nothing more than staking out a place on the beach and deciding on that evening's meal.

The sisters had been making this annual pilgrimage to Ikaria since Nicole was ten and Theodora was eight. When they were young, their grandparents' house was bursting with children every summer. But as their cousins had finished school and married, the number of grandchildren Sophia and Andreas brought had dwindled each year until it was only Nicole and Theodora. These had been some of the best times, with just the four of them.

The summers together here had served to forge an even closer bond than already existed between the sisters. Nicole, bold and daring, and Theodora, the younger and more serious of the two, were known by the doting islanders as "the Parsenis girls." As little girls they had explored the far reaches of the island, discovering hidden trails and paths that took them from verdant and lush greenery to the arid, rocky land on the other side of the hills. Together with their friends, they'd ferried to Mykonos and Santorini and Samos, carrying their lunches of hard cheese, crusty bread and bottled water. Their Greek improved each year until they were able to converse easily, even with the old Greeks that spoke in a whir of syllables. The old grocer in *Ayios Kyrikos* always made sure he saved the ripest and juiciest fruits for them, and Ari, the young gentleman who rented motorbikes, never failed to give them the newest and shiniest of the lot.

They passed their last afternoon in languid pleasure, reveling in the soothing warmth of the sun and each other's company. As others began to gather their belongings and pack up for the day they realized it was almost five o'clock.

"I guess we'd better head back to the house and get dressed for tonight. Yiayia and Papou want to be at the restaurant by seven," Nicole reminded Theo.

Soon they were walking up the narrow cobblestone street that led to the small house Sophia had inherited from her mother. The sun beat down on their bare shoulders as they walked on the hot stones. There were no shade trees or gentle breezes to provide relief from the intense heat that enveloped them. Theodora pulled a t-shirt over her head and handed another to her sister.

"Here, put this on before we get back. Papou will have a stroke if he sees us in these suits."

"Keep it," Nicole answered. "I'm going to die from heat exhaustion before we even get there."

"Not to worry. By the time we get to the house there won't be any hot water left and you can take a nice, frigid shower."

"Oh, now that's something to look forward to," Nicole said as they skipped up the stone steps to the house. When they entered the plain interior, the temperature was at least ten degrees lower than outside. The thick white walls kept the fierceness of the late afternoon sun at bay, and the cool tile floors were an invitation to remove their dusty sandals. It was funny, Nicole thought, how much they loved this unimpressive little island house. Back home in the States, her grandparent's beautiful old home in the city and apartment on the beach firmly established the fact that they had attained prosperity and success in their chosen land, but those places, though modern and comfortable, never got under her skin in the way of this simple dwelling by the sea.

By seven o'clock they were dressed and ready for dinner with their grandparents, who awaited them on the tiny stone terrace.

"Theodora, did you wash your hair again? It will all fall out!" her grandmother scolded.

"You know I wash it every day, Yiayia, and it's fine," Theodora answered.

Sophia shook her head and looked at her husband.

"Come my girls, no cross words, it is our last night here. Let us go have a good dinner," Andreas said.

They walked together to the center of town and the island's largest restaurant.

"So, today you say goodbye to all the island boys whose hearts you break?" their grandfather teased. Gnarled fingers raked through the thick white hair in a familiar gesture. Andreas Zaharis was still a virile and imposing figure. The eighty year old family patriarch was every inch the hot-tempered Greek.

"I'm sure they'll get over it," Nicole laughed.

"I don't know about that. Stefano was pretty crushed when you refused to go to the taverna with him last night. He's been moonstruck ever since you got here," Theodora teased.

"Ach, animal. I do not like these wild boys hanging around you. He has hair like a girl," Andreas grumbled. The hawkish nose gave his face an imperious quality that could be intimidating, but Nicole knew his gruff teasing was his way of showing affection. These two girls inhabited a special place in his heart. When he tried to appear angry with them, the coal black eyes always betrayed him.

"Don't worry Papou, I'm saving myself for someone like you," Nicole replied affectionately.

As the lane narrowed, Andreas put his arm around his wife's shoulder and they moved ahead of the girls. They still made a striking couple. Almost eighty, Sophia moved with an inherent elegant grace. Once considered quite beautiful, she was now indistinguishable from her aged contemporaries. The face reflected in the mirror was heavily lined from years of life and laughter but the eyes were still young. Her zest for living, and ability to embrace life fully allowed no room for vanity or regret. She refused to squander her time at the cosmetic counter or the hairstylist and chose plain and unremarkable clothing. She was more concerned with what she had to say than what she had to wear.

Both had been born on this island and together since their marriage at seventeen and twenty. Although they had spent the majority of their lives in America, they still spoke with Greek accents, Sophia's thicker than her husband's. Their marriage was a strong one, and they were fiercely loyal to each other, different sides of the same coin.

The restaurant came into view and at once fragrant smells from the kitchen filled the balmy evening air. Georgios, the owner, stood outside the door.

"*Yasas, elate mesa*, come inside," Georgios called to them as he waved. "Come see what delicious foods we prepare tonight."

They made their way into the kitchen to look at the evening specials. Heavily seasoned souvlaki rotated on a skewer. Mixed salads of onion, plump tomato and feta cheese sat in large wooden bowls. Fresh cleaned fish marinated in pans on the counter next to the huge oven. The smells melded into one mouth-watering aroma that piqued their collective appetites.

Georgios called a waiter over. "Give my good friends a table overlooking the sea," he told the young boy.

The view from the restaurant was magnificent. Bleached white rocks disappeared into the sparkling blue water, and the setting sun cast its amber glow over the calm surface. Theodora looked around as if to memorize every detail.

"*Koukla mou*, soon we will be dancing at your wedding," Sophia said.

Andreas looked at Theodora. "Well, you did not pick a Greek *gambro*, but at least you picked a nice boy, eh?"

"Of course she picked a nice boy, he comes from a good family and is a hard worker," Sophia replied.

An older woman dressed all in black, Andreas's cousin, stopped at their table.

"*Yasas!* I am so sad to think of your leaving tomorrow." Her gray hair was pulled back tightly into a bun and held in place by a black hair net. She had been a widow for fifteen years and adhered to the Greek custom that dictated the perpetual wearing of black.

"Despina, please sit with us," Andreas said as he stood and pulled over a chair from the next table.

"Just for a minute. I must go back and serve dinner. I will come back later with the others and have coffee with you," she said in Greek.

Looking at the girls, she said to Sophia. "Your granddaughters are very beautiful." Turning to the ground she spat twice "Ftew, ftew." The old Greeks believed in the superstition of the evil eye, fearing that harm would befall the person paid a compliment unless it was followed by this ritual.

Despina stood up. "I will see you later."

Georgios approached the table with a carafe of red wine. "Here, my friends, let us have a farewell drink together," he said as he filled their glasses. "*Yasas!* Here is to a safe trip home and a return to our beautiful island next summer."

"Thank you, Georgios," Andreas said.

He raised his glass to his granddaughters.

"To my two precious gems, thanks to God for the joy you bring to our lives. This is the last trip we will have both our granddaughters to ourselves," he toasted, and his eyes shone with restrained tears.

Sophia's face registered surprise at the sentimental toast. He was softening as he grew older. This summer marked an end to a fifteen-year tradition. To Sophia, this was reason enough to be sad, but knowing her husband as she did, she suspected it was more than the maturing of their grandchildren that was disturbing him. Perhaps it was the knowledge that comes to all men and women past their prime, that their time left on earth is coming to an end. This was something she had been thinking about for some time. Somehow, sensing this sudden revelation in her husband was disconcerting. It made the inevitability of their eventual separation more real and frighteningly closer. After sixty years of marriage, the thought of living without her beloved Andreas was intolerable. She felt her chest constrict and had to press her nails sharply into her hands to dull the sudden emotion that flooded her. She turned her attention to her granddaughters and lifted her glass toward Theodora.

"Let us drink to a long happy marriage for our Theodora," she said with forced cheerfulness.

"*Yasas!*" Papou responded, looking gratefully at his wife.

They spent their last evening in Ikaria, laughing and talking late into the night.

Chapter 2

BALTIMORE - AUGUST

*C*aroline Elliott, Stewart's mother, had decided to have the rehearsal dinner at her home. She hadn't felt up to dealing with all the tedious details of using the country club or even hiring a room in a restaurant. She knew that her husband would lend no support and so the arrangements were all handled by Betty, her housekeeper, who had long ago learned that running the Elliott home was something Caroline was only too happy to hand over.

She rose late on Friday, the day of the rehearsal, and came downstairs to a flurry of activity. The florist was delivering huge baskets of white gardenias in full bloom, and their fragrant aroma filled the dining room. Men and women in black uniforms carried trays of delectable food as they set up the chafing dishes that would keep everything warm. Caroline's china and crystal sparkled on the five round tables for eight that had been brought in, and place cards sat in exquisite Limoges holders. She walked toward the kitchen nodding her head almost imperceptibly at the caterer who greeted her from across the long hallway. The noise and confusion were already getting on her fragile nerves, and she lit a cigarette before pouring her first cup of coffee. She wondered how she would make it through the long weekend ahead without being able to retreat to her bedroom and her secret stash of vodka.

"Betty, did you see Dr. Elliott this morning?" Caroline asked.

"No, Mrs. Elliott, he was already gone when I came."

Caroline couldn't remember anything that had happened after eight o'clock last night. Graham had not come home for dinner, which wasn't unusual, and she had started her heavy drinking earlier than usual. An hour after a dinner she barely touched, she passed out on her bed. She wondered if he had made it home at all. Graham and Caroline had maintained separate bedrooms for the last fifteen years. She drew deeply on her cigarette and exhaled slowly, dipping the ash with a perfectly manicured nail. They had come to a tacit agreement years ago that Graham would leave her alone, and she would pretend not to know about his occasional dalliances. In public he was solicitous of her, but in the privacy of their home they rarely spoke. They were simply two people living under the same roof who had long ago ceased to have anything in common.

"Can I get you another cup of coffee, Mrs. Elliott? Perhaps you'd like to sit by the pool and drink it." Betty wanted her out of the way.

"Yes, that would do nicely. When are these people going to be out of here?"

"I imagine they'll be here 'til late afternoon, ma'am."

"Oh God, I don't think I'll be able to endure all this commotion until then. And there's still the party tonight!" She complained.

She walked out onto the flagstone patio shaded by tall oak trees and down the hill to the swimming pool. The white lounge chairs stood out against the shimmering blue-green water. Large navy ceramic pots were filled with ruby red geraniums and trailing vinca. Caroline walked to the far end of the pool and sat down. From her position she could look straight up to the house sitting high on the hill and watch the activity from a safe and quiet distance. Her parents had built the house for Graham and her when they were newlyweds. It was an immense brick and limestone mansion in the Georgian style that had taken over two years to complete. No detail or expense had been spared in the building of the impressive three-story estate. Looking up at the magnificent structure, Caroline thought how many people envied her, and she laughed bitterly to herself.

Her marriage was a sham, and her son had his own life. Nothing was required of her in managing her home, there was ample paid help for that, and so her days were spent in a hazy, alcoholic blur.

She remembered her own wedding preparations so many years ago. How had the time passed so quickly? She no longer bore any resemblance to that hopeful young woman desperate to leave a household full of quiet strife. Graham's manner had been refreshingly genuine. She had grown tired of the young men in her circle with their prep school accents and identical personalities. Graham had passion and purpose. She admired his zeal for life and desire to help others. He would be her ticket out of the emotional coma she had endured her entire life. How was she to know it would prove to be impossible to shed her upbringing? What a cliché she had become.

The arrival of their son both exhilarated and terrified her. She didn't know how to be a mother. With little familial support she quickly became overwhelmed and depressed. All of Graham's time was spent at the hospital, and Caroline was left alone to ponder her inadequacies. She finally gave in to her mother's insistence that she hire a nanny, and it wasn't long before she turned to her mother's favorite pastime and began to find her comfort in the bottle.

She reached for her coffee cup with a shaking hand and it fell to the ground, shattering into jagged pieces. She stood, staring at the broken china for several moments before going back to the house. The French doors leading from the kitchen to the patio were propped open for the caterers, and Caroline walked over to Betty who was directing the flow.

"There's a broken cup on the deck. See that it's taken care of."

"Certainly, I'll send someone right down," Betty replied.

"I'm going to my room. I don't want to be disturbed." She walked away without a backward glance.

Her bedroom was her haven. She opened the drawer of the night table next to her bed and pulled out a small silver flask, took a long swallow, then rested her head on the pillow. She continued her maudlin reminiscing. Her only passion was her son Stewart on whom she had always doted. Feelings of resentment and jealousy welled up inside her as she reflected on his decision to marry Theodora. She hadn't been alarmed when he brought her around the first time. She was used to beautiful women flocking to her son. She never bothered to remember their names because he always tired of them after a few months. In retrospect, she saw that Theodora was unlike any of the other girls. She was more naive, less worldly and she looked up to Stewart.

Caroline suddenly realized that the look of admiration in Theodora's eyes mirrored her own. Perhaps, she thought, that's part of the attraction - he thinks she will always idolize him. Caroline knew better. There was a time when she had seen that same look of awe in her husband's eyes, but it wasn't long before it was replaced by blankness. How could the same person who once made you feel like the center of the universe suddenly make you feel invisible? It had been that way her whole life. She was never quite special enough. Until Stewart. The look of adoration on his face when she entered a room was unlike anything she had ever known. The one thing of which she was certain was his abiding love for her. She took a long drag on her cigarette. Her love for him was the only thing that had sustained her through the years. If only that had been enough. No matter how great her love, it hadn't been enough to stop her from drinking or from raising him at an emotional distance. Somewhere between feeling and expression, the sentiment was lost. What did they say about the road to hell? She supposed hers was paved with endless good intentions leading nowhere. She took another long swallow. Soon she was in blessed numbness, and the hours passed without her awareness.

A steady, light tapping on the door awakened her. "Caroline, are you up?" Graham never entered her room without an invitation.

She was confused, not knowing if it was morning or night, and turned to look at the clock. Four thirty. Then she remembered. They had to be at the church by six for the rehearsal. She had less than an hour to pull herself together.

"Yes, I'm up. I'll be ready to leave in an hour."

"Caroline, may I come in?"

She quickly glanced at the bedside table to see that her flask was out of sight. "Yes, come in Graham," she answered with annoyance.

He opened the door and came just a few feet into the bedroom. "Have you bothered to check what's going on downstairs?"

"Why, is something wrong?"

"No, everything looks fine, but this is a big night for Stewart. Couldn't you at least have kept an eye on things for God's sake?"

She had meant to rest for only an hour. She rubbed her temples.

"Really Graham, Betty and the rest of them are perfectly capable of taking care of everything. Besides, we certainly haven't any need to impress the Parsenis clan. Now leave me alone so I can get dressed."

He looked at her in disgust, shook his head, and left the room without reply. Why hadn't he left her years ago? Because you liked her money, he reminded himself. It hadn't started that way. He admired her in the beginning. She was everything he had ever aspired to be. Ah, the romantic notions of the young. He was going to show her how to enjoy life, real life, outside the safe confines of her secluded and privileged world. She would smooth his rough edges and together they would have it all. How soon she had tired of his rawness and he of her refinement. Articulating his feelings in an impassioned manner was commonplace to him but completely alien to her. He never knew what she was feeling. Her reaction was always the same, impassivity, regardless of whether it was in response to misfortune or joy.

Their differences were evident early on. He had chosen to ignore them and concentrate instead on his career and his image. He couldn't deny that he had loved living in this house at a time when his colleagues were still struggling to pay rent. Nothing to be done about it now. He was too old to start over.

The first of the bridal party to arrive were Theodora's Uncle Stephan and Aunt Effie. Stephan, solidly built and plain looking, was the only son of Andreas and Sophia Zaharis. His fifty-one year old wife was a statuesque blonde who retained the striking face and body that had attracted him thirty-three years ago during a summer holiday on the island of Rhodes.

"Stephan, grab that little package in the back for Theodora," Effie said as she closed the car door.

He picked up the gaily wrapped jewelry box and thought how typically thoughtful it was of her to do something extra for one of their nieces. There was a real bond between Theodora and Nicole and his wife.

"What did you get for her?" he asked as they started up the long set of steps to the Elliott house.

"Just a gold bracelet for her 'something new'."

"Welcome, come in, come in," Graham Elliott greeted them at the door. "You're the first ones here."

"Hello, Dr. Elliott," Effie said as Stephan shook his outstretched hand. "What a perfect evening for this celebration."

"Please call me Graham." He was instantly charmed by her alluring accent and bearing and allowed himself a moment of envy as he looked at Stephan.

Theodora and Stewart came up the steps behind them.

"Well, here's the couple of the hour," he said, looking past Stephan and Effie.

With his arm around Theodora's waist, Stewart was a striking complement to her. His six-foot frame was tanned and athletic, and his face had the finely chiseled curves and angles of Michelangelo's David. A stray lock of blonde hair brushed his forehead and his crystal blue eyes were startling in their clarity. A ready smile revealed even, white teeth that looked almost too perfect.

"Hey, Dad, point me to the nearest drink. That's one long ceremony I just ran through," said Stewart.

"Don't let it get you down, dear," Effie teased him, "You only have to do it once."

As they entered the large central hallway, Caroline appeared looking drawn and distracted. Her blonde hair was pulled back into a French knot and the belted, blue silk dress accentuated her extreme thinness.

"Stewart, darling," she gushed, as she embraced her son and merely nodded to her other guests. "You look so handsome tonight."

She linked her arm in his as she led him to the bar. After an uncomfortable moment, the others joined them. As the rest of the party began drifting in, the sounds of conversation and laughter filled the house. Theodora's parents, Nick and Eleni Parsenis moved from one group to another, making sure they took the time to greet everyone. They were completely at ease with each other after thirty-five years of marriage. Nick was not a tall man, but his firm build and confident air made him a presence in any room. He exuded a charm and vigor that drew people to him.

Eleni looked up and smiled as their son Paul walked over.

"Well, the big day's almost here. How're you two holding up?" he asked smiling. Paul, the oldest of their three children, was a combination of the best of Nick and Eleni. He had his mother's warmth and his father's quick wit and charisma. Close, deep set eyes and a slightly crooked nose made up a face unremarkable save for the stunning smile that transformed it.

"I've got so much on my mind about tomorrow that I almost wish it were over. I don't remember my wedding being this much work," Eleni said

"Well no wonder," Nick laughed, "We were only engaged for two months. You've been planning this for almost a year and you've spent more money than we knew existed when we got married." He put his arm around her waist, and in automatic response Eleni bent slightly to the other side in an attempt to minimize the surplus flesh around her middle. After years of battling her weight, she'd finally resigned herself to those extra twenty pounds.

"Are you talking about money again, Nick?" Eve quipped as she and her husband Dimitri came up to the threesome. Eleni's sister Eve had an easy relationship with Nick. The two couples were fond of each other and spent much of their free time together. When their children were small, they never missed a summer at the beach, the two sisters going ahead with Yiayia and the children, and the men joining them on weekends. Eve's dry sense of humor and cutting wit were the perfect foil for Eleni's gentle and kind nature. Her reserved demeanor had caused those who knew her to react to her marriage with surprise. Dimitri, a hefty man in his early sixties, would have made the perfect "Zorba."

"This is quite a house," Dimitri commented. "Takes big bucks to keep a place like this running."

"It's magnificent, isn't it? Have you been here before?" Eve asked her sister.

"You remember, Caroline invited me to lunch after Stewart and Theodora became engaged. You should've seen the Christmas tree, at least thirty feet high. The whole place looked like Martha Stewart."

"That's right. If I remember correctly, you ranked the afternoon right above a visit to the dentist," Eve laughed.

"I just love it when Eve's claws come out," Dimitri said playfully.

A waiter approached to let them know dinner would be served.

"You all go ahead. I'll refill this drink and be right in. Anyone else need anything?" asked Dimitri, who enjoyed his whiskey.

"No thanks, we're okay." Eve rolled her eyes at Eleni. "He's in heaven. Two parties right in a row. By Sunday he'll be exhausted."

"He's such fun, always the life of the party," Eleni said as they walked into the dining room.

"Oh sure, but he pays for it the next morning."

Eve always complained, but Dimitris' ability to let go and jump in with both feet was what had fascinated her about him. She looked over at him and winked as he came into the room with his drink freshened. Under the buzz of conversation came the soothing sounds of a four-piece string ensemble. As Dimitri approached, Eleni turned to the Elliotts.

"Graham, Caroline, I'm not sure which of the family you've met. I think you know Theodora's grandparents," she said nodding to Sophia and Andreas. "Have you met all of Theodora's aunts and uncles?"

"I've had a great time wandering around introducing myself to everybody," Graham said. "Now, don't give me a test on how everyone's related, but I think I have the names down."

"There certainly are quite a lot of you," Caroline added.

"You haven't seen anything. Wait 'til the wedding tomorrow," Dimitri gave Eleni a conspiratorial look.

"I'm positively trembling with anticipation," Caroline said.

Graham attempted to soften his wife's rudeness. "Caroline's a little overwhelmed," he said. "I'm an only child and she has just one brother. We're not used to such a big family. I'm a little envious, actually. It must be wonderful to have so many relatives."

"What is wonderful is that we care about each other," Andreas said pointedly. "That is what family is all about. I am surrounded by my children and grandchildren, and they are here to share my Theodora's happiness. God blessed me when he gave me Sophia. I am a lucky man." Andreas smiled at Nicole seated beside him and placed his hand upon hers.

"You are a lucky man, Mr. Zaharis," Graham said. "It's a rare thing to see a family so close."

It was a rare thing, Nicole thought, and she sometimes took it for granted. It was clear from her brief exposure to Stewart's family that his familial experience was vastly different. Nicole's anxiety about this marriage was heightened when she met Caroline. Theodora had her work cut out for her with that one. Her attention was drawn to Graham as he rose from the seat next to her. Despite the receding hairline and the extra weight around his middle, he was still attractive, she thought. Nicole found him warm and sincere and was hopeful that in him, Theodora would find a strong ally. He cleared his throat and raised a glass.

"I'd like to welcome all of you on this happy occasion and present a toast to the bride and groom. Theodora, I couldn't have asked for a more wonderful daughter-in-law, and I welcome you into the Elliott family with open arms. I know my son will be happy with you by his side. You're both very lucky. And Stewart, although it would have been my dream for you to be a part of my practice, in Nick Parsenis you will have not only a terrific father-in-law, but a great boss."

Theodora felt Stewart tense beside her at his father's words. Her hand reached out to his under the table, and she gave it a gentle squeeze. Why was it so difficult for parents to let go of their expectations? And why did it seem impossible for children to rid themselves of the feeling that they could never measure up? Stewart had left the East coast after college and gone to Stanford for his MBA. It was shortly after his return to Baltimore that he had met Nick Parsenis at a building seminar. Nick's vigor and drive fascinated Stewart, and he sought the older man at every break in the sessions. Nick became his mentor and Stewart an avid and dedicated student, with the result that he was now an entrenched member of Parsenis Contracting. His father's pleasure at his return to Baltimore, however, was tempered by the nagging disappointment that he had not followed him into the halls of medicine.

At the sound of glasses tapping, Theodora's father was on his feet.

"Thank you for your gracious words, Graham. The way I feel about Stewart is no secret. He's become a valued part of my company and I'm happy that now he'll also be part of the family." He turned to look at his daughter and Stewart. "You kids have everything going for you. Here's to a marriage filled with health, happiness and prosperity." He took a sip and put down his glass. "Now let's have some dinner and then we'll teach you some genuine Greek dancing."

Nick sat down and turned to Stewart.

"You do know that you'll lead the first circle dance at the reception, don't you?"

"I've been completely and expertly trained by Theodora. No one will suspect I'm not Greek. I even have my handkerchief pressed and ready," and he took it from his pocket and waved it in the air.

"He's asked the ushers to break plates on the floor while he's dancing," Theodora teased.

"Really, Theodora, that isn't funny. We're not in some Ionian village for heaven's sake," Eleni said.

"Mother, I'm only kidding - just a little ethnic humor."

She found it amusing that some traditions were completely acceptable, while others were strictly forbidden. Crashing pottery would horrify her mother, just as she would never permit those little lace doilies on the arms of her furniture. She wondered if there were some Hellenic Emily Post to whom all their mothers referred about just how Greek they should be.

"Theodora, dear," Caroline asked, "Stewart's father and I don't have to do one of those little native dances, do we?"

"My dear lady," her grandfather said to Caroline, "You will not want to stop the Greek dance, you will see. You will cry when the music stops. Come," and he took her arm and pulled her from the table, "I will teach you now."

Caroline looked stricken as she stood rigidly next to Andreas in the middle of the floor.

"Pavlo," Andreas yelled to his grandson Paul, "start the music." And soon the sounds of the rhythmic bouzoukis and mandolins poured into the room.

Andreas held firmly to Caroline's hand. "See, it is not so hard. Watch my feet and follow me."

In the next few moments the entire party was on its feet and a part of the line that wound snake-like around the tables. Those who didn't know the steps danced with the most enthusiasm, their feet tripping over each other as they tried to learn. That's the way it always was, Theodora thought. Once they started they didn't want to stop.

Caroline was surprised to discover she was enjoying herself. As the tempo increased, the sea of laughing faces became a happy blur. Their merriment was infectious, and it felt good to lose herself in the moment. No wonder Stewart spends so much time with them, she thought, they are everything we're not. But her elation quickly disappeared, swallowed up by the old fear that rose within her. She was about to lose the one person she truly loved.

Chapter 3

*T*he music swelled as the chords changed to herald the entrance
of the bride. The white figure filled the frame of the narthex,
and there was an audible gasp as Theodora made her entrance. She
was stunning, Stewart thought as he stood waiting at the altar. He
had known Theodora would look beautiful, but she took his breath
away.

Nicole's gaze swept across the church, filled to overflowing and
bathed in white roses and baby's breath. The magnificent stained glass
windows shed multi-colored facets of light throughout the church,
intensifying the grandeur of gold candelabra and icons. She glanced
down at the white crowns waiting to be placed on the heads of the
bride and groom and was struck again by the ritual of the Greek
Orthodox wedding ceremony. She looked at her sister, staring so intently at the priest, taking in his every word, and Nicole said her own
silent prayer that Theodora would find the happiness she sought with
this man.

The priest nodded at Paul, signifying that it was time for the rings,
and taking them, made the sign of the cross on the foreheads of Stewart
and Theodora. This was performed three times in the name of the
Father, the Son and the Holy Spirit. He then handed the rings to Paul
who stood before the couple and placed the gold rings on their fingers. While the priest chanted a prayer, the rings were interchanged

three times on their fingers. The crowns were then placed on their heads and also interchanged three times.

Sophia dabbed at her eyes with a corner of the lace handkerchief she held in her hand. She looked away from her granddaughter and remembered her own wedding sixty years ago. The small village church had been packed with all those who lived on the island. Her mother had spent months working on the hand-made dress Sophia would wear. She had been just a child, she thought, with no idea of the magnitude of the vows she was taking. It seemed that only a moment in time had elapsed and yet she sat here where her children had been baptized and married. Now it was their turn. How did the years disappear without her noticing? Soon she and Andreas would be gone, a memory to their children, as her parents now were to her.

Sophia had never seen her mother again after she and Andreas had come to America, and she felt the loss deeply through the years. There was no mother to go to when she was unsure of herself, when she needed comforting or support. So many times she felt hopelessly ill equipped and had longed for the relationship that exists only between a mother and daughter. She felt Andreas move next to her and smiled as he covered her hand with his.

Across the aisle Caroline was trying hard to focus but the figures at the altar looked blurred and distant. She grudgingly admitted that Theodora was one of the most beautiful brides she had ever seen. The ceremony seemed interminable though, and she looked down at the program in her lap to determine if it was almost over. Sighing quietly, she tried to concentrate on the scene before her. They look like actors in a Roman play with those crowns on their heads, she thought. It had bothered her that Stewart agreed to be married in the Greek Orthodox instead of the Episcopal Church, but no matter how hard she tried to dissuade him, he remained firm. The final insult had been his decision to convert to Orthodoxy a few months before the wedding. She looked at Graham beside her and was frustrated by the rapturous smile on his face. He'd never had any reservations about Theodora and made it plain from the beginning that he approved of

Stewart's choice. How like him, she thought. He wouldn't listen to any criticism from her, didn't care really, how she felt. When had that happened? On her wedding day hadn't she been as radiant and excited as Theodora was today and hadn't Graham looked at her with adoration in his eyes? What existed between them now could not even be considered friendship. She saw Stewart's wholehearted embrace of Theodora's family and faith as a desertion, a desertion that didn't seem to alarm Graham in the least. The prospect of losing her son to this large and animated family terrified and angered her. I will not cry, she thought, and squeezed her eyes tightly against the hot tears ready to spill over.

The ceremony reached its conclusion with the circling of the altar table. The newlyweds, with Nicole and Paul, followed the priest around the table three times to signify their vow to forever preserve the marriage bond. This was the first time during the entire ceremony that Theodora and Stewart faced the congregation. The beaming couple stood for a moment and then, arm in arm, descended the platform with a light and joyous step.

It was all a blur to Theodora, a warm smile here, a familiar pair of eyes there, the row upon row of faces both disjointed and merging together at the same time. Stewart put his arm around her waist, drawing her closer to him as they reached the back of the church, and she was filled with such an exquisite sense of happiness and contentment she thought she might burst. He leaned down to kiss her lips when they stopped, but they were quickly pulled apart by parents and members of the bridal party eager to embrace and congratulate them. Theodora had no idea how long they stood in the receiving line, greeting guest after guest, but she never tired of hearing the same congratulatory words or the usual expressions of love and best wishes; each one further reinforced the fact that she and Stewart were married, that their future was together. By the time the last guest came through the line, her face hurt from smiling but her spirit was soaring.

"Boy, that one's a cold fish," a guest remarked to her sister-in-law, after shaking Caroline Elliott's hand and reaching the end of the receiving line.

"I hear she's an alcoholic," said the other.

"All that money and a doctor for a husband." She shook her head. "You'd think she'd be able to control herself. What does she have to drink about, anyway?"

"You know how some of these Americans are. Emotionless. They keep it all inside. I bet Eleni just adores her," the woman said sarcastically.

"Well, Theodora married into a good family, and that's what counts. If the mother-in-law isn't the greatest, she'll just have to put up with it. We sure had our share with the dragon," came the reply.

They both made a face at the memory of the mother-in-law they had shared, a demanding, complaining widow who never got enough from her sons, no matter how hard they tried.

"What did you think of Eleni's dress?" The subject of Caroline Elliott being exhausted, the women moved on to a dissection of the bridal party's attire and coiffures.

"Never mind Eleni. Did you see Effie in that God-awful spangled thing she can't breathe in? I'll never understand why Stephan had to pick a wife in Greece. What's wrong with the Greek women here?"

"You can bet he's spent years regretting it," said her sister-in-law. "She sure learned fast, with all her expensive clothes and jewelry and that Vera St. Dougdale as her interior decorator."

The two elegantly dressed women walked out into the glaring sunlight of the church courtyard where the four hundred guests noisily milled about. Only the young and very old indicated this might be an ethnic gathering. The teenagers with their shiny black hair, dark brown eyes and olive skin looked as if they could be brothers and sisters.

At the other end of the spectrum were a few, a very few, of the remaining old guard; those who had left Greece in their twenties and come to America with their husbands to start a new life. They spoke broken English and looked the way one expected grandmothers to. The large group in between, however, this first generation of sons and daughters, was without question mainstream America. Although they clung to their heritage, did in fact consider it their identity, they had already blended into white, Protestant America. There was hardly a dark head of hair to be seen. Frosting and blonde streaks reflected the rays of the late afternoon sun. The dress was elegant and understated, adorned by just a few good pieces of jewelry. Only because it was August and over ninety degrees, were their luxurious furs not in evidence.

The men, all in black tie with hair turning a distinguished silver, looked comfortably at ease. They had graduated from the row houses of their immigrant parents and worked hard to become doctors, judges and business owners. They had given their wives and children the American dream and were fiercely protective and proud of the positions they had attained.

Amid showers of confetti, the bride and groom entered the waiting limousine and sped off to the reception. "Well Mrs. Elliott, you've made me the happiest man in the world." Stewart said.

"Mrs. Elliott! Doesn't sound like it's me you're talking about." She leaned over and kissed him. "I hope I always make you the happiest man in the world."

Chapter 4

*T*he dazzling ballroom of the Hyatt Regency was resplendent with white orchids and candlelight. Lush mounds of fresh tropical fruit were piled high on tables amid the huge assortment of tempting hors d'oeuvres. It was impossible to walk more than a few inches without being met by one of the myriad waiters carrying trays of appetizers.

The bridal party was sequestered with the photographer in a separate room and their guests mingled in noisy prelude. These people had known each other all their lives, had celebrated each other's births and weddings and mourned in loss together. But tonight the mood was festive, and the party spirit infectious. In this close knit community, the grandeur of Theodora Parsenis' wedding would now be included in future discussions of noteworthy occasions. In small clusters, one by one, the guests seated themselves. The music stopped, and as if on cue, conversation dropped to a low murmur.

"And now, for the first time as husband and wife... Mr. and Mrs. Stewart Elliott," a voice boomed over the microphone as the band played a drum roll. When they walked into the room, the crowd stood up to clap and cheer. They were led to the center of the ballroom, and the band played "Unforgettable," the song the couple had chosen for their first dance. Halfway through the song the rest of the bridal party was invited onto the dance floor and the festivities began.

On either side of the dance floor and directly in front of the head table, the immediate family members were seated. The Parsenis table included Eleni and Nick, Eve and Dimitri, Stephan and Effie, and Andreas and Sophia. Convention dictated that the priest be seated at their table, so the addition of Father Vasilios and his wife Esther made the group a little crowded. The spirited talk went back and forth between English and Greek as they recounted stories from their own wedding days. They joked about their innocence and how little they knew when they got married.

"Poor Mom and Dad," Eleni laughed. "They barely knew each other before their wedding."

"That is the good way," Sophia said. "What do young people know about choosing a husband and wife? No, it is much better when the parents decide. They know better."

"I can just imagine who you would have picked for me, Mom," Eve said, "I'll take marrying for love anytime."

"You can learn to love anyone," Sophia insisted, "But if you have your head in the clouds, you make foolish decisions."

"Ach, you have really hurt me," Dimitri teased his mother-in-law. "And here I thought you approved of me all these years."

"Dimitri *mou*, my daughter made a good match, but that is only because she was lucky to have a very smart mother to learn from."

Everyone laughed at Sophia's deft refusal to admit that the old way wasn't necessarily the only way.

"One thing is true," Andreas said, "In our day, when you got married, you stayed married. None of this divorce nonsense!"

"Well Papa, that's because you all came here and left your in-laws in Greece," Eve teased.

Sophia cleared her throat, a sure sign of a coming pronouncement. "You can joke all you wish but I will tell you something. One of the reasons our marriages last is because we are all Greek. Our friendships go back so many generations, and we share friends and relatives we have known all our lives. We share a faith and customs and food and you know, all of you, that I could go on and on about all that we have in common. Having things in common, that is a very important part of success in marriage because the more alike you are, the more you can share, the stronger the bond will grow."

There was an uncomfortable silence until Eleni spoke what most of them were thinking.

"What you say might be true Mom, but look at our kids. Most of them are marrying non-Greeks, and that doesn't mean they can't be happy."

"Of course it does not mean that," Sophia quickly replied, "I am only saying that the more a couple's background is the same, the better they can understand each other. What I am saying, my dear, is that your Papa and I know each other's history inside and out, and that joins us together in a way that would be impossible otherwise. You know what I am talking about - you have the very same thing with Nicko and so do all of you. Why your children have chosen to go in another direction, I do not know, and I hope they will choose wisely and be happy, but I do know they will never have our deep connection."

"Come now," Dimitri jumped in, "We're talking about kids who are American, not Greek. Of course they can have the same bond - they grew up in the same country just as you and Andreas did."

"Dimitri, my boy, you can never shake off your heritage whether it is Greek, Irish, Italian or whatever." Sophia, in her maturity and wisdom, knew that all living beings are inexorably tied to their history. No one exists on only one plane or has roots in only the here and now. The past follows us, is inextricably woven into the fabric of our being until even we no longer recognize the diverse and infinite facets that have come to make up who we are.

They were interrupted by the sound of tapping spoons against glasses, a signal for the bride and groom to kiss.

"Where in heaven's name did this stupid custom start?" Eve asked in irritation.

The American band, who had been playing soft background music throughout dinner, was replaced by the Greek band as the meal ended. The two groups had been hired to alternate throughout the evening. The beginning of the Greek music signaled the leading of the first circle dance by Theodora and Stewart, and they were on the dance floor after just a few bars. In quick succession the bridal party added themselves to the line, followed by the rest of the family.

"*Yasou, koukla mou,*" Andreas yelled to his granddaughter as she once again took the lead.

"Come on, Papou. You lead now." Theodora motioned to him.

The dance floor was never empty, and everyone was surprised when it was time to cut the cake and throw the bouquet. Paul came up behind Nicole and rested his hand on her bare, suntanned shoulder. "Here's your chance, little sister. You could be next."

She wrinkled her nose and gave him a long look.

"I'm quite happy solo, thank you very much. Besides, I hate that gaggle of females squealing and elbowing each other trying to catch the stupid thing."

It wasn't altogether true that Nicole had little desire to follow her sister's footsteps down the aisle to the marriage altar. She did, in fact, feel a bit left out, like an outsider among her married friends, and she hated the idea that her relationship with Theodora was now forever changed. It wasn't just the two of them any longer, no more talks long into the night. Theodora would reserve her first loyalty and confidence for her husband, and although Nicole knew that was right, it didn't make her any less jealous that her sister's attention would be so divided. She wasn't sure she believed she would ever find the man who could inspire her to make that commitment, but weddings have a way of making those who are unattached feel somehow unsuccessful and less than whole. That fact, however, was less on her mind than the echoes of a conversation she'd overheard earlier in the evening. Stewart was huddled at the bar, his arm draped lazily around the shoulder of his best man, Todd Davies, a fraternity brother with whom he had shared countless late nights partying, and the two men were feeling no pain. So engrossed were they in their conversation that they didn't notice Nicole behind them.

"You always were a lucky s.o.b. Should have known you'd go out in style. She's gorgeous." Todd's words were slurred and laden with spittle.

"She's top drawer alright. I'm nuts about her." Stewart grinned broadly. "And it doesn't hurt that her old man's the boss."

They collapsed with laughter into each other's arms and Nicole, white with anger, watched Todd repeatedly pat Stewart on the back as if in congratulations. She quickly walked away, not wanting to hear any more than she already had, wondering if perhaps she was taking too seriously something she hoped was said in jest. Maybe Stewart was trying to be the big man on campus again, reminding his friend that he had it all: a beautiful wife who was crazy about him and a rich father-in-law welcoming him into the family business to sweeten the deal. Stewart's behavior, his tipsiness, his spoiled and immature ranting, disturbed and troubled her, but what troubled her more was how charming and endearing he could be one moment and how utterly caddish the next. How would you ever keep your balance with a man like this, she wondered.

She looked around the large ballroom and saw her father lead Theodora to the dance floor for their last dance. The circle of guests surrounding father and daughter entertained the private thoughts and memories evoked by this sentimental custom. Nicole's eyes filled with tears as she imagined the bittersweet mixture of emotions her father must be feeling.

"I love you, baby. I'm really going to miss you," he whispered in Theodora's ear as they danced. She was so young, he thought as he held her tighter, still a child. But then, wasn't he just as young when he and Eleni married?

Theodora felt a thickness in her throat "I love you too, Dad." She pulled away slightly and looked up at him.

"I'm happy Dad, and excited, but a little scared. I want it to be like you and Mom and Yiayia and Papou. Do you think it will be?"

He looked into her questioning brown eyes and was flooded with a fiercely protective love for this youngest child of his, squeezing her hand more tightly in his own. He wished he could assure her of a future secure in happiness and contentment, that he could wave a magic wand and guarantee nothing would ever hurt her.

"More than anything that's what I want for you sweetheart, a lifetime of happiness." Stewart was a fine young man, he thought, and he silently reassured himself that her future was in loving and careful hands.

She put her head on his shoulder, and he felt an intense and momentary sadness as they slowly waltzed across the shiny wood floor. And then it was over. Stewart was at her side and people were hugging and kissing them goodbye. They walked hand in hand to the elevator that would take them to their suite for the night.

"Do you feel any different?" Theodora asked Stewart.

"Not really, why?"

"I feel like I'm pretending. It doesn't seem real."

"I think we can change that in just a few minutes," he said, putting his arm around her waist and pulling her to him.

The elevator doors opened and they turned down the hallway leading to their room. Stewart unlocked the door and Theodora stood there.

"Aren't you going to carry me in?" She smiled.

"I'm going to carry you right to the bed, my dear, and not let you up 'til it's time to board that ship in the morning."

Chapter 5

SEPTEMBER

*T*heodora looked over the morning paper, finished her English muffin and gulped down the last sip of coffee. She and Stewart were still trying to get used to being back after the long, warm days at sea with the sun on their shoulders and the fresh salt air filling their nostrils. She glanced up at the clock on the kitchen wall. It was just six thirty, but Stewart had already gone an hour ago. If she left now, she should miss traffic on 695 and be in Annapolis by seven thirty. She cleared the table of breakfast dishes, picked up her bag and briefcase and headed to the front door, making a mental checklist of all she needed to accomplish. She had only been back at campaign headquarters a few days, and the work was still piled high from her absence. The big fund-raising dinner was just a few weeks away, and there were countless phone calls to make and details to work out.

She enjoyed the long drive to work in the morning. It gave her time to think and slowly change gears. The true test would come this winter when snow and ice would make driving conditions treacherous and traffic abominable, but right now the weather was beautiful and she drank in the scenery. The landscape changed dramatically from Baltimore County to Anne Arundel County and Annapolis. The land became flat, with more wide-open spaces and water almost everywhere. Small creeks meandered through neighborhoods and emptied into the large Severn River and Chesapeake Bay. Long wooden piers jutted out from private waterfront homes dotting the shoreline, and all manner of sail and motorboats bobbed merrily in their slips like colorful toys. She never tired of the scene when she pulled into downtown Annapolis. The historic City Dock was alive with people and activity, and there were always a few Naval Academy middies wandering around in their crisp, white uniforms.

She turned onto Duke of Gloucester Street and searched in vain for a parking spot, finally pulling into a public lot. The building which served as campaign headquarters for Peter Demetrios was a narrow, three-story house built in the early 1900's. Its grand old interior had high ceilings and beautiful, carved moldings covered with layer after layer of paint accumulated over years of numerous owners. Theodora often envisioned how the house might look with the right hands to restore it to its former grace and beauty.

The front door was unlocked, and she knew that if anyone was in at this hour, it would be Michael Pendleton.

"Morning, Michael. You're here bright and early." She paused for a moment in the office doorway of Peter's chief of staff and campaign manager.

"Look who's talking," he replied with a smile, "I didn't think newlyweds got out of bed this early."

"What can I say? True dedication to the cause," she said over her shoulder and walked down the hallway to her office.

He was glad she was back. Theodora's was a calming and soothing presence in a hectic, fast-paced environment. She had that most uncommon trait of grace under pressure and was able to extend, almost as if by osmosis, a quiet confidence to her co-workers. As the November election for senator grew nearer and the pace and workload intensified, Theodora's competence and efficiency took a tremendous load off him. He looked around his office at the stacks of mail, press releases, campaign photographs, and voter lists and thought wryly that politics was the last place he would have imagined himself when he was in law school. He had joined the Annapolis law firm of Morton, Dunlap & Demetrios right after his graduation from Harvard at twenty-five and had been with the firm for the last six years. Tall and clean-cut, with black, curly hair and lively blue eyes, he was a warm, good-natured man. When Peter decided to run for the U.S. Senate, the natural choice for his right-hand man had been Michael. Their relationship was easy and comfortable, with a mutual respect and regard. As the months of hard work were drawing to a close, Michael realized how disappointed he would be if they didn't win in November. But there were more pressing things to think about now, and he buzzed Theodora's office.

"Theo, when you have time this morning, can we go over some details on the fund-raising dinner?" he asked.

"You're reading my mind again, Pendleton. I've been gathering up a whole pile of stuff to go over with you. How's right now, while it's still nice and quiet?"

"Perfect."

She quickly checked her voice mail then grabbed a handful of folders. The offices were empty, but it wouldn't be long before volunteers would line up at the desks in the front room. The thought of the largest fund-raiser of the campaign filled her with anticipation and excitement for more reasons than one. For Peter and the rest of the staff it would be one of the highlights of the last eight months, but she also had a personal reason. She was hoping that when Nicole and Michael met they would see how perfect they were for each other. After working so closely with him all these months, she had come to greatly admire him. He was very much his own man, secure in who he was and because of that, accepting of others. His easy-going, cheerful nature and natural sense of humor would make him the perfect partner for Nicole. Her whole family planned to attend, and Theodora was careful not to mention Michael to her sister. She knew Nicole's reaction would be to ignore him if she thought she was being set up, so she kept her mouth shut and hoped for the best.

Michael looked up and smiled at her as she came into his office. She looked tired to him, but he supposed she hadn't yet hit her stride after the wedding and honeymoon.

"Let's sit at the table in the corner. I think it's the only surface in the room with a few inches of uncovered space."

"This is starting to look like my brother's bedroom when he was a kid," she said.

"Isn't this where I say, it may look disorganized, but I know where everything is?" He laughed.

"Yeah, that's your line. Here," she handed him some paperwork, "Take a look at these publicity spots and tell me what you think."

He quickly scanned the sheets. "Looks good. How about the news-papers? Are they up to speed on what's going on?"

"They have the press releases, which they'll run next week, and we have coverage promised on the eleven o'clock news from all three T.V. stations," she said

"Good. Looks like everything's on target there." He leaned back in his chair. "How 'bout the fat cat reception before the dinner? Do we have a number on that yet?" This was a select and private recep-tion to be held in a suite of the hotel before the dinner itself. The gathering was for the largest contributors, those who felt their sizable contributions merited more time and attention from the candidate.

"Should be about eighty," Theodora said. "We have the final list and, so far, everyone invited has said yes."

"Okay, great. Peter should be in around ten and then he has an appearance in Silver Spring scheduled for four o'clock. We'll be able to sit down with him for at least an hour sometime through the day."

They sat that way for another half hour. When Theodora got up to leave, the outside offices bustled with activity. She had been so focused she hadn't heard anyone come in. With characteristic warmth, she stopped at every few desks, chatting with volunteers, inquiring about their children and answering questions. Her interest and en-thusiasm made her a popular figure at headquarters and it took her a while to get through the room and back to her own office. The light on her phone had three lines blinking when she sat down at her desk, and she knew there would be no let-up until the day was over. She quickly took care of each one and then dialed her sister.

"Hi, sis. How are you doing?" Nicole's voice came on the line.

"I'm up to my neck with this thing at the Marriott next week. I just wanted to make sure you have it on your calendar. You are coming, aren't you?" Theodora asked.

"I think this will be the fifth time I've told you I'll be there. Does that count for yes?"

"I am getting a little obsessive, aren't I?"

"Just a little. Anyone interesting going to be there?"

"You'll just have to wait and see. Gotta run."

"Okay. Talk to you later," Nicole said.

Theodora picked up the phone again, but before she could dial out, Peter Demetrios stuck his head in the doorway.

"You look awfully busy this morning. Any fires I need to know about?" he asked.

"No, so far everything's on schedule. Are you all set for this afternoon?"

"Michael just briefed me. He said he wanted the three of us to get together today. How about doing it over lunch, my treat."

"That sounds great. What time?"

"Oh, about twelve thirty. We'll walk over to the deli," he said and tapped the doorframe as he walked away.

She watched his figure recede and thought once again what a good senator he would make. He was scrupulously fair, and his idealism was mixed with a healthy sense of reality. His years as a litigator had given him an appreciation of both sides of an issue, and he remained open-minded until all the facts were presented. She had been impressed with him the first time he guest-lectured at her university, and when he had announced his candidacy, she had been quick to offer herself as a campaign worker. Peter was a tireless, dynamic campaigner and the experience had been demanding, exhilarating, fascinating and exhausting, but one she wouldn't have traded. She saw first-hand the political groupies and hangers-on, women who wanted to be near perceived power, and she respected Peter's graceful, yet distant handling of them. His outgoing personality and charm attracted people to him. At first glance, his light coloring belied his Greek heritage, but his dark, expressive eyes were undoubtedly Mediterranean.

Having lived in Annapolis all his life, Peter was not a part of the Greek community in Baltimore, and so a part of Theodora's job had been to woo the support of his fellow countrymen. She had begun with an introduction to her father, who took an immediate liking to Peter and become his entree into that group. Peter now had wide reaching support from the Baltimore region and they would be well represented at the dinner. Her work on the fund-raiser was reaching crescendo proportions, her day racing away from her with non-stop telephone calls and interruptions, and she could hardly believe it when she looked at her watch and saw that it was already five thirty. If she finished up what still had to be done, she could be on her way by six. She wanted to get home before Stewart, and if she hurried, she'd have time to freshen up and have a tidy little dinner waiting for him to boot.

Stewart's car was parked in the garage when she pulled in. Damn, he had beaten her. There was music coming from the bedroom and he was just getting out of the shower as she entered the room. Beads of water glistened on his muscular tanned chest, and a blue towel was wrapped around his waist.

"You look nice and cool, and pretty appetizing, too," she said and went over to give him a kiss. "I'll grab a quick shower, and then we can have a drink before dinner."

"I wish I could, sweetie, but I have a meeting tonight." He saw her expression change and said quickly, "How about a rain check tomorrow night? I promise to be home early."

"Sure, tomorrow. Who's your meeting with?"

"A new HVAC sub-contractor who's been trying to get Parsenis' business for years. I think I can save the company a lot of money on heating and air."

Theodora sat on the bed and watched him knot a yellow and blue paisley tie in the mirror. "Do you think you'll be late? I'll wait up."

"Don't do that. There's no telling how long I'll be." He turned to face her as he put on his navy blazer. "Do I look business-like enough?"

"You look great." There were times that his startling good looks took her breath away. He was in high spirits and seemed anxious to be on his way. He walked over to the bed and leaned down to kiss her.

"I'm sorry, sweetie, this came up suddenly or I would have called to let you know." He massaged her back. "On second thought, why don't you go ahead and wait up for me." His hand moved to the small of her back and he pulled her body close to his. "And if you do happen to fall asleep, I'll wake you in a most delicious manner."

Mollified, she pushed him away with a smile. "Hurry up and get going so you can hurry and get home."

Stewart gently eased his car out of the driveway and headed down Falls Road toward the city. He was meeting two of the principals of the company at a popular Fells Point restaurant. There was no doubt his father-in-law was a good businessman, but he was living in the past. Old loyalties were costing him money. There was no such thing as friendship in business. Stewart would show them all, including his father.

Chapter 6

*T*he floor was littered with boxes and her bed piled high with clothes as Nicole packed up her childhood bedroom. She had already moved most of her things to her new townhouse, but still had winter clothing and a few odds and ends at her parents'.

"Hi, honey, how're things coming?" her mother came into the room.

"Almost finished. I never realized what a pack rat I am. That whole corner is going to Goodwill."

"You get it from me. I think I still have the dress I wore on my first date!" Eleni laughed.

"Well, now you'll have more room to store all your stuff." Nicole said.

"I'd much rather have you living at home. Why do you want to move downtown all by yourself? At least here you come home to a nice dinner after work and have some company. I don't like the idea of your being all alone with no one to take care of you."

"That's the problem. You took care of us all so well I don't know even know how to sew on a button! You've done everything for me." She smiled as she sat down on the bed next to her mother and put her arm around her shoulder. "It's time for me to be on my own, Mom, as tempting as it is to stay here and be treated like a queen."

"What's wrong with that? Plenty of girls stay home until they get married."

"Who says I'll get married anyway?"

"What are you talking about? Of course you'll get married. Everybody gets married. Why wouldn't you want to get married?"

"I didn't say I don't want to get married, but who knows if I will. Maybe no one will come along."

"Don't be ridiculous. Men are like streetcars; another one comes by every minute. You find someone you want to marry and then you go after him. Don't be a dummy. You have to be bold, even do a little chasing."

"Don't you think things should happen a little more naturally than choosing your target and zeroing in for the kill?"

"Let me tell you something," Eleni said, "When Basil and Connie Patrides were dating thirty years ago, her mother went to his parents after six months and demanded to know what their son's intentions were, because she didn't want her daughter's reputation hurt. A month later they were married. And John Sarnas' mother told him she'd drink poison if he didn't marry Mary. I don't have to tell you how long they've been married."

"I would have handed her the glass. He must have been crazy to believe that."

"People listened to their parents in those days. But I'm with you. He should have told the old bat to go ahead and drink it," Eleni laughed.

"If I recall correctly, you didn't orchestrate Dad's proposal." Nicole said.

Eleni smiled at her daughter. "You're right, but I had a crush on him from the time I was sixteen. Every Sunday my girlfriends and I sat in the front row of the balcony at church. Your father always sat on the other side and boy, it was the highlight of my week, seeing him for that hour and a half." She laughed, a faraway look on her face as she visualized the young Nick sitting across from her.

Nicole knew the rest of the story, but she never tired of hearing her mother tell it. "Go on, what happened next?"

"Oh, you know the rest. He finally noticed me, this 'older' man.

Five years is a big difference when you're sixteen and he's twenty-one. Anyway, I was twenty at the time and working at Hutzler's in the perfume department. One day he just materialized at my counter and I thought I would faint. He must have tested thirty different fragrances. Told me it had to be just the right one because it was for someone very special. I can tell you, I was crushed. Imagine helping the man you've always been crazy about choose perfume for another woman. I wanted to break the bottle he finally chose!"

"You're coming to my favorite part," Nicole said.

"Mine too. The bottle arrived the next day with a note asking me to dinner, and the rest, as they say, is history. Your father has always been a man who knows what he wants and isn't afraid to go after it."

Nicole laughed. "That's an understatement. He proposed after your first date!"

Eleni blushed at the memory. "And I said yes."

"And you call me impulsive," said Nicole.

"He wasn't exactly a stranger. You have to remember, our families had been friends for years." Eleni reminded her.

Things had been so different then, Nicole thought. So many times she and Theodora sat in the kitchen with their mother and Aunt Eve and listened to their stories of growing up. They had socialized only with other families in the community. It was like one large, extended family. Something was always going on through the church. There were dances every other month, elegant affairs in hotel ballrooms with live bands. There were clubs for every segment of the church community: AHEPA for the men, Philoptochos for the ladies, and for the young men and women, the Sons of Pericles, the Daughters of Penelope and the Greek Orthodox Youth of America. These clubs hosted annual national conventions, where groups from surrounding states gathered for weekends of parties and fellowship. Their mother told them that as a young girl she had more evening gowns than everyday dresses.

Nicole had listened to the endless stories and envied parts of that by-gone era. Everyone knew where he or she fit, where they belonged.

They were so innocent. At some point in time they had all dated each other until settling down in marriage. Nicole was always amazed when she heard one of them say, "Oh yes, I used to go out with him, and he also used to date Betty Landros and Penny Constant." None of them married outside of the community, and they still socialized almost exclusively with one another.

Nicole's generation had broken the mold. As her parents' circle grew more affluent, they left their small enclaves in the city and spread out into the suburbs. They exchanged their Sunday mornings in church for a game of golf or relaxing at home. They stayed connected with each other, but their children had meshed into the outside world. Now their parents wondered why these children didn't have the same bonds with one other.

"Mom, I almost forgot, today's Wednesday," Nicole said. "What's the latest news?"

Every Wednesday her mother, her Aunt Eve, and four of their closest friends, Georgia, Tessie, Christina and Froso, met for lunch. These sessions lasted well into the afternoon and were guaranteed to provide all of the most up-to-date news on everything going on in the community. These were women who had known each other all their lives. They knew everything about each other; where the family skeletons were and the tragedies each family had survived. They had shared joy and congratulations at each other's weddings, births and christenings, and had grieved with each other at funerals. They considered few details of their lives too intimate to share.

Eleni smiled, "We do notice everything, don't we?"

"Notice? You give substance to the expression 'Telephone, telegram, tell a Greek'!"

They were both laughing now.

They heard the front door open and Nick call out, "I'm home."

"We're upstairs," Eleni answered.

He came into the room. "Hi, sweetie, how are you?" Eleni said to him as he leaned over to kiss her, then Nicole.

"Great. How're my favorite girls?"

"Good," they answered in unison.

"Nicole, are you staying for dinner?" he asked.

"Sorry Dad, I've gotta run. I've still got tons to do at home." They walked downstairs together and Nicole left.

Eleni turned to Nick. "How about a drink before dinner?"

"Sure. I'm going upstairs to change." He stopped before he was out of the room. "Why don't we eat by the pool and have a nice romantic evening?" he said before climbing the stairs.

As Eleni started cooking she thought how far they had come. There had been some tough times through the years, times when she wondered if they'd make it. But they had, and learned in the process to let go and be thankful for the good times. This was a good time and she was grateful.

Chapter 7

*S*tewart paced the floor waiting for Theodora to get home. She was barely through the door when he began an angry assault.

"What the hell were you doing at the office this late?" His face was crimson.

Theodora was shocked. "What's wrong with you? You know we're getting ready for the big fundraiser next week. I told you I'd be working late."

"It's ten o'clock. No wife of mine is going to be out gallivanting until all hours of the night."

She tried to calm him. "Stewart, we worked 'til nine. You know my drive takes an hour. You work late all the time. I don't understand why you're so upset." She fought back tears.

He relaxed slightly. "I'm sorry Theodora, it's just that I worry about you on those lonely roads in the dark. Anything could happen. Why do you have to work somewhere with such a long commute? If you worked around here we could be together more."

Since returning from their honeymoon, the television had been a better companion than he. Now all of a sudden he wanted to be together? She took a deep breath.

"I love my job. I believe in Peter and what I'm doing is important."

"Peter. If I didn't know better I'd say something was going on between you two," he said spitefully.

"Stewart! How can you say that to me. My God, we just got married."

"What do you expect me to think. You're at the office all kinds of crazy hours, you talk about how wonderful he is all the time. Any man would be suspicious. I won't be made into a laughing stock. If you're too selfish to put your husband before your career, there's nothing I can say. Some wife you're turning out to be." He stormed out of the room.

Theodora dropped her briefcase on the hall table and ran into the bathroom. She shut the door and sank to the floor in tears. How could he speak to her like that? She'd never seen him like this. His cruel words reverberated in her mind and she thought she would be sick. Sobs racked her body and she was too hurt to be angry. Was she being selfish? She thought he was proud that she had a career. They had never argued about it before. She thought about her own parents. Were they happy because of their traditional roles? She wondered how her father would have reacted if Eleni had a job that kept her away from home so much. Things were supposed to be different today though. Men didn't expect their wives to sit at home waiting for them. Or did they? Maybe men really hadn't changed all that much.

A light tap on the door made her look up.

"Sweetheart, open up. I'm sorry. I don't know what got into me."

"Go away!" Theodora said quietly.

"Theo, please. Come out. I feel terrible. Please, please talk to me."

She examined her face in the mirror. Her eyes were red and swollen and her skin blotchy. She didn't want him to see her like this. She wet a towel and pressed it to her face.

"Give me a minute."

When she finally opened the door Stewart pulled her into his arms. She tried to move away from him but he held her tightly. He was crying.

"Baby, I'm so sorry. I didn't mean what I said. Please forgive me. I just get so damn worried about you. You're so beautiful and trusting and men can be such bastards. My imagination got carried away. I can't bear the thought of you with anyone else."

She was still upset. "I'm not with anyone else. What do you want me to do, stay in the house all day?"

"Of course not. Let's just forget it, okay? It's stupid of me, but Bob's wife just left him for another guy and I went nuts thinking about what I would do if that were you. Then when you were so late, my thoughts got away with me. I just love you so much, I couldn't bear to lose you."

Theodora was appeased. She allowed herself to relax in his embrace and was relieved the tension was gone. She couldn't bear the thought of losing him either. Maybe she could try to get home earlier on the nights he wasn't working late. She would make an extra effort to cook his favorite meal and make him feel special.

Chapter 8

*T*he suite of the Annapolis Marriott was filled to capacity by six fifteen. Peter Demetrios was scheduled to arrive at six thirty with his wife Pat and have a quick half hour to circulate before going downstairs to the Grand Ballroom, where the dinner for two hundred and fifty was being held. A half dozen waiters circulated throughout the room. The talk and laughter grew louder as the crowd enjoyed the good food and drink and looked forward to the arrival of the candidate.

Theodora worked the room with Michael, making introductions and thanking people for their support. She was talking with the president of Maryland United Bank when she saw her brother and sister come in. Nicole looked magnificent in a strapless, black crepe dress that clung to her body and stopped just above the knee. Her lustrous black hair was piled on top of her head and the minimal make-up she had expertly applied emphasized a face already beautiful without it. Paul's arm was at her back, gently guiding her as they entered. Nicole scanned the room and smiled when her eyes found Theodora.

"Please excuse us," Theodora said to the group. "Someone's just come in I'd like to introduce to Michael. Thanks for coming tonight." She smiled graciously.

"Come on, it's time for you to meet some of the family. My brother and sister just arrived," she said to Michael and led him over to them.

"Finally! I've been looking for you since this started," Theodora said and hugged them both.

"This is some bash." Paul said looking around. "As usual, the two most gorgeous women in the room are my sisters."

"I have to second that," Michael said, captivated by Nicole's presence.

Theodora made the introductions and said, "Michael worked with Peter at his law firm and came on as his campaign manager."

"This must be pretty exciting for you Michael," Nicole said.

He couldn't remember when a woman had made such a powerful impression on him. It was difficult for him to take his eyes off her.

"It's been so busy for the last year I don't know what I'm feeling half the time," Michael said to her. "Your sister's been a life-saver. She was sorely missed when she went on her honeymoon, and I have reams of paper in my office to prove it."

"Theo is definitely the one to count on when you're in a jam," Nicole said with feeling.

There was a buzz of activity at the door to the suite, and the four of them looked over to see that Peter Demetrios was at last making his entrance. In a moment he vanished in the crush. It was clear from the expression on his face that he loved the limelight. Michael reluctantly excused himself and strode over to his boss' side.

"Well, what do you think of him?" Theodora asked her sister.

"I haven't even met him yet," Nicole said.

Theodora looked puzzled. "What are you talking about?"

"The man just walked in the door and you expect an opinion from me?"

"I'm talking about Michael. How did you like him?"

"Oh, he seems nice enough," she said distractedly.

Theodora hid her disappointment. She had seen Michael's face when he met Nicole, and there was no mistaking the attraction. She was sure once Nicole spent some time talking to him she would return his interest.

It suddenly occurred to Theodora that Stewart hadn't come in with her family.

"Where's Stewart?" she asked her sister.

"He called about a half hour before I was leaving and said he had some work to finish up, so he'd get here on his own rather than make us late."

Nicole didn't know what could be so important that he would let it interfere with Theodora's big night, and she could see from her sister's expression that she wondered the same thing.

"Theo, is everything all right?" she asked.

"Yeah, everything's okay, he's just working a lot lately. I never realized what a slave-driver Dad is."

"I didn't have any trouble getting here on time." As soon as the words were out of her mouth Nicole regretted them. "I guess this project is taking more of his time than he figured," she said, trying to recover.

"Don't let it upset you, he'll be here soon. Why don't you take us over and introduce us to the big guy?" Paul said to Theodora.

But Peter and his wife, along with Michael, were already moving in their direction. Peter put his arm around Theodora's shoulder and gave her a friendly squeeze.

"You've done a wonderful job," he said with appreciation. "I don't know what we would do without you."

"I've loved every minute of it." She smiled. "Peter, this is my brother Paul and my sister Nicole," and turning to them, added, "and this is Peter's wife Pat."

"I can certainly see the family resemblance," Peter said. "It's a pleasure to meet you both." His eyes rested a few seconds longer on Nicole.

"Hello," was the simple response from his wife. She was a quiet woman and it was plain to see she was uncomfortable in this large gathering with so much attention lavished upon her. The months of campaigning had been difficult for her, and she had refrained from attending as many political functions as her husband's office would have liked.

"I can't tell you how much I appreciate your support here tonight," Peter said to the group.

"It feels good to be able to back someone whose values you believe in," said Nicole, "And judging from most of the people I've talked to around town, this is going to be a landslide victory."

Peter laughed. "I like your attitude. Have you given any thought to volunteering? We can always use that kind of enthusiasm, can't we Michael?"

"Just say the word and I'll put you right to work," Michael said, and was surprised to realize this wasn't just idle chatter; he was hoping she would volunteer.

"Sounds exciting." Nicole turned to Pat. "I imagine the next two months will be a whirlwind for you."

"I'll be happy when November comes and we can try to settle back into some sort of normal routine again," she said, looking at her husband.

Nicole felt a sudden pang of sympathy for her. It was painfully obvious that while Peter loved the attention and interaction with people, Pat only endured it for his sake. Nicole had the urge to rescue her, to somehow make her feel more comfortable and enjoy the evening.

"Yes, that seems to be a very common feeling among the families of those running for office. It's always a little frightening to be in uncharted waters," Nicole said.

Pat softened and relaxed a bit. "I suppose one of the hardest parts is constantly meeting new people. Peter's a natural, but I've never been very good at that."

"I do think it's something you probably get better at as time goes on. If you think back to how you felt at the beginning of the campaign, I'll bet it's not nearly as intimidating now."

"Yes, I suppose that's true."

Peter looked at Nicole with interest. She was a natural at making others feel comfortable. He was surprised by the poise and grace of this beautiful young woman.

"Theodora always raves about her family, and now I can see why. I hope we'll have the chance to chat again, but right now I think I'd better circulate," Peter said, his attention drawn back to the purpose of this night.

"You go ahead, Peter. We'll catch you later," Theodora said.

"I'm going to do a little wandering too," Paul said to his sisters.

"Checking out the available females?" Nicole asked.

"Can you suggest something more interesting?"

"Go to it, Romeo. We'll watch from the sidelines." Theodora smiled.

"You two are never on the sidelines," he said as he walked away.

"I'm going to get another drink. Do you want one?" Nicole asked her sister.

"No, I'm still working on this one. Well, what do you know? My errant husband just walked in. Excuse me while I see what the big emergency was."

Nicole walked to the bar, nodding hello to familiar faces along the way.

"A glass of Merlot please," she said to the bartender. She looked around the room. Theodora and Stewart were standing off by themselves deep in conversation. She knew things weren't right, and it bothered her that Theodora wasn't being honest with her. They never kept things from each other, but Nicole felt her slipping away.

Many of the guests had moved outside where small round tables had been set on a terrace overlooking the Annapolis harbor. The sun was beginning to set and a cool refreshing breeze blew. Nicole made her way through the crowd and leaned on the balcony. She took a deep breath of the night air and exhaled slowly, enjoying the feel of the light wind on her face. She felt a tap on her arm and turned to see Peter Demetrios standing behind her.

"I guess I'm not the only one who needed some air." He smiled at Nicole.

Suddenly at a loss for words, she simply smiled back as they stood together gazing straight ahead.

"This is such a beautiful city," she finally said, and looked up at him. "You grew up here, didn't you?"

"Yes. I've been a lot places and I haven't seen anything yet that beats it. I love it here."

"I can see why."

He felt himself catch his breath as he looked into her incredible brown eyes.

"This reminds me of Fanueil Hall in Boston. So many places to go outside. We practically lived there once the weather turned warm," she said.

"When did you live in Boston?"

"I went to school there, undergraduate and graduate. I was there for six years. It was hard to leave, but I knew I could never permanently settle that far away from my family."

"We ethnic types do seem to stick close to hearth and home, don't we? I often wonder if my children will feel that way, but somehow I don't think they will. I've never lived away from here, even school was local. I commuted to the University of Baltimore."

"Did you go to law school there too?"

"Yes, law school during the day and work at night to pay for it. There wasn't time for much else. I was a pretty dull fellow in those days."

"I'm sure you were never dull. Probably just tired." She wondered what he had been like, the young and determined law student.

He looked at his watch. "Well, it looks like it's time for us to get downstairs for the dinner." He was reluctant to leave her. He touched her hand lightly. "I've enjoyed talking with you. I hope you'll think about what I said."

"What you said?"

"About volunteering. We treat our workers great," he smiled.

"I'll think about it."

"I hope you will." He hesitated a moment, about to say something more, then reconsidered.

"There you are," Michael said to Peter. "We've been looking for you." He looked at Nicole who seemed flushed and then back at Peter.

"The dinner's about to start. I thought you might want to look over your speech once more before we go down."

Peter turned to Nicole, "I enjoyed our talk," he said before disappearing into the crowd.

Nicole couldn't help but be flattered by the unexpected attention from the guest of honor. Before she could analyze the encounter any further, her parents walked over to her. Aunt Eve and Uncle Dimitri were right behind them.

"Well, don't you look beautiful tonight." Dimitri exclaimed.

"It looks like everyone is starting to go downstairs," Eve observed.

"Well, what are we waiting for? I'm starving, let's go eat before everything's gone!" Dimitri said.

They followed the throng down wide escalators leading to the Grand Ballroom. The entrance was surrounded by hundreds of white and blue balloons. Men in tuxedos and women in glittering evening dresses quickly filled the room. Theodora waved Nicole over to their table and seated her next to Michael.

"Can I get you another drink?" Michael asked her.

"I'd better eat something first. One more glass of wine and you'll have to carry me out of here."

"Anyone else?" Michael looked around the table.

"Vodka and tonic," Stewart answered.

Michael returned with the drinks and sat down.

"Theo tells me you just moved to Federal Hill. How do you like it?"

"I love it. It's great being so close to the harbor."

"That's what I like about living in Annapolis. I spend most of my weekends on my boat."

"That sounds great. Something so relaxing about having all that water around you."

"You'll have to come down one weekend." He smiled at her.

"I might take you up on that."

The voice amplified by the microphone drowned out conversation at the table. The candidate was walking towards the dais. Peter looked around the room smiling at those he passed on the way to the front of the ballroom. His stride was quick and purposeful and charisma oozed from every pore. Nicole was transfixed, her eyes following his every move. He took the microphone and looked out at the crowd.

"Good evening friends, thank you so much for coming tonight and giving me your support..." He spoke passionately for the next twenty minutes, never looking at his notes, and when he was finished the room exploded with applause. As he descended the platform, he was surrounded, and the band moved into high gear.

"Dance?" Michael asked Nicole.

"Love to," she answered.

He put his arm around her waist and led her to the dance floor.

"They make a nice looking couple," Paul remarked to Theodora.

"Don't they!" Theodora answered, looking pleased.

She might have been dancing with Michael, but Peter was never long out of Nichole's sight, her attention involuntarily and continually drawn to his whereabouts. The strength of her attraction to him was both unexpected and alarming. Her reflections were cut short when her father tapped Michael on the shoulder to cut in. As they whirled around the floor, familiar faces smiled at him. Her father always attracted attention. She adored him and was at times in awe of him. He was the yardstick against which she measured all men, and they always came up short. When she was with him she felt like the most important person in the world. She had no doubt that he would lay down his life for her without hesitation. Who would she ever find to love her that way? She rested her head on his shoulder and closed her eyes, relaxing in his protective embrace. When the song ended, she straightened her shoulders and looked up to see Peter standing there.

"Nick, I want to thank you for coming tonight and bringing your family."

Nick grasped his hand in a firm handshake.

"It's my pleasure, Peter. Have you met my daughter, Nicole?"

"Yes, Theodora introduced us earlier. You must be very proud," he said warmly.

"I am. God blessed me with a wonderful family."

"I'm very grateful for all your support. You've opened a lot of doors for me, and I won't forget it. I'm looking forward to speaking at the Home Builders Association dinner next week."

"We're looking forward to it too."

Nicole stood between the two men, thinking how alike they were. Both exuded that distinct aura of complete self-assurance unique to powerful men.

"Excuse me Peter, there's someone I'd like you to meet," Senator Parker interrupted.

Peter turned to Nick and Nicole.

"Thanks again." And he vanished into the crowd.

Soon it was midnight and the crowd had thinned significantly. Theodora finally relaxed. "It's been a total success," Nicole assured her, echoing her thoughts.

Peter came over and smiled warmly at Theodora. "I was just telling Michael what a sensational evening this was. You did a great job."

"Thanks, Peter. You must be exhausted. The only time I saw you sitting was during dinner."

"I could say the same for everyone at your table. I think your group wins the prize for non stop dancing." He turned to say goodnight to Nicole, and once again felt a shock as he looked into her eyes. He knew he shouldn't let his gaze linger, but he could not help himself for a long moment. The air was filled with the attraction between them, feelings of compelling magnetism originating from impulse, and devoid of logic or reason. He finally looked up just in time to see Pat approach.

"Can we go now?" she asked peevishly, ignoring Nicole and Theodora.

The sympathy Nicole felt for her earlier completely evaporated.

"I should be going too, I didn't realize it was so late." Nicole said a hurried goodnight, turned on her heel and walked away.

Chapter 9

*N*icole pulled into the parking lot at six a.m. She smiled when she saw the black Cadillac parked in the first row. No matter how early she got here, he always beat her. That was one of the things that made him so successful, his singular focus. It came naturally to him and she couldn't remember a day when her father hadn't been up, showered and dressed before dawn. Even on weekends, he was already finished breakfast and getting on with his day when she was just rolling out of bed. She had never been a morning person, preferring the quiet dark hours after midnight, but she forced herself to change when she started working full time a few months ago. She was determined to succeed on her own merit, not because she was the boss's daughter.

She knew the business well, had in fact worked on a different housing development project every spring and winter break since she was eighteen. She understood the business from the customer's point of view and kept that perspective in mind when making decisions. Ever since she was a little girl, she knew she wanted to work for her father and remembered fondly the Saturday drives, just the two of them, listening to Greek bouzouki music blasting from his tape player. Occasionally she and Theodora would argue over who would go. More often, though, Theodora was content to stay with their mother. Nick took Nicole with him to each construction site, proudly showing her off. She knew that he wanted Paul, his only son, to take over the business, but when it became apparent that Paul was a gifted artist, with no interest in building houses, Nick had resignedly turned his attention to her. Even though her father loved and respected her, it would take everything she had to prove to him that she was as capable as any man. No matter how enlightened he pretended to be, his heritage had handed down the conviction that the business world was a man's domain. Never one to back down from a challenge, Nicole resolved that she would work harder and smarter than anyone else.

She was hired as an assistant to the Vice President of Marketing. Her boss, McKenzie Winters, was a no-nonsense woman in her early sixties who had been in the real estate business for thirty years and could spot a phony miles away. To those who worked hard and diligently, she was fiercely loyal.

Nicole climbed the flight of stairs to her office and slowed when she heard loud voices coming from the hall leading to Stewart's office. It sounded like Stewart and Phil, one of the purchasing managers. She stood still and listened.

"I don't give a damn what you think, I've already decided to purchase the lumber from Moorstock." Stewart said.

"They're not on the approved sub list. You have to get them cleared through the proper channels first."

"Listen to me. I won't have some junior pencil pusher telling me what to do. Do you know who I am? Don't you dare tell me who I can and cannot do business with. Now if you don't mind, I've got work to do."

Nicole was outraged. The arrogance! Where did he get off behaving that way? She wanted to run straight to her father's office and tell him about it but realized that would be inappropriate. If she really wanted to be treated like an ordinary employee, she couldn't exploit that relationship when it suited her. She would talk to McKenzie about it and keep a close eye on Stewart. She hurried to her office before she was seen and after getting settled went to the kitchen for some coffee.

"Good morning Nicoletta. Are we still on for lunch today?" Constantine Metrolis poked his head around the corner.

"Of course Uncle Costa, I'm looking forward to it."

Costa, Nick's best friend, had been with Parsenis Contracting from the beginning. He was born in Greece and retained the strong accent of his youth. A vibrant sixty-two, he was still a vital part of the company and a loyal friend to the Parsenis family. Widowed five years ago, and childless, he loved Nick and Eleni and their children as his own, taking special joy in his goddaughter, Nicole. Even though he wasn't related, the children had always referred to him as "uncle."

The friendship between Costa and Nick had been forged over thirty years ago when they worked together for a building contractor. Over the years, they had became like brothers. When their boss suddenly died of a heart attack and the company was disbanded, Nick decided to go out on his own. At thirty-four, with a three year old and another on the way, Nick secured a loan by putting his house up for collateral and investing every cent of savings to start Parsenis Contracting. He worked eighteen-hour days over the next five years, with Costa at his side, as they slowly and carefully built the company. He invested the profits back into the business, and when it began to hold its own, started investing in land.

Nick always bought in undeveloped areas, what others referred to as the boondocks. His friends shook their heads and called him a wild speculator, a dreamer. As the years passed, the land he bought increased in value and the wilderness in which he had taken an interest became highly sought after property. Nick never rubbed his success in his friends' faces, but graciously advised them about investments as they began to beat a path to his door. He became a pillar of the community, sought out by Greeks and non-Greeks alike for his business acumen as well as his charisma. It wasn't his money that made him popular, but his ability to make those around him feel more important than himself.

Costa's loyalty was rewarded by a significant interest in the company, which provided him substantial wealth and a financially secure future.

66

Nicole loved spending time with her godfather and listening to his stories about the early years. Her appreciation for her father and her pride in him grew as she learned how he had spent the past twenty-five years. Through her godfather's stories she began to understand the forces that had driven him to spend so much time working and away from his family. She thought about her childhood and how often she had yearned for his attention when he was working late or on the phone with a business associate.

They were an intriguing looking couple as they left for lunch. As usual, Costa was impeccably dressed in a custom tailored suit, and his thick gray hair combed sleekly back. An aura of mystery was enhanced by the dark glasses he never removed and an expensively subtle aroma of citrus which lingered in his wake. He exuded confidence and elan. Nicole, stylish and elegant at his side, completed the picture. They were seated at their usual corner table.

"Well *agapi*, how're you making out working for the iron maiden?" her uncle asked her.

"She's really okay, Uncle Costa. I've learned a lot from her."

"Well, when things got started, it was men who ran the business, not broads. Nothing personal. It's just hard to teach an old dog new tricks. Hell, when things got started, we never even heard of a marketing department. Everything was a lot simpler in the beginning," Uncle Costa reminisced.

"You're forgiven, but only because you're an old dog! Don't let anyone else find out that you said that to me without receiving a feminist lashing," she teased him.

"Ah, Nicoletta, don't become too modern. Things weren't so bad the way they used to be. When your father started this business, your mother was pregnant with you. I'll never forget the first time I met her. The way she looked at your father. My own sweet Argie never looked at me that way. Eleni's eyes were full of adoration and pride. She was supportive of everything he did. My wife sometimes complained about the way we worked constantly. Not Eleni. I once asked if it bothered her that she was left home alone so much of the time.

She looked at me and said, 'I know that Nick is only doing what he needs to be his best.' She believed he could do anything. And your father worked his heart out to live up to her image of him. You don't see much of that kind of love in a marriage today." He was quiet as he pulled out a thick cigar and lit it.

"It's different now, Uncle Costa."

"You don't have to tell me that. But Nicoletta, there's something to be said for the way of the life we old dinosaurs hold dear. You can't look at your parents and grandparents and deny that."

She thought about what he said. Sometimes when societies change and move forward to a better, more equitable sphere, valuable things get left behind. With change comes loss, regardless of the bright future it might promise.

"You've always understood your place in the world, haven't you Uncle Costa?"

He smiled at her and gave her hand a tender squeeze. Costa was a man who seldom indulged in self-absorption. You took what life handed you, did your damnedest to turn it into something good and moved ahead without regrets or recriminations. He'd come to America when he was fourteen, a scrappy, smart aleck kid from a poor Greek village with no indoor plumbing. There was never a question in his mind about what he wanted or where he wanted to go. He felt impatience for those lost souls who got sidetracked and derailed by a lack of purpose. He tapped the ash off the end of his cigar.

"I guess I have, Nicoletta."

She always felt safe with Costa, his strength of character like a swirling cloak of protection around her.

Chapter 10

*A*s Nicole drove home, she thought about how different things were this September. Just one year ago she was in Boston finishing her last year of graduate school, while Theodora was in her senior year at the University of North Carolina. Saturday mornings had been set aside for their telephone visits.

Now they were back in Baltimore, living on different sides of town. Theodora and Stewart had bought one of the Parsenis houses north of Hunt Valley. Their closest neighbor was five miles away, the closest store even further. She remembered the first time Theodora had taken her to see the house. The stone rancher was barely visible from the road, and sat high atop a wooded hill. A long driveway led to the side of the house and a two-car garage. Nicole's townhouse was in Federal Hill, one of Baltimore's oldest and most historic downtown neighborhoods. It was especially nice in good weather because she was close to the Inner Harbor with all its attractions, as well as Fells Point, home to a vast diversity of specialty shops, bars and restaurants. It was an exciting place to live, especially for someone single and energetic. She thought of how much fun she and Theodora could have had exploring all the restaurants and little taverns in the area. She turned the radio up and leaned back in her seat, relaxing a bit. As her car sped along the highway her spirits lifted in anticipation of an evening with her sister. By the time she got home and changed it was close to seven. She was tossing the salad when she heard a voice in the hallway.

"I could've been a murderer! Your door was unlocked," Theodora said.

Nicole laughed, knowing Theodora was joking, imitating their father. He couldn't stand an unlocked door and continually worried about their safety.

"So," Nicole asked her sister, "Are you guys all settled in the house?"

"For the most part. We've both been so busy that we haven't unpacked all our boxes. I still haven't finished my thank you notes, and every time I talk to Mom she asks me about it."

"Why don't you get Stewart to help you?"

"Are you kidding? They'd never get out. I'll get them done. I'm just glad that everything's over and we can get back to normal."

"So, you're happy right?" Nicole prodded.

"Definitely! Married life is great."

"Good."

"Enough about me. How was your blind date the other night? Who was it with?"

"Manny. You remember him, the Greek dermatologist Aunt Eve fixed me up with right before the wedding?"

"Oh yeah, the one who asked you out for dinner and then took you to the Country Buffet," Theodora said laughing.

"That's the one. Old Diamond Jim. Why I let Aunt Eve talk me into it in the first place I'll never know. But you know how she can be. Anyway, I guess the cheapskate figured he'd go the economy route to make sure he didn't waste his money on some dog. All through dinner he kept telling me how attractive I was, how beautiful my skin is, especially for a Greek girl. I guess he thought that was some kind of a compliment. It was all I could do to keep myself from saying how unattractive he was for a Greek man."

"I thought you said he was nice looking," Theodora said.

"He is, until he opens his mouth."

"What a nightmare," Theodora laughed.

"No more blind dates for me. I've had enough to last a lifetime," Nicole said resolutely.

"I feel the same way. I used to hate them. Soon enough, you'll meet Mr. Right and these dating rituals will be history."

"Well, don't get your hopes up. I'm starting to doubt the existence of Mr. Right. But enough of all that. How about dinner?" Nicole asked.

"Yes, I'm famished."

"Good, dinner's ready. Oh by the way," Nicole said casually. "I've been thinking I'd like to volunteer on Peter's campaign."

Theodora was delighted. "What made you decide?"

"I've been doing some research on your Mr. Demetrios and I like what he stands for. I know there're only a couple months 'til the election but I figured better late than never."

"Wonderful. We'll get you started right away."

Chapter 11

*T*heodora took a deep breath, determined to keep her temper under control.

"Why didn't your mother call me about tonight?"

"I'm sure it wasn't intentional. She called me at work last week to talk, and then asked if we'd come to dinner. I forgot to tell you. It's my fault, not hers."

This was the fourth time Caroline had invited them over and each time had done so through Stewart. Twice, Theodora was forced to change other plans because Stewart accepted before checking with her. She had asked Caroline to go through her since she kept their social calendar, but Caroline clearly didn't think it important to honor her daughter-in-law's wishes. It was pointless to discuss it further. She went upstairs to shower and adjusted the water temperature until it was almost too hot to bear. She tried to relax as the hot water beat upon her back. An evening with her mother-in-law was not something she looked forward to. No matter how hard she tried, it was impossible to get close to Caroline. Stewart tried to help, but he had a blind spot where his mother was concerned. Theodora remembered the time she had questioned him about his mother's drinking. His face turned bright red and he gave her an icy stare.

"What are you talking about? So she has a couple of drinks occasionally. It's not like the parties in your family are dry."

She had let the matter drop. She couldn't believe he didn't notice that Caroline always had a drink in hand and how nasty she became the more she imbibed. There had been a particularly upsetting incident shortly before she and Stewart became engaged. They were at the Elliott's house for a party when Theodora walked into the kitchen and heard her name spoken. She hung back and overheard Stewart and his mother talking.

"Well honestly, dear, what do you expect me to think of her? She's hardly social register material," Caroline said.

"Neither is Father but that didn't stop you from marrying him," he shot back.

"Stewart Phillip, I won't have you talking to me that way. Besides, your father's half English. This girl is a Greek peasant." She said the word "Greek" as if it were an obscenity.

"Theodora is hardly a peasant, Mother. Besides, have you forgotten that the Greeks were educated and civilized eons before your precious 'English'." He defended Theodora in a rare show of rebellion.

"I suppose you'll do whatever you want, you always do. Just don't expect me to be happy about it," she said and turned her back to him. Theodora ran from the kitchen in tears, taking refuge in the bathroom until she was composed enough to rejoin the party. When she found Stewart she pleaded a headache and asked him to take her home. Eleni was livid when Theodora recounted the conversation.

"Just who does she think she is? Greek peasant, my foot. Without the Greeks, there wouldn't be half of the words used in the English language today. And just what type of oath does she think her husband took, the English Hippocratic? Never let anyone make you think that they are better than you," Eleni advised her.

"Mom, I don't know what to do. I love Stewart, but how can I marry into a family that doesn't want me?"

"Darling, Stewart's a grown man. It isn't fair to blame him for his mother's ignorance. Why don't you let him know how you feel and see what he says?"

Stewart was mortified that Theodora had overheard the exchange and couldn't apologize enough. He even convinced Caroline to make amends to Theodora, which she did, albeit, insincerely. Theodora had tried to put it behind her, but the memory lived on.

Well, the woman was related to her now and there was nothing she could do about it. She stepped out of the shower and put on her bathrobe. She chose a pair of navy linen slacks and matching blazer.

Stewart stood looking at her as he casually leaned against the door-jamb.

"Honey, why don't you wear the black dress I got you?"

"It's a little cool tonight, I thought I'd be more comfortable in this," she answered.

He went to her closet and pulled out the dress.

"But I can't admire your gorgeous legs in that. I really think you'd look much better in this. Besides, I spent a lot of time picking it out and you've never even worn it." He sat on the bed and waited.

She sighed. He was always encouraging her to wear sexy clothes. This one was a short, backless number that she would never have chosen. She supposed she should appreciate his interest. How many of her friends complained that they were lucky if their birthdays and anniversaries were remembered? Stewart constantly bought things for her. So what if they weren't exactly her taste? The important thing was he cared. She walked over to him and kissed him on the lips, and he slid his arms around her and pulled her to him. She shrugged her jacket off and stepped out of her pants. His hand dropped down to stroke the inside of her thigh.

"Don't get dressed yet," he whispered.

She moved to take her heels off.

"Leave them on," he commanded.

She was overcome with her need for him. He was as essential to her as the sun to the dawn. She was exhilirated by his touch.

They arrived late for dinner.

"Good evening Mr. Elliott, Mrs. Elliott. Your parents are in the living room." The housekeeper greeted them.

"Thanks Betty," Stewart said

"There's the happy couple," bellowed Graham, pleasantly buzzed from his third martini. He shook Stewart's hand vigorously and enveloped Theodora in a bear hug. "Welcome."

"Honestly Graham, don't crush the girl. Hello dear, good to see you," Caroline said as she kissed the air next to Theodora's cheek.

"How are you Caroline?" Theodora asked. It had become quite clear when Theodora and Stewart got engaged that Caroline had no desire to be called 'Mother' by her future daughter-in-law. When they announced the news to them, Graham reacted with delight and immediately welcomed Theodora into the family. He told her he would be very happy if she would call him Father, but before he could go any further, Caroline had cut in.

"Graham dear, don't be so insensitive. Theodora already has a mother and a father. I'm sure she wouldn't feel right addressing near strangers in the same fashion."

When Theodora tried to protest, she cut her off too.

"Nonsense dear, don't try to spare our feelings. Caroline and Graham will do just fine."

Now she answered Theodora with slightly slurred speech.

"Actually, I've been a little under the weather lately, but don't you worry about that. This evening is for you and Stewart, and I wouldn't dream of letting my small sufferings interfere."

Theodora rubbed her temples. She could feel a headache coming. "I'm sorry to hear that Caroline. Please let me know if there's anything I can do."

"I'll be fine dear. You just enjoy yourself."

Betty approached. "May I get you a drink?"

"I'll have a gin and tonic please," Theodora said. She would need it to get through the evening.

"Where's the couple of the hour?" Aunt Peg called when she came into the living room. Peg was a pretty woman in her early fifties, with short blonde hair that framed a kind and generous face. Her bright blue eyes sparkled with energy, and her warm, bubbly personality could always be counted on to liven up a party. Her husband Roger, Caroline's brother, rarely said more than a few words at a time. Theodora had liked Peg instantly, but never understood what she saw in Roger. He seemed a complete boor.

"Theodora, you look smashing!" Peg said as she hugged her. "Looks like you've completely recovered from all the wedding stress. I, however, am still soaking my feet from all that wonderful Greek dancing! That was the most fun I've had at a wedding in a long time." She looked over at Stewart. "Darling, you did a splendid job in picking a wife."

"Here, here," Graham piped in.

"Thank you, Aunt Peg, I completely agree," Stewart said and winked at Theodora.

Caroline walked over to her brother. "Roger, how are things at the Bank?"

"Fine," he answered, looking bored.

"I read in the paper yesterday that you're loaning the Betman Group the money to build that new mall downtown. Isn't it a bit risky putting a mall in that area?" she continued.

"Not really," he said, sipping his drink.

"When will they begin the project?" she probed

"Not sure, I'm not handling that one," he said, looking over her head.

Roger's reserve had always bordered on rudeness. She didn't know why she even tried to engage him in conversation. Exasperated, Caroline stalked off in search of Betty. She found her in the kitchen, pulling out a tray of hot hors d'oeuvres.

"It's about time," Caroline scolded.

"Sorry ma'am."

Sighing, Caroline said, "Hurry and serve them. We'll begin dinner at eight thirty."

She looked around, saw that no one was watching and sneaked upstairs to her bedroom. She shut and locked the door, sank onto the bed and reached under her night table for her bottle of vodka. Raising the bottle to her mouth, she gulped greedily. Small beads of liquid dribbled down the side of her face, and she wiped them away with the back of her hand. She took one more sip, recapped the bottle and put it back in its hiding place. Zigzagging over to the vanity, she barely seated herself without falling and tried twice to steady her shaking hand as she attempted to reapply her lipstick. A generous application of JOY, especially around her mouth and neck completed the ritual. Satisfied, she stood, unlocked the door and stumbled out into the hallway.

"Damn it Mother, you almost knocked me over," Stewart snapped at her disgustedly. "Look at you, you're drunk. You can't go downstairs like that."

"Leave me alone, I'm fine," Caroline slurred, as she tried to push past him.

"You are not fine, and I won't have you embarrassing yourself in front of everyone. I'm putting you to bed. I'll tell the others you got sick," he insisted.

Not strong enough to resist, Caroline allowed herself to be herded back into the bedroom. Stewart gently pushed her onto the bed, removed her shoes and tucked her under the covers. Within minutes, she was asleep, mouth open, the snores loud and irregular.

"Why do you do it, Mother?" he asked in a small voice. He turned away and shut the door.

When he rejoined the party, he pulled his father aside.

"Mother isn't feeling well. She wanted to come back down, but I was afraid she might faint. I've put her to bed," he explained.

A look of anger clouded Graham's face. He quickly recovered and nodded his head. Turning to his guests, he said, "Let's go in to dinner now. Caroline has a migraine and has gone to bed."

It was a charade, of course, that had been played many times before, but appearances took priority over truth. Theodora looked at Stewart. He was clearly upset, and she watched as he struggled to hide his feelings and maintain his composure. She wished he would open up to her. She wanted to erase all the bad memories for him and take away his pain. She was suddenly furious with Caroline. How could she put him through this? It was one thing to ruin your own life, but when you had children the rules were different. A strong urge to protect Stewart arose in her. She couldn't change his mother for him, but she could do everything in her power to lavish upon him the attention he so sorely missed growing up.

Chapter 12

*A*ngry voices echoed from Nick's office, and the door abruptly swung open. Uncle Costa, his face red, quickly brushed past Nicole and nearly knocked her down. She peered in and saw that her father was alone, sitting behind his large mahogany desk.

"Dad, what's going on? Uncle Costa looked like he was ready to kill somebody," Nicole said.

"Costa's a stubborn old mule who thinks we should do business the way we did twenty years ago. He doesn't realize times have changed and we have to change along with them. It doesn't matter what I say to him, he thinks he's right," Nick said.

"Right about what?"

"He thinks I'm giving Stewart too much control, and that he's too green to handle the Manor Hills project. He's being shortsighted."

Nicole felt her anger rise. She completely agreed with Costa's assessment of Stewart, and Nick's blind faith in him distressed her.

"Uncle Costa's been with you from the very beginning. He knows this business inside out. How can you just toss aside his concerns and chalk it up to stubbornness?"

"Let me tell you something, Nicole, Stewart is here around the clock. He's got the new blood we need if we're going to keep growing. Your Uncle Costa has gotten too comfortable."

"Is it comfort or sensible caution?"

"Caution and fear of moving forward are two different things. He seems to forget we took chances in the early days, and that's the reason we're where we are today. Costa would've chewed up and spit out anyone who tried to stand in his way. I almost think he's envious of Stewart's gumption."

"Gumption? The way Stewart rides rough-shod over everyone has a lot of noses out of joint. Costa isn't the only one resentful. Why are you the only one who can't see it?"

"What I see is a bright, forward-thinking young man, full of energy, who's working his tail off. If he ruffles a few feathers, so be it. The company is his first priority."

"First? What about his wife? You remember. Your daughter?"

"Theo will have to get used to it. Your mother did."

"She didn't get used to it. She adjusted her whole life to you. That doesn't mean she liked it or that it was easy for her."

Nick rested his head in his hands and massaged his forehead. "It wasn't easy for either of us, Nicole," he said in a tired voice. "You know, when I was a boy, I worked in my father's vegetable stall in Lexington Market. My brother Jim and I would go there before school at five in the morning to get everything set up and organized. It was dark, and we heard rats scurry around the stalls and felt them run over our feet. It terrified me. I hated it. My father worked like a dog. When this company was started it took every bit of my time. Do you think I enjoyed being away from my family, that I was happy about missing one of Paul's soccer games or a school play you were in? There're a lot of things I missed that I can never recapture, that are gone forever. And maybe the trade-off was too high, but it's too late to do anything about that now. It's pointless to sit here and wallow in regrets. We've come a long way, and I won't make any apologies for it."

"Oh, Dad, I'm not criticizing you or asking for apologies. This isn't about you. We were talking about Stewart. And he's the issue here. It would kill me to see the company you worked so hard to build get into trouble because of his rashness."

"I'm not about to let that happen," Nick said.

"I'm not sure you can prevent it."

"I'm sorry you have so little faith in my judgement," he said quietly.

Nicole went around the desk and leaned down to kiss her father on the cheek. "Dad, I'm sorry. I lost my temper, but please, don't ignore Uncle Costa's concerns."

Nick hugged his daughter. "Stop worrying and get back to work."

Nicole gently closed the office door. Nick leaned back in his chair and thought about his conversation, first with Costa and then with Nicole. They managed to cast some doubts on his confidence in Stewart. He wanted to believe he'd found in Stewart one who would regard Parsenis Contracting the way a son would, someone whose actions would be spurred by a true sense of loyalty and pride in the company. Maybe it was wishful thinking. Was he trying to fit Stewart into the slot he had hoped his son Paul would take?

Nicole walked down the hall to her Uncle Costa's office and was disappointed to see that it was empty. He had probably left the building after the explosion with Nick. Impulsively she grabbed a piece of paper and began to write a note and then thinking better of it, balled it up and tossed in into the trashcan. She pulled his office door firmly shut and headed down the long hallway.

"Good morning, McKenzie," she said walking into her office.

"Hi, Nicole. I put some copy from the ad agency on your desk. And Jim Gannett wants to take us to lunch today. Can you do?" Gannett was head of their ad agency. Nicole knew this wouldn't be a working lunch; it was simply his way of keeping in touch and thanking them for their business.

"I can't today. I'm really jammed and I have to leave a little early to meet Theodora for dinner in Annapolis."

"Why are you having dinner down there when you both have to come back to Baltimore?" McKenzie asked.

"Didn't I tell you? I'm volunteering on the Demetrios campaign. Theodora is giving me the grand tour tonight and deciding what job I'm suited for, if I'm suited for anything," Nicole smiled.

"Does he need a personal shopper?" McKenzie asked. "You'd be dynamite at that!"

Nicole aimed a rubber band at McKenzie and released it, widely missing her. "I don't have time to sit here and be insulted," she said in mock indignation. "I have work to do."

Chapter 13

*B*y the time Nicole left the office, Costa still hadn't returned. She couldn't remember a time he'd stayed away all day.

She slid into the front seat of the car and thought about her confrontation with Nick, reluctantly acknowledging she might be wrong about Stewart. She'd never seen her father make a mistake when it came to business. If only she had someone to talk to, but Theodora was the person in whom she would normally confide and she certainly couldn't discuss this with her. For now, she would put it out of her mind and enjoy the evening with her sister.

Demetrios headquarters was busy and noisy when Nicole arrived. Almost the entire first floor had been turned into a large office, with four rows of desks lining the room. Volunteers sat at every desk methodically going through computer lists of registered voters and calling them to encourage them to get out and vote on Election Day.

Theodora came rushing up to her. "Michael and I are waiting for you. I thought the three of us would go to dinner together, but first I'll show you around the office."

Nicole was disappointed. After the day she'd had, she was looking forward to relaxing with Theodora and catching up, but the whole tone of the evening would change with Michael along.

"I kind of figured it would be just you and me tonight," she said to Theodora.

"We could do that, but since you'll be working with Michael too, it would be good for you to get to know each other. And besides, he's great company. You'll see. We'll have a good time."

Nicole was too tired to argue. "All right. Why don't you give me the lay of the land."

"This is where you'll be working." Theodora pointed to the series of desks where workers were making calls.

"Most of what you'll be doing is telephoning voters. Each night there'll be a report from the person who worked that desk right before you and instructions on where you pick up. There's a prepared script and answers to questions you might be asked. We're trying to get as much of the vote out as possible. We'll even make arrangements to get those people to the polls who can't get there on their own. The key to winning this is going to be a large turnout on Election Day."

"That doesn't sound too hard. I've made arrangements at the office to go in early two days a week so I can get here by around five. I don't imagine you can make these calls much later than nine. I could probably come in on some Saturdays too."

"Wonderful. We can use all the time you can give. I'm going to put you with Theresa Williams at first. She's been here from the beginning and knows the ropes pretty well. She'll seem a little flaky, but she knows what she's doing and she's easy to work with. Come on and I'll show you the rest of the offices."

They walked into Theodora's small cramped office filled with filing cabinets, a large desk littered with papers, and two worn wooden arm chairs covered in a dull brown vinyl. A small window behind her desk overlooked a narrow alley that backed up to rows of houses with tiny yards surrounded by tall privacy fences. The office walls were covered with campaign posters and photographs of a smiling Peter Demetrios shaking hands with voters, posed with elected officials, and with his family. Nicole walked up to the family portrait and studied it. Peter's presence dominated the picture, his magnetism picked up even through the eye of the camera. Next to him was his wife Pat, and on her right a shy looking young boy who appeared to be around sixteen. On Peter's left was a younger child, a daughter who had inherited her father's blonde good looks. Nicole noticed that the arm around Pat was her son's and not Peter's and was unsettled by the fact that she was glad.

"They're a nice looking family, aren't they?" Theodora said coming up behind her.

"Yes, they are," Nicole said with forced cheerfulness. She turned from the photograph.

"I was thinking maybe I should take one of these scripts home with me so I can be a little prepared. Can you make a copy for me?"

"Sure, that's a good idea. I'll go do that now."

Nicole sat down in one of the chairs opposite Theodora's desk. Her neck and shoulders felt tight, still tense from this morning's encounter with her father. She closed her eyes and tried to relax.

"They haven't tired you out already, have they?" The deep voice startled Nicole. She opened her eyes and saw Peter Demetrios standing at the door. Her hand reflexively went up to smooth back her hair. She felt her face get warm and her stomach felt like it was on the crest of a roller coaster, just before the descent.

"I didn't think you were here. I didn't see you when I came in," she stood up.

He walked toward her until they were just a few feet apart. "I came back to pick up some papers. How are you? It's great to see you again." He extended his arm to shake her hand.

Everything left her mind except the touch of his hand. "Fine," she managed, "How's the campaign going?"

"I'm running around in circles. Half the time I don't even know where I am, it's so crazy." He paused and then became serious. "Please tell me you're here to volunteer."

"Yes, on Tuesdays and Thursdays, in the evenings of course, and maybe some Saturdays."

Peter filed that information away.

"Unfortunately, I still have to work for a living. The bank doesn't like waiting for those mortgage payments," she said smiling.

"Theodora told me you've just moved into a new townhouse. Downtown Baltimore, right?"

"I'm impressed. You have a good head for details."

"Certain things stick with me." She was right, though. He never forgot a detail, that was part of what made him such a successful attorney, and he certainly hadn't forgotten anything Theodora told him about her sister.

"How do you like being a homeowner?" he asked.

"I love it. Of course, my mother thought I should wait at least another ten years before leaving home, preferably with a husband, but I expected that. I'm enjoying myself though, puttering around in my garden, wallpapering rooms. I'm even taking gourmet cooking lessons. Pretty soon I'll be ready to test my skills on some unsuspecting dinner guests."

"I have a feeling that whatever you set your mind to, you do well," he said.

"Peter, what are you doing here?" Theodora returned with the copies.

"I left some work here, things I need to go over before tomorrow."

"Pat called about an hour ago and I told her you'd probably go straight home after your meeting. Don't you have a birthday party to go to? She's probably wondering where you are. Maybe you should call her."

"Thanks, Theodora." He turned to Nicole, "It was good to see you again. I'm glad you'll be working here." He was all business again.

"I'm looking forward to it. Good night, Peter," Nicole said, sobered by the mention of his wife.

"Goodnight, Theodora, see you in the morning." And he was out the door.

Theodora handed the papers to Nicole. "Okay, here's your script, now let's grab Michael and go have something to eat."

It was a short walk to the Treaty of Paris restaurant, and the night was cool and pleasant. Nicole couldn't stop thinking about Peter and their conversation. Her responses seemed so flat and ordinary. She wanted to be witty and clever, to fascinate him with her sharp repartee, but she had been almost tongue-tied. Now she could think of a thousand things she might have said. She struggled against this pleasurable and fluttery feeling in her stomach, the feeling that she was on the verge of something exciting and tantalizing, struggled to bring this insanity down to earth and see her interest in this man as the folly that it was. She felt Theodora nudge her and realized Michael had asked her a question.

"I'm sorry, did you say something?" she said to Michael.

"Here I am dropping pearls of wisdom for the last two blocks, and you haven't heard a word I've said. It's enough to bruise a man's ego," Michael said.

Nicole smiled at him. "Most men have egos large enough to handle a little bruising quite easily. It's good for you, it builds character."

"He's already a character," Theodora said.

"Great, I'm being double-teamed."

"We'll try to behave ourselves, Michael," Theodora said affectionately.

The restaurant was a favorite with most of the staff and the hostess smiled and gave them a familiar greeting as they entered "Three for dinner?"

"Yes, is there a long wait?" Michael asked.

"No, we'll get you right in."

"Give us a good table, we're breaking in a new volunteer tonight," he said, looking at Nicole.

"This is great," Nicole commented as they sat down.

"Nicole, I really appreciate the time you're giving us," Michael began. "I know it's a sacrifice to give up your evenings."

"Thank you Michael. I'm looking forward to it.

"Here, here. Let's drink to that." Theodora raised a glass of wine.

They gave the waitress their dinner order, and Theodora excused herself to go the ladies room.

"I think I've just witnessed a first," Michael said with an impish smile.

"What are you talking about?"

"I thought women always went to the ladies room in pairs."

"I'll tell you a little secret. Just when you think you have us figured out, we do something completely contradictory just to confuse you."

"I'm a long way from thinking I have women all figured out. But I sure enjoy the learning process."

"You must not have too much time for that right now. I imagine this job wreaks havoc with your social life."

"It's true, I don't have many free evenings, but there isn't anyone in particular I'd like to spend them with anyway," he said truthfully.

"Yes, I'd just as soon curl up with a good book these days."

"What did I miss?" Theodora sat down and took a sip of her drink.

"Your sister and I were entertaining each other with stories of our wild and busy social lives."

"That must have been a short conversation. You work all your life and Nicole turns down ninety percent of the men who ask her out. You're perfect for each other," Theodora smiled triumphantly.

Michael laughed and turned to Nicole. "Maybe she's got something there. We'll have to coax each other out of this rut."

They had all ordered seafood, because no one would think of ordering anything else in Annapolis. The fish was always fresh and the crab cakes were cooked as only a Maryland restaurant could prepare them.

"These are the best crab cakes I've ever tasted, or else I'm hungrier than I thought," Nicole said.

"No, you're right." Michael agreed. "That's why we're here so often."

"Don't you ever cook?" Nicole asked.

"Certainly I cook. I can heat soup and put bread in the toaster."

"I don't think that qualifies. What can you do with the oven?" Nicole asked.

"I've never turned it on. Don't even know if it works."

"Poor boy. It just so happens I'm becoming an expert cook. Maybe I'll prepare you a nice dinner sometime," Nicole said.

Theodora tried not to look too pleased at the turn the conversation was taking. She wanted so badly for Michael and Nicole to like each other, and it seemed they were hitting it off.

"I'll take you up on that anytime." He hoped it would be soon.

They took their time with the meal and when the waitress began to clear the dishes, Michael asked if either of them wanted dessert or coffee.

"I think I'll pass," Nicole said as she looked at her watch and suppressed a yawn. "It's getting late."

"Are you sure I can't tempt you? They have great cheesecake." Michael grinned.

"I'll take a rain check. I've really got to head home."

"I should be hitting the road too," Theodora said. "Thanks for coming with us Michael. It was fun."

They left the restaurant together. "Where are you girls parked?" he asked.

"I pulled in right behind Theodora on the street."

"Good, I'll walk you both to your cars. Stay with each other on the highway and be careful."

"You sound like our mother." Nicole smiled.

"Mothers usually give pretty good advice. See you in the morning Theodora, and I'll see you Thursday," he said to Nicole.

She eased her car out of the space, rolled down the window and drove up the hill to Church Circle from which she would pick up Route 50. Michael was a nice guy. She could see why Theodora enjoyed working with him, but right now snatches of this morning's argument with her father crowded Michael Pendleton out of her mind.

The house was dark when she finally pulled up. She had meant to leave a light on this morning, but as usual had forgotten. One of her father's lectures on safety precautions played itself in her head as she fumbled with her key in the dark. The house was warm and stuffy. She turned on the foyer light and without bothering to look at her mail, she went upstairs to undress and wash her face. It was past midnight when she finally got into bed and pulled up the covers.

Chapter 14

*T*hursday morning was one of those gray, rainy fall days that is a precursor to the long winter lying in wait. Nicole shivered against the chill and pushed the window down. The fall weather was crazy, one day requiring air conditioning and the next long underwear. She stood in front of the closet and tried to decide what to wear, hoping something would jump out at her. Her whole morning had been like this. Her hair. Her make-up. She did everything in slow motion, not satisfied with the finished product. Tonight would be her first night working at headquarters, and Peter might be there. She hadn't been this concerned about her appearance at her senior prom. Finally settling on a smart black linen suit and cream silk camisole, she began to dress. She added a single strand of pearls and a pair of small pearl earrings and looked at her reflection in the mirror. Satisfied, she grabbed her black leather handbag and left the house.

It was later than usual when she arrived at work, but instead of going to her office, she went directly to her uncle's. The ubiquitous cigar was burning in the ashtray on his desk while he sat deeply immersed in the contract he held before him. He looked up as she walked in.

"Good morning. Come in, come in. Sit down." He took off his glasses and rubbed his eyes. He rarely removed the dark glasses, and his appearance was radically changed without them. His service in

Vietnam had resulted in an eye injury that left them extremely sensitive to light, and the dark lenses were his constant source of protection. They gave him a rakish, enigmatic look and appeared to be an affectation to those who didn't know the reason he wore them.

"Feeling better today?" She sat in one of the chairs opposite his desk.

"Yes, yes. Don't worry your pretty little head with this Nicoletta. It's not the first time your father and I have disagreed, and it won't be the last."

She wondered if men told unattractive women not to worry their ugly little heads.

"Uncle Costa, I adore you, but you are without question, one of the most chauvinistic men left on the planet. One day the feminists are going to have you strung up. Contrary to what you might think, we females are capable of doing something besides looking good."

"Feminists, schmeminists. I'm getting sick of hearing a bunch of whining women tell me how bad they've been treated. Why are they so anxious to be men?

"They don't want to be men. They want to be the best women they can be, with the same opportunities men have. Why is that such a difficult concept?"

"Nicole, don't tell me you buy this radical garbage. God made men and women different. No matter how much you want to change things, you'll always be the ones to have the babies. Men should go out and earn the living, and women should stay home and take care of the family. It's worked for centuries."

Nicole shook her head in amazement.

"We have to get off this subject, or I'll wind up pulling your tongue out of your head. Anyway, the issue here is not your archaic view of gender roles, but Stewart Elliott. I want to know what's going on. Don't just dismiss me as if I were some little fool. I can help you."

"You watch how you talk to your godfather, young lady," he said in feigned anger. "I promise I'll let you in on it as soon as I have all the facts. Okay, *koukla*?"

"Okay," she said frustrated, but knowing she'd get no further. "I'll let you get back to work now."

"Incidentally," he said, making her stop and turn around to face him. "You do a wonderful job of looking good." She shook her head once again as she left his office.

Nicole and Michael laughed as she recounted the conversation with Costa. After three hours on the volunteer desk with no break, Michael had rescued her and insisted she stop and have coffee with him. They had been sitting in his office for the last hour, trading stories, after discovering they'd both gone to college in Boston.

"We probably passed each other a hundred times in Harvard Square," Nicole said.

"Impossible. I would never have let you get past me. Of course, anytime you were ever at the Boston Garden, I can say with confidence I was there," Michael said.

"Big Celtics fan, huh?"

"My world stopped for them. I wanted to be Larry Bird."

"You're much cuter than Larry Bird," she said in a friendly way. "What my world stopped for was a sale at Filene's Basement. I spent more research time there than at the library."

"I'm proud to say I never stepped foot in there. When my mother and sister came to visit and described the scene, I made a solemn vow to stay out." They were both laughing again.

"Sometimes I really miss those years at school. Life was much less complicated then," Nicole said thoughtfully.

"Are things so complicated now?"

"Maybe it isn't that so much as the sense of freedom I had being away from my family. Don't misunderstand. I love them, but it's hard not to fall back into the little niche reserved for Nicole. I find myself reverting to old patterns and ways of thinking. Did you know that one of the lesser-known contributions the ancient Greeks made to the world was the elevation of worry to an art form? Give me a situation and I'll give you a minimum of two reasons to worry about it," she paused a moment. "I mean it, give me something."

"You're serious. Okay, let's see." Michael put his head back and thought.

"Saturday turns into one of those magic fall days that's seventy degrees, and we take the boat out for an evening sail."

"You're making it too easy. I can do this one without thinking. Number one worry - the boat might spring a leak and we drown as it sinks. Number two - the wind dies, the back-up motor is out of gas and we drift into the Atlantic never to be heard from again," she finished.

"Okay, how about this one. It's the first snow of the winter, there's a full moon and we take a walk around the neighborhood."

She smiled. "One of us slips on the snow and breaks a wrist. Or, we get mugged. I'm telling you, where I come from there are dire consequences to any action remotely adventurous. The last words I heard whenever I left the house were 'be careful'. I used to dream one day my parents would say 'Be careless, take a chance.'"

"What would you expect Nicole? No parent wants his kid to get hurt. That's only natural."

"No, you don't understand. This goes way beyond being prudent. This is a fear that is intricately woven into our everyday existence. Not just a fear of trying something new or daring, but this feeling of a black cloud hovering just out of sight ready to steal happiness away. Don't get too content; be watchful, because just when you least expect it, disaster will strike."

She got up from her chair and picked up the empty coffee mug. "Sorry. I don't know what got into me." She looked at her watch. "Gosh, I didn't realize how late it's gotten. I have a forty-five minute drive ahead of me. I'd better get going."

Michael reluctantly got up from his chair. "Are you coming Saturday?"

"Yes."

"How 'bout lunch?"

"Love to." She ran her hand through her hair. "Does Peter usually come in on Saturdays?" She hoped she sounded nonchalant.

"Depends on his speaking schedule. Most of his appearances this weekend are pretty close to home, so I imagine he'll stop by at some point. Let me walk you to your car," he said as he helped her with her jacket. He wanted to put his arm around her and give her some kind of assurance that if he had anything to do with it, no disaster would ever come near her.

"That's okay, I'll be fine. Thanks for everything. Goodnight." She was gone, and he was already counting the hours until Saturday.

Chapter 15

*T*he City Dock was lazily coming to life under the soft autumn sun, the boats and buildings casting shimmering reflections on the still water. A few early risers sat at tables outside the market nursing cups of gourmet coffee, immersed in their newspapers. The scene resembled a muted watercolor. As she strolled past the quiet activity on her way to campaign headquarters, Nicole was filled with a rich expectancy and a feeling that slowly, inexorably, her life was moving toward a maturing and fulfillment. When she arrived at the small house on Duke of Gloucester Street, Theresa and a few of the other volunteers were there, casually dressed on this easy Saturday morning. Nicole wore jeans and her hair was pulled back into a loose ponytail.

"Hey," Theresa was noisily chewing gum. "You look like a teenager today."

"Theresa, I've been meaning to ask how you can talk on the phone with that big wad of gum in your mouth."

"I stick it on the back of my hand while I talk. Just chew in between calls. Keeps my juices flowing."

"I don't think you need anything to keep your juices flowing." Nicole laughed. "You have more energy than all of us put together. Anyone from the back offices here yet?"

"Just Michael. But they'll all be in and out today. They always are on Saturdays. Well, time to get rolling," she said and picked up the telephone.

Once the telephoning began, Nicole became completely absorbed. She stayed on the line longer than necessary, but she found she enjoyed talking to people and hearing their views. The time passed quickly, and it was nearing lunchtime when she heard loud voices and laughter across the room. She looked up from her conversation to see who had come in. Her eyes met Peter's and they held each other's gaze. He broke into a smile, walked over and leaned on her desk.

"Hey, it's good to see you," he said.

Before she could answer, Michael appeared.

"Peter, I've just gotten a call from the sound people for tomorrow. I've got to meet with them to iron out some details." He turned to Nicole. "I have to retract my lunch offer for today, but promise me we'll do it another time?" he asked.

"Sure, no problem. Another time," she said.

"I don't know if I'll be back today or not," he said to Peter. "Anything you need to go over with me before I leave?"

"No, I think everything's under control. You go ahead."

"He is one hard-working guy," Nicole said to Peter as Michael left.

"He's fantastic. I'm lucky to have him. But I am sorry your lunch plans got sacked. Can I make up for it and take his place?"

"I'd love that," she said.

Her chummy lunch with Michael was turning into something much more and she found herself straining to hide her delight at Peter's invitation and ignore the insistent voice telling her this was wrong.

"Great. There's a wonderful place right down the street that makes the best Greek salads in the world. How does that sound?"

"I can already taste it."

"What are we waiting for? Let's go."

They walked leisurely down Main Street stopping along the way to look in store windows. They paused in front of a small gallery and Nicole admired a painting of stark white buildings on the hillside of a Mediterranean island. "That looks like Greece," she said. "Isn't it magnificent?"

"Beautiful. Have you been there?"

"Yes, many times, but it never fails to take my breath away. There's something magical about it. Have you been?"

"Only once. We spent a few days in Athens and then took the boat from Piraeus to some of the islands. I loved it, but Pat thought Athens was crowded and dirty, and the island accommodations crude. I suppose it didn't help that she couldn't speak the language. It tends to dampen your enthusiasm when the person you're with isn't enjoying it. I'd love to go back someday."

Nicole could not imagine anyone able to resist falling under the spell of such an incredible country, but she said nothing.

"My parents were never much a part of the Greek community. I remember hearing stories about Greece from my grandfather, but it seemed like he was talking about some place that no longer existed. I don't think I felt a real identity with it until that trip to Greece. Something happened then," he said.

"Yes. I always feel as if I've left something of myself behind when I leave. There are ties that I just can't explain."

They arrived at the small delicatessen. "Here we are." Peter put his hand possessively on Nicole's elbow as he opened the door for her. "It doesn't look like much, but you won't be disappointed."

"*Yasou* Peter," Chris, the owner of the establishment greeted him. "You come for lunch, yes? We have best table for you." He looked at Nicole and gave her a warm smile. "Peter, *pia eeneh ee kopella?*"

"The girl is Nicole Parsenis, and she works at campaign headquarters," Nicole said in perfect Greek, smiling, as she answered his question.

"Ah, you are Greek eh? Welcome, welcome. I am Chris Stratos. I am happy to meet you. Come and sit down."

He seated them at a small table in the rear of the room and handed them each a menu. "We have excellent kalamari today. Is very, very good."

"Do you want to try it?" Peter asked her.

"No thanks. I'll stick with the Greek salad you raved about."

"Just two salads, Chris." Peter handed him the menus.

"I go to make them myself," Chris said and hurried to the kitchen.

Peter looked at his watch. "I have an hour before I have to be anywhere, and I intend to keep you all to myself until then. Unless, of course, you have any objections."

"You won't hear any argument from me. I can't think of anyplace I'd rather be."

"Good." He leaned back in his chair. "Tell me about Greece."

"If you get me started on that subject, we might be here much longer than an hour."

"We'll keep it unfinished and have a reason to continue, like Penelope and the shroud that she wove and unwove while she waited for Odysseus. So, tell me about those wonderful trips."

"They *have* been wonderful. Theodora and I have spent part of every summer there since we were teenagers, mostly on Ikaria where my grandparents were born. Our parents thought we'd go through culture shock the first time we went. The island's very small, and Yiayia's house there is pretty spartan to say the least, but anything else would seem out of place. The life style is so different from here. We were never indoors, except to sleep, and never afraid to be out walking late at night. People meet at the local tavern for drinks and coffee after dinner and sit for hours and hours visiting with each other. They don't have much in the way of material things, but they take the time to enjoy life in a way that's alien to us."

"I felt the same thing when I was there. Our lives are so busy, and it seems there's never enough time to do the things we really want. We put things off as though we're going to live forever. I'm more guilty of that now than ever. This last year has been one long round of traveling, speeches, and shaking more hands than I care to remember. Half of the time, I don't even know what day of the week it is," he said pensively.

"But there's an end in sight, and when you win the election you can make a difference in people's lives. That counts for something."

"If I win the election. It's nice to know you have so much confidence in me. And you're right, I do think I can have a positive impact on the quality of life in this state, but there're times when I'd like to disappear to one of those beautiful islands and dig a little deeper into the soul of Peter Demetrios." He gave Nicole a long look. "Somehow meeting you has made me feel that all the more."

Nicole thought back to all the times she had discounted her grandmother's persistent conviction that there exists a bond unlike any other between two people of the same background. She'd considered it a foolish pronouncement, fashioned by an old country mind-set, but now the beguiling truth of it struck her.

"Why has that changed anything?" she asked hopefully.

Before Peter could answer, Chris brought their salads piled high with extra olives and feta cheese and placed them on the table with a flourish.

"I make these special for you and some nice hot bread to go with it. *Kali oreksi*, good appetite."

"Mm, these look wonderful. Thank you Chris," Nicole said, both relieved and disappointed that he had interrupted them.

"Chris always takes care of me. I told you he made the best Greek salad in the world," Peter said as Chris beamed proudly.

Peter held up his glass and smiled warmly at her. "Here's to the country of our grandparents. Maybe one day we can raise a glass there."

Nicole saw a sadness in his eyes that had not been there before.

"Well," she said, trying to change the mood. "Let me taste this and see if you truly are a salad connoisseur."

"Was I right?" he asked as she put her fork down.

More than you know, she thought. "You sure were," was all she said.

Chapter 16

*F*rom the moment her lunch with Peter ended, time dragged. He was constantly on her mind. She wondered if he was thinking about her, then reasoned he had more important things to think about. Men could compartmentalize. They put everything in neat little boxes and concentrated on one thing at a time. But for her, thoughts of him were the overriding theme, and it worried her more than she cared to admit. She puttered around the house all day, going from one project to the next, becoming bored with each one. Now she was late for her mother's Sunday dinner, and she dressed hurriedly and left the house. When she arrived at her parents', they were already seated for dinner.

"I was starting to get worried," Eleni said as Nicole came into the dining room. "I left a message on your machine. Where've you been?"

"Sorry I'm late," she said as she kissed both of her parents. "I lost track of time. Hi guys." She hugged her brother and sister and gave Stewart a quick peck on the cheek. "What's for dinner?" she asked as she took her usual place at the table.

"Your favorite, pastistio," Nick said as he pointed to the mouth-watering layers of macaroni and beef smothered in a bechamel sauce. "How are you, sweetie? You look tired."

"Thanks, Dad, just what I needed to hear."

"You do look a little green around the gills," Paul kidded her. "Late night?"

"I stayed home last night, big brother. The only thing I've done all weekend is campaign work on Saturday."

"How was your lunch with Michael?" Theodora asked her.

"He canceled on me. Something came up at the last minute and he had to leave, but Peter filled in for him."

Theodora raised an eyebrow.

"That was awfully nice of him," Eleni said.

"He's married, isn't he?" Nick asked.

"You know he's married Dad." Nicole said. "It was just lunch, no big deal."

There was an uncomfortable silence at the table.

"So, how 'bout that Lakers game?" Paul said.

"What Lakers game?" Nick looked at Paul. "There was no Lakers game. What are you talking about?"

Theodora and Nicole laughed at the standard line Paul used when the conversation got heated. It went over Nick's head every time, and he always responded with the same puzzled, but irritated question.

"What's so funny girls?" Eleni asked.

This caused another burst of hysterical laughter and soon both sisters had tears running down their cheeks. If they looked at each other it started all over again. Eleni looked at her husband and shrugged her shoulders.

"How did you stand these two? They must have really gotten on your nerves," Stewart said to Paul.

"They did. I used to lock them in the basement when I babysat."

"Oh, Paul, for heaven's sake. Stewart might think you're serious. You know you love your sisters," Eleni said.

"I think Stewart knew I was kidding, didn't you old man?"

Stewart, with a mouthful, simply smiled and nodded his head.

"Who'd like seconds? Theodora, see if Stewart would like some more pastitsio or salad," Eleni said.

Theodora gave Nicole an exasperated look and got a sympathetic smile in return. "Mom, don't worry. If Stewart wants more food, he'll ask for it."

Ignoring her, Eleni turned to Stewart. "Would you like seconds, dear?"

"No thanks, Mom. It was delicious, but I'm full."

"I'll get the coffee and dessert," Eleni offered.

"Mom, you sit. Nicole and I will do that. Come on," Theodora said to Nicole.

When they reached the kitchen, Theodora seized the opportunity to speak to Nicole alone.

"Nicole, what's going on with Peter?"

"Nothing. We just had a simple lunch together. You're acting like I had a date with him or something."

"I've seen how you look at him. Are you crazy? What are you trying to do?"

"I'm not doing anything, it's happening without my trying. I can't stop thinking about him, and it's driving me crazy. I look at my week in terms of when I'm going to be in Annapolis next and possibly see him. I've never felt this way before." Her eyes filled.

Theodora put her arm around her sister's shoulder. "I'm sorry. This has got to be tough for you, but my God, Nicole, you need to pull away now, while you still can. Maybe you should stop working on the campaign. If you don't see him it'll be easier."

"Girls, what's taking so long?" Eleni came into the kitchen.

"We're bringing it now. This strawberry short cake looks yummy. Did you make it?" Theodora asked her mother.

"No, it's from the bakery. I made some rice pudding though. Nicole, why don't you grab it from the icebox and bring some small bowls in too."

They followed Eleni back into the dining room and Theodora whispered to Nicole. "We're not finished talking."

But Nicole wasn't listening.

Chapter 17

Nicole deliberately took her time leaving. She knew Peter was still in his office, and she was determined to get a minute alone with him. Theresa looked over at her.

"Wanna walk out together?"

"Thanks, but I've got a couple things to finish. Go on ahead."

Theresa shrugged. "Have a good one. See you later."

Nicole breathed a sigh of relief when the door closed behind her. She hadn't seen him since their lunch on Saturday. She didn't understand why she felt so drawn to Peter and knew what she was doing was wrong, but for some unfathomable reason she found it impossible to walk away. It was as though she had discovered a missing piece of herself and was unwilling to let it go. She became a master of rationalization. Maybe Pat didn't even love him, they certainly didn't seem suited to each other. Nicole wondered what had drawn Peter to her in the first place. What was she doing? She grabbed her purse and stood to get her coat. As she was about to leave, she heard the door to Peter's office open.

He was surprised to see her.

"Nicole, what are you still doing here?" He walked over to her and smiled.

"Just finishing up some last minute things. Didn't realize how late it is."

"We're working you too hard! I was catching up too." His eyes held hers and there was an awkward silence. Finally Peter spoke.

"Why don't you let me buy you a drink? You've been working so hard it's the least I can do."

Nicole was delighted. "That sounds wonderful."

They walked to a crowded pub and he led her into a small room with a long bar and several tables. Peter sat next to her, and she savored his closeness.

"What have you've been doing since I saw you last?"

Thinking about you, she wanted to say. "Working mostly," she said instead.

"You need to relax a little too, you know."

"Look who's talking," she laughed. "When was the last time you took a break from your insane schedule?"

"It is insane, and it's only picking up steam now that we're near the end. Three more weeks and it'll all be over. Are you coming to the hotel for the returns on election night?"

"Are you kidding? I wouldn't miss it for the world. I want to be part of that victory celebration."

"I love your optimism. You make me feel invincible." He reached over and squeezed her hand, then let his hand rest on hers. She made no attempt to pull away.

"You'll win, Peter. I know Theo has no doubts about it."

"She's a great gal. I don't know her husband too well. What's he like?"

"Very ambitious and hardworking. Personable enough but a little too controlling for my taste."

"Does Theodora know how you feel?

"It's funny. We've always been so close, told each other everything. But it's as if this is one subject that's taboo. If I even hint at any kind of reservation about Stewart, she changes the subject or lets me know it's not something she wants to discuss. I worry that he's not good for her."

"Well, I hope you're wrong. If I know Theodora, she'll spend her life trying her damndest to make it work. And believe me, I know how tough that can be."

"You sound as if you're speaking from experience," Nicole said.

He hesitated. "I guess I am. You know, I don't want this to sound like the poor husband whose wife doesn't understand him. No one put a gun to my head and said I had to marry Pat, and I take full responsibility for my decision. But the fact is, my choice might not have been the best one for either of us. I really don't think she's been any happier than I have. We both went into the marriage with good intentions, and I suppose we thought we were in love at the time, but I knew very early that I made a mistake."

"That's awful. Why didn't you do something if you felt that way?"

He sighed. "I've wondered the same thing over the years. I told myself this must be the way things are after you're married, that maybe in time things would get better. I looked at the marriages around me and they didn't seem all that great, so I figured this is what marriage is. After a while, the kids come along, the job takes three quarters of your life, and you don't have time to think about it anymore. You just keep plugging away and the years pass by, and you wind up where I am, asking yourself why you feel so empty inside."

"I can't imagine living like that, Peter. I would rather be alone than with someone I couldn't feel deeply about. How can you live your life that way?"

"Other things fill the void: my children, my work, my friendships. When I look at the whole picture, I would have to say that I have a lot of things to be thankful for. I try not to dwell on what's missing." He took a deep breath. "What about you, Nicole? Is there someone special in your life?"

"No. I haven't done the greatest job of picking men, but fortunately I've been lucky enough to see that before jumping into a marriage." She realized too late how that must sound to him. "I'm sorry. I wasn't trying to sound superior. I've just been lucky so far, that's all."

"You don't have to apologize. I can imagine how it must sound to you. I thought I had accepted the way things were, come to terms with my life more or less. It becomes the norm. You don't even think about it." He stopped. "That's changed, though, from the moment I met you. I find myself looking inside, examining my life as if it were under a microscope. I don't like what I see, and I don't know if I'm willing to tolerate it any longer. But then there's the side of me that says you can't have it all. I have two wonderful kids, a career I love. Pat and I may not have the perfect marriage, but we have a lot of years together, and that counts for something. I don't know. Sometimes it all spins around in my head so furiously that it hurts to think." He smiled ruefully. "You must be thinking this would be the right time to walk away from this confused man."

She could feel herself being pulled under, out of control, and didn't know what to say. She needed a moment alone.

"I think the time has come for me to powder my nose. Will you excuse me?"

"Of course," he said. He stood up and put his hand on the back of her chair.

The rest room was empty, and she leaned back against the wall and closed her eyes. She must be mad. She could feel her heart pounding against her chest and she took a long, deep breath. Every minute she spent with him made her want more. She wanted to walk down the street with him, hand in hand, to dance in his arms, to share with him those private moments of people in love. Get a hold of yourself Nicole, she thought. This is off limits. She was on a slippery slope, one that, she knew, other women had gone down and wound up just as she would if she continued, reaping heartache and regret. She went to the washbasin and held her hands under the faucet. The cold water felt good, and she splashed some on her face. She was calmer now and started back to the bar.

She felt a tap on the shoulder and turned around.

"Michael! What are you doing here?" She felt as if she had been caught stealing.

"What a terrific surprise, but you're the one who's out of her neighborhood. Are you alone?" he asked hopefully.

"No, Peter's here."

"Peter? Peter Demetrios?" His surprise was apparent.

"That's the one. Why don't you join us?"

Michael followed her to their table.

"Peter, look who I ran into."

"Michael." Peter stood up, visibly caught off guard.

"Hi, Peter. What a surprise."

"I missed you at the office tonight. When I stopped in Nicole was the last one there, and I twisted her arm to come and have a drink with me. Sit down. Can I get you anything?"

Michael pulled up a chair from the table behind them and sat down next to Nicole. "I'll just have a club soda. Anything else would probably put me to sleep."

"I really should get going." Nicole stood up and put her coat over her arm. "Goodnight. Thanks for the drink."

"Goodnight, Nicole. I'll see you Thursday," Michael said.

"Excuse me, Michael, while I walk Nicole to her car."

She turned to him as they approached the front of the restaurant. "I feel as if I've been caught with my hand in the cookie jar. It's not a good feeling."

"I'm sorry, Nicole."

"It's not your fault," she said quietly.

They walked slowly along the dark street. When they reached her car she looked up at him.

"Thanks."

He didn't answer but stared at her and time was suspended. As if in a dream, he moved towards her and his lips found hers. She returned his kiss with a passion that astounded her. Their mouths fit together as if they had been shaped and molded for only each other. She didn't want him to stop. Finally, he pulled away gently.

"Can I call you tomorrow?"

"Yes."

He touched her cheek. "Drive safely."

Her stomach twisted in knots. Had she really just been in his arms? As long as her infatuation had remained a fantasy, it was easy to enjoy the flirtation, but this was no game. She had better be damned certain of what she wanted before continuing this dance. She approached downtown Baltimore without even realizing she had progressed from one highway to the next. The ringing telephone greeted her when she entered the dark house. Who would be calling so late? Immediately she began to think of what crisis might be the reason for a call at this hour and hurried in to answer the persistent ringing.

"Hello?" she said shortly.

"Good, you're there. I just wanted to be sure you'd gotten home safely." It was Peter.

"Safe and sound. Thanks for calling. It's sweet of you." She didn't want him to hang up.

Peter cleared his throat. "Will you be here Tuesday?"

"I'm there every Tuesday. I don't see why this one will be any different," she said, trying to sound blase.

"Will you spend some time with me after the office closes?"

Things were moving too fast.

"I don't know, Peter. I don't know what to make of what happened," she said.

"Nicole, I should apologize for kissing you but I can't. I've wanted to do that from the first moment I saw you. It doesn't have to go any further than that. I just want to be able to spend some time with you, that's all. Please?"

"I don't know, Peter. Maybe," she said with uncertainty.

"I'll see you Tuesday," he said, taking her maybe for a green light. "Sweet dreams." She heard the click of the receiver.

Chapter 18

*T*heodora slammed the phone down in frustration. This was the fourth hang up that day. Suddenly she had an idea. She found the number, punched it in the cordless phone, and paced while entering the endless selections required to get to a live operator.

"I'd like to add a service please," she said when she finally got through. "Caller ID."

She sank into the soft cushions of the sofa and sipped her coffee. She was not suspicious by nature and tried to dismiss the nagging anxiety that was beginning to permeate her thoughts. Was she being paranoid? Maybe she had spent too many hours of her childhood around the kitchen table listening to stories of women wronged by cheating men. The implicit admonition in the telling of these tales was to beware of scheming women who were out to get your man. An overly friendly secretary had more on her agenda than work. Ironically, she was almost positive her father had never cheated on her mother. Still, there were enough examples of the baser side of men in their own community to make Theodora skeptical of any behavior that appeared too far out of the ordinary. With Stewart, there was nothing overt, but rather, subtle changes. He, a lifetime devotee of classical and chamber music, suddenly couldn't get enough of country music. He traded his Gray Goose for Budweiser. When she commented on it, he became defensive and called her a snob. He was evasive about phone calls he received on his cell phone, and he was working constantly, or so he said.

This was the first Saturday in a month he had cleared his schedule to be with her. He promised her earlier that morning that he just had to put in a couple of hours at the office and they'd be on their way by noon. It was after one and he was still gone. She'd been unable to reach him at the office or on his cell phone. She looked up when she heard the door open.

"Where have you been?" she snapped at him, despite her best intentions to keep her voice neutral.

He looked at her as if she were crazy. "What do you mean? I told you I had to go to the office." He threw his briefcase on the table and began sorting through the mail, ignoring her.

She walked over to him. "Stewart, you said you'd be home over an hour ago. I tried to call you and you weren't at the office." She sounded like a shrew, even to herself.

"For God's sake Theodora, I didn't answer the phone because I was trying to get some work done. What's the point of going in on a Saturday if you allow yourself to get distracted by the damn phone."

She couldn't stop herself. "Why didn't you answer your cell then? What if there had been an emergency and I needed to get in touch with you?"

He looked at her. "Was there?"

"Was there what?"

"An emergency?" he asked sarcastically.

"No, I'm just saying," she answered, exasperated.

He smiled at her. "You worry too much. Let's not fight. I didn't answer because I wanted to hurry and finish things up to be with you. Here I am. Let's not waste the day on this nonsense." He kissed her on the cheek.

Theodora didn't want to ruin the day and was eager to restore the good humor between them. Still, she felt manipulated. How did he always manage to make her feel as though she were creating the problems? On the other hand, she really had no reason to suspect him of anything. She forced herself to sound cheerful.

"You're right. I was thinking we could go to the Walters to see the Van Gogh Exhibit and then have lunch."

"Sounds terrific. Let me jump in the shower and then we'll get going." Halfway down the hall, he turned around. "Care to join me?"

Sex was the last thing she was in the mood for. "Wonderful as that sounds, I'd better not or we'll never get out of here." She made her voice light.

He flashed her a charming grin. "Come on Mrs. Elliott, don't you take your vows seriously? You don't want me to have to find satisfaction elsewhere do you?"

Theodora could hide her feelings no longer. "That's not funny Stewart. Are you trying to blackmail me?"

His face fell. "I was only kidding Theodora. My God. What's the matter with you? Do you think I'd actually say something like that if I meant it?"

She didn't know what to think anymore. Now he was angry again. She followed him upstairs.

"Stewart, I'm sorry. It's just . . ."

He interrupted her. "Just what? You've got to lighten up. I love you and would never hurt you. Why is that so hard to believe?"

She laid her head on his chest and he stroked her hair. "I don't know," she whispered.

He held her for a long time and then they were lying together on the bed. He made love to her tenderly and reassuringly until she could no longer remember why she had been angry.

"Much better than an art exhibit, don't you think?" He whispered right before he fell asleep.

Chapter 19

*F*or the past three weeks Nicole's world had revolved around her work at headquarters and her time with Peter, everything else a mundane and tedious obligation to be endured. Whenever possible, he made it a point to be there on the nights she volunteered and if they didn't always have time alone together, they at least saw each other. And then there were those few precious evenings when they'd managed to have some time, just the two of them. It soon became obvious that the safest place to meet was her house.

When they were apart, she saw him everywhere, in the sudden glimpse of a stranger's similar frame to a gesture that mimicked his. A part of her was continually with him, leaving inside her an emptiness whose vastness she had never before experienced. On the evenings they did not see each other, she waited impatiently for his phone call, unable to give her attention to anything else until they'd spoken. It didn't occur to her that perhaps her sister had felt this way about Stewart, or her mother this way about her father or, for that matter that anyone had experienced quite what she was feeling. She tried not to dwell on how things might change after the election was over and the campaigning ended. And she especially tried not to think of the family he had at home or what her family would say if they knew.

She rose early on Election Day so that she could vote before going into the office. The polls were already filling with people, a good sign because a heavy voter turnout was expected to work in Peter's favor.

The hours at the office dragged. She had taken clothes to change into for the celebration tonight, and called Theodora for the fourth time in the last two hours. By late afternoon she was so edgy, she had to get out of the office. She walked the two blocks to a small convenience store and poured a hot cup of coffee for herself. While she was paying the cashier, she noticed the Sun with a photograph on the front page of each candidate at his polling place. There were Peter and Pat getting ready to cast their votes at the high school in Annapolis. She turned away, paid for her coffee and left the store, blinking to keep the tears back.

At five-thirty she poked her head into her father's office.

"How's it looking in there Dad? Will you be ready to go soon?"

Nick and Eleni were coming to the hotel to wait for the returns. The four of them, Nick, Eleni, Stewart and Nicole, planned to drive to Annapolis together and have dinner with Theodora in the hotel. Since the polls closed at eight o'clock, most people would arrive at the hotel sometime between eight and nine.

"I'll be finished in ten minutes. Why don't you give Mom a call and see if she's ready? Tell her we'll pick her up in about half an hour. I'll buzz Stewart and make sure he's ready to leave too."

Within an hour and a half, the five of them were seated at their table for dinner.

"It must have been crazy today," Nicole said to Theodora.

"Actually, just the opposite. It was almost eerie after all the noise and commotion that usually goes on. It was kind of sad to know today was the last day."

"The last day. You're talking like he's going to lose," Nicole said.

"No I'm not. I know he's going to win. But it is the last day of campaigning and all the strange and funny things that have happened along the way. Some of us won't be working together any more even if Peter wins. It won't be the same. It'll probably never be as much fun. We'll never duplicate this past year, and I guess everyone was feeling that today, including Peter," Theodora said.

"How was he today? Was he nervous?" Nicole asked.

Theodora looked at her sister. "I didn't see that much of him but he seemed okay. He went to a number of polling places with his family," she said quite deliberately. The last thing she wanted to do was hurt Nicole, but perhaps tonight, seeing Peter with Pat and the children, would show her that this infatuation was dangerous and futile.

"I'm hungry," Stewart said. "Do you think we could put Peter on hold until we order some food?"

The large room at the hotel was filled with huge clusters of navy and gold helium balloons. Tables were placed to allow plenty of room for walking, and drinks were served from two bars at either end of the room. Nicole knew that Peter, with his family and a few close friends and workers, was upstairs watching the returns in a small private room. He would join his workers and supporters in the main ballroom as the outcome of the election became clearer. In the meantime, people milled around and watched the first returns trickling in from precincts around the state. So far Peter was leading but it was far too early to claim victory. Nicole wandered aimlessly around the room. Would this day never reach its conclusion, when Peter arrived downstairs and they would finally see each other? She glanced again at the group of people with her family and saw that Michael had joined them. She was surprised. Michael should be upstairs with Peter. She made her way across the room, and he left the group to meet her.

"Hi. How come you're not upstairs?" Nicole asked.

"I wanted to see how things are going down here. Besides, how could I stay up there when I knew you were here all alone?"

"Such gallantry. I don't know how I've resisted you all this time," she bantered.

"Quite honestly, I don't either."

"Is Peter feeling good about the returns so far?" she asked.

"Pretty confident. I think it's obvious we've got it wrapped up. He should be here soon. He asked me to let you know that."

She felt a mild shock, since she and Michael hadn't discussed her relationship with Peter. "Thanks, Michael. You're a good friend."

"See you in a little while," he said and left the ballroom.

"Nicole," Theodora called to her. "Come on over. We need you to settle a bet."

"What?" she said coming over to the group.

"Dad and Stewart have been going on and on with this ridiculous drivel that men are better drivers than women. We're comparing driving records. I know you've never had an accident, but how many tickets have you had?"

"I haven't had any. Does that settle it?" Nicole smiled.

"No way," Stewart said. "How many times have you been stopped?"

"What's that got to do with anything?" she asked.

"That has everything to do with it. Cops are usually men, you're a gorgeous woman, hence you talk your way out of a ticket," Stewart replied.

"For your information, I've never been pulled over," Nicole said smugly.

"There goes your argument," Theodora said.

"I could have told you you'll never win an argument against these two," Nick laughed. "I've tried for years and haven't had success yet."

"I'm not budging. My argument makes perfect sense," Stewart continued.

His words were drowned out by the band, who turned up the volume and played "When The Saints Come Marching In" as Peter Demetrios made his entrance. All eyes turned to him, and the clapping that began to ripple through the room turned to thunderous applause. He walked to the microphone, followed by his wife and two children. With Pat at his side, he held his hands in the air in a gesture indicating he wanted quiet so that he could speak.

"Good evening everyone. As I look at the faces in this room and see so many loyal friends and supporters, it occurs to me that I could never thank you enough for your hard work and dedication throughout this campaign. You made it possible. I have just received word that my opponent, Kenneth Anderson, has conceded the election." With those words a tremendous roar went up. Peter waited for the noise to die down. "I thank each and every one of you for what you have done to make this victory possible, and I will do everything in my power to live up to your trust and belief in me." He was greeted with more applause and whistles. "Now the work really begins. We have much to do, and we will go forward together to make this a better place for every citizen of this great state. Thank you."

The room was filled with the sound of deafening applause and shouts of victory amidst the strains of "For He's A Jolly Good Fellow." People cried and embraced. Some began dancing around the room. Peter enthusiastically made his way into the crowded mass to shake hands and thank people personally. Nicole moved to the back of the room, watching from a distance. She felt such a mixture of emotions; happiness and pride in his victory and a melancholy in knowing how much on the periphery of his life she remained.

Suddenly he was standing in front of her. Aware of the cameras and reporters following him, he carefully avoided any acknowledgement of her as anything more than another loyal campaign worker. She was crushed. But, what kind of fool was she to expect anything more? If she didn't know before, it was all too clear now exactly where she stood. It was here, in the back of the room and up against a wall, on the outer fringe of Peter's sphere, looking in but never a part of his life. It was not Nicole by his side, but his wife, with her hand in his and a wide smile on her face. She felt discarded and dirty like a pair of soiled and tattered garden gloves that have outlived their usefulness.

No one noticed her leave the room. The air outside was bracing, just what she needed to clear her head and take away the queasiness in her stomach. She looked out over the quiet water, bathed in silvery moonlight, and never felt more dejected or alone.

Chapter 20

*N*icole read the same sentence for the fourth time. Concentration eluded her and she glanced quickly at the gold carriage clock sitting on the mantle to see that it was past eleven. She rubbed her tired eyes and closed the book. The sudden sound of the doorbell startled her, and her brow wrinkled in puzzlement. When she looked through the peephole, she saw Peter standing there. For a moment she hesitated, trying to decide whether to answer the door or pretend she was in bed, but she knew she would never sleep if she let him leave without knowing why he'd come. Her hands shook as she opened the door.

"Nicole. May I come in?"

"What are you doing here, Peter? She stood in the doorway and pulled the door close to her body, refusing to open it in welcome. With her face freshly scrubbed and clad in an oversized t-shirt, she looked even younger than her twenty-six years.

"Nicole, I have to talk to you,"

"I don't think we have anything to talk about," she replied, still holding the door firmly.

"I have a lot to say to you. The first is I'm sorry. Please Nicole, let's talk."

Feelings raged inside her. He looked so unhappy that she felt pity for him despite her anger and resentment. She wanted to scream at him and tell him how much he'd hurt her. She wanted him to take her in his arms and assure her that everything would be all right, but the thought fled as quickly as it came, replaced by the pain that was her constant companion since election night. Now he wanted to walk back into her house as if he belonged there. He stood waiting, silent and patient, like a man facing the jury about to sentence him.

"Let me put a robe on." She opened the door all the way. "I'll be right down."

Peter walked into the room and felt cheered by the warmth and ease of the surroundings. The faint smell of sage emanated from the cluster of lighted candles on the Regency desk, and as he breathed in the pleasing scent, he sank back comfortably into the soft, leather sofa cushions.

Peter looked as the woman with whom he was falling more and more in love came into the room.

"Come here and sit with me so we can talk." He held out his hand in invitation and smiled calmly at her.

Deliberately ignoring his outstretched hand, she walked over to the fireplace and sat in the wing chair facing him. A fresh wave of anger washed over her when she thought about how he'd treated her and at his brazen presumptuousness in showing up at her door this way.

"What makes you think you can come knocking on my door whenever you feel like it? You have no claim on me, you know. You're married, remember?" She lashed out.

He sat still, waiting for her to go on, to get it all out.

"You made me feel like some insignificant volunteer last night." She hurried on, "All you cared about was your precious image. You, Mr. Senator, Mr. Family Man. I hated you. I wanted . . ." She couldn't continue, the sobs making her words indecipherable. Peter drew her gently out of the chair and into his arms, but her body remained rigid in his embrace.

He sighed. "I'm so sorry, Nicole. The last thing I ever wanted was for you to be hurt." He touched her cheek. "You know, I'm falling in love with you. I feel like I'm twenty years old again."

"Oh Peter." She felt herself softening. She wanted to melt into his arms and tell him she was falling in love with him too, but what good would that do? There would still be a wife to whom he belonged and went home every night.

He sensed her indecisiveness and rushed on.

"I've missed you Nicole. I feel as though I've known you for years instead of months. From the first time I saw you at that fundraiser, I knew you were someone special. Politics has a way of impersonalising your life. So many relationships are superficial, built on a system of mutual advantage. But when I'm with you, I feel as though you're interested in Peter the man, and that feels good."

Nicole was quiet. "Peter, I'll never forget how it felt on the night of your election. I've been kidding myself. I want much more than you'll ever be able to give me."

He continued to watch her. He knew she was right, but he wasn't willing to give up that easily.

"I despise the thought of never being able to spend time with you again. I would be satisfied with the tiniest piece of your world. Just to be able to see you once in a while and talk with you, be with you. Don't say anything now. But promise me you'll consider it." He was begging her. He touched her face affectionately. "I'll call you." He kissed her cheek and left before she could answer.

She sat down on the sofa and hugged her knees to her chest like a little girl. She was exhausted, her emotions battered and confused and yet being with Peter felt so good. Now the anger began to dissipate and all she could think about was the wonderful way he made her feel. I'll just play it by ear, she thought, intoning one of her father's favorite expressions.

Chapter 21

DECEMBER

*S*he was late. Nicole walked as fast as she could to the food court. Weaving in and out of the frantic mass of Christmas shoppers, she searched for Theodora and felt a yank on her hair.

"I guess I know what to get you for Christmas. Would you like a Timex or a Bulova?" Theodora teased.

"Sorry," Nicole said out of breath. "I saw something for Dad and lost track of time."

"That's okay, I've been entertaining myself people watching. Do you want to eat in this madhouse or should we try one of the restaurants downstairs?" Theodora asked

"Let's go downstairs, I've had enough of crowds."

They got on the escalator and began the descent to the next level.

"Hey there Nicole, how's it goin?" called an attractive woman from the escalator going up. She wore skintight jeans and a body hugging pink sweater.

Nicole forced a smile and waved as the escalator took the woman up and out of sight.

"Who was that?" Theodora asked.

"One of our new agents, Heather Daniels."

"A bit much, isn't she?" Theodora said.

Nicole laughed. "A little flamboyant for my taste, but the customers seem to like her."

"How does this place look?" Theodora asked, pointing to the open cafe style restaurant on her left.

"Perfect."

"So, what did you find for Dad that was so fantastic?" Theodora asked after they'd ordered.

Nicole pulled out the antique pocket watch and showed it to her sister.

"Oh Nicole, it's perfect. He'll love it. What a lovely idea," Theodora exclaimed.

"You really like it?"

"I love it! He'll be thrilled. He always is, you can do no wrong in his book," Theodora said, without envy.

"So tell me, what are you giving your husband on your first Christmas together?"

"It doesn't sound very romantic, but what he really wants is a tread-mill. Says he doesn't want to develop the married man's pouch." Theodora patted her own midriff as she spoke.

"Hmm."

"His mother, however, is a different story. I haven't the slightest idea what to get her."

"Why don't you get her a yearly pass to the zoo so she can visit her relatives in the snake pit," Nicole said.

"She really is difficult to like, isn't she? Every time I start to feel something even bordering on affection, she says or does something to make me want to wring her neck. I don't know how Stewart stood it, growing up with such a bitter woman. Of course, he's no help. When I asked for his input, he just shrugged and said, 'That's your job babe.' In any case, I know that no matter what I get her she'll make some comment about its inappropriateness."

"How about a bottle of her perfume? She can't make a disparaging comment about that," Nicole suggested.

"That's not a bad idea."

Two crispy green salads arrived at the table topped with walnuts and Gorgonzola cheese.

"Mm, looks yummy." Nicole took a forkful. "So, what did you get Peter?"

"I'm going to send a gift basket from Baltimore Coffee and Tea to the whole family." Theodora said.

"Do you see much of his wife?" Nicole asked casually.

Theodora put her fork down and looked at her sister. "Nicole, what's going on? I thought you had put this behind you."

Nicole hadn't told Theodora how far things had gone, but she found it impossible to keep quiet any longer.

"Theo, I think I'm in love with him." Nicole whispered.

"What? Nicole, what are you saying?" Theodora's eyes filled with concern.

"All right, listen, I'm going to tell you everything, but promise me you'll try to understand and not get angry." She waited and when Theo nodded silently, Nicole continued. "Theo, you know there was an attraction the very first night I met him. Then we kept seeing each other all the times I was at campaign headquarters and it seemed like we always wound up spending time together after everyone else left. And you know that time we had lunch together, the time I told Dad it was no big deal? Well, it was a big deal. It was the beginning of really getting to know each other and seeing how much we love being together. I've been seeing him ever since. We both tried to stop it, really, but it was impossible. The first time he kissed me I knew I was lost. I'm crazy about him, Theo, and he feels the same way about me, I know he does." She stopped, trying to gage her sister's reaction, then rushed on.

"You know that his marriage was in trouble long before I came along. Is there some law against our being happy?" She leaned back in her chair and looked at her sister expectantly. Had she finally gone too far? Would Theodora comfort or condemn her?

Theodora reached across the table and squeezed Nicole's hand. "Oh, Nicole, what have you gotten yourself into? I hoped it was just a passing infatuation. You know I want you to be happy. But, I can't imagine you'd let yourself break up a marriage. You've always had such a strong moral compass."

Nicole's expression was bleak.

"If they were truly happy, would he have ever looked at me?"

"I don't know. I've never seen him even flirt with anyone. I do believe he has feelings for you. But that doesn't make it right. If his marriage is over, let him end that and then start something with you."

Nicole nodded absently. "He's worried about the children."

"And about his political career." Theodora couldn't help adding.

"No, the children are the driving factor." Nicole insisted.

"Regardless of his personal feelings he is a politician and he'd never get a divorce if he thought it would damage his career. His career is number one, and nothing's going to change that. Please get out now before it goes any further." Theodora pleaded.

"Don't ask me that and please don't be mad, okay?" Nicole said as she looked at Theodora.

"I'm worried, not mad. Come on, let's walk and have a look at the Christmas decorations."

Theodora was lost in thought. She knew troubled times lay ahead and there was nothing she could do about it.

Chapter 22

*T*he flight to Boston was crowded with students heading home for Christmas, but Nicole had most of the first class section to herself. She sat back against the unyielding leather airplane seat and closed her eyes. She hated landings. Her stomach lurched as the plane descended faster and faster toward the ground. The wheels hit the runway and she felt the familiar staccato of bumps until it gradually slowed to a halt. She opened her eyes and stretched. Picking up her leather briefcase, she moved into the aisle and nodded at the flight crew as she deplaned.

"Happy Holidays," the flight attendant recited to each passing passenger.

She took the escalator to the ground level and stepped outside. The cold air caused a sharp intake of breath, and she shivered under her light trench coat. She hailed a taxi.

"Prudential Center, please," she told the driver as she slid into the back seat.

They sped off, weaving in and out of the heavy Boston traffic.

By eight, she was seated in the ornate mahogany conference room of Creative Concepts, the advertising agency that had been wooing Parsenis for the past five years. Recent changes in top management at the firm Parsenis currently used had necessitated a search for a new agency. Creative had jumped at the chance to pitch Nicole, and had offered to fly her to Boston for their presentation. The meetings went on all day, with only a brief respite for lunch. By five Nicole was exhausted.

"I can take you to the airport. What time is your flight?" Ed Miller, the company's president asked her.

"That's okay Ed, I can just grab a cab."

He started to protest but she insisted. The last thing she was in the mood for was small talk. She wanted to relax on the way to the airport.

"All right, if you insist. I'll have Kathy call you one. Should be about ten minutes."

"Thanks Ed. I'll be in touch."

She made it to the airport with an hour to spare and went to the counter to present her ticket to the agent. The woman typed into the computer then looked at Nicole.

"You called this morning to cancel. We've released your reservation."

"What are you talking about? I never called. There must be some mistake," Nicole answered.

The woman typed something more into the keyboard. After a few moments she shook her head. "I'm afraid it's no mistake. We've already reassigned your seat. This is a full plane," she said apathetically.

Furious, Nicole looked at the woman with murderous eyes. "This is absurd! I never canceled my reservation."

"No. I did." A deep voice came from behind her.

She spun around. "Peter!"

"I thought I'd better step in before a fight broke out." He grinned at her.

Shocked by his sudden appearance, she was momentarily speechless.

He led her to the seating area.

"What in the world are you doing here?" she asked incredulously.

"When you mentioned your trip to me last week, I thought it would be nice to surprise you and take you to dinner."

"But what about my flight home?"

"Don't worry, I've taken care of everything. I promise you'll be home in time to get to the office by nine tomorrow." He laughed.

Nicole was stunned. She was ecstatic to see him, but slightly miffed at the way he had so cavalierly changed her plans without consulting her.

"I don't know what to say."

He noticed the hesitation in her voice.

"You're not angry are you? I know it was impulsive, but I've missed you so much." He looked at her plaintively.

She melted. "Of course not, it's wonderful." She threw her arms around him then quickly pulled back, aware of their public surroundings.

Peter looked around nervously. "Why don't we get going, I've got a car downstairs."

A silver limousine waited and they settled into its plush interior. Peter pushed a button and the privacy window opened.

"Our reservations aren't for another hour, so drive around a bit." He closed the window, and they were alone again.

"Champagne?" He held a glass out to her.

"Mmm, thanks."

They toasted each other.

"Where're we going?" she asked excitedly.

"How does Anthony's sound?"

"Wonderful! It's one of my favorite restaurants. When I was in school, I only went there when my parents visited. I could never afford it. I loved looking at the photographs of all the celebrities."

Her comment reminded him again of their age difference, and he felt a stab of guilt. He watched her as she leaned against the leather seat and sipped her champagne. Her skirt had inched up above her knee. His gaze traveled the length of her legs and he felt a warmth flood his body. He couldn't help imagining the soft feel of her skin and wondered how those incredible legs would feel wrapped around him. He was consumed with desire for her and wondered if she could sense how aroused he was. It was all he could do to keep from reaching for her then and there.

Nicole was unaware of her effect on him. Visions of romance and professions of love filled her head as she fantasized about what the evening would bring. Ever since the night Peter showed up at her house unannounced, they spoke on the phone daily and met when they could, usually late in the evenings. They still referred to their relationship as a friendship, but they knew it was a pretense. So far they had managed to limit their physical relationship to no more than a few kisses and touches, but it was only a matter of time before they would take it further and pull the veil off to expose their true feelings. It terrified her. Her worldview was black and white, and she found women who coveted other women's husbands beyond contempt. She would have bet her life that she'd never wander down that crooked road. Yet, here she was, teetering on the edge, ready to violate every principle she'd ever held dear. Still, a voice inside wouldn't be quieted; the voice that stopped her each time she started to let go and reminded her of who she was and what she was made of. But Peter's presence drowned it out, and Nicole was becoming increasingly willing to let that happen. He placed his hand on her knee, and she turned to look at him.

"Now I can give you a proper greeting," he whispered huskily as he took the champagne glass from her hand and put it down. He moved toward her and pressed his lips to hers.

She gave in to his embrace and relaxed happily in his arms. She was acutely aware of his hand on her leg and it sent shivers of delight through her. The only voice Nicole could hear was the one telling her how wonderful this felt.

Chapter 23

*T*heodora opened the bedroom window and took a deep breath of the fresh cold air.

"Look, snow! So perfect for our first Christmas together." She came back to bed and snuggled close to him. "Let's exchange gifts," she smiled seductively, wrapping her leg around his.

They made long, slow love, aware that they had the rare luxury of time on this snowy Christmas morning. When Stewart finally got up and put his robe on, Theodora was still in a half sleep with sheets and blankets wrapped around her in a disordered jumble. He reached down and patted her behind, "You're the messiest sleeper I ever saw," he kidded.

She stretched lazily and with her leg tossed the blanket off the bed in his direction.

"Come on little girl, let's go see what Santa brought you."

She put on a fluffy, terrycloth robe and together they went downstairs.

Theodora sat on the floor near the tall, luxuriant Christmas tree and breathed in deeply the wonderful fragrance of fresh pine. A huge pile of packages of every sort and size sat under the tree, all brightly wrapped in red and green foil bedecked with enormous gold ribbons. She loved the ceremony and splendor of the holidays and this was reflected in the decorations throughout their home. Stewart reached under the tree and brought out a very small box.

"I hope you like it," he said as he handed the present to Theodora.

She turned the box around in her hand and slowly began unwrapping to reveal a black velvet jewelry box. It must be the necklace they'd seen together months ago, the one she thought was so beautiful with the sparkling blue sapphire and thin gold chain. When she pulled the top up and saw what the box held, she looked up in surprise.

"It's lovely Stewart." She hoped he couldn't hear the disappointment in her voice.

He rose eagerly and came over to where she sat so that he could look at the necklace with her. "I know you were looking at the one with the sapphire, but I think this one with the emerald and heavier chain is so much nicer, don't you? Here," he said, taking it out of the box, "let me help you."

She turned so her back faced him and held her hair off her neck while he clasped the heavy links. He put his hands on her shoulders and gently turned her to face him.

"Ah yes, beautiful. Go look in the mirror."

She rose automatically and walked to the evergreen draped mirror on the far wall. She leaned in closer, examining her reflection and fingering the band of gold. It was pretty, she thought. Maybe Stewart was right. Perhaps the other chain was a little too delicate and the emerald was probably a better color for her than the sapphire. One thing was certain. He had put some thought into it, not like most men who grabbed a list and mindlessly checked things off just to be done with it.

He came up behind her, put his arms around her waist and looked over the top of her head into the mirror. "Do you like it?"

"Oh Stewart, I love it. You're right, it's perfect!"

She walked over to the tree and picked up a small package for him. "Now it's your turn." She handed him the box.

He opened it and found a certificate inside. "My treadmill! Great. Thank you, sweetheart."

"That's not all," she said pushing him back down on the sofa. She handed him an even smaller package.

"Theo, I love it," he said quietly. "How did you know?" he asked as he lovingly fingered the gold signet ring with his initials.

"Know what, darling?"

"I thought maybe Mother had told you the story. She bought my father his signet ring on their first Christmas together." He slipped the ring onto his pinkie finger and held his hand out to admire it. It was difficult for him to imagine that his parents' first Christmas might have been filled with the same warmth as his and Theodora's. But his mother must have been happy and in love when she gave Graham that ring so many Christmases ago. God, what happened to people that they could turn something wonderful into spitefulness and ultimately to indifference? That wouldn't happen to him because he would always hold a little bit back. No one, not his mother or his father or his wife was ever going to own all of Stewart's heart. He would never allow himself to be hurt the way his parents had hurt each other.

"Thank you, sweetheart. It's a wonderful gift. I'll never take it off." He kissed her and abruptly got up. "Hungry? How about I cook us some breakfast?"

Theodora could see that he was touched by her present, but didn't know how to express it and so changing the subject was his way of not appearing too childishly happy or sentimental. She wished he trusted her enough to reveal those sentiments, but she was beginning to realize that it was going to take a long time and lots of loyal assurances from her before he ever let her glimpse the whole Stewart Elliott. One day things would be different.

She made coffee while Stewart cut up onions, peppers and cheese for the omelets. She poured them each a steaming mug and sat at the table to talk to him while he cooked.

"It's so wonderful to have three whole days together, with no work," she said.

"Isn't it? Things have been nuts ever since we got back from the cruise." He stopped chopping and turned around to face her still holding the knife in his hand. "I know it seems like we hardly see each other, but it'll be worth it in the end. Your father's really starting to depend on me. I've got a vision that will take that company places he's never dreamed. It's not the kind of thing that's accomplished in an eight hour day." He was excited.

"I understand. Dad was gone by five in the morning and usually not home until seven. I know how demanding business is, and it's not as though I work a forty hour week either."

"I worry about you, you know. I really don't like your driving alone at night. It was bad enough from Annapolis but now that you're working in Washington I like it even less."

"Whoa. How'd we get on to that subject? If we're going to take a three-day vacation from work, let's do it mentally as well, okay?"

He was reluctant to let this go. "I don't think you understand. It's not safe for you to be on those roads all alone at night. I don't like it one bit. I've been thinking that you should consider changing jobs, you know, get something closer. You don't even have to get another job, Theodora. We're not exactly hurting for money. There's really no reason for you to work at all."

She stared at him in astonishment. He couldn't be serious. Did he really expect her to give up work she loved, to sit home and do nothing?

"Stewart, you must be kidding. I can't just quit my job." She took a sip of coffee. "I don't want to talk about this anymore."

The pungent aroma of peppers and onions filled the room, but she no longer had an appetite. He could see that she was upset.

"I'm sorry honey. I only worry because I love you. No more talk about work, I promise." He turned back to the cutting board.

They finished their breakfast and lounged in robes as long as they could before it was time to dress for the day of visiting ahead of them. Theodora showered and put on the elegant black silk suit she had just bought. Around her neck she wore the emerald necklace Stewart had given her.

He whistled as he walked into the bedroom. "Don't you look sexy?"

The tension between them disappeared and she sat on the edge of the bed while he finished dressing. He made final adjustments to his tie and turned to face her.

"Well, do I pass muster?"

"You look great." She didn't recognize the tie he wore. It was different from his others, a flashy jumble of bright colors blended to form a spin art design. The most predominant color was hot pink in jagged zig zagging lines.

"What's wrong?" he asked, noticing the look on her face.

"Where'd you get that tie?"

"Pretty wild huh? One of the agents gave it to me, a sort of combination thank you and Christmas present. I figured if I can't wear something bright on Christmas, when can I?"

Theodora felt a pang of uneasiness.

"What agent?" she asked in what she hoped sounded like a casual voice.

"Her name's Heather. I met her at the Builder Mart a few months ago. She was selling five million a year with Carter Realty, and I lured her away to Parsenis. Says she likes it much better with us, and has more income potential because of our size. So, she gave me this tie as a token of her gratitude." He put the finishing touches on the knot.

"I saw her at the mall the other day. She seemed a little tacky."

Stewart turned from the mirror to face her. "That's a crappy thing to say. Not everyone grew up with an unlimited shopping allowance. Besides, she's good at what she does."

"What did you give her?" Theodora asked, more sharply than she intended.

"Nothing. What's the matter with you? It's just a stupid tie, don't make a big thing out of it."

"I'm sorry." It felt like she kept running into minefields today. "Well, we'd better hurry up, you know how your mother hates it when anyone's late."

They each picked up two large shopping bags full of presents and were soon cruising down the road, listening to Christmas carols. Theodora's mood lifted, and she forgot the tie.

"Merry Christmas!" Graham's booming voice greeted them. He opened wide the huge double doors. "Come on in, we have some

Elliott eggnog with your names on it." He kissed Theodora and patted Stewart on the shoulder.

"Merry Christmas Dad. Where's Mother?"

"She'll be right down. Come into the living room and relax. Your Aunt Peg's anxious to see you both."

The fireplace crackled and glowed, its ornate mantle festooned with a lively assortment of German nutcrackers. A sedate but elegant Christmas tree stood in the corner and strains of Bing Crosby's "White Christmas" filled the room. Theodora couldn't help but wonder if her mother-in-law had put this picture perfect scene together or if it had been left, as usual, to the help.

"Here you are, Theodora." Graham handed her a crystal punch cup filled with eggnog.

"Thank you, Merry Christmas." She held her cup up to his.

"Hello, my darlings, Merry Christmas." Aunt Peg rose from the sofa and held out her arms for a welcoming hug. "Theodora, you look lovely today," she said, pulling Theo to her in a warm embrace.

Theodora felt a familiar rush of gratitude and fondness for this genuinely nice woman who never failed to make her feel valued and appreciated.

"Merry Christmas, Aunt Peg. It's great to see you. Tell me that's not a Christmas gift from Uncle Roger," Theo said, pointing to a string of Christmas lights blinking crazily around Peg's neck.

Peg's deep, booming laugh filled the room. "You know better than that. Why, Roger would be embarrassed to even pretend interest in something like this in a store, much less buy it." She enjoyed teasing her somber and gray husband, and Theodora thought she saw just the tiniest spark of a twinkle in his normally impassive eyes.

"Peg turns her lights on in bed when she wants me to find her in the dark."

No one spoke at first, and then Stewart burst into surprised laughter, joined heartily by the others. Perhaps there was more to Roger and the marriage than there seemed.

"What's so funny?" Caroline called as she entered the room, sweeping past Theodora and going directly to Stewart for a kiss.

"Merry Christmas, everyone." She turned to Theodora. "You look festive, dear."

"Merry Christmas, Caroline." Theodora kissed her lightly on the cheek.

"Well, now we can start to open our presents. What fun," Caroline said dryly as she positioned herself in the wing chair nearest the tree.

The mood was effectively broken. Roger sank back into his posture of detached indifference and Graham became stiff and guarded. Peg alone seemed unaffected.

"So, Stewart, how did you two enjoy your first Christmas as husband and wife?" asked Peg.

"Blissful, Aunt Peg." He stood up and walked over to where Caroline sat and leaned down. "Look Mother, this was my present from Theodora." He showed her the ring.

Caroline paled slightly. How was she to endure this constant assault upon her relationship with her son? Who did this girl think she was? She'd only known Stewart a few years for heaven's sake. Caroline was the one who really knew him, the one who should be the most important person in his life. She could kick herself for not having given him such a ring herself. "Well..." she stumbled for words. "How delightful my dear. I suppose Stewart told you I gave one to Graham our first Christmas."

"Yes, he did, just this morning. I had no idea when I chose it."

"Okay, everybody sit down. It's time for the good stuff," Graham ordered, as he put a Santa hat on his head. He handed Theodora a box wrapped in hunter green paper with a thick grosgrain ribbon around it.

"How lovely. Thank you very much Caroline and Graham." She forced a smile as she held up a red and blue plaid knit skirt and matching top, an outfit obviously and completely unsuited to her.

"Get one of ours Graham," Theodora said.

"Okay, this one is to Caroline," he handed her a shiny red package with a bright gold ribbon.

"What extravagant wrapping. It's beautifully done my dear."

Caroline unwrapped the perfume. "Thank you both, you know I can never have enough JOY," she said.

The next half hour was filled with more of the same. When they finished, they sat down to dine at the long formal table covered with a starched white damask cloth. The sparkling crystal and china gave the holly boughs in the center of the table an even more festive look. A large china platter held roast beef with horseradish and walnut sauce, another smoked salmon, while yet another held sauteed chestnuts and brussels sprouts. Buttered brown bread nestled in a beautifully woven basket. The meal was quite different from those to which Theodora was accustomed.

"We'd better start, Stewart and Theodora have to rush out by four to have Christmas with her family," Caroline complained.

"That gives us plenty of time Caroline," Graham said sharply, annoyed with his wife's hostility toward Theodora.

Caroline was quiet, galled at being publicly reprimanded.

"Here's to many more Christmas celebrations and to some future little Elliott additions," Peg said, holding up a glass of red wine.

"Here, here. I hope you two are working on that," Graham said.

"My God," Caroline said. "Must you be so vulgar? Is nothing private for heaven's sake?" She was unable to comprehend the vague, but pervasive sense of distress she felt at the mention of Stewart and Theodora starting a family.

There was only the sound of silverware against china as they all concentrated on the food before them, then Peg cleared her throat and pointed her fork at Theodora.

"You know, I have to tell you how proud I was of you when your man won the election. I know you worked damned hard to get him elected. Why, I told my book club, you should see the little spitfire of a gal working for Demetrios. How are things going for him anyway?"

"He jumped in with both feet, Aunt Peg. He cares about people and the problems created by poverty. I really believe he'll make some very significant changes, changes that will make a difference."

"No matter how sincere the man is, there will always be those who depend on others to support them. Certain types just don't want to be self sufficient," Caroline said.

"Well that doesn't mean we just give up and stop helping people reach self-sufficiency," Graham began. "Look at my family; my grandfather was a poor potato farmer from Ireland who came here without two nickels to rub together. A friend of his gave him a job in his grocery store, and he was able to raise a family and put my father through school. Now look at his offspring only two generations later. What if there hadn't been anyone to help him?"

Caroline winced. "Must you bring up that wretched story? We don't need to be reminded of your humble beginnings."

Theodora's face flushed with embarrassment. She avoided looking at anyone and hoped the awkward moment would pass.

Graham laughed. "I forgot, you descend from royalty. Guess you don't want me to mention the horse thieves in your family tree?"

"Oh yes," Peg joined in merrily. "Roger has the old 'Wanted Dead or Alive' poster of your great, great grandfather to prove it."

"That's quite enough. It's Christmas. You'd think you might all be civil," Caroline said in a hurt voice, ever the victim.

"Come on. Mother's right, it's Christmas. A time for happiness, not fighting," Stewart said. He didn't remember a holiday that hadn't been stained with argument and antagonism. Why should it be any different today?

"Okay, I apologize. How about dessert for everyone?" Graham said heartily.

A spiced currant cake with rum butter was served. It was three thirty by the time they finished dessert, and Theodora and Stewart prepared to leave.

As they drove towards her grandparents' home, Theodora felt a keen sadness for her husband. Christmas in her home had always been a time of joy. She was used to a lot of family around, everyone cheerful and boisterous. It was a wonder Stewart even enjoyed the holidays.

"I guess we're the last ones to arrive," she said when she saw all the cars parked in the driveway and along the curb.

They walked up the steps to the large front porch where a cheerful wreath with red ribbons and holly adorned the front door. The house was alive with activity, and the smells of Yiayia's cooking wafted into the hallway from the kitchen and filled the house.

"Merry Christmas!" Theodora called cheerily and hugged her parents.

"Hi Darling, Merry Christmas. You look beautiful. Hello Stewart, Merry Christmas," Eleni said, hugging him.

"Merry Christmas to both of you! How about a drink?" Nick said.

"Nothing for me thanks, I'm going to go say hi to everyone," Theodora said.

"I'd love one, Dad. Whatever you're drinking," Stewart answered.

He walked over to the bar set up in the living room and poured two scotches, one for himself and one for Stewart. Nick handed him the drink and put his arm around him.

"I want to give this to you in private," he said, handing him a plainly wrapped box.

Stewart opened it and looked at Nick quizzically. Inside was a key.

"It's to your new office. I'm moving you to my floor, to Alex Fibern's old office. You're doing such a great job on the Manor Hills project, I decided you needed a bigger office. Congratulations."

"I don't know what to say." He ran a hand through his hair. "I feel like going over to the office right now and moving in!"

Stewart was elated. Alex had been the senior vice president in charge of construction. Since his death a year ago, his old office remained vacant. It was almost as large as Nick's and decorated with the same thick Persian carpet and antique furniture. Stewart knew this symbolized Nick's growing faith in him and his intention to share more authority with him.

"First things first. Today is a family day, go enjoy your wife!"

It pleased Nick that Stewart was so devoted to the business. For the last two and a half years he had demonstrated a ceaseless determination to learn and advance. The construction department flourished under his leadership; projects were always completed on time, often at a substantial cost savings due to Stewart's careful management of expenses. Since becoming part of the family, Stewart was even more eager to perform. His ambition and drive reminded Nick of himself at Stewart's age, and he intended to do everything in his power to foster that ambition and shape Stewart into a good leader.

"Merry Christmas Dad." Nicole walked up to him.

"Hi darling. Merry Christmas." Nick put his arm around Nicole as they headed to the dining room.

The scene was in sharp contrast to the one Stewart and Theodora just left. An overflowing spread of sumptuous foods was the backdrop for noise and confusion as the family seated themselves around the crowded dining room table. Lamb, beef tenderloin, spanakopita, tiropita, stuffed grape leaves, pilafi, green beans, home made bread and a large salad with onions, cucumbers, tomatoes and feta cheese made up the feast. Yiayia worked for days preparing all the food except for the lamb. That was Papou's specialty.

Here the talk and laughter mixed in rising and falling crescendos of excitement and pleasure. Scraps of wrapping paper remained scattered along with discarded boxes. The children greeted the gift exchange with shouts of delight, and the celebration continued well into the evening. Finally they began to gather coats and packages, reluctant to see another Christmas come to an end.

Nicole was the last to leave and she was feeling pleasantly tired from a long, happy day. When she opened her storm door a package fell to the ground. It was wrapped in gold paper and tied with a thick velvet ribbon. There was no card. She unlocked the front door and hurried into the warmth of the dark quiet house. She took the package into the living room, turned on a light and sat down. When she unwrapped it, she held in her hand a beautiful leather tooled copy of Elizabeth Barrett Browning's Sonnets from the Portuguese. She opened the book to the first page and read the inscription written in large, bold script.

My Dear Nicole,

Please accept this gift of poetry that I know you love so well, and think of me when you read "How do I love thee? Let me count the ways . . ." I could never count the ways if I lived to be one hundred.

You are never out of my mind. I am thinking of you now as you sit and read these words. I miss you more than you will ever know.

Merry Christmas, sweet Nicole. I wish you peace and happiness in the year to come.

Always,
Peter

Memories of Boston flooded Nicole's mind. She saw his face, the way he smiled at her in that private way. She could almost feel his arms around her, his body touching hers. The familiar ache returned once more. Would the time ever come when she wouldn't miss him, not think about him, when everything didn't remind her of him? She hugged the book to her chest and then the tears came. More tears than she ever imagined, and she helplessly abandoned herself to her grief. She cried for what she couldn't have, for what would never be. And with her sorrow was the bitter irony that the one man she could love was beyond her reach.

Finally, there were no more tears. Just an empty, hollow feeling in her body. She rose from the sofa and walked aimlessly to the window. She was so tired. Depleted. The bright moonlight washed over the snow-covered ground. It was Christmas and she was alone. She looked down at the book clutched in her hands and read once more what Peter had written. Her eyes rested for a moment on the last line, "I wish you peace and happiness in the year to come."

"What happiness, Peter?" she asked aloud and closed the book.

Chapter 24

JANUARY

*T*heodora watched the waves crash against the beach and was struck by the change Ocean City took on in wintertime. She was curled up in one of the huge swivel chairs that sat in front of the porch window, sipping a steaming cup of hot chocolate her grandmother had made. The furious northeast wind rattled the storm windows, and she instinctively wrapped the heavy afghan closer around her. She loved it here any time of year. Each season brought its own mood and feeling. Her problems always seemed smaller against the background of the steady sea, its majesty and infiniteness always dominant.

The weekend trip had been hastily arranged only a day before, the night she dined at her grandparents' home. She told them Stewart would be in Pittsburgh on business for the next few days. What she hadn't told them was that Heather Daniels would accompany him. She'd discovered this quite by accident when the travel agency through whom the tickets were booked, had mistakenly called the house instead of the office to see if someone would be picking up the tickets for Ms. Daniels and Mr. Elliott or if they should be delivered by messenger. The scene that followed when Stewart came home that night was still painted in her mind.

"Is anyone else from the office going? She had asked him.

"Nope, I'll be all on my lonesome."

She felt panic and anger vie for supremacy as he calmly lied to her.

"Really." She tried to keep her cool. "Then I can't imagine why the travel agent called here with tickets for Mr. Elliott and Ms. Daniels. What the hell is going on Stewart?"

"Nothing's going on, but I knew you'd react exactly the way you're reacting, with suspicion and jealousy, if I told you Heather was coming, and quite frankly I didn't want to have to go through all these dramatics with you."

"Don't you understand that keeping it a secret makes it look suspicious? What am I supposed to think?"

"You're supposed to think you've got a husband who's never given you a reason to doubt him and who loves you more than any other man would. Why do you have to create problems?"

"Stewart, I'm not the one creating problems. I'm not flying off somewhere with a man from my office."

As if speaking to a child, he had said very slowly. "Theodora, I am not flying off somewhere. I am attending a builder convention and seminar, and the person in the department whose attendance will benefit the company is coming along. It just happens that person is Heather. If it's going to upset you so much, I'll call her and tell her she'll have to stay behind because my wife doesn't want her to go."

The argument had continued in their usual manner. He interpreted anything Theodora said as an attack and then smoothly side stepped the real issue at hand. No one won an argument with Stewart Elliott.

She leaned her head against the back of the chair and looked around the familiar room. There were so many happy memories crammed into this apartment, sunny days spent with her brother and sister and their cousins. They were on the beach by nine o'clock every morning and didn't leave until the sun began to set over the building. The beach boy marked their spot with two umbrellas side-by-side and tagged with the name Zaharis. Once they arrived, the site looked like an encampment, with blankets and beach towels spread out, canvas bags filled with lotions, t-shirts and toys for the younger children, and a variety of goodies to munch on. The rented canvas lounge chairs were reserved for the adults, and sprawled around the perimeter sat rafts for surfing the waves. At night they walked the boardwalk, agonizing over which rides to choose with their limited funds for the night.

She looked past the sofa to the kitchen that opened off of the large living area. Sophia was bustling around, more at home in that room than anywhere else.

"Yiayia, stop working and come sit down and talk to me," Theodora called.

"I will be right there. I am almost finished." Sophia was a few more minutes, then came to sit with her granddaughter. She still had her apron on, and Theodora smiled as she realized she didn't even own one. They sat in easy silence, watching the scene outside. An adventuresome couple, bundled heavily against the cold, strolled along the shoreline, the lone human beings for blocks and blocks. Sophia turned away from the window to look at Theodora.

"You are very quiet. Something is bothering you, yes?" No one was ever able to hide anything from Sophia. She watched her brood like a mother hen and was acutely aware of every small nuance of behavior.

"Yiayia, you and Papou have always seemed so happy together. You really love him don't you?"

"Ah, Theodora, I think there are not too many men like your grandfather. I was very lucky."

"So was he. I look at you and wonder what I'm doing wrong. I've only been married six months and half the time I'm miserable. It's as if Stewart and I speak two different languages. What's the secret?"

"There is no secret, *agapi mou*. You learn. You learn when to keep your mouth closed and when to open it. I always put your Papou first, before my children even. There were times he made me angry, but I knew he never did those things intentionally. I remember when he brought his sister, *Thea* Anoula, from Greece. She was just a few years younger than I and single. She lived with us for two years while my children were still little ones. Your grandfather, he was a member of many organizations, and there were always dinners and events to attend. In those days no one hired baby sitters. When we went visiting, we took our children with us. Your Papou wanted Anoula to meet a husband, and so he took her with him to all of these gatherings. I stayed home with the children. She never once said to me 'You go with your husband, Sophia, and I will watch the children for you.'

"That's terrible. Why didn't you say something to him?"

"It was her place to offer. Men do not think of these things, but Anoula should have known better. She was selfish, just as my mother-in-law, Anoula's mother, was selfish."

"If you want to trade mother-in-law stories, I'll bet I can top yours every time."

Sophia shook her head. "Yes, that one of yours is an unhappy woman. She is not a kind person."

"That's putting it nicely. But back to you and Papou. Are you telling me that I should just keep my mouth shut if I'm upset about something? That sounds like a high price to pay for harmony."

"I said you must know when to open your mouth, not that you never open it. But you do not see one very important thing. Your grandfather is a good man. He is generous and kind, and these things are behind all that he does. I know in his heart he always wanted only the best for me and for his family. There was one time when your mama misbehaved, and Papou tapped her little behind with his slipper. Your mama, she was so ashamed. Papou never scolded this way. Later I said to her, 'So Eleni, your papa gave you a little spank,' and she said to me 'My papa didn't hit me, his slipper did.' He would never do something from a mean spirit or because he wanted something for himself. A woman is able to overlook many things with a man like that."

Theodora pondered her grandmother's words. Was she implying that Stewart was not that kind of man?

"And you know," Sophia continued in her heavy accent. "We did not have the time you young people do to wonder if we were happy or not. All day I took care of my children, I cooked and cleaned and sewed. Our house was never empty of relatives your grandfather brought from Greece. Barely would one move out when another would arrive. Sometimes your mama and aunt had to sleep on the floor. My house was always full."

"That doesn't sound very appealing."

"It was not so bad. Your grandfather worked long hours those first years and I always had *parea*, company. They played with my children and our dinner table was a lively place with much talk and laughter. While Anoula was here there were many suitors who came, and your mother and Aunt Eve, who were just little girls, loved to watch her get ready for these occasions. Anoula was ahead of her time. She became friendly with the Greek girls who wore much make-up and tight dresses. They smoked and drank and went to one party after another. Of course, she never lit a cigarette in front of your Papou. She was too smart to let him see that. She finally picked one of the boys who followed her around like a small puppy and married him. You were not born when her husband Giorgios died. He worshipped her always and made a very good living for her. You see all that she has, her beautiful home and fine things."

"I remember her in wonderful clothes that showed off her figure and lots of noisy jewelry. She didn't look like most of the other yiayias," Theodora said.

"She was not like most of the others. Anoula and her group, they were the fast ones. They dyed their hair blonde, they went on trips alone together, they even had boyfriends while they were married."

"You're kidding! I can't believe it. What did Papou say?"

"Your Papou talked and talked to her, but she never listened. He was happy to have his sister in this country with him, so he stopped looking at the things of which he did not approve."

"You must have had your hands full while she lived with you."

"There were problems, but all in all they were good years. You make them good."

"I don't know how you did it Yiayia. Maybe I'm not ready to be married," Theodora said.

"Theodora, I want to tell you something. In my day, when you married, you married forever. No one thought about leaving an unhappy marriage. That would be unheard of. And I do not say a woman should stop trying just because there are a few problems or things she does not like. Life is like our circle dance. When you are behind someone who knows the steps, you follow. When the leader stumbles, you step in and show the way. But sometimes, when the leader takes you too far in the wrong direction, you must break off and start a new line." She got up from her chair. "Now come and have lunch. You will feel better." Food was always the magic balm.

Theodora lay down for a nap after lunch. She wondered what Stewart was doing right now. He knew she was at the beach for the weekend, but hadn't bothered to call yet. She stared at the swirled ceiling, and her eyes formed faces and animals out of the random designs. Her grandmother's words troubled her. Her father and grandfather were very much alike, both strong men with an underlying core that was gentle and kind. She had thought Stewart was a page out of the same book, but it was becoming clear to her that he was quite different. She remembered comments she had chosen to ignore while they were dating, incidents that she had shoved to the back of her mind. All along, there had been that small, still nagging feeling in her gut that something was not right, but she had foolishly disregarded those feelings. She thought back to the times he disapproved of her choices - her clothes, the Christmas necklace - and tried to remember whether he'd always been so controlling. Had she just been too high in the clouds to see it? She wasn't comfortable in her home any longer, knowing the slightest comment might start an argument. She was off balance and tense. The crazy thing was that if anyone asked her to articulate what she was feeling, she would be at a complete loss. She didn't know how to fix things any longer. Maybe time would take care of it. Maybe if only she tried a little harder, things would get better. She drifted off into a fitful sleep.

Stewart and Heather got back to the hotel a little before five o'clock, drained from an eight-hour day of non-stop meetings and teaching sessions. They had continued right through lunch, cold sandwiches eaten on the run.

"Why don't we grab a couple hours of down time," he said to Heather in the elevator. "We can meet in the lobby around eight o'clock and go have a relaxing dinner."

"Whatever you say. See you at eight," she said as the elevator stopped at their floor.

Stewart went to his room and flopped on the bed. He should call Theodora, but he was all talked out. The last thing he felt like doing was answering more questions.

He stretched out contentedly on the king size bed. They had decided to skip the association-sponsored dinner tonight so from here on out his time was his own. Now he had the rest of tonight and all of Sunday to do whatever he wanted before returning to Baltimore. He thought of Heather just down the hall. The more he thought about her, the more excited he became at the prospect of spending tonight and tomorrow alone with her.

The ringing telephone roused Theodora from a light sleep. Darkness enveloped the room, although it was only five o'clock. She got out of bed and went to the kitchen to answer it.

"Hello?" she said, anticipating Stewart's voice at the other end.

"Hi, what are you up to?" It was Nicole.

"I was sleeping. The phone woke me. I thought you might be Stewart."

"No, just me. Are you having a good time?"

"We've been kicking back, talking and relaxing. You know it's pretty dead here this time of year. I wish you had come with us. What's this hot date you've got? Anyone I know?" There was a brief silence on the line.

"Yes, as a matter of fact you do know him. Now don't lecture me, Theo, but I'm going to dinner with Peter tonight."

Theodora's heart sank. "Oh, Nicole, why are you doing this to yourself? You're just going to get hurt. I've watched you agonize over this thing for the last three months. It's only going to get worse if you keep seeing him."

"I asked you not to lecture me. I have to see where this might lead."

"You know where it will lead. Nowhere."

"Just trust me okay? I'm not going to do anything foolish. I've gotta go." She hung up.

"Oh Nicole," Theodora whispered, "what are you doing?"

Chapter 25

*P*eter wouldn't be here for another hour. Nicole went into the living room, put some music on and sat down to wait. Only Michael and Theodora knew that she and Peter had been seeing each other. She was thankful for Michael's friendship over the last few months. Unlike her sister, he listened without judgment or pronouncement and was the confidante upon whom she depended on those too frequent occasions when Peter had to put his family before her. It was to Michael that she was able to pour out her feelings of anger and frustration on the nights Peter stayed at home with Pat or they, together as husband and wife, attended a political function or social gathering. She envied Peter his lack of jealousy in knowing she was, unlike him, alone when they were apart, waiting impatiently for the hidden moments they could be together.

She hadn't seen him since the week before Christmas, a mere twenty-one days ago, but it seemed to her a time without end. Her family and their merry celebratory mood had gotten her through the holiday, but the days following were torture. She went about her routine of work, meetings and appointments completely distracted by images of Peter, Pat and the children together in New Hampshire where they were spending Christmas and the New Year with Pat's parents. She realized more and more that she wished to share Peter with no one.

It was impossible to sit still, and she looked around the room without taking anything in. Her hand tapped a nervous beat on the sofa's arm and when she glanced at the double French doors, she saw that a light snow had begun to fall. A picture began to form in her mind, of snow-covered streets made impassable, a roaring fire in the fireplace, and Peter stranded here with her. She sipped her wine, rose and walked over to the mirrored wall for another appraisal. She frowned. The dress was all wrong. For the fifth time she returned to her bedroom and flung open the closet door. She could kick herself for not having gotten something new for tonight. She began to grab and discard garment after garment until finally she pulled out a black knit dress. She hurriedly threw off her sweater, let the black pants drop to the floor and pulled the dress over her head. The clinging knit hugged every curve of her body as if in adoration, and she gave the reflection in the mirror a satisfied nod. She changed into her slender high-heeled black pumps and just as she added gold hoop earrings the doorbell rang. Her heart beat faster, and she ran downstairs. A rush of cold air as she opened the door made her take a step back. The temperature had dropped quickly and dramatically.

"Peter, come in." She threw her arms around him and felt the cold from his body through the thin knit.

He wrapped her in a tight embrace. "How are you, darling? It's wonderful to see you." He stood back and looked at her for a long moment. "I've been looking forward to this all day."

"So have I," she said, shutting the door against the cold and taking his hand. "Shall we have something to drink before we leave? A little something to warm your bones?"

"You're what can warm my bones," he said in a playful voice and pulled her to him once again.

She pretended to struggle in protest and they fell, laughing and pleased with themselves, onto the sofa. Nicole pushed him away, holding a hand against his chest in restraint and said in pretended seriousness,

"You just have a seat, Mister, and I'll be right back."

"Yes, ma'am, whatever you say." He gave her a smart salute and settled back against the cushion.

The room invited sitting and relaxing. Dark green walls accented with white molding and a long wall of built in cases filled with books and photos gave the room a warm, cozy feeling. A small corner fireplace with carved wooden mantle was visible from any seat in the room. The wood floors were polished to a high gloss and partially covered with an oriental rug in deep greens, blues and burgundies. He looked up as she came back with the wine.

"I love this room. I always feel so comfortable here."

A disconcerting rush of resentment stirred inside as it occurred to her that they would never be sitting in his house having this conversation. She looked up to see him staring closely at her.

"I can't tell you how good it is to see you. It feels like a year instead of a couple weeks. I could sit here and look at you all night," he said, and she merely smiled at him and shook her head.

"It was a strange Christmas. I never stopped thinking about you. It was hard not being able to talk to you," Peter said.

Nicole was quiet for a moment. "Spending the holidays without you gave me a lot of time to think. Too much time. This is not the way I want to spend my life."

A worried look creased his brow. "I know this isn't fair to you darling. I was miserable too."

"How long are we going to go on being miserable?" she asked.

"Please give me time. You don't know how hard this is for me. I love you. I'll work this out, I promise." He embraced her and she rested her head against his shoulder, doing all she could to hold back tears.

"It's all right darling. We're together now," he whispered.

She pulled away.

"What time do we have to leave for dinner?"

"Whenever we want. We have a private room at a restaurant downtown. We can be all alone, even a private entrance."

Perhaps he'd intended his arrangements to be special and romantic, but Nicole saw only the back alley entry and out of the way room that would keep her hidden and unseen.

The snow had stopped falling when they left the house but the sidewalks were covered with a fine layer of powdery dust. Peter held Nicole's arm and she shivered as the wind whipped against her.

"The car should still be warm. Heat will be coming in just a minute." He pushed the button on the dashboard.

"Each year when winter comes, I wonder why on earth my grandparents decided to settle in Maryland. Wouldn't you think that people from the Mediterranean would go someplace like Florida?" she asked, trying to lighten the mood.

"So you're a sun worshipper, eh?" he asked, laughing. "I don't mind the winter that much. I guess I'm used to it."

Peter pulled up to the restaurant and surrendered the car to the parking valet. They were assaulted again by the biting wind and he hurried her to the restaurant's private side door and up a narrow staircase. A discreet waiter stood at the top of the stairs and escorted them into an elegant, low-ceilinged room bathed in pale gold light. He led them to a small linen covered table and held the chair for Nicole. A bottle of champagne sat waiting, nestled in an ice-filled silver urn. She was overwhelmed.

Peter poured them each a glass and raised his to her.

"What shall we drink to?"

"Would it be trite to say to us?" she asked softly.

"Nothing could be less trite. To us."

Nicole took a long swallow and enjoyed the tickling sensation as the bubbles traveled down her throat. She was already a little tipsy from the wine and the feeling of Peter so close at last. She drank in every detail of his face and couldn't resist the urge to reach out and touch his cheek. He pulled his chair closer to the table, and she could feel the heat from his leg next to hers. His hand reached out for hers and their fingers intertwined in a tight embrace. Now she was glad he had arranged for them to dine alone. She didn't think she could have stood being this close to him and not be able to touch him.

"I missed you," he said.

She felt the burn of desire in her body.

"Oh Peter, I've missed you too. So much."

She wanted to be with him all the time, not just the rare moments he could steal away from his marriage and his work.

He took her hand in his.

"You know, it's never occurred to me to question my personal life. Somehow I've always kept anything having to do with my emotional side at arm's length because it was something I didn't want to deal with, but I'm seeing that eventually everything catches up with you. I can't ignore my feelings anymore, and I know that more and more each time I'm with you."

"What is it exactly that you're saying to me?" Nicole put her elbow on the table and rested her chin in her hand.

"I'm saying that you've awakened feelings in me that I've never felt, never thought I would feel. There's a freedom to be myself with you I've never felt with anyone else. You understand me because we come from the same soil. When you talk about your family, the years growing up, the holidays, I'm there with you. I did the same things, had the same family. We're connected by so much. I never thought that was important, that it didn't much matter one way or another, but I see now I was wrong. It matters, and it's something I've missed because of my own lack of judgment. So many times I look at you and know you know exactly what I'm thinking." He smiled at her. "We've been brought up to respond to people and situations in the same way."

The arrival of their meal and the savory aroma of foreign and exotic spices interrupted them.

"Let me divide this up so we can each taste everything," Peter said with gusto.

"I think we're going to have a pretty hefty doggy bag to take home." As soon as the words were out of her mouth, she was reminded once again that they kept very separate homes. Nicole looked out the window to the sparkling Christmas lights still decorating the trees and buildings. She always thought the lights looked a bit forlorn and shabby once the holidays were over, like actors with wildly overdone make-up at the end of the final act.

"What are you thinking about so intently?" Peter asked her.

"I was just thinking how bleak it seems when December is over. All the excitement and anticipation leading up to the holidays, and it's over in the blink of an eye. Now we have the long, cold winter to look forward to." She felt an unaccountable sadness. "I'm counting the days until spring. My mother would tell me I'm wishing my life away."

"Your mother's a smart woman," he said.

Nicole put her fork down and looked at him. "She would also tell me I'm a fool to be out with a married man."

He leaned forward and reached his hand across the table to hers.

"Nicole, I can't say anything to you that will make everything all right, but I can tell you one thing. I'm in love with you. I haven't thought beyond that, about what that does to my world, my family. It didn't occur to me that I wouldn't stay married to Pat forever even though it hasn't been the happiest of marriages. We made a commitment to each other when we said our vows. Now all of a sudden, I'm questioning everything in my safe, orderly world. Can you understand that I'm at a place where I feel like I'm on the brink, but can't make a move? Kind of like standing at the open door of the airplane with your parachute on, but paralyzed by the thought of putting the leg out that will start your fall. I don't know what to do, but I do know that the thing I want least is to lose the chance to love you."

They weren't the words Nicole wanted to hear. She wanted him to say they had a future together, without complications and difficulty, that she was all that mattered. It was unrealistic, but it didn't stop her from feeling hurt and resentful.

"Nicole," he started. "I can see you're upset, and I know this isn't fair to you, but please give me time. I don't know what I would do if I couldn't see you again."

She thought about his wife and children waiting at home for him.

How would she feel if she were the wife whose life could be turned upside down by the decision of a stranger who had entered her husband's life? If she ignored her misgivings and continued this relationship, how would she ever face her father or herself for that matter? She was being torn in two and realized this would become an all too familiar state of mind if she chose to continue seeing him.

"Peter, I wish things were different. It makes me angry that we can't be together, that I could only share a part of your life. It seems so unfair. One part of me says to hell with whoever gets hurt, we deserve some happiness. But deep down I know I could never live with myself and I don't think you could either. I could never endure being your mistress." Her laugh was filled with irony. "God, that word sounds so ridiculous. It's a no win situation, no matter how I look at it. We're in the wrong place at the wrong time.

"Nicole, there are certain things we have no control over. It's not our fault that we didn't meet until now. You're my soul mate. I didn't even know I believed in that sort of thing, but now I know it's true. We're unbelievably lucky to have even found each other. Can you honestly tell me you don't feel it too? You're the missing part of me. Aren't I that for you?"

What was he doing? When she gathered the courage to stand behind her convictions, he said things that made her falter. Her thoughts were as confused and turbulent as two raging bodies of water colliding in their struggle for dominance. She looked down at the table and back at Peter.

"You're the missing part of me, too, Peter, and that's what makes it so hard. Can't you see? How are we lucky? You're married." She paused. "Maybe I'm just some little distraction for a bored husband."

He was shaken. "How can you say that? Darling, it's more than that, and we both know it."

"Peter, you say these things to me, but they're empty words with nothing behind them."

"My heart is behind them. But, Nicole, my life is more complicated than yours."

"More complicated? Because you have a wife?"

"Because I have two children. If it were only Pat, I'd leave tomorrow, but I can't hurt my children to satisfy my own happiness. Can you understand that?"

"What are we doing here then? You're cheating your children anyway, they just don't know it."

"I'm not saying I'll never leave, but I need some more time. I never imagined I was the kind of man who'd be unfaithful. But I also never knew I could feel this way about someone. Please, give me time."

Nicole wanted to believe him and wrestled against her feelings of guilt. She was filled with heady satisfaction in knowing that she alone was able to evoke such a deep degree of emotion in him. It wasn't her fault that Pat didn't understand him and had emotionally abandoned him. Nicole believed that she could make him happy in a way Pat never could. She had begun to define herself according to Peter's needs and desires, much as the lone note has meaning only in its contribution to the entire symphony. She forgot there were others in his life he loved more, and it was agony to realize his children would always come first. She couldn't compete with them and she knew in her heart it was wicked to try. Still, that didn't prevent her from feeling jealous of them and wishing their existence was not a reality she had to face. They were innocent players in a cast of masqueraders and frauds and she wanted no part in their duping. On the other hand, was it fair to them to grow up in a household laden with apathy and disharmony? Wouldn't their own adult relationships be doomed to failure, modeled after the imperfect example of their parents? If she walked away from their father now, would it really benefit them? She told herself that his happiness was a bigger factor in their long-term well being than his staying with their mother out of obligation. For now at least she would give him the time he asked for.

"Come on, let's get out of here. I need to be alone with you," he said to her.

When they reached the main level of the restaurant and he helped

Nicole on with her coat, he saw a look of alarm on her face when she turned to face him.

"I don't believe it. What on earth are they doing here?" She barely moved her lips as her Uncle Dimitri and Aunt Eve approached them.

"Nicole, what a surprise," Aunt Eve looked coldly at her niece.

"Hello Aunt Eve, Uncle Dimitri," Nicole had no idea what to say next. Peter dove in for the rescue.

"I'm glad to see someone else wasn't afraid of the weather tonight. My aide, Michael Pendleton, was supposed to join us, but he backed out when he saw the snow. He called after we got here to cancel."

Nicole looked at him in amazement. She couldn't believe how smoothly and quickly the lie came from his lips and found herself annoyed at the bad light in which the lie placed Michael.

"Well, perhaps it was a bit fool-hardy to come out on a night like this," Eve said. "It was nice to see you Peter. Nicole, I'll call you tomorrow. We'll have lunch." It was not an invitation, but a command.

"I'd love to, Aunt Eve. Be careful driving home."

"Goodnight dear. Goodnight Peter," she said.

Uncle Dimitri looked at her and winked.

"Take care, sweetie. Goodnight Peter."

As they walked away Dimitri said to his wife. "What do you think that's all about?"

"I don't know. But you can bet I'm going to find out."

"Of all the people in the world to run into. This is just great," Nicole said.

"I'm sorry, Nicole," he shook his head. "I feel like I'm always apologizing to you."

"If I needed anything to convince me this is wrong, bumping into my aunt and uncle was it."

Nicole was silent on the way home, and when they pulled up to the house, she said to Peter, "Please don't come in. Let's say goodnight."

"You're not going to let what just happened interfere with our happiness are you?" He caressed her back, pulling her body close to

his. With his head buried against her neck, he could smell the familiar scent of her perfume. He held her for a long moment then lifted
his head to look at her.

"I love you, Nicole," he said quietly, and pressed his lips against
hers. They held each other for a long time, and the figures of her aunt
and uncle receded further and further in her mind until they became
insignificant and forgotten. It was Peter who finally pulled away and
opened the car door. Slowly, arm in arm, they walked together into
the warmth of the townhouse.

Chapter 26

*T*rue to her word, Eve had awakened her early the next morning with a phone call to set a time for lunch. Nicole was already late for their twelve-thirty meeting and was still in her office, on hold for the advertising department of the Sun newspapers. She hung the phone up in exasperation, telling herself she would rather miss the deadline than incur the wrath of her aunt. Grabbing her coat and bag, she hurriedly left the building. By the time she parked and walked the short distance to Casa Mia's, it was almost one o'clock. She spotted her aunt in a booth near the back of the restaurant and walked over.

"Sorry I'm late. Things got a little crazy at the office and I couldn't get out as early as I'd hoped." She sat down opposite Eve.

"That's all right. I haven't been waiting too long. Why don't you have a look at the menu and we'll order. Then we can talk," she said.

They placed their order and Eve leaned back in the booth, her hands clasped tightly in her lap. "I'm not going to beat around the bush, Nicole. I was quite surprised to see you out with Peter Demetrios on Saturday. I haven't said anything to your mother yet."

Thank God for small favors, Nicole thought.

Eve continued. "Just what is this all about?"

"I think Peter explained it to you at the restaurant. The three of us made plans, and at the last minute Michael couldn't make it."

"This is your Aunt Eve you're talking to. I didn't just come over on the boat. Michael was never part of your plans on Saturday, was he?"

Nicole was becoming angry at her aunt's insistent probing. It wasn't any of her business, she thought.

"There's nothing going on between Peter and me, and so there isn't anything to discuss."

"I hope that's true Nicole, because getting involved with him would be the biggest mistake of your life. This city is too small. It would be a huge scandal, and you know as well as I that the woman always gets the raw deal. His life would go on as usual because people will always want to be near someone they think is powerful. You would be the one talked and whispered about. Even if he left his wife and married you, people would always say, 'You know, she's the one he had an affair with and left his wife for.' Is that what you want?"

"I'll tell you what I want. I want to live my life without wondering what other people will think. I refuse to make my decisions based on what other people will say about me. I've told you nothing is going on. I'm not having an affair with Peter Demetrios, he's not going to leave his wife, and that's all there is to it. As a matter of fact, I have a date with Michael Pendleton this weekend." She made up the last part.

Eve looked skeptical. "Good. I'm glad to hear you're going out with him. He's a nice young man, the kind of man you should be seeing. But for your own good, don't be so cavalier about dismissing what other people think. The way you appear to the world is very important."

Here it was again. Live your life for an invisible audience who knew your every move and judged whether it was a wise or foolish action. She would be damned if she would turn herself inside out to fit into that little box or if she would give up Peter so easily.

Nicole looked at her aunt. "Aunt Eve, I hope you're not going to mention any of this to Mom."

Eve took her time answering. "If what you tell me is true, I see no reason to tell your mother." She took a sip of her water. "However, if I find out you are seeing him, for your own good, I won't keep quiet about it."

Chapter 27

APRIL

*S*tewart hung up with Theodora and turned back to the paper-work stacked on his desk. He shuffled through the subcontractor bids and divided them into two piles.

"Burning the midnight oil again?"

He looked up. "Hey Heather."

"How long are you gonna be? I'm starving!" she whined.

His eyes traveled the length of her body, a body with which he was now intimately familiar. Heather had been coming on to him for months, and he'd kept her at arm's length for quite a while. There was no denying his attraction to her; she possessed a certain raw sex appeal he found extremely alluring. He had known when he married Theodora that it was only a matter of time before he would be unfaithful to her. The thought of sleeping with only one woman for the rest of his life was ludicrous. He just hadn't expected to tire of his beautiful young wife so quickly. Theodora and Heather were like night and day. Heather had none of the ingenuousness inherent in Theodora. Her cynicism and wit challenged Stewart and he enjoyed their flirtatious bantering immensely. Despite the fact that her taut body and jutting breasts were achieved through the surgeon's knife, he was captivated. Still, he had been cautious, not wanting to jeop-ardize his future by getting involved with someone this close to home. Then the risk became a turn on, almost as strong a lure as Heather herself. He had established the ground rules before their union and was satisfied that she, like him, was interested in nothing more serious than a sexual fling.

"Let's go." Stewart turned off the lights and locked the door. As they left the building, he secured the front door, then walked Heather to her car.

"I'll follow you," he said.

He slid behind the wheel of his new BMW and she took off, leaving him to chase her down the road. She stopped in front of a brick apartment building and jumped out of the car. They walked up two flights of stairs until they reached her apartment where the furnishings were sparse and mismatched, a hodgepodge of garage sale rejects.

"Want one? " she asked as she fixed herself a Tia Maria on the rocks.

"Sure."

"Coming right up." She brought their drinks to the sofa, along with a bag of Doritos. She turned on the stereo, and the sound of soft rock filled the room. They sat talking and eating and before they knew it the bag was almost empty.

"Geez. I guess I should order the pizza. I didn't realize how hungry I was."

"It can wait. The chips stemmed my appetite. How about another drink?" he said.

"You know where it is, help yourself. I have to pee." She got up and disappeared into the bathroom.

A few minutes later, she emerged, wearing nothing but a black lace body suit and spiked heels. She dimmed the lights and lit a few candles.

"Come here, gorgeous." Stewart said.

She walked to him, grabbed his face in her hands and kissed him, parting his lips with her tongue and thrusting it far into his mouth. He returned the kiss greedily, and within minutes they were rolling on the floor. They were rough with each other, taking their pleasure with no tenderness or affection. When they finished, they lay on the floor next to each other, out of breath, looking up at the ceiling.

"Better than I expected," she said with a grin.

"I should hope so. But I think we're going to need a lot of practice to achieve perfection. I'm willing to make the sacrifice, how about you?"

"Definitely. We should practice daily. Don't want to get out of shape," she giggled.

He ran his hand through her short blonde hair. "I could go for that pizza now," he said, and started to put his clothes back on.

"I'll go order it. But don't get dressed, I'm not through with you yet."

It was after midnight when Stewart left. He pulled into the garage, took his shoes off and tiptoed into the hallway, trying not to awaken Theodora. The house was dark. He climbed the stairs to the second floor, and softly slipped into the bedroom. Intent on opening the door without making any noise, he turned the knob slowly. Theodora was still asleep. He disrobed in the bathroom, and gently pulled down the covers as he slid into bed next to her. She stirred slightly, but did not awaken. Breathing a sigh of relief, Stewart closed his eyes and fell asleep with a smile on his face.

Chapter 28

*N*icole yawned as she finished reviewing the monthly advertising schedule. She had been running since seven this morning, going from meeting to meeting and had finally gotten a few quiet minutes in her office. She glanced at her watch and saw that it was past noon. Her stomach was rumbling and she decided to go across to the deli and pick up a sandwich for lunch. She called into her boss's office.

"McKenzie, would you like anything from across the street?"

"No thanks. Dear old hubby is picking me up for lunch."

"Lucky you."

On a whim, she poked her head inside her father's office. His secretary, Linda, was typing at her desk. She was a stocky woman in her late forties who had been with Nick for the past fifteen years and was as loyal as an old watchdog.

"Hi Linda, is he busy?"

"I'm sure he has time for you. Let me buzz him. Mr. Parsenis, Nicole is here to see you." She put down the phone. "Go right in Nicole."

"Thanks."

Nick opened the door, as Nicole was about to turn the knob.

"Well, this is a pleasant surprise." He smiled.

"I was on my way to grab a sandwich from the deli, and I thought I'd invite you to lunch if you aren't too busy."

He looked at his watch and thought for a minute.

"Tell you what, give me about twenty minutes and you're on. But lunch is on me. We'll go over to the Bluestone, and then stop by the construction site at the new development on the way back. Can you be away for a few hours?"

"Yes. All my meetings for the day are finished. Just call me when you're ready." She gave him a peck on the cheek and went back to her office, pleasantly anticipating the time with her father.

Theodora was on the phone when she returned.

"Hi. What's going on?"

"Not much, what's wrong? You don't sound too great."

"I've been better," Theodora sighed. "Stewart and I don't seem to be connecting very well lately and it's got me down."

Nicole was surprised at this admission. "I thought you guys were having a romantic dinner last night."

"That's difficult to do when you're all alone. I rushed home, had everything ready, then he called me at seven thirty, and said he had to work late. I finally went to bed at ten thirty, and he still wasn't home. When I woke up this morning, he was already showered and dressed and heading out the door. I feel like I have a roommate instead of a husband."

"That's crazy. Even Dad doesn't work that late. Have you talked to him about it?"

"Sort of. He just gets defensive. Talks about how it's all on his shoulders to make sure we have a secure future. He's really caught up in this drive to succeed. It's the only thing he seems to care about and it's hard to argue with him when he keeps saying he's doing it all for us."

"I'm sorry Theodora. Try talking to him again."

"It'll work out somehow, but it's a drag right now. Well, gotta run, Peter's holding a staff meeting in a few minutes. Talk to you later."

"Bye." Now it was Nicole's turn to feel depressed. Why did Theodora have to mention Peter? She had actually gotten through the entire morning without thinking about him. Now she pictured him in his office, wondering what he was wearing, and what kind of mood he was in. She rubbed her temples, as if trying to erase the image. Her intercom buzzed and she picked up the receiver.

"Yes?"

"Ready?"

"Sure Dad, I'll be right there."

She hung up the phone and left the office, determined not to let thoughts of Peter ruin her lunch with her father.

They drove in silence for the first few minutes, each winding down from busy mornings. Nicole put her window halfway down, and enjoyed the feel of the cool spring breeze on her face.

"I remember when you were a little girl, you used to love to stick your head out the window and feel the air on your face. We were always afraid you'd fly out of the car!"

"Paul used to tell me that if I wasn't careful, a truck would come by and knock my head off!"

"My God. That's horrible. I don't remember that," Nick exclaimed.

"He always teased us. I didn't pay much attention." Nicole laughed. "Actually sounds like something you would say."

"What do you mean?" he asked.

"Well Dad, you do tend to overreact."

"Like?"

"Like the time you took me to the emergency room for a bee sting. Or when you insisted that Theodora and I carry a police whistle on our walks around the neighborhood or when..."

"All right, all right," he interrupted, "So sue me, I care about my children," he said pretending anger.

"And we appreciate it, really we do," she smiled.

"We're here."

The hostess greeted them. "Hello, Mr. Parsenis. Nice to see you. Your usual table?"

"Yes Nora, Thank you."

They were seated at a table by a window. "Your waitress will be right with you."

"So what are you going to eat?" Nick asked.

"I'm going to splurge and have the Thai calamari. How 'bout you?"

"I'll stick with the crab cake. So, what's going on? Now that you've moved out, I can't keep tabs on you anymore. Are you seeing anyone?"

Nicole was quiet. She wanted to pour her heart out to him and tell him all about Peter. She longed for him to comfort her and assure her everything would be fine but she knew that if she did, he would blame Peter for taking advantage of her. She wouldn't allow that to happen. Instead, she just shook her head.

"What's the matter with boys these days? They must all be blind."

The waitress brought their lunch, and they dug in heartily. When Nicole looked up, she was startled to see Heather Daniels walk in with Stewart. She stared openly, arousing Nick's curiosity, who turned his head to see the couple as they were seated.

"Isn't that sweet. He doesn't have time to see his wife, but he can go out to lunch with that bimbo," Nicole remarked angrily.

"Nicole. What a thing to say! She works for us. I'm sure it's perfectly innocent," Nick rebuked his daughter.

"What could be innocent about it? She has nothing to do with the construction department. There isn't any reason for their paths to cross."

"That's not true. She's working Manor Hills, which still has quite a few condos left to be built. Since she sits in the model, some of the residents are bringing their complaints to her. Stewart probably wants some feedback from her."

Nicole didn't bother arguing further, even though she wanted to remind her father that there were already processes in place to ensure that Stewart received that feedback daily from marketing. One of her father's best qualities was his unfailing loyalty to his friends and family. It was also his biggest fault, for it often prevented him from seeing when that loyalty was ill deserved. Nicole decided she would keep a closer eye on Stewart and see what he and Heather were up to.

"You may be right Dad. Guess I shouldn't jump to conclusions.

Just to prove I'm a good sport, I think I'll go over and say hello." She was up and halfway across the room before Nick could object.

"What a pleasant surprise." Nicole said to Stewart.

"Nicole...hello," he answered, flustered.

"Heather, how nice to see you again."

"Likewise," she said indifferently and looked away.

"Dad and I were just having lunch, would you care to join us?" Nicole asked with feigned sweetness.

"Thanks, but I don't want to interrupt. I just came from Manor Hills and was on my way for a quick bite. Heather wanted to talk to me about hiring her brother. Insisted on taking me to lunch in exchange for my time."

Nicole looked at Heather expectantly.

"Eddie's been in construction a long time, getting a raw deal at his current job. The pay's lousy so I'm hoping he can work for Stewart."

"Well, I'll leave you to your interview by proxy." She turned on her heel and returned to her table.

"Feeling better now?" her father asked her sternly.

"Not really."

"Nicole, you've got to get that temper under control. Your impulsiveness worries me."

"I'll try to be more restrained. Can we drop it now?"

"Sure."

Nicole was furious at how Stewart's presence seemed to contaminate all her family relationships and tried to think of something to say to relieve the tension.

"Dad, I'm sorry. I don't want our lunch ruined, we have so little time together. Can we back up to ten minutes ago?" She looked at him imploringly.

He paused. "I never could say no to that face. We were talking about your love life."

"Tell me about how you felt when you asked Mom to marry you."

"The same way that I do now. From the first time your mother and I went out, I knew I would marry her. She had this innocent quality about her that was so endearing. Still does actually. I knew when I looked into those eyes that I could trust her with my soul. I never looked at another woman again and I've never regretted it."

Nicole stared wistfully at her father.

"Oh Dad, that's so romantic. Did you ever tell Mom that?"

He thought a moment. "You know, I haven't, not in so many words. I guess I feel it so strongly, I assume she knows."

They finished their lunch, and Nick picked up the check. He left the waitress a twenty five percent tip. He had always been a generous man, and it was a quality Nicole admired. Stinginess was a major character flaw in her book, and she had determined long ago that she would never end up with a cheap man.

It took them less than five minutes to reach the model unit at Parsenis' newest project. Manor Hills was a mid-rise condominium development tucked away behind an abundance of trees and shrubbery. The model units were completed a few weeks ago and the marketing efforts now in full swing. When completed, the development would have five hundred units. So far, construction was halfway finished in the first one hundred group, and fifty-two units had been sold to date. Nick had handed over the bulk of the responsibility for the project to Stewart and was trying his best not to interfere. He was good at delegating authority but was used to keeping some measure of control. In the past, all major decisions had to be approved by him. At Stewart's entreaty, however, Nick was allowing him to run the project with full authority. Stewart had come to him and made the case for himself, reminding Nick that he had been with Parsenis for several years prior to becoming Nick's son-in-law. He pointed out that Manor Hills was the perfect opportunity for him to cut his teeth while he could still call upon Nick if necessary. The unspoken implication was that Stewart would one day assume control of the company. Nick had agreed to Stewart's plan with one provision. Stewart was to supply weekly progress reports on the project, bringing Nick up to date on all phases of construction, sales, and budget. He reminded Stewart that he would still be visiting the site, as was his habit on all Parsenis projects. So far,

Stewart was coming in well below budget, and everything was going according to schedule. Heather was doing a terrific sales job as were the two other part time agents assigned to the project.

Nick parked in front of a row of units under construction. A gust of wind lifted a cloud of dirt around their legs when they got out of the car. The open structure contained several workers, covered in dust, busy with their tasks. Trucks pulled in and out of the site as materials were unloaded and hauled off by the workers. Nicole looked at the familiar scene. She suddenly noticed a discordant note. A large truck with the name "Cherry & Sons Concrete" emblazoned in red, was parked in front of the building. Ever since she could remember, they had used Tarpon Concrete.

"Dad, Did Tarpon go out of business?"

"Of course not, why?"

She pointed to the concrete truck in front of them.

"Oh. Stewart thought that Cherry & Sons was a better choice for this project."

"But we've been using Tarpon for twenty five years. You're always telling me how important it is to establish good relationships with all the subs, and how if you're loyal to them, they'll be loyal to you. How could you let Stewart bring in some unknown company?" she asked hotly.

"It wasn't my decision. I'm not disputing what you're saying, but I gave Stewart my word that I wouldn't interfere with his running of this project, and I can't go back on it now."

"Even if his decisions have a harmful effect on the company?"

"That won't happen. This is only one project. I've already talked to Manny at Tarpon and explained that we aren't changing suppliers. He understands this is a one time thing."

"He may have told you that, but don't you think word will get out that your son-in-law is getting his hooks in and that once he's in charge they're all out?"

Nick stiffened. "Nicole, like it or not, Stewart is your brother-in-law and nothing's going to change that. I'd suggest that you do your best to rid yourself of this animosity. He's family now, and we don't speak unkindly about our own. Is that understood?"

She took a deep breath. "Loud and clear."

Nick walked off ahead of her and said a few words to the foreman. She knew it was useless to try and sway her father. The smart thing would be to play along, pretending to like Stewart, until she could gather enough proof that he was indeed only looking out for himself. The problem was, she never was much good at hiding her feelings. She resolved then and there, that she would beat Stewart at his own game and play it close to the vest. From now on, she would act as though she'd turned over a new leaf and embrace her brother-in-law with open arms. She'd be damned if she would sit back and allow that snake to take over her father's business.

Chapter 29

Nicole had made up her mind that it was time for Peter to choose. It was no longer possible to deny the shame and guilt that ate at her with an increasingly relentless insistence.

He was due any moment and every few minutes she peeked through the curtains to watch, unseen, for his arrival. Her breath caught in her throat when he pulled up. She felt her palms moisten in nervous anticipation and went to open the front door.

"You're a sight for sore eyes." He looked at her hungrily and handed her a single red rose to make the eleven he'd sent earlier an even dozen.

"Thank you." She took the flower and gently slid it into place amid the others.

"You're always more beautiful than I remember." He tried to put his arms around her but she turned away.

"What is it, darling?"

She deliberately avoided a direct answer to his question, and he uneasily followed her lead in keeping things light and impersonal.

"Would you like a glass of wine?" she asked.

"Please. It smells wonderful in here, what are you cooking?"

"Moussaka. An old Ikarian recipe."

"My favorite. I haven't had it home cooked in years."

"It'll be ready in about a half hour."

They sat in the living room, and he looked expectantly at her, waiting for her to speak. She cleared her throat and tried to bring to mind all the words she had so diligently practiced beforehand.

"Peter . . ." She hesitated for just a moment. "I can't live like this anymore. You said you needed time and I've given you that, no pressure, no questions asked. But it seems to me you're content to comfortably float along with one foot in each camp. I'm not willing to share you any longer. It's turning me into a jealous, possessive, complaining woman, and I don't like who I've become. The only thing that keeps me sane right now is my work. Thank God for that and the networking and socializing it requires. Otherwise I don't know what I'd do.

Peter was at a loss. He didn't want to respond to her charges, choosing instead to focus on the last thing she'd said.

"That's one of the things I admire about you and your work. You're always at ease in a crowd. You would make a perfect politician's wife."

Nicole stiffened. "Or a perfect politician."

He looked embarrassed. "I'm sorry. I didn't mean it the way it sounded. I was just thinking how wonderful it would be to have you by my side. You wouldn't look at it as a tedious obligation but would enjoy it."

"Compared to Pat who doesn't?"

"Well, yes. She isn't cut out for this. She's extremely shy and detests having to accompany me to the dinners and parties. She avoids the ones she can, and when she's forced to come, can't make it unless she takes a few valiums beforehand."

"Didn't she know you had political aspirations before you were married?"

"We talked about it, but we were so young, it seemed unattainable. I don't think she really believed it would happen. But that's all water under the bridge now. I'm different, she's different. There should be a law against getting married younger than thirty. I'm sure if we met for the first time today, we wouldn't be the slightest bit attracted to each other."

"Are you saying that if I were older, I might not be attracted to you?"

He was quiet for a minute. "Maybe you wouldn't," he answered thoughtfully. He walked over to the stereo, scanned the selections and inserted a Craig Chaquico CD into the player. He sat down close to her, took the glass from her hand and touched her face tenderly.

"Peter, we have to talk."

"Shh," he came closer towards her.

She backed away. "Please, nothing has changed.

"I'm sorry Nicole. Of course, we'll talk." He breathed a heavy sigh. "I've been thinking the same things you have. Pat has even noticed a difference in me, but the last straw was when I found out that my friend Tom was in the hospital. I went to see him, but they wouldn't let me in. He was in intensive care for three days before he died of a massive coronary. I just had lunch with him two weeks before and he seemed fine. I kept thinking that could be me. That's when I realized that life is too short to waste. I haven't been happy in a long time, but I've ignored it. Pat and I lead our own lives, we don't share the same dreams anymore. Our marriage has become nothing more than a convenient arrangement. My children have been the only bright spot in my personal life, until you came along. I won't deny myself that happiness anymore."

"What does that mean Peter?"

"It means I want to be with you today, and the next day and the next. I don't know how we'll accomplish that in practical terms, but I believe we can figure it out somehow."

"I want to be with you too, more than anything else. But are you really prepared to put an end to an eighteen-year marriage?"

"I haven't thought that far Nicole. I just know I can't put an end to seeing you."

Nicole felt a knot develop in her stomach. Part of her knew she was setting herself up for a fall, but she wasn't ready to believe it. He knows how he feels about me, and he's seen that life has no guarantees, she thought, reasoning that it would only be a matter of time before he would set the wheels in motion to be free. Still, her conscience tugged at her.

"Peter, does Pat still love you?"

"Not in the way you're asking. She loves that I take care of her and that I'm the father of her children. I don't think she's been in love with me for a very long time. There isn't any passion left between us; that died long ago. Pat's a very sweet woman who's afraid of change. I don't believe she's any happier in our marriage than I am. But she chooses to ignore her feelings. It's easier for her to live her life on auto pilot."

"What about you? Are you sure there's no love left in your heart for her?"

"Oh Nicole. How can I make you understand? Of course I love Pat, I always will."

Nicole felt the pain tear at her like a knife.

Peter continued. "But it's not the same kind of love I feel for you. She's been a loyal wife and good mother all these years. I can't just forget that and rid myself of those feelings. The love I feel for her is similar to the love I would feel towards a sister. I don't want to hurt her or see her unhappy, but if I could choose, I wouldn't want to be married to her anymore."

If I could choose, Nicole thought, as though everything were out of his control. The conversation wasn't going at all the way she had hoped.

"Trust me Nicole. I won't leave you out in left field. I need some time to sort this all out. The only thing I know is that I love you with all my heart, and I'll do whatever it takes to be with you. Just give me some time."

"Peter, I don't know what to say..."

"Then don't say anything."

He pulled her to him and kissed her lustfully. His arms encircled her in a vise like embrace, and she felt the room spin. He kissed her hard while his hands moved over her body languidly, back and forth like a wave taking possession of the wet sand beneath it. She lost all sense of time and abandoned herself to the passion raging through her. He unbuttoned her shirt slowly, and lifted it from her shoulders. She was hypnotized, lost in his gaze, unwilling to stop him.

"You're so beautiful," he marveled.

She lifted his sweater and he shrugged it off. He pulled off his shirt and hugged her to his chest. The feel of their bare skin touching was like sizzling hot coals, and Nicole surrendered to his embrace. He pushed her down and moved on top of her. Her arms encircled him as he kissed her deeply and hungrily.

"I love you," he whispered to her over and over. As his hands caressed her face, she noticed the light catch something shiny and saw it was his wedding band. She mustered every bit of strength she possessed and pushed him away.

"What's wrong baby?"

The tears began and she was unable to contain them. Peter wrapped his arms around her and held her shaking body against his.

"I'm sorry." She pulled away. "I never cry in front of people."

"Don't apologize, my love."

"I can't do this. I want you more than I've ever wanted anybody. When you touch me the feelings are overwhelming. But when I looked at your hand and saw your wedding band, it was just one more reminder that you don't belong to me. No matter what your heart says, right now, you belong with your wife. However much I want you for myself, I've no right to ask you to leave her, and I love you too much to share you. I know in my heart that if we make love, I'll be lost forever. I don't know if I'd have the strength to do the right thing. This has to be goodbye. Really goodbye. Can you look me in the eye and honestly tell me that you are ready to divorce her?"

Peter looked at her for a long time. "I don't think I can. I wish I had met you eighteen years ago."

"I would have been eight years old." She laughed weakly. "It isn't meant to be Peter. I'll never forget you, you'll always be right here." She pointed to her heart as tears ran down her face.

"Nicole, I'm so sorry I put you through this. I'm supposed to be the older, wiser one. I should never have started something I couldn't finish. I just..."

She put her finger to his lips. "Stop. No regrets. It's been wonderful. All the talks, the time together. At least I know I'm capable of feeling all these wonderful feelings. Don't say anything to ruin our memories. Please go now."

"I don't want to leave you like this."

"Please Peter, before I change my mind."

He hesitated then picked up his jacket. "Goodbye *agapi mou.*" He took one last look at her, head down on her knees crying, and left. She heard the door close and lifted her head. She felt bereft, her stomach in knots, and was afraid she'd never know happiness again.

Slowly, she dialed Michael.

"Nicole?"

"I'm sorry to bother you." her voice broke.

"Nicole, are you all right? What's happened?"

"Oh Michael, it's all over. For good this time."

"What are you talking about?"

"Peter. Peter just left here."

"Damn. So that explains it," he muttered under his breath. "Just stay where you are, I'm coming over."

"But you're all the way in Annapolis."

"It doesn't matter. You sound like you need a friend."

"No. Just talk to me for a few minutes."

"Give me a minute to drop someone home, and I'll be there within the hour."

Nicole had forgotten he was out on a date. "I can't let you do that. I'm sorry I called. Go back to your date."

"Listen to me. I'll be there by midnight."

She was too distraught to argue. She hung up and was ashamed of being so weak. She wasn't used to asking for help, and she hated herself for depending so heavily on Michael. She lay down on the sofa, and thought of Peter and how she had thrilled to his touch. She couldn't imagine any other man evoking that degree of passion in her. She wondered if Pat had felt that way when she had first married him. Maybe marriage was the death knell for passion. Her own sister seemed unhappy and hadn't hit her first anniversary yet. Her parents were happy but their relationship was born of a different time. She curled up on the sofa and fell asleep. Finally she was awakened by a knock at the door and wearily rose to answer it.

"Thanks for coming Michael."

He saw the red-rimmed eyes, the disheveled hair and felt his heart break. He took her in his arms, and this touch of kindness brought on a new rush of tears.

"Dry your eyes, and I'll go make us some coffee," he said, and went to the kitchen.

"Do you want to tell me what happened?" He sat the mug down in front of her.

With difficulty, she managed to recount the events of the evening. "What a fool I am. I expected him to come here and tell me his marriage was over and the way was clear for us."

"Don't be so hard on yourself. Peter can be pretty convincing. And don't forget, he's a lot older than you. I'd say he has a slight advantage."

"You make it sound like a game, Michael," she said, getting angry.

"I wasn't implying that. I just don't want you to blame yourself for everything. Go on."

She continued. "He kept telling me he that he loves me and wants nothing more than to be with me, yet he isn't anywhere near ready to leave Pat. He talked in circles."

"I don't think he's ready to leave her either. She's too dependent on him. When he campaigned and was away overnight, she went to pieces. He's the glue that holds that house together. Those poor kids wouldn't have any stability if it weren't for him. No matter how he feels, he'd never do anything to destroy Pat, and believe me, his leaving her would. She's very fragile, Nicole, always has been. I'm sure one of the things Peter finds so captivating about you is your independence. His feelings for you are strong enough to balance his guilt about disappointing Pat, but I don't think his conscience would allow him to leave."

"Are you saying he was planning to spend time with me until he got tired of me and then go back to her?"

"Nicole, I don't know what he's thinking these days. I've never seen him like this."

"He's so torn, Michael, but I can't live that way anymore. I feel sorry for him, especially now, hearing what Pat is like, but I can't sacrifice my own happiness. I'd never be able to live with myself if I was the cause of his leaving and it destroyed Pat's life or his children's."

She looked at Michael with new purpose

"He's out of my life for good and that's the end of it. I just need some time to get over it. Don't ever mention his name to me again."

"Do you think it's healthy to just push him out of your mind?"

"I've spent the last few months trying to sort things out, and it's made me miserable. It's over. There's no going back. I don't see any point in wasting one more minute analyzing it. Besides, I'm sick of acting like a hurt puppy. Peter will get on with his life, and I'll get on with mine. No matter what he says to you or asks about me, I don't want to know. Okay?"

"If that's the way you want it. For what it's worth, I think you've made the right decision."

"Like my father always says, you have to know when to cut your losses. I've been sitting at the table with a losing hand for too long."

"I won't bring him up again, but if you need to talk to me about it, you always have an ear."

"Thanks. I'm feeling better already," she lied.

"Just the same, I think I'll stick around for a while."

"Why don't you stay in the guest room? There's no point in your driving all the way home tonight. I'll make some popcorn and we can sit up and watch a movie."

"Sounds good to me. I'll check the T.V. guide."

A few minutes later, she brought in soda and a large bowl of popcorn and settled on the sofa next to Michael. Within minutes Nicole was asleep. Michael looked at her and felt a strong desire to shield her from any more pain. He had been powerless to do anything but stand on the sidelines as Nicole was slowly transformed from the vibrant, happy women he first met to the emotionally wounded one she had become. Peter's behavior distressed and sickened him to the core. He thought back to the heated exchange that took place a few months earlier. Peter had kept his relationship with Nicole clandestine until he was in need of Michael's help. Even then, he made a vain attempt to deceive Michael by denying his true intentions. It was right before Peter decided to surprise her in Boston. He was going to be gone overnight and had asked Michael to cover for him if Pat called with a question about his schedule. He finally admitted to Michael that he was going to spend the night with Nicole. Michael recalled bits and pieces of the conversation.

"Peter, what are you doing? How can you take advantage of her in this way? And what about her family?"

Peter had the grace to look ashamed. "I love her. I didn't plan for it to happen but it just did."

Michael was horrified. "Are you going to leave Pat?" He saw no point in mincing words.

"I haven't thought that far yet. I just know I need to be with her. See where this leads."

Michael's disillusionment grew stronger as their conversation progressed. This wasn't the same man for whom he'd campaigned and believed in so passionately. This was a man in the throes of a classic mid-life crisis, the embodiment of a tired cliché. He was sorely disappointed and wondered if his judgment was flawed or if Peter had indeed changed. He struggled to find some justification for Peter's behavior. His loyalty was so strong that he found it impossible to condemn him so quickly. He desperately wanted to believe he was a good man, that somehow he would redeem himself by doing the right thing before it was too late. He tried again to reason with him.

"If you really love her, leave her alone until you figure things out. You know it's wrong. Peter, this isn't like you at all."

Peter was getting impatient. "You can't possibly understand. Just tell me whether I can count on you to cover me with Pat," he finished curtly.

Michael was shocked by Peter's rebuff. His growing antipathy for him was increased by the fact that the woman he was so cavalierly toying with was Nicole, someone Michael could love and offer the life she so richly deserved. Only for Pat's sake had Michael relented.

"Just this once and only to spare Pat. Don't put me in this position again," Michael replied coldly and walked out of the office.

Nicole shifted in her sleep. He sighed deeply. What a mess you've made of things Peter. And who's there to clean up for you as usual? Not anymore, Michael decided. Tomorrow he would tell Peter he needed to find himself a new errand boy.

Chapter 30

*T*heodora and Stewart were meeting Caroline and Graham at the Hopkins Club at seven. It was already six thirty and Stewart wasn't home. Theodora was getting frantic. She didn't know if she was more concerned over Caroline's ire if they were late or the details of Stewart's whereabouts. She dialed his cell phone again and paced the floor.

"Yes?" he answered out of breath.

"Stewart, where are you? We're supposed to be meeting your parents in half an hour!" She was incensed.

"I had to stop at Manor Hills on my way home. There's a problem with one of the units. I'm on my way now, babe."

"We're never going to make it on time," she exclaimed.

"Why don't you go on ahead and I'll meet you there. That way Mother won't be upset."

She shook her head in disgust. "Hurry up!" She hung up.

He must think she was an idiot. Did he really expect her to believe there was anything going on at a construction site on a Saturday night? For God's sake, she was Nick's daughter. Where the hell was he?

Caroline and Graham were already seated when she arrived, and Caroline raised her eyebrows in inquiry as Theodora approached.

"Stewart's going to be a little late. He had to stop by one of the projects before coming home," she explained.

"Your father is quite the task master," Caroline replied.

"Stewart sets his own hours, Caroline," Theodora answered shortly.

Caroline was surprised by Theodora's tone. Was it possible things weren't as idyllic between them as she thought? The possibility pleased her. Perhaps Stewart was beginning to realize he'd make a mistake marrying outside his class. What did the girl know about their world? Caroline had done her best to be a good mother-in-law. She tried to get Theodora involved in her charity work and to introduce her to the women who held important social positions in town. Theodora was too busy with her job and some Greek women's guild to care about Caroline's organizations. Why did she have to work anyway? A girl with any sense would realize the rare opportunity Caroline's connections afforded her, but it was all wasted on Theodora. She simply hadn't made any effort to assimilate into their milieu.

Graham attempted to lighten the mood. "Come now, I'm glad to hear Stewart's a diligent worker."

Caroline sniffed. "Yes, you would. Nothing is more sacrosanct than work." She took a sip of her martini and pointed to the chair next to Graham. "Theodora dear, have a seat."

Graham smiled at her. "What would you like to drink?"

"Club soda, please." She was still seething but struggled to appear unperturbed. The last thing she wanted was to reveal her marital problems to Caroline. What a pity it had to be this way, she thought. How comforting it would be if Caroline was the sort of mother-in-law who would reassure her of Stewart's love and fidelity. She wanted so much to believe that he was the man of integrity she first thought him to be, but, she would find no such assurances here.

They made small talk, ignoring the growing lateness of the hour and Stewart's continued absence. He finally appeared and walked toward them smiling broadly.

Caroline rose immediately and embraced him. "Darling, come and sit, you look tired." She put a possessive arm around him.

"Sorry to have kept you waiting. This project is all consuming." He gave Theodora a peck on the cheek. "I need a drink."

"We should order dinner soon, the kitchen will be closing in a few minutes," Graham said.

Stewart was in a jovial mood. He excitedly relayed his latest accomplishments to his parents. His self-important chatter annoyed Theodora, and she could barely look at him. He finished his drink in a few gulps and ordered another.

"Better take it easy, you do have to drive," Theo couldn't resist.

Caroline shot her a look.

Stewart chuckled. "Such a worry wart." He looked at his mother. "It's a Greek thing." He dismissed Theodora's concerns.

Theodora's cheeks flushed. "Actually it's a legal thing. This state has some of the stiffest penalties for D.W.I.'s in the country. Not to mention, a moral thing."

"I guess you think because you work for the great senator you're now an expert on the law," Stewart baited her.

"You don't have to be a lawyer to know it's wrong to drink and drive. Excuse me!" She threw her napkin on the table and stalked off to the ladies' room.

"I'll be back." Caroline said and followed her.

Caroline found her dabbing at her eyes in front of the mirror.

"Theodora, you must try and control your emotions. You made quite a scene out there."

Theodora was appalled. "I hardly raised my voice. I'm sorry if I embarrassed you but some of us have feelings, you know."

Caroline tried to soften her tone. "You may have been brought up to express yourself in any circumstance, but Stewart isn't used to that. I'm only telling you this for your own good. There are certain ways to behave in public, and angry outbursts are unacceptable."

What was the use, Theodora thought. They were from different planets.

"Caroline, I appreciate your concern, but Stewart knew who I was before we got married. I'm not going to change my entire personality now." She paused, "But out of respect for you, I'll be more restrained in your presence."

I've done all I can, Caroline thought. I try to give her some motherly advice and she snubs it. She was on her own; Caroline was through trying to help.

When the women returned, it was as if nothing had transpired. Stewart was laughing at something Graham had just said, and flagged the waiter for another drink. So much for her advice, she thought wryly. It would serve him right if he got pulled over. She was hurt that he appeared to care so little for her feelings. He hadn't glanced her way once in the past half hour. Finally it was time to leave, and with relief Theodora said her goodbyes to her in-laws.

"I'll stay behind you on the way home." Stewart said.

Theodora gave him a cold look. "Don't bother. I'll see you at home." She slammed her car door and peeled out of the parking lot like a rebellious teenager. Pent up tears of frustration and anger bathed her face. She couldn't go on like this any longer. She would force the issue tonight.

Stewart's car was already in the garage when she got home. He wasn't downstairs, and Theodora climbed the stairs, dreading the impending confrontation. Her blood boiled when she saw that he was sprawled on top of the comforter, snoring loudly. She walked over to him and shook his arm in an attempt to rouse him. He shook his head and uttered something incoherent.

"I hate you!" she screamed childishly, but he didn't stir. She stormed out of the bedroom and went back downstairs. She wondered if Nicole was alone. She needed to talk to her, pour out her heart and have Nicole tell her everything would be okay, but this was something she couldn't share with her unless she wanted to turn Nicole completely against Stewart forever. Waves of loneliness overcame her. For the first time in her life she felt totally abandoned.

Chapter 31

*T*he wind and rain whipped violently against the windowpanes. Nicole looked up from her paper at the relentless downpour. She got another cup of coffee and sat back down. When she came to the "Today" section her heart stopped. Smiling up at her was a picture of Peter shaking hands with a tall, silver haired man. They were both in tuxedos and Peter looked even more handsome than she remembered. The caption read, "Senator Demetrios donates time and money to a good cause." The article described the senator's unfailing support of The Special Olympics, and his earnest desire to enlist the support of others within the state.

Throwing the paper down, she got up from the table, grabbed the phone and dialed. Michael's voice answered. "How are you?" he asked.

"I've been better. I saw Peter's picture in the Sun. Just when I think I'm starting to forget about him, all these feelings come rushing over me again. Tell me I did the right thing by ending it."

"Nicole, I can't tell you how to live your life. It's no secret how I feel about you, but despite my feelings, I want your happiness. It seems to me you haven't resolved things in your heart one way or the other."

"You're right." She paused. "I don't know what I would've done without you. No matter how low I get, you're always there to pick me up. And what do I give you in return? It's not fair to you."

185

"Let me worry about that. You know you can call me anytime, and I'll be there for you."

"What are you doing tonight?"

He hesitated. "I have a date."

Nicole paused, surprised by his answer.

"Oh. That's great!" Trying to sound enthusiastic she continued. "Who's the lucky girl?"

"Her name is Alicia. Pat has been trying to fix me up with her for months. I finally agreed."

At the mention of Pat, she felt her breathing become shallow and her body grow rigid.

"Are you going out with her alone?"

Michael sighed. "No, Nicole. We're going with Peter and Pat. I'm sorry."

"It's okay. It's better for me to realize that Peter isn't sitting at home pining over me. It's just what I needed to hear."

"If you need to talk later on, just call me on my cell phone. If the night starts to drag, you can rescue me. Promise me, you'll call if you need me?"

"Sure. Talk to you later." She hung up the phone with a heavy heart. She was surprised to discover that the thought of Michael with another woman disturbed her. Was she actually feeling a little jealous? What's wrong with me? Why shouldn't Michael be dating? It wasn't fair of her to expect him to spend all his time comforting her. She wondered where they were going. The thought of Peter enjoying himself without her sickened her, and she found herself second-guessing her decision to end things for the hundredth time.

She thought back to the last time she'd seen him. Somehow, she had stuck to her guns and refused to reconsider, despite his numerous efforts. For the first month, she found a message from him on her answering machine every night, his smooth deep voice pleading with her to change her mind. She was so often tempted to relent, but drew strength from the fact that his messages never asked her to call him at home, but at the office, hidden and secret from the rest of the world. She stopped turning on her machine. She also stopped answering the telephone, using her caller ID to screen calls. When it became evident that he couldn't reach her by phone, he started sending cards and notes. For the entire month of February she found a different card from him every day. She told herself she should throw them away before opening them, but she couldn't bring herself to do so. She pored over them again and again until she knew them all by heart. Some were funny, some romantic, but all shared the same underlying message, which told her that he loved and missed her terribly. She hadn't responded to his cards either, and they had stopped a week ago. She was both relieved and dejected when she realized Peter's campaign to win her back had ended. She knew she was near the breaking point, ready to give in at any time. The fact that he had given up without more of a fight made her feel that his declaration of undying love was nothing more than a passing infatuation. Now she had the added burden of picturing him on a cozy foursome with Michael tonight. She picked up the phone and dialed Theodora's number. Stewart answered.

"Hi. It's Nicole, How are you?"

"Fine, thanks. I guess you're looking for Theo."

"Yes, is she around?"

"You just missed her. She went to the grocery store. You might be able to get her on her cell phone."

"Thanks, talk to you later." She dialed the number and when she got Theo's voice mail, slammed the phone down.

She took a quick shower, dressed and was ready to head out the door when the phone rang. Thinking it must be Theodora returning her call, she picked it up.

"Hello."

"Please don't hang up."

"Peter."

"I can't believe I'm finally talking to you. Nicole, I miss you so much."

She sat down, her mind numb. "I can't talk to you."

"Are you telling me that you've been happy these past two months?" he said.

"I've got to go. Have fun on your double date tonight."

"What?"

"Michael told me about your plans."

"Oh, that. Pat can't stand to see anyone unattached."

"How nice. Does she know anyone for me?" she asked sarcastically. "I really have to go now."

"Nicole wait. I'm miserable without you. I can't live like this. You're all I think about We must talk. Won't you at least think about it?"

"What do we have to talk about? I'm free and you're not. What's the point?"

"I promise, I won't ever bother you again if you just see me one more time. Maybe there's a way to work things out. Don't we deserve a little happiness?" his voice caught in his throat.

She wavered.

"Oh Peter, I'm so confused. I've been so unhappy. Everywhere I look, I see you. I can't hear a song on the radio without thinking about you. I'm tired of feeling bad all the time."

"What are you doing tonight?" he asked.

"Why?"

"I want to come and talk to you."

"At midnight? I don't think so."

"No. I'll cancel out on tonight. Please."

No, her head screamed, but she heard her voice say yes.

"Thank you. You won't regret it Nicole. I'll see you at seven. I love you." He hung up before she could reconsider.

I've got to talk to Theo, she thought, as she dialed her house again. This time Theodora answered.

"Peter's coming over tonight," she blurted out, not bothering to say hello.

Theodora was silent.

"Did you hear me?"

"I heard you. Nicole, what are you doing? I swear, he's taking advantage of you. I don't understand how he could put you in such a terrible position. Don't you realize that nothing good can come from your seeing him?"

"Oh Theo, I've been so unhappy without him. I'm starting to think that you've just got to grab what little happiness you can. Who knows, I could be hit by a truck and be dead tomorrow. I've tried to stay away from him, but he just won't let up."

"Is this really what you want, a relationship you have to hide and be ashamed of?" Theodora asked.

"No, that's not what I want. Peter knows I won't live like that. He called me this morning and begged me to let him come talk to me one more time. He says we'll work things out. Maybe he and Pat are going their separate ways. All I'm saying is I'm willing to hear him out."

"Nicole, you know how much I love you? I have to tell you, that even though I respect Peter, I've seen the smooth-talking side of him, his talent for appeasing people, and turning them around to his point of view without their even realizing it. He knows people, and he knows how to turn on the charm to get what he wants. I'm not saying he doesn't love you, but that doesn't mean he'll forsake everything he's worked so hard to accomplish to be with you. I don't believe for one minute that he'll leave Pat and even if he did, I don't think you could live with yourself, knowing that you were the cause."

"A part of me knows that you're right, but there's this other part that can't stop. No matter what, I've got to see him one more time and hear him out. If I don't, I know I'll spend the rest of my life wondering what could have been. I don't know how it'll end, or even what I want to happen. The only thing I do know is that I must see him. Don't worry, all I plan to do is talk."

"I can't help but worry."

"I'll be fine. I'll call you tomorrow."

She put on an old Sinatra CD and lay across the bed to relax and wait, recalling their phone conversation. He had sounded so desperate, and she realized she, too, had been squandering her days by moving through them in a dull haze. Depression was new to her; she had never understood people who wallowed in their sorrows. Until now, her inner core of strength and resilience had served her well. This was the first time she found herself yearning for something out of reach. She was beginning to see that she was living with a lid on her feelings. She didn't know where this holding back, this resolve not to show the world any weakness came from. She found herself on unfamiliar ground, unsure of her next move. It was like dancing on a mountaintop with your eyes closed.

And slowly, as she lay there meditatively, it became clear that no one else could pull her out of the miasma. With stunning clarity she saw what she had become. How had she allowed herself to travel so far from her values? She would reclaim her morality and close the door on that part of herself that had blindly ignored what was right and true. She would have to muster all the inner strength she possessed, a strength she believed formidable, and continue to move forward with her life. She reminded herself that in her genes was the strength of Andreas and Sophia and Nick, power sufficient to rise above anything, even Peter Demetrios. And finally, she admitted, a power greater than all these things was available to her if only she would accept it. Tears of repentance cleansed her soul as she poured out her heart to God and confessed her wrongdoing.

Night came, shrouding the house in darkness. She remained in her room, lights out, at ease once again with her conscience. When the doorbell rang at seven o'clock, it appeared that no one was home.

Chapter 32

MAY

*I*t was a perfect Saturday in May, one of those rare Baltimore days when the sun shines brilliantly and no humidity hangs in the air. Nicole and Theodora sat at a sidewalk cafe sipping diet cokes between bites of pizza. They had spent the morning shopping, and were now enjoying a leisurely lunch.

"How long since we've done this? I miss it," Nicole said.

"Too long. We're both always so busy, I feel like we haven't really talked in ages. How are you, anyway?" Theodora asked her sister.

"You mean am I getting over Peter? I think so. Oh, I still think about him, but it's not the way it was in the beginning. I've spent a lot of time with Michael. He's been a great friend."

Theodora smiled. "You do know he's crazy about you? Who is this Alicia that calls the office for him all the time? I haven't met her."

Nicole hadn't met her either, but already she didn't like her. Michael didn't say much about her other than to casually mention they had seen a movie or gone for a bite to eat. It bothered her that he was seeing someone, and she realized she was afraid he might become serious. She was surprised by how much she didn't want that to happen.

"Does he talk about her?" she asked Theodora.

"Not really. He doesn't seem that interested, but she must like him. From what I gather, half the things they do are concerts or plays she's gotten the tickets for. I think he goes because he has nothing better to do. With the exception of you, that is, but he knows that's hopeless." She stopped a moment and stared at her sister. "It is hopeless, isn't it?"

"I don't know anymore. I suppose I think of him as more than a friend. Whenever I hear about Alicia I feel myself getting bothered."

"If I didn't know better, I'd say you were jealous."

Nicole looked out past the wide sidewalk to the street beyond. "If I didn't know better, I'd say the same thing."

"Well, then let me give you some motherly advice. If there's the slightest chance you're interested, you'd better do something before this girl gets her hooks all the way in."

"Do you think I'm just being possessive about the friendship? You know, like when your best girlfriend starts getting friendly with someone else and you start to panic?"

"I don't know. Only you know that. But I'll tell you one thing. If there's any doubt in your mind, you'll never forgive yourself if you don't go for it."

"Maybe you're right. I do look forward to the time we spend together. He's easy to be with, and we've had great fun together."

"Why don't you invite him for Easter at Aunt Effie's?"

"And expose him to the whole tribe at once? That could be a little intimidating. It might scare him off."

"He's already met half the family, and anyway, it would take a lot more than our clan to intimidate Michael. He can hold his own."

The more Nicole thought about it, the more she liked the idea.

"Are you and Stewart going to the Elliotts' for American Easter?" Because the Orthodox religion followed the modified Gregorian calendar, their Easter fell on a different Sunday of the month than the Protestant and Catholic holiday.

"No, I managed to convince Caroline to come to our house, so I'm cooking."

"Lots of work, isn't it? Do you have time?"

"Not really, but it beats having to sit through another holiday at the Elliott's. I'm hoping Caroline won't get drunk if she's away from home and can't keep ducking into her bedroom for a drink."

"That bad, eh?" Nicole sympathized.

"You have no idea. Oh, don't get me wrong, Graham is wonderful, always saying how glad he is to see us, but her, she makes it clear that if I dropped off the edge of the earth tomorrow it wouldn't be soon enough."

Nicole shook her head, laughing. "Poor Theodora. How can you stand it? Isn't there some way to get out of it?"

"None whatsoever. She'd never speak to me again."

"Well, that might be progress. What about Stewart? Does he mind it as much as you?"

"It must seem normal to him. He doesn't even notice how rude she is to me. To tell you the truth, there are a lot of things he doesn't notice. He works so much, I hardly see him anymore. But I think maybe that will change."

"What makes you say that?" Nicole asked.

Theodora hesitated. "I haven't told anyone yet. I'm pregnant." Nicole couldn't tell if Theodora was excited or troubled.

"Are you sure?" Nicole asked.

"Positive. I got the results of the blood test yesterday. The baby's due in December."

Now that she'd said it out loud, told another living being, the pregnancy seemed more real. How could she be so stupid as to let this happen? The timing was all wrong. She and Stewart couldn't get along with each other, how were they going to care for this helpless, dependent little creature who would soon be the hub around which their every waking moment revolved. She wasn't sure she had enough in her to give to this child when Stewart needed so much of her. On the other hand, it might be the very thing they needed, to take attention off of their problems while they lavished their love on the child they had created together.

"We weren't planning this so soon," she admitted to Nicole. It was impossible to overlook the expression on Nicole's face. "I can see you're not overflowing with enthusiasm."

Nicole was overcome by feelings of tenderness and support for Theodora. "I think it's wonderful news. When are you going to tell Stewart?"

"Tonight. We're going out for dinner, just the two of us. It's been so long since we've spent an evening out together, I'm not sure I'll know how to act. Things are so different than I thought they'd be."

"What do you mean? You're not becoming disenchanted, are you?"

"I wouldn't put it that way exactly. Maybe a better way of describing it is that I've come down to earth. I must've thought marriage would be one long, extended honeymoon. I took the last line of all those fairy tales seriously, 'they got married and they lived happily ever after.' Those writers certainly had a sense of irony," she said wryly.

"Are you saying you're not happy?" Nicole asked.

Theodora tilted her head to one side and thought about the question. "I'm not happy or unhappy. I guess I'm in neutral. I keep thinking surely things will change, this can't be all there is."

"I suppose any observations coming from me are pure supposition since I've never been married, but what you're describing doesn't sound like the way it should be. You haven't even been married a year."

"Well, isn't the first year supposed to be the hardest?" Theodora asked.

"Hard, maybe, but not miserable. Have you talked to Stewart about how you feel?"

"I can't talk to him. He would see anything I say as criticism and an attack on him. He gets defensive, as if I'm blaming him for any problems we might have. I have to figure this out on my own."

"Theo, listen to me. If things aren't good, you're right to be asking questions and examining what's going on, but you have to work this out together, you can't do it by yourself. How many times have we talked about how different we would be? That we'd never tolerate a marriage where we would have to be anything less than who we were, where we could openly and honestly reveal our inner selves and want and accept the same thing in return. What happened to that?"

"What happened is it's not possible. At least not for us."

"I don't buy that." Nicole was angry now. "It is possible, and you know what? If being with Stewart doesn't allow you the kind of integrity you need to be who you really are, then you're in the wrong place."

"That isn't quite what I wanted to hear as I sit here pregnant," Theodora said.

"I'm not telling you to leave him. I'm only saying your problems are not going to be solved by you alone. This is something you've got to work on together or it's futile." She could tell by Theodora's restlessness that she didn't wish to pursue the subject any further. "Okay, enough. How about a cup of coffee? Or do you have to rush off?"

"No, I'd love one as long as it's decaf." Theodora gestured to the waitress. "So, what have you decided? Are you going to bring Michael on Easter?"

"I'll ask him tomorrow night. We're going to the Harbor."

"Good." They sat in silence for a while, sipping their coffee and watching the people walking by.

"Did Aunt Effie call you about bringing anything?" Theodora asked.

"No, did she call you?"

"Yeah, she asked me to bring a vegetable dish."

"Maybe she thinks only the married ones can cook. I'll probably just take a bottle of wine and some flowers."

"Flowers? You know Aunt Effie; there will be vases and vases of fresh flowers everywhere. Everything is always perfect." Theodora said.

Nicole took the last sip of coffee. It was relaxing and pleasant to spend time with Theodora again, and she was reluctant to get up from the table. She smiled at her sister.

"It's after three o'clock. I'm afraid they'll kick us out if we don't give up this table voluntarily."

"I guess we should get going. I could use a nap right about now. I'm so tired by afternoon. It must be the pregnancy."

They left money on the table and walked to the lot where their cars were parked. Theodora unlocked her door and turned to give

Nicole a hug goodbye. "Bye sis. It was fun. Have a good time tomorrow with Michael."

"I will. Good luck tonight with Stewart. Hope everything goes well. Now go home and get some rest."

Theodora got in her car and Nicole walked to the door marked 'Stairs'.

By the time Theodora reached the house, she felt as if she could go to sleep and not get up until the following morning. She put the mail on the kitchen table without looking at it and didn't bother to retrieve any messages from the machine. Going directly to the bedroom, she closed the blinds and pulled down the spread. She slipped off her jeans and turned the ringer off on the telephone before getting into bed. Just before falling asleep, she set the alarm for five o'clock. She didn't want that dull headache she got if she napped too long and wanted ample time to dress for her evening out with Stewart. As she drifted off to sleep, she silently rehearsed what she would say to him tonight.

Nicole took off her shoes and sat down in the soft armchair next to her bed, putting her feet up on the hassock. She leaned her head against the high back of the chair and closed her eyes, thinking about the child her sister was carrying. It was strange, but she realized that when she tried to imagine her yet unborn niece or nephew, Stewart had no tie to the child. She thought of it only as Theodora's. Her dislike for him was becoming so powerful, she didn't want to acknowledge his connection to this baby. She smiled thinly as she realized that Stewart would probably pick a thousand other people as an aunt to his child before her. They were like oil and water, and they both knew things would never change between them. So far it hadn't harmed her relationship with Theodora, but she feared it was only a matter of time before the effects would be felt between them. Theodora would choose a loyalty, and Nicole understood the loyalty would have to be to her husband, as much as it grieved her. She tried to imagine how Stewart would react to the news tonight. She hoped for Theodora's sake that he would be happy. More than that, she hoped she was wrong about Stewart and Heather, that nothing was going on between them. She decided she would tell her sister if she found out he was being unfaithful, then thought better of it. Follow Dad's advice, she thought, and play it by ear.

She picked up the Time magazine on the nightstand and became so engrossed that the sound of the telephone ringing next to her made her jump.

"Hello?" she said a little impatiently.

"Am I getting you at a bad time?" It was Michael.

"No, not at all. I was just reading."

"Oh. I won't keep you. I'm calling to let you know I'll pick you up around seven o'clock tomorrow night. Does the Harbor still sound good?"

"Yes. Hopefully the weather will be nice," she hesitated a moment, wanting to ask if he was free tonight, and then thought, why not. "Hey, I know it's last minute, but, are you free tonight?"

He hesitated. "Sorry, I've already got plans."

"Oh, well that's okay. Have a good time," she spoke quickly, eager to get off the phone.

"Is everything okay?" he asked.

"Of course. I'll see you tomorrow."

She put the phone back in its cradle and sank into the soft cushion of the chair. What did she expect, that he would come running the minute she indicated any interest? She supposed she did. She had come to depend on his deep fondness for her, a comfort and reassurance to her bruised ego after the anguish she had gone through with Peter. Selfishly, she hadn't given much thought to his needs. All right then. Tonight he was with Alicia. But tomorrow night he would be with her. She would invite him to her aunt's and uncle's for Easter dinner with the family. It was time for Alicia to exit the picture.

Chapter 33

*T*he insistent buzzing of the alarm awakened Theodora from her nap. She looked at the clock, disoriented, and couldn't remember if it was morning or night. As the numbers on the LED came into focus, she began to get her bearings. There was a stale taste of coffee in her mouth and her throat was dry. She threw off the white duvet, swung her legs over the side of the bed onto the carpeted floor and headed to the kitchen for something to quench her thirst. She grabbed the pitcher of orange juice and poured herself a tall glass. Small pieces of pulp swirled around her tongue as she took a long swallow. She turned her head at the sound of the garage door opening. It must be Stewart. She hadn't expected him this early and was pleasantly surprised.

"Hi sweetie," she said as he came into the kitchen. He seemed surprised to see her standing there. "I'm bushed," he said and dropped his briefcase on the kitchen table. He hadn't even bothered to say hello.

Theodora tried to hide her annoyance and smiled sympathetically. "Why don't I fix you a nice cool drink and you can sit down and relax awhile. Our reservation isn't until eight o'clock. We have loads of time."

"Would you be awfully upset if we stayed home tonight?" He had just come from a long afternoon with Heather, and the last thing on his mind was a candlelight dinner with Theodora. He just wanted to go to sleep.

She bit her tongue. She'd be damned if she'd spend another Saturday night in front of the television with Stewart snoring away beside her. She tried not to sound sharp. "I was looking forward to an evening out with you. Why don't you rest a little bit. I'll get you a cup of tea with some honey. You'll feel refreshed before you know it."

"Why do you sound like June Cleaver? The only thing missing in this sunny little picture is the starched shirt-waist dress. I don't want a nice little cup of tea with honey. I just want to lie down after a long day and rest without my wife pouting and complaining."

This was too much. She wasn't going to let him turn this around and make it her fault. "I'm not pouting and I'm not complaining, although if anyone has something to complain about, I do. You come in and don't even say hello and then you bite my head off when I try to do something nice for you. I almost believe you'd be happier if I left. If I weren't pregnant, I think I'd do just that." It came out in one long breath.

He stared at her, saying nothing. Theodora waited, but he continued to stare. "What are you looking at?" she asked indignantly.

"What did you just say?" he asked.

"You want me to repeat all that?"

"What did you say at the end? Did you say you were pregnant?"

Had she said she was pregnant? "Did I say that? I was going to tell you tonight over a quiet, romantic dinner together. So much for candles and roses."

He walked over to her and put his arms around her slender waist. He moved one hand to the front of her body, down to her stomach and gently rubbed in a circular motion.

"I can't believe it." He felt an incredible surge of power and potency such as he had never experienced. His creation was a living, moving being inside of her. His heart raced and he felt the blood pounding as it pulsed in his veins. His would be the first Parsenis grandchild. Nick would be overjoyed, and Stewart's place in the old man's affection would be assured.

The white Land Rover hummed along smoothly at an even seventy miles an hour, the route so familiar to Michael that concentration was not required. He recalled his date with Alicia last night. She was a nice woman and their time together was easy and pleasant, but he knew he could never love her, and she deserved a man who could. She'd made it easy for him, telling him she understood, he couldn't help it, after all, if he didn't feel the way she did, that they might still be friends and she wished him well. Her kindness extended so far that it felt as if she offered consolation to Michael for hurting her. He was truly sorry. Sorry that she was in love with him and Nicole was not.

The days were getting longer now, and when he arrived at Nicole's house it was still light and the temperature a pleasant seventy degrees. He sprinted up the front steps and rang the doorbell.

"Welcome!" Nicole smiled widely as she opened the door for him. "Come on in and sit down, I'll just be a minute." She was holding one sock and a white Reebok in her hand. They sat in the kitchen and Nicole put on her other shoe. "Grab a coke out of the fridge if you'd like," she looked up at Michael as she tied the laces.

"What do you feel like doing at the Harbor?" he asked.

"I thought we'd just walk around, maybe get some fattening and delicious Thrashers french fries, and sit and watch people. If we get bored we can take the water taxi over to Fells Point and have a Latte. And there's always Ben and Jerry's for ice cream. What do you think?" She stood up, both shoes now on.

"I think it sounds like we're going to gain a hundred pounds!"

The change into spring weather always brought huge crowds of people into Baltimore's Inner Harbor. It was a popular tourist attraction as well as a favorite haunt of the locals. Nicole and Michael sat on a bench near the water, eating fries soaked in vinegar from a large cardboard container and watched the throngs of people parading in front of them.

"Okay, what does he do for a living and is that his wife or girlfriend with him?" It was Michael's turn to guess. They had been playing a game, choosing an interesting or unusual looking couple walking by, and then constructing a background.

Michael studied the tall, skinny man with a balding head and thick horn-rimmed glasses. He appeared to be around forty years old. The woman next to him was plump and fair-haired. She wore no make-up and her plain cotton dress looked homemade. "Let's see," Michael said. "He's an accountant with a grocery store chain and she's his second wife. They just got married, after a long torrid affair which took place mostly behind the meat counter."

Nicole laughed at the picture Michael painted. He leaned the cup of french fries toward her. "Have the last one," he said. She picked up the limp fry at the bottom of the container and put it in her mouth.

"Thanks. Good to the very last drop. Want to walk?"

They strolled along the water's edge talking and watching boats come in to anchor for the evening. When they had covered the entire area, Michael suggested they have a drink at one of the outside cafes on the Light Street Pavilion, and they seated themselves at a round wrought iron table outside and on the second floor of the harbor building. Nicole looked across the table at Michael whose gaze was on all the activity and twinkling lights on the water, and thought again how nice looking he was. She noticed the second glances from women who passed, something to which he seemed completely oblivious. She liked that about him. He was at ease with himself, had a healthy self-image without being egotistical. He felt her eyes on him and turned to look at her. He smiled as their eyes met.

"Penny for your thoughts," he said.

"I was thinking how much I enjoy being with you. You've been a great friend to me these last few months. I don't know what I would've done without you," she paused, took a sip of her drink. "For a long time I've thought of you as my best friend next to my sister, but you know what? Something's changing. Did you have a date with Alicia last night? Never mind, don't answer that," she said before he could reply. "I kind of figured you did. I guess I'm jealous thinking of you with someone else."

"Nicole, for the first time in my life I'm at a loss for words. I never imagined you'd think of me as anything more than a friend."

"Michael, don't misunderstand. I need to take things slowly, but I know I like being with you and I find myself looking forward to seeing you more and more."

Michael smiled at her and squeezed her hand.

"We're agreed. We'll take this slowly and see where it goes."

Impulsively, she placed her hand at the nape of his neck and pulled his face close to hers, putting her lips against his. She closed her eyes and felt the warmth and moistness of his mouth on hers and let herself enjoy how good it felt. They parted slowly and looked into each other's eyes. Yes, she thought, Michael had definitely moved from the ranks of friend into a whole new realm.

Chapter 34

*T*he delicious aroma of the traditional Easter lamb filled the house. Effie was firmly in control in her magnificent kitchen filled with the most modern and ingenious cooking devices. One corner of a wall was devoted to her impressive collection of cookbooks, with floor to ceiling shelves for housing the assorted and sundry display. Eleni had stationed herself in the kitchen too, and helped each one as they brought their assigned dish into the room. No matter how large the gathering, no one would dare serve a catered meal on a holiday. Certain foods were expected.

Sophia was busy at the stove wearing an apron from home. She could never find one in these kitchens of her children. She cursed under her breath at the counter top stove she was trying to work on. What was wrong with the old stoves, where you could see the fire and make it higher or lower depending on what you wanted to do with your food? You couldn't even tell if these things were turned on. She always felt like she was in a space age movie when she came to Effie's. If it were my daughter, I could say something, she thought to herself. But since it was her daughter-in-law, she felt she must suffer in silence. "*Vre, zon,*" she spat at the stove once more as she tried to heat the pilafi.

In the living room the atmosphere was calmer. The room seemed to go on forever, with billowing white seating upon which the bright afternoon sun threw sparkling cubes of light. Nicole and Michael sat with Stewart and Theodora on large, overstuffed love seats facing each other. A glass table was between the two white sofas and on the table sat a multi-faceted leaded glass box of the most dazzling blue imaginable. The delicate, long-stemmed glasses they drank from were the same incredible turquoise.

Stephan and Effie had planned together every detail of the house that took a year to build. It was a huge contemporary structure of stark white stone, with geometric and circular windows throughout. The inside of the house was cool and airy, with large rooms laid with marble terrazzo floors. The furnishings and rugs were in varying shades of white and the occasional splash of color was a stunning turquoise. The feel was fluid and elegant. The house sat high on a hill and on every level, oversized glass double doors led to terraces overlooking the valley. Nicole and Theodora always imagined they could hear the sounds of the warm Aegean Sea lapping at the shore.

Although there were forty for dinner, Effie's dining room was large enough to accommodate them with only the addition of one round table for ten. She put the very young children at this table and the adults gathered around the massive glass dining room table specially ordered and made to her specifications. The talk was continuous, loud and boisterous, and no one made a pretense of holding back an unpopular opinion or comment. They were noisily debating a case of adoption revocation.

"I think it's terrible," Eleni said. "Giving birth doesn't make a woman a good mother. Any animal can give birth. The courts should never have given her back to her birth mother."

"But there are other things to consider," Nicole put in. "After all, the mother does have some rights, too. She was in a very unstable emotional state at the time of the child's birth. And the father was never given the knowledge of his child or the opportunity to decide whether or not he wanted it."

Eve picked up, impatient with her niece. "Oh for heaven's sake. The mother didn't even name the right father at the time the child was born. After two years she decides she wants the child after all. What if she gets tired of her in a few years? Is she going to give her back? Who gives a damn if the father never knew? They shouldn't have been sleeping with each other anyway." Eve's voice grew louder as she hammered her point home.

"Aunt Eve, there's no reason to get hostile," Nicole shot back. "And why shouldn't they have slept together. They weren't hurting anybody."

"Ach, *Theo mou*," Eve said, imitating her mother's mournful cry to God for help. "If I say any more, some of us may not be speaking by the time the next holiday rolls around."

"Michael," Nick's voice boomed across the table. "Tell us how things are going in Washington. Any impending legislation we should be worried about?"

Before Michael could respond, Nicole cut in.

"I'll tell you what we should be worried about. Military spending is increasing and welfare money is decreasing. We're the richest country in the world and we have the poorest record in the civilized world on social reform. It's a disgrace," Nicole said.

"And tell me, *pethaki mou*, what have you done to increase the treasury of this great country?" Andreas asked her. "You are so ready to give away money? When I came to this country fifty years ago, no one handed me anything. I worked like a mule to give my family food to eat and a roof over their heads. And so did everyone who came over. We did not expect anyone to give us something for nothing, but we knew if we worked hard enough, we would be successful."

"Papou," Theodora said patiently, coming to her sister's defense, "There are some people who are unable to work. They come from disadvantaged backgrounds where education hasn't been an option and crime runs rampant in their neighborhoods. These people need our help to rise above their circumstances."

"*Koritsi mou.*" He used the fond diminutive for 'my girl' in Greek. "I had no education. I barely spoke the language, but that did not stop me. There is a saying in my little village, '*An then vrexis kolo, then tros psari.*'" There was a roar of laughter all around the table. Michael looked at Nicole with a puzzled expression.

"I'll translate for you. 'If you don't get your ass wet, you don't eat fish.'" She smiled. "That's the work ethic according to Andreas Zaharis."

"Seems to have worked for him," Michael said looking around the room. The scene was one of abundance and affluence. The grandchildren reaped the benefits of long hours and grueling work, but along with the advantages had come the problems associated with them. Already, two of the families had been touched by divorce. Harry, Stephan's son, sat at the end of the table with his date of the week, a young waitress from the restaurant. Since the break-up of his marriage, he managed to bed every new waitress who walked through the door, and they were only too eager to be with him. One glimpse at his parents' lifestyle was enough to convince them he was worth going after, and he exploited it to the utmost. Effie had long since ceased asking him to bring his dates by, but she was unable to keep them away on holidays. The heavily made up girl with him today hardly spoke, obviously overwhelmed by her surroundings and the sheer force of this huge family.

"Theodora, have you and Stewart decided who you will ask to be godparents?" Sophia asked.

"Not yet, Yiayia."

Nick, beaming at the mention of his first grandchild, said. "I intend to lavish every spare minute of time and attention on this incredible child."

Theodora laughed at her father's enthusiasm. "Dad, how can you be so sure this child will be incredible?"

"What a question. Of course it will be incredible. How could it be anything else with genes like this?"

"How indeed," Paul patted his sister on the back. "Just look at its mama."

Theodora looked into her brother's kind, gentle eyes. She had always adored him. She looked past him to the blonde sitting on his right. What was her name? Theodora thought he had said Marjorie, but she wasn't sure. Just as they got used to whomever he was dating, someone new came into the picture. She was sure he had left many a disappointed young woman behind, and she couldn't understand why he hadn't found someone to whom he could commit himself.

"Now don't everyone get up," Effie said as she began to clear the table. "We'll break the spell. Eve and I will bring out coffee and dessert. You all just stay put," she commanded them.

Groans of delight greeted the profusion of sweets brought to the table. There were kourambiedes, baklava, and koulourakia, the traditional Easter cookie, an elaborately braided confection. In addition to the Greek selections, there were pies and cakes.

"Let me divide a piece of lemon meringue pie with you and then we can have some baklava too," Eleni said to Eve.

"I want a little piece of the cheesecake too," Eve said, cutting a small portion.

"Speaking of cheesecake," Nicole said. "Has anyone eaten at Mike's Diner yet? You know, the new place that opened on York Road? They have the most fabulous Mississippi mud pie in the entire world."

"What's that got to do with cheesecake?" Paul asked her.

"What do you mean, what's it got to do with it? It's a dessert, isn't it?" Nicole replied.

"I was there for lunch the other day," Dimitri said. "They have wonderful food. Had one of the best crab cakes I've ever eaten."

Stewart looked around the table in disgust. "You know, I've never met a family who talks about food as much as you. You talk about other food while you're eating this food. It's incredible."

"And tell me, Stewart, what is the scintillating table conversation at your family gatherings?" Nicole glared at him.

Eleni pushed her chair back and rose from the table. "Theo, Nicole," she called, "Aunt Effie's done quite enough. Let's finish in the kitchen." There was no mistaking the tone in her voice, and in unison, they rose.

"Yiayia, go sit down," Nicole said as she went over to the sink. "We'll do this."

"No, no. I know you will throw food away. You will waste things if I am not watching," she said to her granddaughter.

Theodora looked over at Nicole and smiled. Their grandmother never threw anything away. In her kitchen the top drawer was reserved for mounds of rubber bands from the daily newspaper, used aluminum foil she smoothed out and refolded for future use, and other odds and ends with which she couldn't bear to part. She recycled long before it became politically correct. The food she saved was often what her daughters and granddaughters would have thrown out, but they admitted that her meals made of leftovers were usually better than anything they cooked from scratch.

"How come we always wind up doing the dishes at these things?" Nicole said to Theodora as she loaded the dishwasher.

"Because we're the good granddaughters," Theodora said.

"We're the only granddaughters. Do you think that could be the underlying cause of our unpredictable behavior?" Nicole joked.

"Who told you your behavior was unpredictable. I can predict everything you do."

"Oh you can, huh? What do you predict I'll do with Michael?"

"That's easy. You'll marry him." Theodora put the soap in the dispenser and shut the door of the dishwasher. "Well, we're finished. Let's go back inside."

"Wait a minute. Not so fast. What do you mean I'll marry him?"

"Just what I said. You'll marry him. And you know what? You couldn't find a nicer guy."

"You're right about the last part. I've never met anyone kinder than Michael, and the good part is I'm starting to like that."

"Take it from me, there's nothing more important than that. Nice, that small, slightly boring little word, is the bottom line. Without it, the rest means less than nothing." She looked Nicole straight in the eye. "Don't throw him away."

Chapter 35

JULY

*T*heodora hated herself for what she was doing, but she couldn't stop herself. Stewart was upstairs sleeping, and she was sitting in his den, briefcase open, reading his American Express receipts. She was determined to find out once and for all if he was cheating. She had hoped that her pregnancy would change things and bring them closer, but with the exception of his initial delight, it had changed nothing between them. He refused to attend Lamaze classes with her, claiming to have better things to do than sit in a room and listen to a bunch of whales breathe heavily. That comment had stung, and it didn't take Theodora long to realize that Stewart was one of those men repulsed by pregnant women. He had already warned her that the minute she began to balloon out she could forget about any sex until she was back to normal. She was beginning to feel that it would be fine with her if they never had sex again.

In front of her family he acted the loving and attentive husband, and she played along, too embarrassed to let them see behind the facade. Her youthful idealism had been shed with her virginity. If she was a naive twenty-three when she married him, she was certainly grown up now. No more turning a blind eye to his flaws. From now on she would listen to her instincts, which were screaming that something was very wrong.

She continued to sort through the receipts, but found nothing questionable. She put everything back into the envelope and moved to their VISA bill, but found nothing peculiar. She looked in the pockets on the side of the briefcase and came up empty. Suddenly feeling rather silly, she zipped the briefcase and sat it back down on the floor. As it fell to its side, a key fell out. She picked it up and inserted it into the middle desk drawer and heard a click. Lying face up was another American Express bill, this one in Stewart's name and billed to his office. There were at least six months of statements. She opened the statement with the most recent postmark. Her heart sank as she read it, its meaning unmistakable. Three hundred dollars at Victoria's Secret; receipts for dinners at restaurants; days at hotels and finally three thousand dollars for jewelry just last week. The bill fell from her hand and she sat as if in a trance. Her cheeks burned with shame. Unable to look at any more, she fled from the room. She leaned over the toilet and was sick, and then sat on the bathtub's edge, catching her breath as beads of perspiration dotted her face. After a few minutes, she felt strong enough to stand. She went back to his den, locked the drawer and returned the key to his briefcase. She turned off the light and went to the family room to lie down. Not trusting herself to see Stewart, she slept there, hoping that the morning would bring inspiration.

Chapter 36

A grim-faced Theodora awaited Stewart Sunday morning. "What happened to you last night? I never heard you come to bed," he said distractedly while he fixed himself a cup of coffee.

"I was reading," she answered flatly.

"Oh. What?"

"Cheating, lying scumbags masquerading as husbands," she answered.

He winced. "What kind of man-hating garbage is that?"

"I found your American Express bill."

He spun around to look at her, and his eyes narrowed. "What are you talking about?"

"I went through your desk and I found the separate account you have. I notice you've spent a small fortune on her. Who is she?"

"How dare you go through my personal things? What gives you the right to invade my privacy?"

"Look Stewart, don't insult my intelligence. I know you're having an affair, so don't bother trying to deny it, and don't try hiding behind some self-righteous anger either. I have every right to look through whatever I want in this house. I want answers and I want them now. Now tell me the truth." Her eyes blazed.

Realizing she had the advantage, he tried a different approach. He hung his head and looked at the floor.

"Theo, I don't know what to say. I've been such a shit. I never meant for it to happen. I don't love her. It's just one of those things. Things have been so strained between us, and I was lonely. She moved right in for the kill, and I was too weak. I've been so ashamed of myself; I haven't been able to look you in the eye. I'm glad you know. Now I can get rid of her. I was planning to end it as soon as you told me you were pregnant. I told her I couldn't see her anymore, and she threatened to tell you about us. I didn't want to risk upsetting you and possibly hurting our baby. I've been trying to figure out what to do ever since. Thank God you know. Please say you'll forgive me and give me another chance."

She looked at him with disgust. "You still haven't told me who she is."

"What difference does it make? It's over. Why do you want to know the details?"

"Because I do. Wouldn't you want to know who I was sleeping with if the situation were reversed?"

"Please don't even say that. I can't stand to think of another man touching you."

"Oh really. Well, let me tell you, it doesn't exactly thrill me to picture you with another woman. Now who is she?" she demanded shrilly.

"Someone at the office."

"Let me guess. Heather Daniels. Little miss tie giver and trip companion. Tell me Stewart, when did it start? Christmas? New Year's? How long have you been betraying me?"

"It's only been a couple of months," he answered wearily.

"Only a couple of months. Gee, what does that translate into? Fifty times, forty times? How could you?" She was crying now.

"Please, Theodora, I told you I was sorry. What more do you want from me?"

"More than you have to give, obviously. I want to understand what drives a husband of eleven months to go out and cheat on his wife. Wasn't I exciting enough for you?" she asked as tears of hurt and anger rolled down her face. "Maybe I should've gone out and gotten a lot of experience before marrying you. Is that what you want? A woman who's slept with a hundred men, like Heather?"

"Of course not. I'm so sorry. It doesn't have anything to do with you. I can't explain it. She just wouldn't give up, everywhere I looked, she was there. She flattered me and made me feel like the sexiest man in the world. I'd come home, and you'd be asleep on the couch, or working on something you'd brought home. I couldn't resist the attention. I know it was wrong, I should've come to you and talked to you about our relationship, tried to put it back on course. It will never happen again. We're a family, Theodora, please give me another chance."

"I need some time to think." She picked up her purse and ran to her car. His admission heightened the sense of violation she already felt, his betrayal stinging anew like alcohol on an open wound. Images of Stewart and Heather taunted her. It sickened her to think of him coming to their bed after making love to another woman. She drove with no destination, knowing only that she had to be alone. No matter what she decided, the relationship was irrevocably changed. Broken trust, like fine porcelain when it is repaired, retains forever a hairline crack. She wiped the tears from her face. Her eyes burned, felt swollen with grit. It was difficult to see, but she didn't care. As far as she was concerned, she might as well be driving into oblivion.

Chapter 37

*N*icole and Michael pulled up to her grandparents' house at precisely eleven thirty. At Michael's insistence, they had stopped by a roadside vendor where he purchased a bunch of yellow daisies for Yiayia.

"*Yasou koukla*. Hello Michael. Ella, come in," she kissed them each on the cheek.

"These are for you, Mrs. Zaharis," he handed her the flowers.

"Thank you, they're lovely. And please, call me Yiayia, everyone does."

"Okay." He smiled.

"I have a surprise for you." The aroma of fresh baked bread filled the kitchen, and Nicole felt her mouth watering in anticipation. Yiayia handed them each a plate of hot bread covered with butter and sugar.

Michael took a bite of his. "Mmm, this is wonderful. You made this?" he asked incredulously.

Yiayia laughed. "Of course *pethi mou*. You do not think you get bread like this in the store? I am glad you like it. I will get you more, you could use a little more meat on your bones."

Nicole laughed. "Watch out Michael or she'll have you weighing three hundred pounds."

"I hear an angel's voice, ach, no it's my Nicole," her grandfather came in to the room. Nicole stood up and hugged him.

"*Yasas*, Papou. You remember Michael don't you?"

"Of course. How do you do sir?" He winked at Michael and shook his hand.

"Fine thank you. I was just having some of your wife's delicious bread. I had no idea what I was missing all these years."

Andreas chuckled. "My Sophia is a beautiful cook. It would be good for all women to know how to cook like her." He looked pointedly at Nicole.

"Message received. I've already made a date with Yiayia to learn how to make spanikopita."

"Bravo. You should get your mother and aunt to come too."

Andreas sat down at the table and looked at Michael. "So Nicole tells me that you are a lawyer. How long have you been with the Senator?"

"About five years. He hired me as his aide when he began campaigning."

"Demetrios is a good man, I was happy to see him win. You are happy working for him?"

Michael was quiet. He hadn't yet told Nicole about his resignation. He was worried that she would blame herself. The truth was, he could no longer work for a man he didn't respect. He supposed this was as good a time as any to come clean.

"Funny you should ask," he began. "Actually, I've decided to take a position with the Justice Department."

Nicole was flabbergasted. "What?"

Michael turned to her. "I'm finishing up with Peter next week, and then I'm starting my new career. It's time for me to move on. Peter doesn't need me anymore. They've been after me for some time, and I feel I'll make more of a contribution there."

She was stunned.

"I thought you were happy where you are." She couldn't bring herself to say Peter's name.

"Perhaps Michael wants to be his own man," Andreas interjected. "This country could use more honorable men fighting for it. Bravo to you."

"Enough talk of work," Sophia declared. "Michael, tell me about you. Where do you come from, and what is your family like?"

Michael smiled. "I grew up in Philadelphia with three brothers and two sisters. Most of my family is still there with the exception of my sister who lives in San Francisco."

"Is your family close?" Sophia asked.

"We are. Of course we had our share of disagreements as kids but we've always looked out for each other over the years. Everyone still goes to my parent's house for Sunday dinner. Every time I go home they try to talk me into moving back." He paused. "They remind me a lot of your family."

It was Sophia's turn to smile. This was a good one, she thought, and hoped Nicole would realize it. He wasn't Greek, but Sophia had seen enough over the years to realize that wasn't always the most important thing. He had similar values to theirs and was a respectful boy. It sounded like he came from a nice family. Nicole could do worse. She had been paying close attention to him and liked what she saw. She was worried about Nicole. It hadn't escaped her attention how drawn and unhappy she'd been looking. Sophia didn't know the cause of her granddaughter's sorrow but she could guess that it had to do with love. She was beginning to regain her spark, and Sophia hoped her difficulties were behind her. She knew she must keep quiet about her opinion of Michael. Nicole was even more headstrong than Sophia had been in her youth. When the time was right, she would plant a seed.

She turned to Nicole, but before she spoke the phone rang, and Sophia stood to answer it.

"Hello."

The color drained from her face and she crossed herself. "Oh *Theo mou!*" she cried.

"What is it?" Andreas asked in Greek.

"Theodora was in a car accident. She is at the hospital. Eleni says she will be all right but they do not know about the baby. I told her we would come now."

"Oh no!" Nicole cried.

"We can take my car," Michael offered.

Twenty minutes later they pulled into the parking lot of Greater Baltimore Medical Center and went to the emergency room.

Nicole's parents were already there and she ran to them. "Is she okay?"

Eleni had been crying. "She has a mild concussion and they're checking for internal injuries. We're not sure about the baby yet."

"What happened?"

"She was driving down Falls Road and ran a stop sign. Another car hit her, on the passenger side, thank God. She didn't have her seat belt on."

"Can I see her?" Nicole asked.

"Not right now honey." Nick answered.

"Where's Stewart?"

"He's with her."

The doctor came out and motioned for Nick and Eleni to follow him. Nicole joined her grandparents and Michael on the cold vinyl chairs in the crowded emergency room. Michael put his arm around her and patted her shoulder.

"What is happening?" Andreas asked.

"They're going in to see her now. They'll call us when we can go in," Nicole answered.

Sophia was crying, "My little Theodora."

"I'm sure she's going to be fine," Michael said, hoping to encourage them.

"I don't understand what happened. It isn't like Theodora to run a stop sign. She's one of the most careful drivers I know." Nicole said.

A half hour later, Nick and Eleni re-emerged with Stewart. "She's sleeping now. They want to keep her under observation for at least twenty-four hours, maybe longer. It looks like the baby's fine, thank God." Nick told them.

Nicole breathed a sigh of relief.

It was hours before they were allowed to see her. The family was taken to a smaller waiting area closer to her room and Caroline arrived.

"Is the baby okay?" Caroline asked frantically.

"Yes," Stewart answered.

Caroline sank into the nearest chair in relief. Ever since she found out she was expecting a grandchild, she had been filled with a renewed sense of hope. She reluctantly admitted that Stewart's marriage might not be such a bad thing, and that rather than taking her son from her, Theodora was now providing her with the opportunity for a fresh start. She was beginning to see her daughter-in-law in a new light and hoped it wasn't too late to try and forge some sort of relationship with her. She wasn't naive enough to believe that a true friendship would ever blossom between them, but perhaps in the budding of this new life, they could build a bridge upon which to share their love with this child. Caroline wanted desperately to try.

The doctor came out.

"She's asking for Nicole," he said.

Nicole jumped up.

"What about me? I'm her husband." Stewart said, annoyed.

"She wants to see Nicole."

Nicole opened the door to Theodora's room, and was relieved to see her looking alert.

"You gave everyone quite a scare. When did you become Mario Andretti?"

"Hi," Theodora answered weakly.

"The doctor says you're going to be just fine. Thank God. You'd better start wearing your seat belt," Nicole said, trying to appear stern, but unable to hold back the note of relief.

"I almost lost the baby." Theodora's voice trembled.

Nicole walked over and took her sister's hand in her own. "But you didn't. Everything's going to be okay."

"The accident was all my fault. I was so angry I couldn't think straight."

"Why? What happened?"

Theodora told Nicole what had transpired that morning.

"That bastard. I could kill him!" she exploded.

"Calm down, they'll hear you. I don't want everyone to know," Theodora pleaded.

"I'm sorry. What can I do?"

"Don't say anything to anyone until I can sort it out. I don't want to see him right now."

"Okay, we'll call the nurse and ask her to tell everyone you're too tired for any more visitors."

"It would never have happened if I hadn't run that stop sign. The horrible thing is, I was so mad at him for what he's done, that I was wishing I wasn't pregnant, and now all I care about is that the baby lives." She started to cry.

"Oh Theo. What you wished for in light of the circumstances is perfectly normal. Anyone would have thought the same thing. That doesn't mean you wanted to lose the baby. It only means you were feeling hurt and betrayed. The pregnancy made you feel vulnerable, and no one wants to be vulnerable with someone they can't trust."

Theodora nodded her head. "I really am tired."

Nicole gave her a peck on the cheek and left the room.

"How was she?" Stewart asked.

"She's been better," she answered, looking at him coldly.

He averted his eyes. "Thanks. See you tomorrow," he said as he walked toward his parents.

Sophia slipped past the family. When she went into the room, Theodora was lying back with her eyes closed. Assuming she was sleeping, she turned to leave.

"Yiayia, wait," Theodora said softly.

Sophia knew Nicole had left unsaid much of what really happened, but she was nevertheless shocked at the puffy, red-rimmed eyes confronting her. She hurried to the side of the bed and closed her hand over Theodora's.

"What is it, my Theodora." She pronounced the name in Greek.

"You are safe. You did not lose the baby. What is so terrible to make you cry like this?" She caressed Theodora's brow.

"Oh, Yiayia, everything's such a mess. How could I have been so stupid?"

Sophia waited for her to go on and when she finished the telling, her grandmother rose from the edge of the bed, walked to the window and looked out over a large cluster of pine trees. She stood straight, back rigid in her habitual stance of perfect posture. What could she possibly say to this child who had learned too much too soon? It was unimaginable to her that a husband could so betray his wife. She never, in the sixty years she and Andreas were married, considered that he might be unfaithful to her. It was inconceivable. His fidelity was motivated as much by his own honor as by his love for her. His faultless integrity would never allow it. Stewart had seen a very different picture, however, in the home of his alienated parents and Sophia sensed he had never received the kind of nurturing that would foster his own strong principles. Sympathetic as she was, however, Sophia was not prepared to watch Theodora be the sacrificial lamb while Stewart learned. She turned from the window.

"Dear one, I will tell you what I think. You have learned very quickly that marriage is hard work. Give and take, compromise, usually more on the woman's side than the man's. Unfair, but that is the way it is, no matter what the new books and so-called emancipated women say. Each person must give not fifty percent but one hundred percent, that way no one is counting, no one can say 'I am giving more than you.' But Theodora, there are times when compromise is impossible and you will know those times because your heart will be sick and your soul will be empty. Look inside, my girl, and let your spirit speak to you. One of the truest signs of growing up is to trust what your spirit is telling you. Listen and you will do what is right."

Chapter 38

*N*icole looked up from the report she had been poring over for the last hour and rubbed her tired eyes. After Michael had taken her home from the hospital last night, she tossed and turned until almost three in the morning. Finally, after another fitful two hours of wakefulness, she got into the shower at five and headed to the office. There were questions she wanted answered, and there would be no interruptions at this hour of the morning.

The first things she gathered were the homeowner files from Manor Hills, the condominium development on which Stewart was project manager. The job had been completed well ahead of schedule, which was an enormous cost savings to Parsenis, however, resident complaints had poured in from the day of the first move-in. As she meticulously read each file, she began to see a common thread running through the grievances. In every case, the mandatory walk-through with the new owner generated an unusually long punch list of items needing attention. They were not the customary, incidental problems associated with new construction. Many of the needed repairs were major undertakings, and from the follow-up letters in each file, most had not been taken care of prior to move-in. What puzzled her was how the turnover of units from construction to sales and management took place with so many problems unresolved. Never had they had such a large percentage of unhappy and dissatisfied buyers. What was even more alarming was that the homeowners were now talking to each other about their frustrations, and some had put their condominium fees into an escrow account. It was just a matter of time before they retained an attorney to represent their demands for a settlement of their difficulties.

She slowly closed the file on 38 Larkspur Way, the most recent move-in this month and already bulging with correspondence. She got up and walked to the window. Something was terribly wrong. She was overlooking something very obvious but couldn't put her finger on it. She needed more pieces of the puzzle. Going back to her desk she reached for the phone and dialed Accounting. No answer. It was just seven thirty. No one would be in that department before eight, and she impatiently tapped her pen on the desk as she sat waiting.

A steady clicking sound from the hallway grew louder until it stopped right outside the suite of marketing offices. Nicole recognized it as McKenzie's trademark spiked heels echoing along the empty corridor. Her pace was always breakneck, and Nicole marveled more than once at her ability to walk for hours of inspections in those incredibly high heels, while workers along with her, shod in construction boots, had a hard time keeping up. "What are you doing here so early?" McKenzie balanced a cup of Seven Eleven coffee and large portfolio in one hand and a briefcase and umbrella in the other.

"I couldn't sleep. Besides I wanted to go over some of these Manor Hills files while it was quiet. McKenzie, have you seen all of these complaints?"

She dropped her briefcase and laid the portfolio and umbrella down on the chair next to Nicole's desk.

"Not only have I seen them, I've spent the better portion of every day talking to these people trying to calm them down. I don't want to go over anyone's head, but I'm getting nowhere with Stewart and the Construction Department. I was thinking when I left on Friday that it might be time to talk to your father. This is getting out of hand, and with my leaving, your hands will be full enough without this mess added to it."

"I think there's more here than meets the eye. I'm going to do some digging," Nicole said.

"What are you implying?" McKenzie asked.

"Nothing yet. It just seems strange that all of a sudden we have so many dissatisfied buyers. We don't build garbage. There isn't any reason to have all these complaints. Maybe it's just inexperience on the part of the project manager, but then again, maybe something else is going on. In any case, I intend to find out what it is."

McKenzie had never been crazy about Stewart, but she also knew that Nicole's assessment of him could be colored.

"Don't jump to any rash conclusions. Make sure you have all your ducks in a row before you make any accusations," she advised her.

"Don't worry. I've learned not to shoot my mouth off until I can back it up. Well, it's ten after eight. Somebody should be downstairs by now," she said and picked up her phone.

"Let me know what you discover."

Nicole heard the phone being picked up at the other end and nodded her head as McKenzie walked away.

"Hello, Louise?"

"Yes, can I help you?"

"Louise, it's Nicole. Can you get me some information?"

"Sure, what do you need?"

"I'd like to see the job cost analysis to date on the Manor Hills project. And can you also get me copies of each sub-contractor file? I really only need the copies of the original contracts and any change orders for right now. If I need more than that, I'll let you know."

"When do you need it?" Louise asked, trying to calculate how long it would take to gather this for her and who she could free up to assemble the information.

"As soon as possible. I know it's a pain in the neck, and I really appreciate anything you can do," Nicole implored.

"I think we can get it all to you before lunch today. I'll call you in a little while."

"You're an angel. Thanks." Nicole hung up the phone and picked up 38 Larkspur again. Something between the lines had triggered a suspicion in her, and she scrupulously reviewed every word trying to discern what it was. She had gone over it three times before it finally hit her. The couple who had purchased the unit had been told settlement would not take place until September. They made their plans accordingly and were suddenly contacted in late May with the news that construction was in the finish stages and they should be ready to settle at the end of June. After hastily rearranging their original plans, they went to settlement almost three months ahead of schedule. The fact that everything had been pushed ahead for them, served to make the problems they were now encountering all the more vexing. Nicole leaned back in her chair. That was it. In nearly all of the cases, the original completion date had been accelerated by two to three months. How had Stewart managed to bring everything in so far ahead of schedule? Maybe the reports coming up to her later today would shed some light on the matter. She decided she would try to get some work done and then go see Theodora in the hospital. Maybe when she returned, Accounting would have the data she'd requested.

After her visit with her sister, Nicole stood at the elevator down the hall from Theodora's room and watched the numbers light up as they climbed to six, the floor she was on. The doors opened and two nurses stepped out followed by a nice-looking young doctor. He looked appreciatively at Nicole and nodded his head, smiling as he passed her. His attention made her think of Michael, and she realized that she missed him. It was a nice feeling.

She pulled into her marked space and walked into the lobby of the building. Louise Phelps stopped her.

"Nicole, I was just bringing these up to you. I think everything you asked for is there."

"I can't thank you enough," she said as she took the large bundle of papers. "I owe you one."

"No problem. Let me know if you need anything else," she said and headed toward the stairs.

Not knowing quite what she was looking for, Nicole pulled out the job cost sheets first. As she looked them over, she realized the information was worthless to her without being able to compare costs to previous projects already completed. She could see that none of the usual sub-contractors had been awarded the contracts on this job, but she had no way of knowing if they represented a cost savings. She picked up the phone and called Louise again.

"I hate to do this to you, but could I have the old cost sheets on Timber Ridge and Valley View?"

"Those are easy. They're finished and wrapped up. I'll send someone up with them right away." If she was curious about what Nicole was after, she didn't betray it.

"Great, thanks," Nicole said.

Moments later, there was a knock at her door and she had the additional information she sought. Now we're cooking, she thought.

After an hour of comparing, and a trashcan filled with scrap paper from mathematical calculations, Nicole hadn't found anything to raise alarm bells. The thing that mystified her was that Stewart hadn't saved any money by using these new sub-contractors. Their prices for materials and labor were no lower than those Parsenis had been charged on previous jobs with their regular and loyal subs. She thought that was the whole point of his changing horses. Putting the long computer print-outs to the side, she reached for the first contractor folder on the pile, Masterson Flooring, who had supplied and installed the tile and carpeting in all of the units. There didn't seem to be anything unusual with the bid or contract. She went through more files and could find nothing amiss. She sat back in her seat and thought. I need to go back further, she thought. For the last time, she hoped, she rang Louise. "I'm sure you're sick of the sound of my voice by now," Nicole began.

"Not at all. What can I do for you?" Louise was a gem, Nicole thought.

"Can you get me the spec book on Manor Hills and also all of the original bids submitted to us?"

"It's on its way."

"I promise this is the last time I'll bother you today." She held the button down on the phone and lifted it once more to hear a dial tone. She buzzed her assistant.

"Nancy, will you please call Jeppi Nut Company and have a candy basket delivered to Louise in Accounting? Just have the card say "Thanks for all your help, Nicole."

"Sure, Nicole."

When the last material she had called for was finally sitting on Nicole's desk, there wasn't an inch of empty space. She took the divisions one by one and compared each bid against the specifications called for in the thick book compiled by the architectural firm who designed the job. At first everything seemed in order. On closer examination, however, she began to see small differences. The carpeting being supplied by Masterson was the same carpet called for in the specs, and it was the same carpet other sub-contractors had bid, but the padding was a different story. It was of a much lower grade, and yet the price was the same as that of the higher grade padding bid by others. She frowned and pulled out the HVAC and Mechanical files. Once again, there were differences in what had been proposed and for what Stewart had actually contracted. The condensers were not the size originally specked out. The job called for ten ton, but seven and a half ton units were installed instead. The price had been lowered so that this portion of the job came in under cost. Now the complaints about insufficient cooling made sense to her. She knew before opening the folder that she would find the same type of switching for the painting contractors. But what was Stewart trying to accomplish, she wondered? In some cases he was paying top price for inferior goods. It didn't make any sense. She got up from her chair and stretched. Her neck was sore from leaning over her desk for such a long time. She tried to massage the ache away, and walked around the room. It was after five and she hadn't made a dent in the papers piled high in her in-box. She resigned herself to a long night and cleared her desk of the Manor Hills figures so she could get to work.

By eight she could almost see the bottom of the box. A growl from her stomach reminded her that the only thing she had eaten today was the half piece of toast at the hospital this morning. She was deciding whether to finish and grab a bite on the way home, or call and order a sandwich delivered, when the phone rang.

"Hello."

"I thought I might find you there. I tried you at home." Michael's voice came over the line.

She was delighted to hear from him.

"Hi, Michael. I was just finishing up, as a matter of fact. I was debating whether to order some food or just get out of here."

"You haven't eaten yet? I just got out of a meeting in downtown Baltimore. I'm only twenty minutes away. Could you wait that long and have dinner with me?" he asked.

"I'd love to. Shall we meet somewhere?"

"Good idea. What do you suggest?"

"Have you ever eaten at Ikaros in Highlandtown? They have the best Greek food in town. It shouldn't take you more than fifteen minutes."

"I'm on my way."

Nicole arrived first and got a table for two. She saw Michael walk in and waved to him as he looked around the room for her. He smiled when he saw her and quickly walked over to where she was sitting, and leaning down, kissed her.

"I'm glad you were free," he said, looking around. "This is nice. Looks like we're in Athens."

"The food's wonderful too. I ordered some *saganaki* and *dolmathes*. Is that okay?" She said.

"I've had the stuffed grape leaves, but what's the other thing I can't pronounce?"

"Well, take a look." She pointed as their waitress lit the block of

Kasari cheese and the blue flame rose high. "This is the best cheese you'll ever eat."

He took a bite. "Mmm. You're right." He put his fork down. "How's Theodora. Have you talked to her today?"

"I saw her this morning. She seemed better. I think she's going to be released tomorrow morning."

"That's good news, but you don't seem very excited."

"Of course I'm thrilled she's okay. She could've been killed running a stop sign. What I'm worried about is her emotional state. She's pretty fragile right now."

"She'll be okay, Nicole. She's stronger than you give her credit for."

"It's more than that, but it's not something I can talk about right now. I promised Theodora."

He respected her reluctance to discuss the matter and didn't press the issue.

"So, how come you're working so late? Are things that busy at the office?"

She wanted to talk to someone about everything she'd found, to try and get some intelligent feedback from someone in whom she had confidence. She looked at Michael and hesitated only a moment. She could trust him and believed his clear, logical thinking might help her sort things out. She recounted in detail all she had discovered, the shoddy workmanship, the complaints of homeowners, the disparity between bids. When she finished, it still didn't make any more sense to her than it had before.

"What do you think?" She asked him.

"Have you talked to anyone else about this?"

"No, not yet. Do you think I should go to my father with it? I really don't feel like I have the whole picture yet."

"I was thinking more in terms of talking to Stewart. Maybe he has some sort of explanation," Michael offered.

"I can't imagine what that could be, although I guess talking to him first would be the fair thing to do."

"At least you'll have the advantage of catching him off guard. I'm sure the last thing he's expecting is that you would have scrutinized everything his department has done on the job. You'll be able to get a good read from his initial reaction to your questions."

"Spoken like a true attorney," she laughed. "I don't think I'd want to be cross examined by you."

"Any cross examination of you would be of the most exquisite variety, not to be found in the average courtroom."

"I think I might enjoy that after all, counselor."

Chapter 39

"Good morning Ingrid," Nicole greeted the receptionist. "Will you do me a favor and buzz me when Stewart comes in?"

"He called in already, Nicole. He won't be in until nine. I don't think he'll be here long. He's supposed to pick your sister up from the hospital around noon."

"Oh, that's right. I'll just look in a little after nine and see if he's here. Thanks."

Damn, she thought as she walked up the stairs. She had rehearsed over and over how to approach him this morning. She wanted to get it over with, and now she had at least an hour to wait before he arrived. Well, that would give her time to get all of the files back to Accounting. She didn't want him to know she had been combing through them. She settled in at her desk and began to return the phone calls she had never gotten to yesterday. At nine she walked upstairs to the Construction Division where Stewart's secretary was sitting at her desk working on a long requisition form. She looked up as Nicole came in.

"Can I help you with something, Nicole?"

"I was wondering if Stewart is in yet."

"No, not yet, but I'm expecting him any time. Do you need to see him?"

"Yes, I do. Could you..."

"Here he is now," the girl interrupted, looking past Nicole.

Nicole spun around, taken off guard.

"You're looking for me?"

"I'd like to talk to you if you have a few minutes," she answered.

"Sure," he said off-handedly. "Jo, can you see that these go out in this morning's mail." He handed his secretary a stack of envelopes.

"I'll take care of it. Oh, by the way, Mr. Parsenis called and asked if you would stop by his office this morning. He wanted to know what time his daughter is being released from the hospital," she said to him.

"Thanks. Come in, Nicole." He sat at his desk and indicated a chair in front of it for her. "I don't have much time. Will this take very long?"

"I don't think so. I'm concerned about the complaints we're getting from Manor Hills. I wanted to come to you before I talked to anyone else."

"Who else would you talk to? Manor Hills is my job," he said impatiently. "What complaints are you talking about?"

"They're major. Cooling problems with the air conditioning units, large cracks in the ceilings, sloppy paint jobs. We're getting more letters and telephone calls than we've ever had. There're a lot of unresolved maintenance issues. And from what they're writing to us, nothing is being addressed."

"That's ridiculous. I've walked every single unit prior to settlement. I would've seen problems like that. And when there is a problem, we're in there within twenty-four hours to take care of it. New home buyers are a bunch of whining cry-babies. You should know that. You can't take half of what they say seriously."

"Stewart, these are not the complaints of cry-babies. They are very real problems. We've even got someone threatening to sue us."

"I can't believe they've got you running scared. That's the oldest line in the book. No one's going to sue us."

"How can you be so sure? And even if there are no lawsuits, we don't need this kind of publicity. The Parsenis reputation for quality building has always been a core value."

"Listen, I've brought this job in way ahead of schedule without sacrificing quality. I don't need you to tell me how to do my job. Go back to your Marketing Department and figure out how to sell these things as fast as we build them. I have to go see your father." He marched out of the room and left her standing there.

That settled it. She was going to get that son of a bitch if it was the last thing she did.

Chapter 40

Stewart pulled into the visitor parking lot at GBMC and slipped the receipt from the gate into his sun visor. Theodora had left a message on both their home phone and at his office, asking him not to come to the hospital until this morning when she would be released. He was uneasy, not knowing what to expect. They hadn't spoken since their fight over Heather, and he had no idea what she planned to do. He hated being at her mercy like this. He was used to calling the shots, and it infuriated him when he made this kind of misstep and allowed someone else to be in control. He walked toward her room, hoping none of the family was around. To his relief, he found only Theodora when he entered. She was dressed and waiting for him.

"Hello Stewart." He could feel her wariness.

"Theo, I've been so worried about you." He looked pitiful.

She faltered a moment, but thinking back to that awful scene helped her to stand her ground. She couldn't let him just come waltzing back without some assurances that things would be different.

"I'm very tired. Can we check out of here and go home? We have a lot to talk about, and I'd prefer to do it in the privacy of our home."

"Sure, whatever you say, honey. I've taken care of everything. We're out of here."

They drove home in silence. Theodora stared out her window

and as they pulled into the driveway, she had the feeling that she'd been away for a very long time and was suddenly extremely weary.

"I think I need to rest for a little while," she said as they got out of the car.

"You go upstairs, honey. I'll fix us a nice dinner, and we can spend a quiet evening relaxing."

She began to feel encouraged. Maybe he was ready to make amends, to start again on the right footing. She wanted to bring this child into a marriage that was solid and committed. If he was willing to do all he could to make things work, she was ready to give it one hundred percent, as much for her sake as the baby's.

"That's sweet of you," she said to him. "If I'm not up in a few hours, wake me," she said, and went upstairs.

Stewart looked in the freezer and cabinets for something easy to fix, and becoming more frustrated at his lack of cooking expertise, decided to order Chinese carryout. There was a limit to how far he was willing to go. Having disposed of the dinner problem he settled down with a beer and the Wall Street Journal. In the midst of all this strife, he hadn't checked his stocks since Friday afternoon, and was anxious to see what was happening. He'd been quietly investing for the last six months and had acquired quite an impressive portfolio. He made sure all the certificates were in his name alone and tucked safely away in a safety deposit box, the existence of which no one had any knowledge. After scanning a few news items he put the paper down. He should get the table set for dinner, he thought, rising from the sofa. He took the plates into the dining room and tried to make it look cheery by bringing in the pink hibiscus from the kitchen windowsill and placing it in the center of the glass table. At five o'clock the doorbell rang and a young boy stood outside holding large brown bags filled with spicy smelling dishes. Stewart paid him and proceeded to transfer the food onto serving dishes. Looking at the scene he had set in the dining room, he was satisfied at the atmosphere created and went upstairs to awaken his wife.

"Theodora." He looked down at her sleeping face. She was beautiful, he thought. It had been a long time since he'd really looked at her. Gently shaking her shoulder, he said. "Time to get up. Dinner's ready." She opened her eyes.

"Okay. Let me splash some water on my face, and I'll be right down."

He left the room and went downstairs. As an afterthought, he grabbed two candlestick holders and candles from the china closet and put them on either side of the plant. When Theodora walked into the dining room, Stewart was lighting the candles.

"This looks beautiful." She looked at him approvingly.

"Only the best for you. Won't you sit down?" he said, pulling out her chair.

"You're not going to tell me you cooked this wonderful meal, are you?"

"I cannot tell a lie. It's carry out. I don't get any of the credit."

"Oh, but you do. Your thinking was inspired and the table is positively elegant."

"Here, let me serve you some of this," he picked up the platter with Egg Foo Young.

They ate leisurely, with measured small talk, feeling each other out. Theodora began to relax and by the time the meal was finished she felt up to some serious talking.

"Stewart," she began. "We need to talk about what's happened between us and figure out where we're going."

"That's all I've thought about since your accident. I know I've hurt you. I would do anything to undo everything I've done. This thing with Heather meant nothing to me. You've got to believe me," he begged.

"Why did it happen, Stewart? Were you that unhappy with me?"

"I love you. You had nothing to do with it. She's a man-chasing little tease, and I was stupid to get involved. She's hounded me since the day she came to work at Parsenis. You won't believe this Theodora, but one day she walked into my office and standing right in front of my desk, told me she had something very important to show me. She had a dress on that buttoned down the front. She unbuttoned it and pulled it wide open. She was completely naked underneath."

Theodora's stomach turned at the picture of Stewart staring at another woman with mounting excitement. "What did you do?" she asked coldly.

"I told her to get out, of course. But you can't imagine the tricks she used. I'm not saying I'm guilt free in all of this, but I am a normal man."

"What does that mean, Stewart? That if someone tempts you in the future you won't be able to resist? Am I supposed to keep you in a cage somewhere and only let you out on a leash?"

"I deserved that. But it doesn't make it any easier to take. No, I'm not telling you I can't be faithful. I've learned my lesson. My God, when I got the call about your accident and thought I might lose you and the baby, it brought me to my senses. Theodora, I give you my solemn promise, this will never happen again. You have my word."

"I really want to believe you Stewart. I want more than anything to make our marriage work, to be a family."

"I want the same thing. Can't we start over? Please give me another chance. I don't know what I would do if I lost you."

"Things would have to change, Stewart. No more of this working around the clock. You have to make time for us or we'll never make it."

"I will. I know I've neglected you. All of that's going to change. We'll take some weekends away together before the baby comes. Meet for a romantic dinner after work. I don't want to lose you. I want a family with you Theodora. I've changed. You'll see, if you'll just forgive me and give me another chance."

These were the words she longed to hear. She wanted to put away her reservations. Was it fair to deprive this child of its father because of her pride and unforgiveness? If she intended to work on this marriage, she would do it all the way, without any hidden agendas or resentments. She would forgive him from the core of her heart and put the past behind her.

"I do forgive you," she reached out to hold his hand. "I'm ready to go forward and not look back."

"Thank you. I promise you won't be sorry." He leaned over and kissed her lips. He had forgotten how warm and full her mouth was and the pleasure it gave him. His hand moved down to open the first button of her blouse. She wore nothing underneath, and he slowly caressed her breast, kissing her neck and shoulders. He could hear her breathing become shallow and more rapid. He pulled back from her and looked into her eyes.

"I want to make love to you more than I ever have."

She rose from her chair, and holding his hand, led him to the sofa. She stood over him, undressing slowly while he watched her every move. Finally, unable to resist any longer, he pulled her down next to him, holding her close. They stayed together that way for a long time and Theodora thought she had never felt closer to him. The desire to take him back exploded inside of her, and with it Theodora relinquished her last uncertainty.

Chapter 41

*N*icole gathered her papers and walked to her father's office. "Hi Dad, ready for me?"

"Sure, come in."

Nicole took a seat in one of the leather chairs.

"What's so important you had to schedule an emergency meeting?" he asked.

"You're not going to like what I have to tell you, so I want you to make me a promise before I begin." She paused. "Promise me you'll hear me out to the end before you say anything."

"Come on Nicole, what's this all about?"

"Promise first."

He sighed. "All right, I promise."

She took a deep breath. "It's about Manor Hills. We've been getting major complaints about the finished sections, the ones completed in April and May. The air conditioners are conking out, the carpets are sub-standard and the paint jobs are shoddy. So far, forty percent of the new residents have outstanding complaints and they aren't being addressed. I've tried discussing this with Stewart, but he refuses to explain anything and he's told me it's none of my business."

"I inspected a few of the first finished units with Stewart, and they looked great," Nick said surprised.

"With Stewart? I'm sure he wouldn't take you through anything that looked less than perfect. All I know is that if something isn't done soon, Manor Hills is going to become a significant public relations problem. Dad, I've never seen dissatisfaction of this proportion. McKenzie's been tearing her hair out. We've sold fifty of these units. Once word gets out about the quality, we'll be lucky if we can give them away. The crazy thing is, he's used all different sub-contractors and none of them was cheaper than our usual subs. In fact, in some cases, he paid top dollar for inferior goods. It doesn't make any sense."

Nick was frowning. He was still resistant to the idea that Stewart was anything but a dedicated company man. "You think perhaps your feelings toward Stewart are coloring your perceptions a bit?"

"Not this time. Look at this." She handed him a photocopy of a letter.

It was from a lawyer and his wife, addressed to Nick. The letter contended that they had complained about the condition of their condominium prior to settlement. The agent had written a punch list, detailing all the outstanding repairs and signed and dated it. They were assured all repairs would be made within thirty days. Settlement had occurred in May and as of July, not one item had been repaired. They had called the management office daily to no avail. The letter served to notify Parsenis they were moving into a hotel, and all charges for food and lodging would be billed to the company. Their management fee was being held in escrow until repairs were completed, and if their letter did not result in resolution of the problem, they would be suing for damages. Attached to the letter was a copy of the punch list, outlining repairs ranging from paint in the outlets to cracks and chips in the walls and ceilings.

Nick massaged his temples as the meaning of the words sunk in. Pain clouded his face. "This was written over three weeks ago. When did you get it?"

"I didn't. I found it hidden under a bunch of papers in Stewart's in-box. I copied it last night and put it back. I was going to wait for McKenzie to come back from vacation so that we could see you together, but once I saw this letter I knew it couldn't wait," she confessed.

Nick looked at his daughter with a raised eyebrow. "So Stewart doesn't know you've seen it?"

"No one does. Only you."

"Good. Here's what I want you to do. Leave the letter with me. Don't say anything to anyone. I'm going to do a little poking around. I think Stewart's gotten in over his head and is too proud to ask for help. Maybe I was hasty in letting him shoulder this project alone. He was so eager to bring this in early that he lost sight of other factors."

Nicole was floored. Even after everything she had shown him, her father still had blinders on.

"What about the fact that he buried this letter! These people are threatening a lawsuit. When was he going to tell you?" she cried out, her face blood red.

"Nicole, get a hold of yourself. I'm not letting Stewart off the hook. I just don't want to go off half-cocked. Before I go storming into his office, accusing him of God knows what, I intend to find out what really happened. In the meantime, to a point, I must give him the benefit of the doubt. Aren't you the one who's so big on 'innocent until proven guilty'?"

She looked down at the floor.

"Trust me. Go back and take care of your job, which is getting these things sold. And work on that temper," he said, not without affection.

She rose and left the room.

As much as he hated to admit it, Nick's confidence in Stewart had been slowly eroding. He'd gotten good feedback about Stewart in his first few years with the company. Back then, when he was on his way up, he had a reputation for giving his all. Since Nick had promoted him, he'd started to notice a more arrogant manner in his son-in-law. Other people in the company seemed uncomfortable around Stewart, and although they wouldn't criticize him to Nick, he noticed that no one sang his praises any longer. It bothered him that Stewart had chosen to use all new subs on Manor Hills, but he chalked it up to Stewart's wanting to be his own man. Nick had always been a leader and felt he shouldn't squelch that same spirit in his protege. The conflict between Stewart and Nicole distressed him, but he felt powerless to change it. Nick had great respect for Nicole's talent and brains, but deep inside, he believed she would leave the business when she married and had children. Now things had gotten way out of control, and he needed to take whatever steps were necessary to assess and contain the damage.

Chapter 42

*N*ick slid behind the wheel of his Cadillac and drove to Manor Hills. He'd brought the complaint letter with him and decided to take a look at this particular condominium on his own. He parked outside the management office and walked up to the woman behind the counter.

"Hello Mr. Parsenis, how are you today?" she asked, flustered by his unexpected visit.

"Hi Sarah. Fine thanks. I'd like the key to Unit 73 please."

She opened the gray lock box on the wall and located it.

"Here you are sir."

"I'll bring it back in about a half hour."

He passed several different work trucks and noted that he didn't recognize any of them. He pulled up to the building and looked around. The exterior looked fine and the landscaping was well groomed. He unlocked the front door and walked into the common hallway to the middle unit on the right. He pulled out the punch list and looked at the first item. Windows painted shut. He walked over to the large windows in the living room and tried to open them. Painted shut all right. He made a note in the margin. He looked at the next item. Paint in the outlets. Sure enough, most of the outlets were covered in paint so thick it would be hard to get a toothpick in. What kind of morons had Stewart hired? The next item was listed as unsightly cracks in the ceiling. He looked up and didn't see anything unusual. He walked into the kitchen, then the bedrooms and looked for the cracks. The last room he checked was the large dining room. Ah, here we are. He looked up to see several long, deep ridges in the ceiling. He went back to the living room, took the poker from the fireplace, and bringing in a chair from the kitchen, stood on it and pushed up through the ceiling. A cloud of white drywall rained down on him. Seconds later, a large chunk of the cement ceiling was dislodged and knocked Nick from the chair. He fell to the ground and tried to get up just as another piece fell and hit him hard on the back of the head, knocking him unconscious. He was out cold before the largest piece came down and landed in the middle of his back.

Chapter 43

*T*heodora got the call at five o'clock. She ran through the house in a frenzy trying to find her car keys and then remembered Stewart had her car. She grabbed his spare set of keys and ran to the garage. Her father was in critical condition at Sinai Hospital.

Please God, don't let anything happen to him, she prayed over and over, afraid if she stopped, he would die. She was still ten minutes from the hospital when the cell phone sitting on the passenger seat rang. Theodora picked it up.

"Stew? Stew Honey, it's your pussycat. You were supposed to be here over an hour ago."

"Who is this?" Theodora yelled.

The woman hung up.

In a fury, Theodora swore at the faceless voice and hurled the phone out the window. "Stewart, you son of a bitch!" she screamed aloud, "I wish it was you in that emergency room."

She parked the car and with shaking fingers stuffed the keys into her handbag and rushed into the hospital. When she got to the bank of elevators in the lobby she waited, watching the light move to each floor and then stop. She stood there tapping her foot impatiently on the tired linoleum when finally the damn thing opened and she hurried inside. The waiting room on the sixth floor must have had ten empty chairs, but Eleni and Nicole were pacing the floor. Theodora ran to her mother.

"Is he okay?" Theodora asked.

Eleni breathed deeply. "All I know is he's alive, thank God. A ceiling caved in. Some cement fell on him. The doctors are examining him now."

Paul came over from the nurses' station.

"They couldn't tell me anything," he said anxiously. Theodora turned to her sister. "How did he get here?"

"It's so awful. He was inspecting a condo and pieces of the ceiling fell on top of him. The woman upstairs was home and called 911."

"I don't understand. How could the ceiling just cave in? Was the building still under construction?"

"No. It was a finished unit. The police are investigating." Nicole stopped, reluctant to bring up Stewart's name.

Theodora sat down to wait with them. Each time the double doors leading into the hallway swung open they looked up expectantly, hoping for news. One hour passed, then another.

"This is ridiculous. What's going on?" Nicole strode angrily to the nurse's station.

"We still haven't heard anything on my father's condition," she told the nurse accusingly.

"Just a moment please." The nurse picked up her phone and spoke into it quietly.

"The doctor's on his way out."

"Thank you."

Moments later a man with kind eyes in hospital blues walked through the door.

"Mrs. Parsenis?" he asked, looking at Eleni. "I'm Doctor Silvers."

"How's my husband?" The words came out in a breathless rush.

Paul put his arm around his mother as the rest of the family gathered around to listen.

"Come and sit down," the doctor said, gently guiding her to one of the leather chairs. This was always one of the most difficult parts of his job. He looked into her worried eyes and knew his words would not ease her fears. Nick had been gravely injured, with the very real possibility that he wouldn't pull through. He cleared his throat.

"Your husband has suffered a very serious head injury, Mrs. Parsenis. He is comatose and the injury has caused severe cerebral contusion, bruising if you will. He's developed a blood clot on the brain which must be removed. The imminent danger is swelling of the brain which is life threatening. It's fortunate that the injury is to the right frontal lobe. With an injury to this part of the brain there could be long-term neurological deficit, but it is possible that he may recover fully. We're preparing him now for surgery to remove the clot."

Eleni couldn't believe what she was hearing. How could he have been laughing and joking with her this morning and now lie between life and death? She wrapped her fingers tightly around the arms of the chair and tried to push down the noxious taste of fear rising in her throat. She swallowed in what seemed a gargantuan effort and looked at Dr. Silvers, fearing to ask the question.

"Is he going to live?"

"His condition is critical, Mrs. Parsenis." He paused a moment and added quietly, "There is a chance he will not survive the operation."

"Oh God." The words were an anguished cry that cut through the room and filled him with pity.

He rose, anxious to leave the heavy pall surrounding them and get back to his patient. "The surgery will take two to three hours and then he'll be moved to ICU. Someone will come and get you as soon as you can see him."

Eleni watched his back as he walked away and disappeared through the swinging doors that led to an unseen world filled with chilling machines and monitors. She didn't want him to leave. Nick was still alive, waiting for surgery. Surely he couldn't die before the doctor got back to him. As long as he stood there talking about Nick, time could stay suspended and she didn't have to worry.

Her sister Eve had come to help her keep watch. "Come on Eleni, let's go up to the cafeteria. You look like you could use some coffee," Eve said.

"No, I don't want to leave in case they need to talk to me." She was afraid Nick would slip away while she was gone, and she would never see him again.

"How about if I bring you some then?"

"Fine," Eleni answered distractedly. She sat down and tried to clear her head. She was in shock, and couldn't believe that her husband lay beyond those doors, fighting for his life. She wished she could be with him, fighting right along side of him. Instead, she sat and waited, powerless to do anything. She quieted herself, closed her eyes, said a silent prayer, and begged God to make him well. She wouldn't allow herself to think of losing him. Life was so ironic. Just this morning she had asked what he wanted for his birthday. He would be fifty-nine in two weeks. He'd laughed and told her that what he wanted was no more birthdays, to stop aging. Eleni prayed with all of her heart that he would live to see another one.

The hours dragged as they waited for the doctor to return. The harsh light of the waiting room was giving Nicole a headache. She sat uncomfortably in the rigid chair and inclined her head against the wall, closing her eyes against the intrusive glare. She pictured her father on the operating table, draped with white sheets, the drill boring a hole into his skull. She wondered if he was aware at some level. Was he in pain? Was he afraid? If only she hadn't taken that damned letter to him he wouldn't be here right now. She should have checked the unit out herself, with a qualified construction crew. She was filled with regret when she remembered how she'd pleaded with him to investigate the project. How would she ever forgive herself if he died? She couldn't imagine existing in a world that didn't include her father. Her love for him defied depth or breadth or boundary. She kept telling herself he would be fine, he had to be, and forced herself to believe that any minute the doctor would push through those doors and bring good news.

Eleni checked the clock on the wall every few minutes. It had been two and a half hours, and Nick was still in surgery. She prayed continually, unconsciously holding her breath each time the doors swung open, afraid of bad news. She must have had ten cups of coffee already. It was impossible to sit still and she absently twisted her watch around her wrist, crossing and uncrossing her legs. She couldn't rid herself of the image of Nick lying on a table with his head cut open. Another hour passed and when there was still no word, she jumped up from her seat and began once more to pace.

"What's going on? I can't stand it anymore!" she cried to no one in particular.

Andreas came to her side.

"It is almost over *agapi*, just a little longer." He looked at his wife and they exchanged sympathetic looks. Eleni rested her head on Andrea's shoulder and he hugged her to him. His sweet Eleni. He still remembered the day she was born. Everyone wished them a son. It didn't matter to Andreas; he was concerned only for the well being of Sophia and their first child. When he held her and felt the strength of her tiny fingers grasping his, he swore that he would always protect her. How easy for the young to believe in their omnipotence he thought. His best intentions to keep her safe had failed when she came down with pneumonia and they had almost lost her. Over the years, they had endured many storms that he was powerless to prevent. At such times he learned the necessity of surrendering to God and begging Him to intervene. He looked at his wife and nodded his head. Sophia took his place next to their daughter and squeezed his hand as he rose. He reached the nurses' station.

"Could you please tell me where the chapel is," he asked.

Eleni looked up to see Dr. Silvers walking toward her and tried to read his face. The tension was unbearable. The few seconds it took for him to reach her seemed suspended in time.

His expression was serious. .

"He pulled through." He saw the tension leave her body. "We

removed the clot and the damaged tissue on the tip of the frontal lobe. We'll monitor the inter-cranial pressure now, but we won't know more until he regains consciousness."

She cried with relief and hugged him.

"Oh thank God. When can I see him?"

"In a few hours, when he's out of recovery. You can even stay at the hospital tonight if you'd like," he offered.

She looked at him gratefully. "Yes, I would like that very, very much."

A frown creased the doctor's forehead. "Mrs. Parsenis, we've gotten through the first hurdle, but his condition is still critical."

Eleni fought the feeling of deflation his words provoked. "My husband's a real fighter. He'll recover."

Dr. Silvers knew it would take every bit of fight Nick had in him, and he smiled at her with compassion.

"The nurse will let you know when you can see him." He turned to the rest of the family. "I know you're all anxious to see him, but it would be best if only Mrs. Parsenis went in tonight." He walked back through the doors.

"We'll stay with you until you can see him Mom," Paul said.

Later that evening, Eleni was escorted to the intensive care unit. She stopped just outside the door and took a deep breath, pushed the door open and walked to the bed. Nick's translucent pallor was alarming and the tubes in his nose and down his throat emphasized the severity of his condition. His head was covered in white bandages, his arms lay limply by his sides and the steady hiss and click of the respirator gave the cold cubicle an eerie, other worldly feel. He looked painfully vulnerable. She took a seat in the chair next to his bed and put her hand on top of his.

"I'm here darling. Everything is going to be fine. You just keep on fighting, you hear me? I love you. We all love you." She brushed the tears from her cheeks with her free hand. When she looked at her husband's face, she imagined she saw just the slightest hint of a smile.

Chapter 44

*B*y the time Theodora left the hospital she still hadn't heard from Stewart. She thought about the phone call. She'd known who it was the moment the woman uttered her first word. Heather's brash New York accent was unmistakable, and her words left no margin for misinterpretation. Stewart had never ended the affair as he'd promised. The voice on Stewart's car phone had been pushed from her consciousness, but it was a voice she would never forget. In those few short seconds, the words Heather had spoken irrevocably changed Theodora's world. She realized the only certainty was change, whether you were ready or not. Life was a continual passing from one plane to another, and the best one could hope for was the wisdom to fully savor the good times. One second could have made the difference in her father's accident and he wouldn't be lying comatose with tubes and needles all over his body.

She slowed the car as she approached Heather's apartment complex. She knew in her bones that Stewart would be here, but she needed to see his car sitting in the parking lot. Despite her certainty, there was a small part of her that hoped she was wrong. When she turned onto Heather's court, her heart was beating so fast she was having trouble breathing. She slowed to a crawl and scanned the jammed lot.

When she spotted the black BMW with the familiar SGE tags her heart raced and became a throbbing roar in her ears. She looked up at the building and tried to guess which apartment might be Heather's. It looked so ordinary. Everything she had held dear was crashing down around her, and it all looked so ordinary. Her husband was somewhere in that building with another woman, the man she had persuaded herself to trust once more, the father of her unborn child. He couldn't even be there for her while her father fought for his life. She felt something wet on her cheek and was surprised to find that she was crying. The tears wouldn't stop and soon there were wrenching sobs coming from somewhere deep within her.

She looked at the building through her tears until every detail was indelibly stamped on her mind. She let herself feel all the pain she had bottled up, and her grief enveloped her. She grieved for the death of her marriage. She became very still and a wave of infinite sadness filled her. She closed her eyes and thought back to her wedding day. She had felt like a fairy princess, had followed all the rules, done everything she was supposed to. She had stood at the altar feeling that she had come to the part that was promised to her all her life, the happily ever after. But her prince had vanished, and she knew now there had never been one. And then a curious calmness descended upon her and with it, a strong determination. Her destiny had never been in the hands of anyone other than herself and her God. She would take back her life. She eased the car into drive and pulled out of the parking lot and the warm air rushed against her face through the open window. By the time she stood at the threshold of Nicole's front door and rang the bell, she knew what she had to do.

"What's wrong? Has something happened to Dad?" Nicole asked alarmed.

"No. This is about Stewart. It's a long story, Nicole. Are you up to hearing it?"

Nicole looked at her sister's tear stained face and red eyes. "Of course. Come in and sit down."

Theodora followed her into the living room and Michael got up from his chair. "I'll leave so you two can talk."

"No Michael, stay," Theodora said. "I consider you part of the family. I want you to be here."

He looked at Nicole and she nodded her assent.

"Do you mind if we sit in the kitchen?" Theodora said to her sister.

They sat down at the oval table, and Nicole poured a third cup of coffee. Theodora sat with one leg under her and leaned forward with both elbows on the table. "I don't quite know where to start."

"Take your time," Nicole said softly. "We have all night."

Theodora turned to Michael and for his benefit repeated what Nicole already knew.

"I'm confused," Nicole said. "What's happened since the accident? I thought things were getting better."

"When I came home he was all sweetness and sugar. Begged me to forgive him and told me he couldn't live without me, that Heather was the biggest mistake of his life. He swore nothing like this would ever happen again. I guess I wanted to believe him. I told him we'd work it out, put all the bad stuff behind us and start fresh."

"And now you've discovered that the affair never stopped." Michael had not asked a question.

She looked at him. "Yes. He's with her now."

She ran her hand through her hair and pushed it away from her forehead. Nicole got up and put her arms around Theodora.

"I'm so sorry. I wish I could do something." As layer after layer was peeled from Stewart's facade, she wondered if there was any goodness at all to be found in him.

"What are you going to do?" Nicole asked.

"It's over. I want him to leave. The problem is I know how valuable he is at Parsenis, and I don't want to do something to put the company in a bind, especially with what's happened to Dad now." She looked at Nicole. "Any suggestions?"

"I think it's time you let your sister in on what's going on." Michael touched Nicole's hand.

Theodora, frowning, looked from one to the other. "What is it?"

"Something's very wrong with the project Stewart's been running."

Nicole recounted for her, one by one, all of the puzzles she'd found in searching the files.

"I went to Dad about Stewart quite a while ago and complained, but he wouldn't listen. The only one who agreed with me was Uncle Costa. In fact, he and Dad fought about Stewart. When he got the call from Athens that his sister was ill, I think he was almost relieved to be able to leave, even though he was worried about her. I've really missed him. A lot of what I looked at in those files doesn't add up for me, but he'll be able to put the pieces together. I'm going to talk to him the minute he gets back."

Theodora sat back, stunned, trying to digest it all. Why did it surprise her that Stewart would lie and cheat in business? Wasn't it the same thing he had done in their marriage? Suddenly, she remembered Nicole's words about Stewart's purchase of inferior goods, and a thought struck her.

"Do you think Stewart's responsible for Dad's accident?"

"I don't know. I've wondered the same thing. I know I've agonized about giving Dad the letter that caused him to go over there that day," Nicole said.

"My God. It isn't your fault any of this happened. You were the one trying to fix the problem," Michael said to her.

"He's right Nicole. Stop beating yourself up. It's a waste of energy."

"I know, I know. But it's still hard not to feel responsible."

Yawning, Theodora moved her leg out from under her and hugged her knees to her chest. "I'm exhausted."

"Are you going to talk to Stewart tonight?" Nicole asked.

"I doubt he'll be home."

"Why don't you stay here for a while?" Nicole suggested.

Theodora agreed. That would allow her to postpone the inevitable confrontation with Stewart. Right now, she had only enough energy to concentrate on her father's recovery.

"I'll let Stewart know I'm going to stay here for a few days."

Michael leaned over and kissed Theodora's cheek. "I'd better be off. Try to get some rest and remember we're with you."

"Thanks Michael. Goodnight."

Nicole walked him to the door. She leaned up to kiss him. "You're wonderful. Thanks for everything."

"Go to bed and get some sleep. I'll call you tomorrow." He walked to his car, and Nicole closed the door.

Chapter 45

*I*t had been two days and Nick was still in a coma.

"Mom, why don't you go home and get some rest? We can take shifts here," Nicole suggested.

Eleni shook her head. "I can't leave Dad alone. I need to stay."

Andreas looked at her kindly. "Eleni *mou*, Nick's going to need you to be strong when he comes out of this. Go home and come back in the morning. There's nothing you can do tonight."

"I'll come over and stay with you," Nicole offered.

"All right," Eleni agreed reluctantly.

Once they got home, Nicole made a pot of coffee and looked through the refrigerator for something to eat. She found a coffee cake in the freezer and put it in the microwave to defrost. She went upstairs and called to her mother.

"Mom, can I borrow one of your robes?"

"Sure honey, help yourself."

She grabbed a long cotton robe and quickly changed.

"How are you doing Mom?" She sat down at the kitchen table where Eleni had already placed two cups of black coffee.

"I feel like I'm walking around in a bad dream and the next minute I'll wake up and everything will be fine," Eleni said.

"I know. I feel so terrible," she began to cry.

"He's going to be all right sweetheart." Eleni consoled her daughter.

"Oh, Mom, that isn't it. I'm the one who told him about the problem on the project, even gave him the letter from the owners of the unit where he was hurt. If I hadn't done that, he'd be okay right now."

"Nicole Sophia, you stop thinking like that right now! It's not your fault. You had no way of knowing what would happen. And besides, your father would've been furious if you'd tried to keep that information from him."

"You're right, Mom, he's going to be fine." She heard the hollowness of her words and wished she believed them.

The phone rang and they both jumped. Nicole picked it up with trepidation.

"Oh, Michael. Hi," she said, relieved.

"I won't keep you, I just wanted to tell you my thoughts and prayers are with all of you."

"I appreciate it." She walked into the hallway with the phone, out of Eleni's earshot.

"Michael, I'm really scared. I couldn't stand it if something happened to him."

"Nothing's going to happen. You've got to keep the faith."

"I'm trying. Thanks for calling Michael."

"He's such a nice boy." Eleni remarked when Nicole hung up the phone. "How are things going with him?"

"I like being with him. I could see this lasting a while."

"What do you mean a while? What about forever?"

"I don't know Mom. I don't think I'm ready for that kind of commitment. Michael's great and everything, but I'm not head over heels in love with him. To tell you the truth, I don't know if I want to be head over heels."

"Now why would you say that? Don't you want to spend your life with someone?"

"I guess I just don't want to get hurt. It seems the more you love, the more pain you get."

"Honey, we're all hurting right now, but I can't believe for one minute that even if you never saw your father again, you would've chosen not to have him for the years you did."

"Of course not. I wouldn't trade having him for anything in the world!" Nicole cried passionately.

"Well darling, it's the same with all kinds of love. There's a risk, but it's worth it. Don't you think I'm scared to death that I'll lose the love of my life? All day long I've been thinking how much a part of me your father is. It's like the air I breathe. I can't imagine going on without him. You know in the back of your mind life is temporary and you always run the risk of losing someone you love, but you don't really believe it. Not until it happens. Then you can't believe you ever took it for granted. I've watched some of my friends lose their husbands, and I've held their hands as they mourned and grieved. I told them I understood, and that time would ease the pain, but I didn't understand. I had absolutely no idea what they were going through, I only imagined I did. None of that's prepared me even the tiniest bit for the possibility of losing your father. I can't imagine never hearing that deep laugh again, or seeing that sparkle in his eyes when he looks at me, feeling his arm around my waist or his lips on mine. But for all that, and the undeniable heartbreak I would feel should I lose him, I would never choose not to have loved him." She stopped, unable to continue.

Nicole got up and put her arms around her.

"We're not going to lose him, not now," she said fiercely.

Eleni looked at her daughter. "I want you to experience that same kind of love. Don't close your heart Nicole."

Nicole hesitated, wanting to tell her mother about Peter, but afraid of her reaction. "Well, I think I have felt that kind of love, but things didn't work out."

Nicole sat down and Eleni looked questioningly at her.

"Peter Demetrios." She watched her mother, waiting for a reaction. Eleni's face registered surprise and disapproval.

"Do you want to tell me about it?" she asked quietly.

It took her a few hours to tell her mother the entire story. "I'm afraid I'll never experience those feelings with another man," she finished.

Eleni shook her head sadly.

"Nicole, what on earth were you thinking? Those are not the values you grew up with. I've always been so proud of you, but you've really let me down this time."

She would have preferred anger to the quiet disappointment her mother expressed.

"I'm not proud of it Mom. I couldn't help it. I fell in love," she said simply.

Eleni softened as she saw the pain reflected so poignantly in her daughter's eyes.

"Oh Nicole, in many ways you're still so young. I'm sorry you were hurt. So often, we mistake excitement and adventure for true love. Love isn't so much a feeling as it is a commitment. There are times when you think the sun rises and sets on the man you love and other times when you're almost indifferent. Love is like life, it has seasons. The beauty of love is in knowing that you'll both be there for each other at the changing of each season, no matter what. Knowing that you can bare your soul to your mate and regardless of what he sees, he won't run away. Love isn't about looking at each other and being blinded to each other's faults, but rather seeing each other's faults and loving each other anyway."

"That's all well and good, but you've told me how when you and Dad were dating, you used to thrill to his touch. How you felt like there were a thousand butterflies in your stomach when you were with him. I felt that way with Peter."

"Honey, I did feel that way, but things were different when we were dating. A kiss was as far as any respectable girl went before she married. The way you date today, you wear out those feelings before you ever get to a serious point in the relationship. There was so much more mystery and intrigue. I've learned over the years that the excitement comes and goes, but it's the love that lasts. Are you saying you aren't attracted to Michael?"

"No. I'm very attracted to him. I just don't get that same giddy feeling I had with Peter. Peter had so many characteristics that reminded me of Dad, I really looked up to him."

"Darling, Peter couldn't be very much like your father if he would allow his weaknesses to take advantage of you."

Nicole started to protest, but Eleni continued.

"You're a very beautiful and intelligent young woman. Your adoration would be difficult for any man to resist. But you are sixteen years younger than he. Aside from that, he knows your family, and he had to know we wouldn't approve. Even if your father and I had a terrible marriage, he has too much integrity to ever get involved in that type of situation. I'm sure to you, it must have seemed even further proof of Peter's love, that he would take such risks. Sweetheart, that is not the hallmark of a strong man, but a weak one."

Nicole was quiet, upset by her mother's words.

Eleni continued. "Let me tell you a story. When your father and I were first married, he worked constantly. In the beginning I adjusted, especially when you kids were small, because that kept me plenty busy. Once you were in school and I had more time on my hands I went through a period where I felt dissatisfied. Oh, I still played bridge and had lunch with the girls, but a part of me knew there was more to life. I started spending my time in the library and art museums, trying to drink up culture and expand my horizons. After a few months, I noticed a particular man at the Walters Gallery. No matter when I went, he was there. One day he approached me and asked if I'd like to have lunch. Flattered and nervous, I politely said no. We talked for a few minutes and then I left. I stayed away for a few days, but then, unable to resist, went back the following week. He was there. I had decided that if he asked me again, I would go. He nodded hello, said a few words to me and that was it. I was so disappointed, then immediately felt guilty for even considering spending time with him. After a few more weeks, he asked me again and I went. He was fascinating. Here I was, a young housewife in her early thirties, having lunch with a dashing man in his late forties. He seemed so worldly, unlike any other man I'd ever met." Eleni stopped a moment and took a sip of her coffee.

Nicole listened to her mother in astonishment.

"He was a writer from New York here on sabbatical. He wrote books on art and culture. He was mesmerizing. He had traveled all over the world and regaled me with anecdotes from his many trips."

"What did he look like?" Nicole asked, enthralled.

"He was thin and he had round wire- rimmed glasses. Nothing out of the ordinary. Until he spoke. Then his eyes sparkled with passion and his whole face came alive. He was one of those men you'd never look at twice, but once you got to know him you'd think he was the most handsome man around."

"Did Dad know about him?"

"We'll get to that. I started meeting him for lunch every Tuesday and Thursday, and we'd spend hours talking at the downtown cafes. I could never figure out what interested him about me. I felt so ordinary next to him, so very pedestrian. He would ask me to tell him about the three of you, how you were doing, what funny things you had said that week. He made me feel as if my life and my experiences were riveting. On the weekends, I found myself looking forward to the week, so that I could see him."

"Were you in love with him?"

"Patience, patience. After about three months of this, your father started noticing a difference in me. I was using phrases I'd never used before, talking about new things. My attitude was different too. I had more confidence, more self-esteem. I guess it was attractive, because it sparked a whole new flame in him. He made more time for us to be alone, took me out to dinner more often, paid more attention to me. He was really listening to me, interested in my views and what I had to say. It was then that I slowly realized the root of my attraction to Max. It was not just his attraction to me, but the way he encouraged me to cherish my curiosity and expand my mind. I had lunch with him one more time, thanked him for what he had done for my marriage, and never saw him again."

"That's it? What about him? Was he upset?"

"No darling, he understood who I was. He knew from the start that an affair was completely out of the question. He enjoyed our friendship for what it was, and never tried to take advantage of my inexperience. He was my 'older man' and for a while he brought out all those same feelings that you described earlier. There's something very exciting and a little scary about an older man taking an interest in you. It's not hard to confuse those feelings with true love."

Nicole smiled at her mother and thought about her words. She could almost picture her sitting at a cafe with Max, so young and innocent, drinking in his every word. The picture was similar to her memories of herself and Peter. Perhaps her mother was right, there were many faces of love. Maybe she hadn't seen them all yet.

Chapter 46

*T*hey were back at the hospital early the next morning. Eleni pulled a chair next to the bed, and stroked her husband's cheek.

"Nick, I know you can hear me. Darling, I know it's terribly difficult, but you must wake up. You have to fight. I need you and I will not let you go! It's not time, my darling. You belong here, with us." She had to get through to him. Years of memories flooded her mind and she was unwilling to concede his absence from her future.

She spoke with greater urgency. "Do you want to miss the birth of your first grandchild? Remember how bittersweet Paul's birth was for you? How it broke your heart that your father hadn't lived to see his own eyes reflected in his grandson's? Please be here for yours."

She was unable to contain the sobs that escaped her lips and she ran from the room and cried unashamedly until she could cry no more. She felt a hand on her shoulder and turned to see her son standing behind her. He opened his arms and she was encircled in his loving embrace.

"It's going to be okay Mom. I promise," he whispered.

"Oh, Paul. What if it's not? I don't think I can live without him."

Costa saw the huddled figure of Eleni as he emerged from the elevator and rushed to her.

"Eleni *mou*, if I had known I would have come back sooner." He had just gotten in from Athens last night.

"Costa, I understand. I'm glad you're here now."

"How is he?"

"Still in a coma."

He shook his head. "It should never have happened. Well, our Nicko, he's gonna be just fine." He sat down next to Nicole and squeezed her hand.

Soon the entire family had gathered.

As the day progressed, family members and friends stopped by to inquire about Nick and comfort Eleni.

"Tessie stopped by this morning with a casserole for you, Eleni. I took it over to the house and put it in the fridge. She asked me to tell you to let her know if there's anything she can do," Eve said.

"That was sweet," Eleni said.

"My phone's been ringing off the hook. All the girls send their love. They're all pulling for him."

"I spoke with John Longaris and asked him about this doctor. Says he's got a great reputation and that he would pick him if he needed a neurosurgeon," Dimitri told Eleni.

"Thanks Dimi, I appreciate it."

Eleni thought again how grateful she was for her friends. Her mother had always stressed the wisdom of staying in touch with her girlfriends and how important they would become over the years. She had been right. She looked over at Sophia and smiled.

Sophia was proud of her family in this time of uncertainty and apprehension. They had drawn together around Nick and Eleni, supporting them with their prayers and their presence. She was thankful to be alive to see the fruits of the teaching she and Andreas had tried to instill in their children and grandchildren. Sophia's own mother, Vasiliki, had not been so fortunate. By the time Sophia and Andreas could afford to make the long voyage back to Greece, Vasiliki was dead. She never saw her daughter's children. It was only now that her own children and grandchildren were grown that Sophia fully appreciated just how much her mother had missed. Perhaps she was too busy as a young woman to give it much thought or perhaps it was too painful to dwell upon in those days when there was nothing she could do to remedy it anyway. But now she realized the emptiness that she and all the other immigrants left in the souls of parents who knew they would very likely never again set eyes on their offspring, their parenting abruptly terminated and ended forever. Her mother had never challenged her decision to leave for America and never, she now realized, allowed her to see the sorrow she felt at her departure. They were brave, these parents who were left behind alone and childless. And they were openhanded in their unstinting generosity to let go.

Chapter 47

*T*he next morning finally brought the dawn. Eleni's call awakened Nicole at six thirty.

"Your father's out of the coma!" She was jubilant.

"Oh Mom, thank God! I'll be right over."

Nicole freshened up as quickly as she could, threw on a pair of jeans, grabbed a sweatshirt from the top of her dresser and ran down the stairs. She couldn't wait to see him and the sense of urgency mounted with each passing minute. What if he slipped back into a coma before she got there? She tapped her fingers impatiently on the steering wheel as she waited for the light to change.

Nick tried to ignore the dull throbbing on the top of his head and pay attention to someone who was speaking to him. She was squeezing his hand so tightly that it hurt. He blinked his eyes several times, trying to focus, but everything remained blurry.

Eleni watched him apprehensively. When she had gotten the call that he was awake, she envisioned a joyous reunion. After so many days of agony, living in terror that he would be forever lost she anticipated . . . if not a celebration, at least a smile. Looking at him, she suddenly realized how unrealistic she had been. It didn't keep her from being disappointed, however, and her heart had broken when she walked in to see him and he stared blankly at her. She was relieved to see him off the respirator and breathing on his own, but there had been no tears of joy, no smile of recognition or embrace, only his ability to follow the simple command to hold up two fingers. What would she do if he no longer knew her? She rose wearily and walked out to the nurses' station.

"Is Doctor Silvers here this morning?" she asked.

The nurse consulted a clipboard. "Yes."

Eleni looked up to see Nicole approaching. Nicole's step quickened when she saw her mother.

"How's he doing?" she asked breathlessly.

Eleni hugged her. "He's resting now."

"Can I go in?"

"Sure honey, just don't expect too much."

They continued back down the hallway arm in arm. When they reached his room, Nicole walked over to the bed and took Nick's hand in hers. She gave it a gentle squeeze and felt him respond. She wished that he would open his eyes. He looked so vulnerable and she had the feeling that he was very far away.

"Dad, it's Nicole. We're so relieved that you're okay. I love you." Her voice broke.

His eyes fluttered and with effort he opened them. As if from a great distance, he saw two fuzzy figures and opened his mouth to speak but the words wouldn't come. He felt as though he were floating in a pool of marshmallows, every effort to hoist himself up failing as he sunk into their soft substance. Somewhere in the recesses of his mind, he knew he had to break out of the fog. If he surrendered to the seductive beckoning of this slumber, he would never awaken again. But it would be so easy to relax his mind and drift away. Why wouldn't they leave him alone? The dizzying feeling was both exquisite and excruciating. His attempt to attain coherence required him to summon every bit of strength he had, but still, it was inadequate. It was so much nicer gliding on the clouds. Nick struggled to emerge from the deep. He was hundreds of feet underwater in a dark, muddy cave.

He swam furiously, kicking up the mud until he couldn't see in front or behind him. A small voice called from the distance and he was determined to reach it. His lungs were ready to explode and he thrashed violently, striving to surface from the murky nadir. He continued to press on, the voices in the room a foghorn summoning him to safety. He could see rays of sun painting the top of the water. Suddenly, with great force, he broke the surface and greedily gulped the sweet air. He opened his eyes and looked at his wife. He was back.

Chapter 48

*T*hat afternoon Nicole went to her godfather's office. He was sitting at his desk studying a long document. "Nicole. Have a seat."

"Boy am I glad you're back. We've got a lot to talk about."

"Tell me about it. Something is rotten in Sweden," he said.

She laughed. "I think you mean Denmark, Uncle Costa, but you're right, something definitely stinks."

She handed him a copy of the letter she had given to Nick.

"This is my last copy, so we should make another. I went to see my father the day of the accident and left this with him."

Costa read the letter and quickly reviewed the attached list.

"I found it hidden in Stewart's in-basket. I'm sure there are more like it."

Costa shook his head slowly as he read.

Nicole hurried on. "I've been through all the cost sheets and things don't add up. The first thing..."

"I know. I've been here all night. Who the hell are all these new subs Stewart hired? I've never heard of half of them, and the ones I have, I wouldn't use for free. I've been through the job folders over and over, and it doesn't make sense. Either Stewart is the biggest pigeon anyone's ever seen, or he's on the take."

"My money's on the latter." Nicole remarked dryly.

"There's no other explanation. Stewart's been around the block. He's no dummy. He paid full price for garbage. The flooring alone was over three million dollars. With what he put into this job, he should've brought it in at half the price. And the timing doesn't add up. I've made a few calls to some friends. I think we'll have more answers by the end of the day."

"What kind of answers?"

"Let's wait until I know more," he replied cryptically.

"If he has been taking kickbacks, there's got to be some kind of a trail. These aren't tiny companies. They can't just have cash sitting around for the taking."

"I was thinking the same thing," he said. "I don't know. I've searched every nook and cranny of this place, including Stewart's office. Nothing. Completely clean."

"Uncle Costa, why do you think that ceiling collapsed?"

"That's what I intend to find out. You just sit tight. If he did what I think, he'll be paying for a long time."

It was useless to try and get information from him before he was ready.

"When will you hear from your friends?"

"This afternoon. In the meantime, keep thinking about that trail. We must be missing something."

"Okay. Call me as soon as you hear anything."

He nodded his head, already immersed in whatever he had been reading when she came in.

When Nicole reached her office it was buzzing with activity. Two of the marketing assistants stopped her to ask if they could have some time with her that afternoon. She pulled out her Palm Pilot and scheduled them in.

"Any messages Nancy?" she asked before going into her office.

"I've put some on your desk but here are two more that came in just a few minutes ago."

She shut the door, sat down and massaged her neck. As much as she disliked Stewart, she had never imagined him to be a thief. If their suspicions turned out to be correct, the ramifications were mind-boggling, but they couldn't voice their concerns without proof. Then it hit her. She picked up the phone and dialed the familiar number.

"Hi. How're you doing?" Nicole said.

"I'm okay."

"Have you confronted Stewart yet?"

"No, I was going to talk to him tonight"

"Could you hold off a day or two?"

"Why?"

Nicole repeated her conversation with Costa. "What if Stewart has the records somewhere in his office at home? If he has been taking money, there must be some kind of proof. I don't know, phone records, odd deposits, something. If you could pretend that everything was okay for a couple of days, we could look through his things and try to find some evidence."

"Yeah, I can do that if it'll help. Come on over. We have to be careful though. Does he have any idea you suspect anything?" Theodora asked.

"I don't think so, but I may have tipped my hand a little. I talked to him a few days ago about the complaints we've been getting on Manor Hills, but he doesn't know I've pulled all the records," Nicole said.

"Well, it wouldn't be hard for him to find out. Hopefully he won't give you enough credit for checking up on him. He told me he's got a dinner meeting tonight and won't be home until after nine. Why don't you come over this afternoon and we'll see what we can find?"

"Good." Nicole was a little worried. Maybe she was asking too much. She was filled with concern for Theodora and the baby.

"Maybe you shouldn't stay there. He could be dangerous."

"I'll be fine. He's not going to do anything to me."

"I'm serious. Maybe you should come home with me tonight."

"Don't worry. He'll be out of here soon enough."

"Well, all right. I'll see you this afternoon. Be careful." Nicole said.

"You too."

Nicole hung up and couldn't shake a premonition of danger. She hoped Theodora was right and that there were limits to what Stewart would do. She was beginning to wonder if he even possessed a conscience.

She picked up her phone again and dialed Costa's extension.

"Yeah?"

"I just got off the phone with Theodora." She gave him the highlights.

"Good. I have a feeling we'll find the final pieces of the puzzle there."

"We?"

"You don't think I'm letting you go over there alone do you?" Costa said protectively.

"It would look a lot less questionable if Stewart came home and only I was there. If he sees you, he's going to know there's something going on."

"Well, we'll have to be fast then. You may not know exactly what to look for. Besides, I don't feel comfortable with the two of you all alone at that deserted house."

"You're starting to make me feel creepy. Is there something you're not telling me?" Nicole said.

"I don't like the picture that's developing of your brother-in-law. I would just feel better not taking any chances. Humor an old man, okay?"

"I'll come by and get you at three thirty."

"See you then," he hung up.

She looked at the stack of messages on her desk, and systematically returned each call. For the next few hours she buried herself in her work, happy to be busy and to have a temporary respite from the disturbing thoughts that plagued her.

Chapter 49

*C*osta shook his head as he listened to the voice at the other end of the line.

"When will you have the final results, Sam?"

"The report will be completed this afternoon."

"Any way you can stall the insurance company a few more hours? Just 'til tomorrow morning?"

"I don't know..."

"I wouldn't normally ask this of you Sam, but there're some things I need to check before this becomes public. As soon as this hits the street, the people responsible will start covering their tracks, and it may be impossible to nail them. I'm hoping I can get a jump on them and prevent that from happening."

The man hesitated only a moment.

"What the hell? What difference will a few hours make? Sure. I'll put the guy on another case for the rest of the day. But that's the best I can do. Tomorrow morning it's out of my hands."

"Thanks Sam, I owe you one."

Costa hung up the phone, and made his next call. Disguising his voice to hide his accent, he asked for Mr. Miller.

"I'm sorry sir, Mr. Miller isn't here today," a nasal voice informed him.

"Do you know where he can be reached?" he asked.

"I don't have that information, would you like to speak with his supervisor?"

"Yes, please."

A few minutes later a man with a high-pitched voice answered.

"Dwayne Ingerman, may I help you?"

"I hope so. This is Dr. Logan calling," Costa lied. "Brian Miller is one of my patients, and he's missed his appointments several weeks in a row. I'm getting concerned about him."

"I don't know what to tell you, doctor. I'm a little concerned myself. He didn't show up for work on Friday or today. I've tried calling his apartment but there's no answer. If he doesn't come back tomorrow, that will be three days absence without calling, and he'll be automatically terminated."

"Is it like him to miss work?"

"Well, I shouldn't really say this, but he hasn't been the most reliable worker. Pretty smart guy but a little on the lazy side. Missed a lot of Mondays, I guess partying too hard on the weekends. Always called though. Would you like for me to have him call you if I do hear from him?"

"No, thank you. Maybe I'll just check back in a few days. Thank you for your time."

"Sure thing."

Costa hung up. He grabbed his car keys and left the office. He had one more stop to make.

He turned the air on full blast as he pulled out of the parking lot. In the short time it had taken him to walk to his car, the hot muggy air had caused beads of perspiration to run down his neck. He couldn't wait for fall, he thought, as he wiped his neck with his handkerchief. Thirty minutes later he pulled into the parking lot and slid his car into a space marked 'visitors.' He looked up at the white stone building as he approached the entrance. A navy blue sign over the door read 'Barley & Summers Testing.' He walked up to the receptionist and stated his business.

"Just a moment please." She made a quick call, and then motioned for Costa to sit down. "Mr. Ingerman will be right with you."

Costa sat down, picked up the latest Fortune magazine and flipped through the pages, too distracted to concentrate.

"Mr. Metrolis?"

Costa looked up to see a rather slight man standing in front of him. He stood up and shook the man's hand.

"Yes. Nice to meet you."

"I understand you have a question about a slump test our company performed?"

"Yes. It would've been back in March." He pulled the certificate out of his pocket. "Here's the certificate attesting that the cement was up to par. I'd like to see the actual results of the cylinder tests."

The man examined the certificate with a puzzled look. "This is odd. I'm familiar with all the cases I've assigned to my people, but I've never seen this one. I'll be right back."

Costa sat back down. Fifteen minutes later Ingerman was back.

"I'm sorry Mr. Metrolis, but I have no record of performing that test for your company. There is no file."

"What about this certificate?"

"It's signed by Brian Miller, but he obviously never submitted the samples to the lab." A look of worry flashed across the young man's face.

"Does this have something to do with that accident I heard about on the news? Something about a ceiling caving in. What was the name of the development where it happened?" He suddenly looked alarmed. "Look Mr. Metrolis, I don't think I'd better talk to you anymore. If you have any other questions, you'll have to talk to the president."

"Thanks for your time," Costa said, and walked down the steps and out of the building.

As he drove toward the beltway, a deep frown furrowed his brow. He could have sworn he saw a paid bill for the slump test in the job folders. He would have to find the check and see if it had cleared, and to what account it had been deposited. He thought of his best friend lying in the hospital and was filled with sadness. Oh Nick, what happened? You should have seen this one coming a mile away. He sighed deeply. He really couldn't blame him. He supposed you should have a blind spot where family was concerned. One thing was for sure, he was going to get to the bottom of this and do whatever he could to help his friend.

He looked at his watch. He had forty-five minutes to get back to the office and meet Nicole. He looked ahead and saw the flash of red brake lights in every lane. Great, he thought. He slowed his car to a stop and tried to see ahead to the cause of the delay. The cars weren't moving. He cursed out loud as he looked at his watch again. After ten minutes, the cars began to creep forward. At this rate, he'd be lucky if he made it back to the office in an hour. By three thirty, he had gone another three miles and could see ahead to the accident that had caused the backup. The three right lanes were closed and all traffic was forced to merge into the remaining lane. Fifteen minutes later he had passed the accident and was moving again, doing seventy to try and make up for lost time. He was already fifteen minutes late and no matter how fast he drove, he knew he wouldn't make it in less than another fifteen. Come on Nicole, wait for me. This was one of those times he regretted his resistance to new technology and wished he'd gotten a cell phone.

Chapter 50

*N*icole buzzed her godfather's office for the fifth time. Exasperated, she stood up, grabbed her purse and punched Theodora's number on the phone.

"Hi. I don't know where in the world Uncle Costa is, but I'm leaving without him. I should be there soon."

"Fine. I've already started looking through his desk. So far I don't see anything to ring alarm bells."

"How did you get it unlocked?"

"Found his spare. He hid it under the computer monitor. Not very original."

"I think you're in the wrong line of work! All right, I'm leaving now. You're sure Stewart's not coming home early?"

"Yup. I called him a little while ago and asked him if he was sure he couldn't come home and have dinner with me. He apologized and took a rain check, the jerk."

"Okay, I'm on my way."

She hung up and walked out the door. As she backed her car out, she heard a horn blow and looked up to see Costa roar into the parking lot. She put the car into park as he hurried over.

"I'm glad you didn't leave yet. There's an accident on the beltway." He opened the passenger door and got in. Moving around uncomfortably, he found the knob to move the seat and slid it all the way back.

"We should have taken my car. This one's made for a midget," he grumbled as they pulled out of the parking lot.

"So, any news yet?" she asked

"I've found out a few things. Let's wait until we get to your sister's house. I don't want to have to repeat myself."

Nicole turned the radio on and they drove the twenty minutes without speaking.

Theodora had a pot of coffee waiting for them. They sat at the kitchen table and looked at Costa expectantly.

"Okay, here's the situation. We all know Stewart brought in a bunch of strangers for this job, right? Well, the way I see it, some he brought in because they were low bid and saved money, and some he brought in because he knew they could be bought. The HVAC contractor has a reputation for paying kickbacks. A lot of the purchasing agents for the big builders have supplemented their incomes with his little bonuses for years. Nicole, as you saw from the cost sheets, we didn't get any breaks on the HVAC/Mechanical costs, in fact, they seemed a little inflated to me, almost twenty six thousand a unit. On the surface, it looks as though they delivered as promised."

He turned his attention to Theodora and explained. "The sinks are pretty and all the fixtures work, but try and get cool on our typical ninety five degree days and forget it. The condenser units for the A/C are too small to properly cool the units. All in all, I'd say Stewart made a deal with the guy to take a percentage of every dollar charged, and that's no small change, let me tell you. Now we get to the flooring. Again, same thing, at first glance, everything looks great, beautiful marble flooring, lush thick carpet, until you look at the padding, total trash." He paused, letting his words sink in.

"I'm with you so far, but all that proves is that Stewart acted like an idiot. We still don't know if he's done anything illegal," Theodora said.

"We're coming to that. Nicole, remember how we discussed the construction schedule and how the finish dates all moved up?"

She nodded her head.

"Well, after your father's accident it hit me. It had to be the concrete. Stewart must have had the sub-contractor add accelerator to make it cure faster."

"What do you mean?" Theodora asked.

"It normally takes concrete about twenty eight days to fully cure and harden. If you increase the portion of a substance made with anti-freeze, called accelerator, the concrete will cure in seven to eight days. The problem is that it compromises the integrity of the concrete."

"What good does that do if the concrete doesn't hold? Didn't he know he'd be found out?" Theodora asked.

"Not necessarily. In the Manor Hills case, there was a grand piano sitting right above where the floor caved in. The excessive weight of the piano was too much for the weakened concrete to hold. It's possible that if nothing heavy was placed there, it never would have happened."

"Are you saying that Stewart knowingly put peoples' lives in danger just to finish a job early?" Nicole asked appalled.

"I'm saying that Stewart worried only about making a profit and getting ahead. He knew that by finishing the job early, he would save Parsenis plenty of money in loan interest, not to mention an earlier return on investment. He wanted to look like the fair-haired boy."

"Do you have proof that the concrete was tampered with?" Nicole asked.

"Not yet but we will. The insurance company hired an independent lab to test a core sample. I spoke to a friend of mine who works there. The concrete broke at 1800 psi."

"Is that bad?" Theodora and Nicole asked in unison.

"Normal is 3500, and after it's set this long, it should've been even higher. It's real bad. As a favor to me, he's holding the results from the insurance company until tomorrow. Once they get the news, it will leak out and be all over the papers."

"What about the lab that certified it for the bank?" Nicole asked.

"I took the certificate back to the company that issued it. They have no record of doing the test. The guy who signed the cert hasn't showed up for work since Thursday. If you ask me, he caught the story of the accident on the news and took off."

"This is unreal! If you're right, then it's Stewart's fault that Dad is lying in a hospital bed right now," Nicole exclaimed.

She was too upset to speak, overwhelmed by the magnitude of what she'd just learned. Not only had Stewart wreaked emotional havoc on those closest to her, he had brought them all perilously close to financial ruin. If what her godfather said was true, they would have to go back to the finished units and replace all the concrete. Thank God they had discovered it now, instead of after everything was finished. With luck, they would be able to repair the damage before anyone else was hurt.

"Are you ready to have a look?" Theodora asked.

Nicole and Costa followed her down the narrow hallway to Stewart's study. She turned the computer on and they sat in silence as it booted up.

"Where do we start?"

"Let's have a look at his word processing files," Nicole suggested.

Theodora selected word processing on the menu and brought up a blank screen. She hit the function key for the directory and they looked over the list of files, finding nothing suspicious. Most were business letters or proposals he had written. They returned to the main menu.

"How about his spreadsheet programs," Costa suggested.

Theodora hit the selection for spreadsheets and the screen changed, asking for a password.

"It figures. Let me see if I can guess." She typed his initials and got an error. Then she tried "SAIL" and "BOATING", "HUNT", thinking he might use a hobby. She continued to try new words for the next twenty minutes.

"I'll bet I know." She typed "HEATHER" and the screen changed again. She was in the program.

"I'm hating him more and more every minute," Nicole muttered.

Costa just looked at her.

"Now what?" Theodora asked.

Nicole sat down in front of the computer and began looking through the files. "This one looks good." It was saved under "MONEY." Nicole retrieved the file and the screen was filled with columns of numbers. It was the household budget.

"Let's try again." For the next hour they retrieved file after file, still finding nothing. Costa stood looking over Nicole's shoulder the entire time.

"What's that?" Theodora asked pointing to the screen.

"What?"

"That sub-directory. Bring it up."

Nicole did as she asked. There were four files under the subdirectory "SES." She pulled the first file up, labeled "ONE". The three of them were quiet as they looked at the screen.

"Bingo," Costa said.

"What's the S.E. Supply Company?" Theodora asked.

"A little invention of Stewart's," Costa answered.

Nicole printed the spreadsheet. On it were various dates showing payments received. The payments were approximately two weeks apart and had started back in January. The total was over a half a million dollars. Nicole printed the rest of the files in the directory. They looked like invoices with the S.E. Supply Company name on top and a P.O. Box for an address. The invoices were for different kinds of building materials, and Nicole printed those also.

"If we can find this account I think we've got him," Nicole said.

"I think we have enough leverage to get him to spill everything. It'll be up to your father whether or not he wants to press charges," Costa said.

"I think he should rot in jail," Theodora said stonily.

"I agree *agapi*, but your family might not. Think of what this would do to them if it got out, not to mention the company. Don't forget, he's the father of that baby you're carrying. No, we've got to talk to your father, and let him decide," Costa insisted.

"But Uncle Costa, Dad's in no condition to deal with this right now. We can't do anything that would jeopardize his recovery," Nicole said.

"I know. That's why we have to keep quiet until I can take it to him."

"I don't know if I can stay under this roof for another minute with him." She was sickened by the discoveries.

"Maybe you don't have to. I don't see any reason you can't confront him about Heather. We don't have to let him know we're on to his business dealings," Nicole said.

Costa looked confused. "What are you talking about? Who's Heather?"

"The woman Stewart has been having an affair with," Nicole told him.

"*Vre Zon*, he's scum," Costa exploded.

"No. If I start, I'm afraid I won't be able to stop and I'll give everything away. I'll tell him I need to get away for a few days, maybe go to the beach," Theodora said.

"You're not going to go down there by yourself are you?" Nicole asked.

"It might do me some good, help me to sort my thoughts out. Besides, I think Yiayia and Papou had planned to go down last week, but didn't because of Dad. Maybe they'll come with me."

"That would solve one problem," Nicole looked at Costa. "You said the lab hired by the insurance company was putting their report out tomorrow. That's going to cause quite a stir. Don't you think we need to get a handle on this before the press gets it?"

"I've already started taking care of that. I talked to our attorney and some of our usual subs. I've had a statement prepared explaining the measures we're planning to take to correct the problem. The occupants of the sold units are being contacted and will be taken care of while the units are rebuilt. Luckily, there are only about fifteen. All the buildings under construction will have the foundations reinforced with caissons and steel beams. All in all, this will be a major financial undertaking, but we'll be fine. Thank God it was discovered at this stage of the project and no one else was injured. I don't even want to think about the consequences if it had gone on much longer."

"Uncle Costa, how are you going to do all of this without Dad?"

"I have his power of attorney. I don't need to talk to him about making restitution. I know it's the way he'd go and besides, we don't have a choice. He's conscious now, which means he could see the news or read it in the papers. I've got to talk to your mother and let her know what's going on. I think we may be able to keep it from him for a few days at least."

"What do you think Stewart will do when all this hits the fan tomorrow?" Nicole asked.

"Try to cover his tracks. I'm hoping he'll lead us to the rest of the proof we need. I plan to watch him very closely."

Theodora looked at the clock on the wall.

"It's almost nine, you'd better get out of here.""Are you sure you won't come home with me?" Nicole asked.

"I'll be fine. I'll plead a headache and turn in early. He won't even notice."

"No way. You leave him a note and come with us. You'll stay with your sister," Costa commanded.

Chapter 51

JUNE

*I*t had been one week since the night they discovered Stewart's scheme, and Costa was on his way to see Nick in the hospital. Theodora was now in Ocean City safely tucked away with Sophia and Andreas. As predicted, Stewart was behaving like a cornered animal. When the insurance company received the results of the core sample, Stewart put on a performance that far exceeded even Costa's expectations. He immediately began pointing the finger at the company who had sold them the concrete, claiming they had sold him the weakened mixture in order to make more money. It was difficult, but Costa and Nicole said nothing and deftly handed him another length of rope. The concrete had been purchased from Cherry and Sons, a reputable firm in business for over fifty years. In response to his accusations, they produced a cylinder they had taken before the concrete had been poured. Unbeknownst to Stewart, it was their practice to keep a cylinder from all the truckloads they supplied to protect themselves in situations such as this. The concrete was tested, and it was found to be perfect. He had really started scrambling then, coming up with a wild theory about a competitor sabotaging the job. Costa took over then, and relinquished the insurance claim, telling the investigator the company would take full responsibility for the damages. Stewart hadn't argued, obviously relieved to have the insurance investigator off his back. He also didn't argue when Costa told him he was off the project.

Costa tapped the breast pocket of his jacket. It contained the piece of paper they had been looking for. They now had all the evidence they needed to put him away for a long time, and Costa was on his way to the hospital, faced with the unhappy task of telling Nick that his son-in-law was a crook.

He had told Eleni there were problems with the job and warned her that soon everyone would know about the bad concrete, but spared her the details of Stewart's involvement. She and Costa spoke with Nick's doctors and asked them to forbid him television or newspapers. When Nick objected, the doctor explained that he needed complete rest for a full recovery. Visitors were restricted to Eleni only. The high dosage of pain medication caused him to spend most of his time asleep.

Costa had spoken with the doctor last night and was pleased. Nick was making good progress and would soon be transferred to a rehabilitation center for intensive physical therapy. Not wanting to do anything to hinder his friend's recovery, Costa asked the doctor if Nick was strong enough to handle some bad news. He recalled their conversation from earlier that day.

"What kind of bad news are you talking about?" Dr. Silvers wanted to know.

"There've been some serious problems with a development project which is going to cost the company a lot of money. It's not going to put him out of business by any means, but it'll be costly. There's already been a lot of press about the safety of the development and now we have reason to believe that there was criminal activity involved. There will be negative publicity once the entire story is out."

"I'm not sure anyone is prepared for that kind of news, but as long as there's nothing heroic required of him, I see no reason to keep it from him."

"No, no. I can take care of everything. I just can't in good conscience keep my friend in the dark. You don't know Nick, but I can tell you, he'd never let me forget it. He's a stubborn customer," Costa laughed and then his expression grew serious. "There's more, though.

I'm not at liberty to go into the details, but the rest of the story could implicate someone very close to Nick."

Dr. Silvers stared at him. "Are you sure about that?"

"Yes."

"If he's going to find out anyway, I think it would be better coming from a friend. Just take it easy and try to break it to him gently. What time are you going to see him?"

"Around six."

"I'll still be here. I'll stop by and see him later tonight."

"Thanks doc."

Costa sighed as he pulled into the hospital parking lot. He was assaulted by the alcohol and antiseptic smell when he entered the lobby. Unconsciously wrinkling his nose in distaste, he walked toward the elevator. He stopped as he passed the gift shop, turned around and went in. Impulsively, he purchased a colorful bouquet of fresh flowers, walked out of the shop and made his way to Nick's room.

The door was open, and Nick was lying in bed, talking to Eleni. His color was good and the sparkle had returned to his eyes.

"This is for you," he said awkwardly, as he handed the flowers to Nick.

"Costa, you shouldn't have," Nick said, mimicking the high-pitched voice of a woman, and they all laughed.

Costa kissed Eleni and walked over to pat his friend on the shoulder.

"When are they gonna let you outta this palace?"

"The doctor just left. It seems that my husband here will be walking in no time! He starts physical therapy soon." She looked at Nick, and they smiled at each other.

A broad smile appeared on Costa's face. "Thank God!" he boomed. "I was afraid to ask. Good thing too, who else would I do the sailor dance with?" he quipped.

Costa and Eleni exchanged glances, and she knew it was time. "Well boys, why don't I go to the cafeteria and get myself something to eat while you two catch up," she said.

"Okay honey. See you later," Nick said.

Costa pulled a chair up to the hospital bed.

"So, how are you really feeling?"

"Not too bad. Still some pain, but happy to be alive."

Costa just shook his head.

Nick's expression became serious. "Okay Costa, now that that's out of the way, what's really been going on? I feel like a sequestered juror, no T.V., no newspaper. Did the world blow up while I was out?"

"There are some problems," Costa began.

"Go on."

Slowly, Costa recounted the events of the past few weeks.

Nick was silent for a long time while he absorbed everything Costa told him.

"How is Theodora?"

"She's doing okay. She's at the beach with Sophia and Andreas. Apparently, she was ready to leave him before she even found out about his business scam."

"What do you mean?"

Costa paused. "He's been cheating on her Nick. From before her accident."

Pain filled Nick's face.

"That son of a bitch! I treated him like a son." Nick absently shredded into pieces the paper cup he was holding.

"How could I have been so blind? Both you and Nicole kept warning me, and I just wouldn't listen..."

"Nick, stop. You can't blame yourself. He's your son-in-law for God's sake. Even Nicole and I never imagined him capable of this. It's not your fault."

"You've done a good job," he said to Costa. "Exactly what I would have done. Thank you. Thank God no one else was hurt. When I think of the possibilities. Everyone is out of there, right?"

"Yes. We've moved them into temporary housing while the units are re-done. You okay?"

Nick sighed. "A few weeks ago I would have been a raging maniac, maybe I still will be when the full impact of this hits. Right now, I'm just grateful to be alive, that no one else was hurt, and that my daughter is safe. Facing death has a way of rearranging your priorities."

"What do you want me to do about Stewart?"

"Do you have any hard proof, other than the spreadsheet?"

Costa reached into his breast pocket. "Here's the canceled check for the concrete certificate. It was deposited into S.E. Supply Company, Stewart's bogus company."

"Good. First, get all the details out of him. Then I want to put him and whoever else was in on it away for a long time, so that they don't have the opportunity to jeopardize anyone else's safety."

"What about the publicity? Are you sure you want to expose the family to this kind of scandal?"

"No. But I don't want to be responsible for someone else lying in a hospital bed or worse. What choice do we have?"

"I guess you're right. I'll talk to Stewart tomorrow. It should be at least a few days before we have to get the police involved. When will you tell Eleni?"

"Not tonight. I don't have the strength, and after everything she's been through, I'd like to spare her for as long as possible. I'll talk to her after you fill me in on what happens with that filth."

Costa stood up. "I'm sorry Nick. I would've given my right arm to prevent this."

Nick looked at his friend of thirty years. "I know. You're a good friend. We'll get through this. We've made it through rougher waters."

When Costa left, Nick closed his eyes. Suddenly he was very tired.

Chapter 52

*C*osta dialed Nicole's extension and impatiently tapped his pen against the phone while he waited for her to pick up. After three rings she answered.

"What took you so long?" He asked peevishly

"I was getting something out of the file cabinet. What are you in such a pleasant mood about?"

He immediately felt apologetic for his curtness. "Sorry, I'm a little on edge this morning. Why don't you come over to my office? I think we're finally ready to pull the rug out from under your brother-in-law."

Her heart raced.

"I'm on my way." She replaced the receiver before he could respond. She had been waiting for this day for the last week, but now that the time had come to confront Stewart, she felt her palms sweating. She was glad her godfather was running the show.

He was looking out the window with his back to her when she came into his office. When he heard her enter, he turned around and Nicole admired the well-cut black silk suit and starched cream-colored shirt he wore. Small gold cuff links reflected the light, the only pieces of jewelry other than the thin Swiss watch on his wrist.

"Sit down, Nicole, and I'll bring you up to date."

She sat down and waited.

"I spoke to your father yesterday and told him everything. He wants us to go all the way with this, even if it means putting Stewart behind bars. We've got all the proof we need. I left a message with his secretary that I want to see him the minute he comes in."

Nicole looked at her watch. It was noon. "Where is he?"

"I don't know. His girl told me he wouldn't be in until after lunch. He'd better not be at Manor Hills. I told him I'd have him physically removed if he stepped one foot on that job site. What does your schedule look like today? Do you have any meetings outside the office?"

"Nothing I can't rearrange. I'll clear my calendar and stay on stand-by. Call me as soon as he comes." The voice on Costa's intercom interrupted them.

"Mr. Metrolis, Stewart Elliott is here to see you."

"Thanks, Joseph, send him right in." He looked at Nicole. "Are you ready, *koukla mou?*"

Stewart was taken off guard by Nicole's presence in the room. He looked at Costa and then back to Nicole trying to assess the situation.

"What did you want to see me about Costa? There's a lot I need to take care of today. I haven't got much time for a meeting," he bluffed his way through.

"You don't know how little time you've got Stewart. Sit down," Costa ordered.

"Now just a minute," Stewart began and Costa's deep voice interrupted him.

"Shut your mouth Stewart, because I'm getting tired of you, and believe me, that's not good." He went to his desk and picked up a thick mound of papers. Walking over to the sofa, he tossed them onto the mahogany table in front of Stewart.

"Did you really think you would get away with this?"

"I don't know what you're talking about Costa," Stewart said indignantly.

"Give it up, Stewart. It's all there. The bogus little supply company you set up, deposits into that account from sub-contractors. You scammed that job from every end. I've looked over every inch of it. You did some pretty fancy footwork, but you got in over your head when you tampered with the concrete, Stewart. Now we're talking more than just greed. You almost killed someone."

Stewart snapped forward to the edge of his seat in alarm. "I didn't do anything with the concrete. If Cherry & Sons poured bad concrete, I swear to you I had nothing to do with it. You've got to believe that. You saw the report. Yeah, I took money from those guys. But Costa, they came to me. They begged me for the Parsenis account and told me they'd make it worth my while. I know now it was wrong, but I was thinking of Theodora and the baby and how much I could do for us."

Nicole wanted to knock his teeth out. "You've never thought of anyone but yourself," she said.

Costa put his hand up to silence her.

"It's no good, Stewart," he said, pulling the canceled check from his pocket and waving it in front of Stewart's face. "The final piece is right here. You never called for a test on the concrete. You had a phony bill sent to us from the lab and you deposited the check we issued to your own account. You knew someone would get suspicious if the check never cleared."

Stewart's face turned scarlet and his lips drew back in an ugly sneer. He looked at Nicole.

"You've never accepted me. I wasn't good enough for your precious little sister. No matter what I do, you're always looking down on me, condemning my very existence. I'm sorry she didn't marry a nice Greek boy. That's what you really wanted, isn't it?" He continued to rant. "You framed me. You'd do anything to be rid of me, you hypocritical, prejudiced little bitch." He was drenched with sweat.

"Enough!" Costa yelled and pinned Stewart against the wall, his hands around Stewart's neck. He leaned close to his ear. "You'd better shut up before I kill you, you bastard. You have no one to blame but yourself. You are lower than scum." Costa turned his head and spat on the floor as he released Stewart.

Nicole rose from her seat and looked her brother-in-law in the eyes. It took everything she had to remain calm and speak in even tones. She drew a deep breath.

"I've wanted nothing more than to be wrong about you Stewart. Do you really think I want my niece or nephew to grow up without a father? But you are right about one thing. I haven't approved of you from the beginning though it has nothing to do with your not being Greek. It has to do with you not being human. You have no decency or kindness in you. You're a selfish, unfeeling monster who has almost destroyed my family. I feel sorry for you. You have no idea what it is to love and be loved." As the words left her lips, she realized that they were true. Rage and indignation still filled her, but pity had also taken up residence in her heart.

Stewart knew he was defeated and tried to appear remorseful. He hung his head "Costa, I'm sorry. I was out of control. Please give me another chance. I'll change, you'll see," he begged.

"Give you another chance? My dearest friend almost died because of you. You put countless lives in jeopardy. We're looking at millions of dollars in costs to repair the damage you've caused. It took us years to build the reputation we enjoy in this city, and you've almost destroyed it. What should I give you another chance to do Stewart, slit my throat?"

Stewart made no reply and Costa went on. "No, your chances are over. Here's what you're going to do. You're going to go to the police and confess everything. I want to know who was involved with you in mixing the concrete. They're going down, Stewart. If you go to the police voluntarily and name them, maybe you can cut a deal. You're still going to serve time, but it might go a little easier for you. You've got twenty-four hours to decide if you go freely or we have you arrested."

Stewart stared down at the floor, his face ashen. He looked up at Costa. "What about Theodora? And the baby? Have you thought about what this is going to do to them? How can you send her husband to jail? I thought you people stuck together."

"We do," Costa answered. "But you're not one of us anymore."

Chapter 53

S tewart left the building without bothering to go back to his office. He had to get a hold of Theodora. She would feel sorry for him and talk to her uncle. She would smooth everything out for him. He got into his car and picked up his cell phone as he pulled out of the company parking lot. What was the number in Ocean City? He pulled his briefcase onto the passenger seat, keeping one hand on the wheel. With his eyes fixed on the road in front of him, he felt around inside for the small black telephone book that contained the phone number of the apartment at the beach. He waited until he was stopped at a red light and opened the book to the page he wanted. He dialed the number and cursed under his breath as it rang unanswered for the seventh time. Where the hell was she? He glanced at the clock on the dashboard. Just one o'clock. He pulled into The Still and went inside to have a beer and think.

The telephone rang in Nick's hospital room. "Hello."

"Nicko, it's Costa."

Nick's hold on the receiver tightened. "What happened?"

"It's over. He denied it at first, but we had him dead to rights. I think he'll go to the police of his own free will. Anyway, I gave him 'til tomorrow. If he doesn't do anything, we'll have him picked up."

"Good. Make sure someone watches him, Costa. I don't want any more missing movements."

"I already took care of that Nick. You get some rest. I'll call you tomorrow."

Nick put the phone down and leaned back against the pillow. The pains in his back were starting to burn again, a signal that the nurse would soon be in with a shot. He closed his eyes and tried to ease into a more comfortable position. He decided he wouldn't tell Eleni anything until Stewart went to the police.

Stewart dialed the Ocean City number every half hour. Three hours and six beers later there was still no answer. He ordered another cold draft and once again dialed the number. He was about to hang up when he heard Theodora's voice.

"Theodora," he cried. "I've been trying to reach you all afternoon. I have to talk to you."

"What is it, Stewart? You sound upset." Her voice remained neutral.

"Theo, I'm in big trouble. You gotta help me. He'll listen to you, and everything will be okay then."

"What are you talking about Stewart? What kind of trouble? Who will listen to me?" She goaded him on.

"Your Uncle Costa. He's accusing me of stealing from the company and doing something to the concrete that made it collapse. He wants to put me in jail, Theodora."

"Did you do those things Stewart? Are his accusations true?" she asked already knowing the answer.

"Theo, I did it for you and the baby. So we could do the things we wanted, go the places we wanted to go. If you talk to him, he won't press charges. He'll listen to you," he was pleading with her.

"You did it all for us? Did you sleep with Heather for us too, Stewart? You never stopped seeing her. She called your cell phone, Stewart, the day I took your car to the hospital. She wanted to know where you were, why you were late. Tell me Stewart, were you just going to go on pretending things had ended, leading a double life? How could you look me in the eye and tell me you loved me? Whatever happened to turn you into such a monster?"

"Theo, don't do this to me. How many times can I say I'm sorry?"

"You could never say it enough. I'm leaving the beach now and I'm going home. I want you out of there Stewart. You have three hours to take what you want and get the hell out."

The line went dead. He gulped down the rest of his beer, threw a twenty dollar bill on the bar and left. He felt a little dizzy and fumbled with the key as he tried to put it into the ignition. He knew where he would go now. It was all Heather's fault, the scheming bitch. He'd make her tell them it wasn't his fault, that she had seduced him. Her apartment was just a few blocks away, in Timonium. He blew his horn impatiently at the moron in front of him doing twenty-five miles an hour. The driver slowed down even further, and Stewart pushed down on the gas and swerved to the side, yelling obscenities as he passed. Her car was parked in front of the building, and he pulled crookedly into the space next to it. In a matter of seconds he was at the top of the stairs banging wildly on her door and drunkenly yelling her name. Heather opened the door and faced him.

"What the hell's wrong with you? Are you crazy or something?" She spat at him.

He pushed past her into the apartment.

"It's all your fault," he screamed at her. "They know everything and it's all your fault," he repeated.

"You're drunk," she said disgustedly.

"And you're a manipulating little slut. You deliberately let my wife know about us."

"I've never talked to your wife in my life."

"She answered my cell phone when you called. And you, you stupid cow, couldn't keep your big mouth shut. They kicked me out. First Costa, then Theodora, and it's all your fault." He wasn't making any sense to her.

"What does Costa have to do with this?"

"He fired me today. He found out I took payoffs. You know what that money went for? All the crap you wanted. The jewelry and the trips. I did it because of you, and now I'm paying for it."

Her eyes widened in disbelief. "You miserable prick. You've conned your wife, you've stolen from your boss and now you're trying to blame me. I never asked you for anything. You were the one who needed to flash that platinum card around, Mr. Big Shot." She was seething now.

"Don't try to turn things around," he sneered. "You're going to tell them all that if it hadn't been for you none of this would've happened. I'm not taking the fall for you."

"You're crazier than shit. Get out of here before I call the police." She picked up the telephone and looked at him threateningly.

Stewart backed toward the door. "You won't get away with this," he hissed at her.

"Get out!" She screamed.

He tripped down the last five steps on his way out of the building and stopped his fall when he grabbed onto the metal railing. The sun was setting and soon Theodora would be back at the house. She had told him to be out, but he would go there and wait for her. He'd convince her to take him back. He started the car and jerked out of his parking space, heading toward York Road, his head throbbing and eyes blurred. Traffic was heavy and he made a left turn onto a side street taking a seldom-used route to Falls Road. Within five minutes he was on the familiar street, where no traffic lights would impede his progress. He picked up speed as he raced around the curves doing seventy miles an hour, straddling the line in the middle of the road, when he saw the truck. Instantly time moved in slow motion. The truck grew larger and larger, becoming a giant monolith about to engulf him. He heard the shrieking sound of metal crushing metal and then silence except for a low, persistent hissing. He was trapped, pinned to the back of his seat by the steering wheel pushing against his chest. When he tried to breathe the pain sliced through him like a liquid fire. Then he felt nothing. Only coldness. He knew it was over. Scenes from his life exploded in his brain with stunning velocity. Himself as a small child. Crying at his mother's feet while she lay in an alcohol-induced coma, oblivious to his terrified screams. His college graduation. Father absent from the happy crowd — tending to someone else's heart that day. His wedding day. Theodora's radiant face, full of hope and expectation for the future.

In those final moments, the realization of all he had foolishly thrown away became agonizingly clear. He had betrayed the woman who loved and believed in him. His blind greed almost killed the man who had treated him like a son and had stood ready to hand his kingdom to him. The family that embraced him in ways his own never did had all suffered greatly at his hand. And now it was all ending on this deserted country road, and they would never know how sorry he was. He heard the distant wailing of a siren. He would never see his child. He prayed then, with an intensity he had never experienced. He prayed for his sins and what he had done to the people he loved. He could barely think anymore, and his vision blurred. Then everything became dark. Theodora's image appeared before him, and he silently begged her forgiveness. Love our child for me, he implored. The sirens were deafening now, but Stewart heard only the sound of silence.

Chapter 54

*T*he service was almost over. Theodora sat ramrod straight, looking to neither side. The coffin was closed. It was customary in the Orthodox Church for the casket to remain open, but Stewart's injuries had been so extensive that she had insisted he be shielded from the scrutiny of the curious.

The priest now asked the mourners to come forward to pay their last respects, indicating the ceremonial portion of the service was finished. Theodora watched as they lined up to pay their last respects. She was surprised at the numbers. The church was filled, and many stood outside. The sad thing was that they were here not for Stewart, but for his families. Graham's patients and colleagues, friends and relatives of the Parsenis and Zaharis families. They came to pay their respects to them and to her. Most of them had hardly known Stewart. *She* had hardly known Stewart, she thought ironically.

Her family and Michael were the only ones who knew the truth about the events surrounding Stewart's death. She felt like an imposter over the last two days, accepting people's sympathy and condolences, and yet as much as she hated everything he had done, she didn't want his dishonor made public.

They filed past one by one. They kept coming. Many people she didn't know. She didn't have any tears left. They had all been used the first time he died for her. A heavy sigh escaped her lips, and she felt her mother's soft, slender hand come down to rest on hers. Eleni was so faithful and dedicated to them all. She was strong, like her Yiayia was. Theodora wondered if her child would be able to say the same thing about her, that she could always be counted on.

When she had gone to her mother's house the night after Stewart's accident and told her everything, Eleni listened quietly, without one word of reproach or questioning. She took Theodora in her arms and told her that it was finished now and time for Theodora to grieve and heal, assuring her she would be happy again. Theodora stayed there that night, sleeping in her old bedroom. It looked exactly the same as the day she had left it to go to her own new home, the same posters on the walls, the familiar bedspread and curtains at the windows. Her old stereo from high school days sat on a low table in the corner of the room. When she was ready to go to bed, she opened the closet to hang her dress and discovered clothing bags filled with her mother's winter clothes had moved into the space. She felt oddly dispossessed, as if she had been moved out without her permission. But as she looked around the room, at the empty bureau top where jars and bottles and trinkets once sat, she could feel that she didn't belong here any longer. This was not her home any more. She would forever be only a visitor in her mother's house.

She was pulled back to the present by the faint sound of her mother's whisper. She was saying something to Nicole seated on her other side. Theodora turned her attention back to the line at the casket and saw her Uncle Stephan. If the immediate family was now in line, that meant they were the last ones. Soon it would be her turn to walk up the three steps of the platform to her husband's coffin.

Eleni looked at her daughter. Theodora's face was pale and drawn. Around her eyes, the skin was slightly darker, giving her the look of one in chronic pain. She hurt for her. She thought of her own husband lying in his hospital bed. She had thought a hundred times today that it might have been him in that casket. He wanted to be here today, and she missed the strength on which she had come to depend. She couldn't imagine a world without his enormous presence. He was so much a part of her sometimes she didn't know where he finished and she began. How many times today had she turned to tell him something, only to realize he wasn't there? She had always hoped her daughters would find the same quality in their husbands, but she knew that times were different. No matter how modern she and Eve and their stylish friends seemed, underneath the veneer were still the girls who believed and lived what their immigrant mothers had told them about virtue and hard work and family. You took care of your children and your husband. You put them first and you made sure you kept a nice house and a hot meal on the table. You over-looked the things you could and you didn't complain. What you got in return was a comfortable home, a man you could depend on, and the time to be with your children. It seemed old-fashioned and out-dated to their daughters, this next generation. But something no one would have expected happened along the way as the years passed. Yes, there were many times they took each other for granted, but they grew to love each other in a deep and abiding way. She recognized it as the same love her mother and father shared. She finally knew that it was a love born of commitment, of knowing that no matter what, the other one would be there. Walking away from the relationship was unthinkable. And this formed the bond that held them together. The years had softened the love, but the glue underneath had only strengthened with time.

It was time for the immediate family to pay their last respects. They stood up together and Eleni saw Graham Elliott put his hand under his wife's elbow to steady her as she rose. She felt deep compas-sion for her and the suffering she was going through. Caroline had no one, Eleni thought sadly. The days ahead of her would be lonely and tormented. She studied Graham. The sparkle had gone out of those lively blue eyes. He would deal with this by working harder, Eleni thought. He would immerse himself in his work, saving more and more lives to make up for the one lost here today. She wondered if there was any way these two could bridge the massive chasm they had allowed to grow between them. She was glad the full truth had not been revealed to them. They should have their own memories of Stewart, ones that were not tarnished by the greed to which he had succumbed. They would have enough to get through in the months ahead.

At last it was their turn. Eleni rested her hand at the small of Theodora's back.

"I'm okay, Mom," she whispered softly. Theodora touched the top of the casket with a trembling hand and looked down at the shiny black box. The last time she had stood here was on her wedding day, filled with joy and hope for the future. She felt the baby kick. A fresh wave of sorrow swept over her, and she wanted to cry out to him, why, why did you let things happen this way? She turned away. As she descended the stairs, her eyes met her brother Paul's, waiting there with the other pallbearers. They were filled with sympathy and compassion. At the end of the aisle she stopped and waited to follow the coffin as it was carried from the church. In the distance she heard the sound of the tower bells, signifying the end of the rites performed here today. In a few moments she would be sitting in the cocooned relief of the darkened limousine.

The long line of cars began its slow crawl to the cemetery almost a half hour away.

"How are you doing?" Nicole gently asked her.

"I'm holding on."

Just barely, Nicole thought, and looked worriedly at Eleni.

"It's almost over, darling," Eleni said.

"I know Mom. I'm okay, really," Theodora stared out the window. It seemed somehow incongruous that outside people were going about their normal business. People were at work, stores were open, news was being made. It seemed to her that everything should have stopped, suspended, as she was right now.

She turned her head from the scenes outside. "Caroline called me last night," she said.

"Oh," Eleni said. "What did she have to say?"

"She talked about when he was a little boy, some of the funny things he did. She laughed and cried. It was probably the first real talk we've ever had."

The car turned and passed through the tall wrought iron gates at the entrance to the graveyard. They inched along the narrow and curving lane to the top of the hill, where rows of chairs sat beneath a green canopy. They stayed in the car while the casket was carried to the burial spot, and others began to take their places under the awning. Costa opened the car door and bent down until the three women were in his sight.

"Are you ready *pethia*? Everyone is waiting." He extended a hand to Eleni.

"Thank you Costa. I want you to sit with us." He had been their mooring through these last awful weeks, filling the void left by Nick's absence. She looked at him gratefully, thinking of all the times he had been there for this family.

He put his arm around his friend's wife and with his empty hand, took Theodora's. The threesome walked up the short hill and took their places next to Graham and Caroline. It was approaching noon and the sun's intensity was at its peak. The air was muggy, with no movement, making it difficult to breathe, and the canopy provided only slight relief.

Seated next to Theodora, Caroline wept softly. Theodora reached over to hold her hand, and her mother-in-law clung to it tightly. It was ending now, ashes to ashes, dust to dust, the familiar words that meant nothing until they affected you. They were taking flowers now, each one placing a single stem on the casket as they left. Theodora walked over to a large arrangement of white roses and took two. Walking back to where her husband's body lay, she put them down with the others.

"From me, Stewart, and from your child."

Chapter 55

*N*ick was packed and ready to go when the nurse wheeled in the chair that would take him for his final ride here. There was no question he was glad to be going home, but part of him clung to the safety and protection he felt here among professionals who anticipated his every need.

"Can't wait to leave us, huh?" the nurse asked with a smile.

"Not that I haven't enjoyed the treatment Sue, just ready for a change of scenery."

The nurses had come to care about him during his stay at the rehabilitation center. He was a great kidder and his mood was always cheerful, no matter how arduous the therapy. They looked forward to his jokes and light-hearted ribbing, and although happy at his progress, they were sad to see him go.

"We'll miss you around here," she said, giving his shoulder an affectionate squeeze as he settled into the wheelchair. He was overcome, unable to stop the tears of relief and apprehension that filled his eyes. But there was no time to dwell on these ambivalent feelings as Eleni and the girls burst into the room carrying shiny helium balloons of red, purple and yellow and talking all at once.

"How're my girls?" He reached out to Eleni, and she leaned over and wrapped her arms around him.

"Wonderful, now that you're coming home." His wife looked into his eyes with tenderness.

Nick's heart swelled with gratitude as his eyes drank in the stirring sight of his family. He looked at Theodora. She's starting to look better, he thought. Their lives were beginning to get back to normal. Theodora had come to see him in the hospital the day after the funeral and they had talked for hours. It had been a liberating experience for them both. As much as he regretted Stewart's untimely death, he was thankful that Theodora would be spared the additional pain of a divorce and the humiliation of her husband going to jail. He still couldn't understand why Stewart had done it. The experience had shaken Nick and caused him to re-evaluate his faith in his own judgement. It was impossible not to be left with a degree of cynicism.

He was forever indebted to Costa who had taken the reigns and settled everything for him. The public had never learned the full truth, only that there were structural defects with the building that had been fixed. The publicity had hurt them, and it would take a concentrated public relations effort to restore faith in the company. Since Parsenis had relinquished the insurance claim and made restitution on its own, there was no investigation. It had cost them plenty and it would put Nick's retirement off for a good many years, but he was grateful to be alive, to have his family and to still have a company to salvage.

He was home at last. As they walked to the front door, he pulled a leaf off a bush, rubbed it between his fingers and held it up to his nose, inhaling deeply.

"It's good to be home," he said

Eleni looked at her husband. He looked tired. "Okay, time to rest."

He started to protest, but she wouldn't hear it. "You're still the patient," she declared.

"You win," he relented, suddenly exhausted.

She helped him into the bed, arranged the covers around him and pointed to a porcelain bell placed on the table next to him.

"Remember that?"

Nick had bought it for her years ago when she came home from the hospital with Paul. He told her to ring it whenever she needed something. It had driven Sophia crazy when she came to stay with them to help with the baby.

"Of course," he smiled.

"Now it's my turn to come running when you ring."

In a few moments he was asleep and the girls went into the living room with Eleni.

"Thanks for helping me this morning," Eleni said to her daughters.

"Of course. We wouldn't dream of not being here," Nicole replied.

"I'm so happy to have your father home. One thing I have enjoyed is all the time I've been able to spend with him. I almost feel like we're newlyweds again. We spend hours just talking and holding hands. I've never felt closer to him," Eleni reflected.

Nicole thought about her mother's words and wondered if she could have that kind of relationship with Michael. She was startled to realize that she was beginning to think of him as a permanent part of her life, not able to imagine his not being there. Still, there was a part of her that resisted complete commitment.

Later in the afternoon, she tiptoed to her father's room to check on him. He appeared to be resting peacefully, and she was turning back to the kitchen when she heard his voice.

"Caught you. Checking to see if I'm still breathing?"

Nicole sat down by his bed. "Just making sure you were okay."

He took her hand in his. "It's been a pretty rough month, huh?"

She shook her head, too overcome with emotion to speak.

"What's the matter sweetheart?"

She began to cry. Nick tightened his grip on her hand.

"I was so scared I was going to lose you. Every night I prayed God would keep you alive. And then when we couldn't see you, I had this crazy fear that something had happened to you but the hospital wouldn't tell us. I'm so relieved."

"I'm not going anywhere honey. Promise. I've got to be around to walk you down the aisle one day."

Nicole was quiet. Nick looked at his daughter, this child who was so like him, and was overcome by his love for her. They had always shared a special relationship. She had been a daddy's girl from the moment she was born. He thought of how close he had come to dying and silently thanked God for his life and the family with which he was so richly blessed.

"Dad, none of this would have happened if I hadn't come storming into your office with that stupid letter." No matter what anyone told her, she still felt responsible for his accident.

"Nicole, that's crazy. You had nothing to do with it." Knowing his daughter and that she wasn't convinced, he continued. "Eventually, someone, possibly many people, would have gotten hurt or killed as a result of Stewart's actions. I couldn't live with that."

She was silent.

He continued. "No, there's a grand design, and we're all part of it. You did what you knew was right, just as I've taught you. I would've been disappointed if you had done anything else."

"But you always got so angry at me every time I tried to talk to you about Stewart."

"I know, and I'm sorry. I misunderstood your intentions. Please forgive me for not trusting your judgement. I still see you as my little girl. It's hard for me to admit you're a grown woman, a business-woman at that. I had a hard time casting you in the role of my protegé. I thought you were just biding your time working for me until you got married and started your own family.

"You mean you haven't been disappointed in me all this time, thinking Stewart could do a better job?"

He looked genuinely surprised. "Disappointed? I've never been disappointed in you. I've always admired the way you go after everything you want with both hands. I never compared you to Stewart. The old fashioned Greek in me was convinced I needed a son to take over my business. Stewart got the job without an interview. I see now how unfair it was to you. I didn't realize it meant so much to you."

"Dad, it's not the business that means so much to me, though of course, I care about it. I've wanted to do well to please you, to be a part of the world that you created. All my life I've watched you and the things you've accomplished with your incredible energy. You've built this hugely successful company; people look up to you and seek your counsel. You've always been a visionary. Since I was a little girl and you took me with you to job sites, I've wanted to grow up and prove to you that I could do a job you could be proud of. Everywhere I go in this town, people know and respect you. I'm so proud to say I'm your daughter. You're the most extraordinary man I know."

He made no attempt to hide the tears. "Do you know what accomplishments I'm most proud of?"

She shook her head.

"The three wonderful children your mother and I made. Everything else is just icing on the cake. There was one thought that kept me going in that hospital. It wasn't that I had a business to run, or a meeting to go to. The only thought that filled my every waking minute was that I couldn't bear to die without seeing you all again. I would have gladly given up every last penny for one more touch, one more kiss, from those I hold so dear. Nicole, never, for one minute, think that anything else means more to me than you."

Her heart swelled with love and gratitude. She stood up from her chair and hugged him.

"You should rest now."

"No more misunderstandings. If something's bothering you, I want to know. Okay?"

"Okay."

"By the way, are you still interested in running the business one day?"

She smiled at him through her tears. "You know I am."

"Good, this time I'm placing my bets on a winner."

Chapter 56

OCTOBER

*T*he gentle rocking of the boat lulled Nicole into a kind of half sleep. The sun was beginning to set, and in the stillness she could hear the lapping of water against the hull. She opened her eyes and looked up at the sky to see thin, pink clouds gliding like streams of ribbons across the blue. She hadn't felt such peace in a long time. The sailboat was anchored in a small cove off the Severn River. 'Gunkholing', Michael called it. There was something very soothing about being surrounded by only water and sky.

"Thought you might be getting thirsty." Michael offered her a tall glass of lemonade and sat down next to her on the deck. The cool liquid relieved her dry throat.

"Delicious. Thanks."

Michael wore white shorts and his sun-tanned chest and arms shone with a healthy glow. Nicole smiled as she looked at the familiar black lock of hair that never behaved, but rested instead on his forehead. She liked his face, the high, strong cheekbones, the full lips, always ready to smile. She was comfortable with him, more comfortable than she had been with any man. He almost made her forget Peter. Almost.

"Getting hungry?" he asked.

"A little."

He took a sip of her lemonade. "We can cook here or head into the marina for dinner. What do you feel like?"

"Let's cook," she answered, not wanting to leave.

In the galley below they prepared the meal with the easy efficiency born of many days spent together on this thirty feet of utopia. Nicole lit the small oil lamp as Michael brought the dishes to the table. He poured a few inches of merlot into their wine glasses. His hands were strong, reassuring, Nicole thought, watching. How would she have gotten through these days without his support and understanding? She looked appreciatively at him.

"I think these times on the boat have been some of the happiest days I've spent."

"I don't have to think about it. I know they are for me. I've watched you become more and more like the girl I first met," he paused. "But he's still there, isn't he?"

Nicole's eyes clouded. "Sometimes I wonder if I'll ever be able to forget him." She saw the pained look that crossed his face and hurried on. "It's gotten better, Michael, and your friendship has helped me more than you'll ever know. I can never repay you for your kindness."

He didn't want any repayment from her. He wanted her to know the incredible magnitude of his love for her and to return it. But he knew she needed time and he wisely held back.

"You don't have to thank me, Nicole. I'd do anything I could for you. You know that."

"There're times I wonder why you put up with me."

He put his glass down and looked into her eyes.

"I wouldn't be here if I didn't want to be."

She fingered the stem of the wine glass and turned it slowly in circles.

"I don't know if I can ever open my heart again, Michael. I won't lie to you, I still think about Peter and if he were free, I'd be with him no questions asked."

They were both quiet. Her words hit Michael with a force that surprised him. Somehow he'd always held out hope that one day she would come to him, finally over Peter, and tell him she loved him, but he realized now that day would never come. Whether she truly loved Peter or not, she believed she did and seemed almost to enjoy her role as the suffering muse. He was merely a diversion for her, a tonic she used to assuage the pain while she marked time waiting for the man she really loved. He would always be second best, runner-up, and even if she one day came to him, Peter would be there in the shadows, always a part of her. When he told Alicia goodbye, he did so because she deserved more than he was able to give her. Should he be any less kind to himself? He took a sip of wine and let the pleasant warm tartness linger on his tongue before he spoke.

"I don't know how to say this, Nicole." He paused. So sure was she of his unwavering devotion that she missed the edge in his voice and failed to see the determined look in his eye.

"What is it, Michael?" She smiled at him.

"I can't do this anymore." He took her hand. "You know the way I feel. The more I'm with you, the stronger my feelings are. But it's pointless, Nicole, because you're in love with Peter. I just can't do this anymore."

She was stunned. She had complacently assumed he would be there for her as long as she wanted him to be. In the single-minded focus she lavished on her own hurts and disappointments, she had been unmindful of Michael's frustrations, content in his care and affection. His words brought clarity. Of course it must end. There was no way to justify her holding on and continuing to hurt him, as much as it saddened her to admit it.

She took her hand from his. "I understand, Michael. I hate the thought of losing you, but I don't want to hurt you any more."

"Well," she said, changing the mood, "Let's get these dishes cleared up and head back.

On deck a million stars glittered in the dark October sky, and the water was still and flat. A cool western breeze swept over their skin. Nicole shivered, and Michael put his arm around her shoulder protectively. She nestled against him.

"My father's doing better. He's walking with a cane." She closed her eyes. "He's been so strong."

"You have that strength too, Nicole." He gently massaged her shoulder. "You'll make it through this."

Chapter 57

NOVEMBER

*C*aroline waited nervously for Theodora to arrive. She looked around the tiny room and thought it ironic that here, surrounded by walls painted a nauseating institutional green, she was finally beginning to find some peace. Stewart's death had rendered her paralyzed in a rigid vise of grief from which she thought she would never emerge. She existed, zombie like, able to continue breathing only because of the strong prescription Graham daily administered. Somewhere, somehow, she had found a tiny kernel of resilience and with it a determination to face the truth. Her son had died because he was drunk and behind the wheel and Caroline was to blame. All those years of self-delusion, believing that her drinking hurt no one but herself. She had been a horrible mother, allowing her addiction to take priority over the well-being of her son. Her method for compensating was to spoil him and give him anything he wanted. She had turned him into the shallow, weak man he'd become, and all for a lousy drink. She was unable to grant herself any clemency, and tears of guilt and shame sprang from her depths in an endless torrent. How would she ever forgive herself? She shook her head in sorrow and was flooded with regrets. For the first time in her life, she was seeing things clearly, but it was too late. Her son was gone forever, and nothing she did now would change that.

She recalled Graham's shock when she'd announced her plans to him.

"Are you crazy? Haven't we gone through enough without your giving everyone more to wag their tongues at?"

She had remained eerily calm. "Graham, I'm through living a sham. It's high time I took some responsibility for myself and admitted I have a problem. I'm finished living for the approval of others. I'm sorry if it embarrasses you, but I can't do it alone, and I won't continue like this any more."

"Why can't you just stop for God's sake? Ever the self-indulgent child. Is this another way for you to be the center of attention?" he asked angrily.

Caroline didn't have it in her to argue. "Think what you like. I'm checking in to rehab tonight, and I'm staying there until I get this life-shattering disease under control."

She had been here over three months, and he had yet to visit her. It didn't really surprise her. She wasn't angry with Graham. She was just as guilty as he in the disintegration of their marriage. Her drinking gave him the excuse he needed to cheat on her just as his cheating gave her an excuse to drink. What fools we've been, she thought sadly. When this was all done with she didn't know if she would have a marriage to return to, but she knew she'd have a life.

There was a knock at the door. She stood, inhaled deeply, and opened it. Theodora entered tentatively, searching Caroline's face for some indication of her mood. Caroline felt a stab of guilt as she realized how cruel she'd been to her daughter-in-law. She embraced Theodora and was relieved to feel her hug back.

"Theodora, please forgive me for how hateful I've been to you," she said without preamble.

Theodora's eyes widened in disbelief. Caroline laughed. "You're not dreaming dear. This old witch is really apologizing to you. Please come sit down and get off your feet."

Caroline reached out for her hand. "How are you feeling?"

"Tired mostly." Theodora patted her belly. "This little angel kicks all night. I haven't been getting a whole lot of sleep."

Caroline looked at Theodora's full stomach. "Not too much longer.

Savor every feeling, it goes by so fast." She began to cry and Theodora squeezed her hand.

"How are you doing? I can't imagine what you're going through." Caroline composed herself.

"Some days are better than others. So many memories go round and round and the recriminations are so difficult to take. I try to think of the good times and hold on to those." Her voice caught and she was quiet.

"Theo, I hope we can get off to a new start. I haven't had a drink in eighty-nine days and I'm going to do whatever I must to keep it that way. I failed Stewart but I want to be a good grandmother to his child and a good mother-in-law to you. Is it too late?" Her eyes beseeched Theodora.

"Oh Caroline, of course not!" Theodora blinked back tears. "I want nothing more than for my child to know his father's parents and to be loved by them. Despite everything that's happened, it would make me very happy if we could be close," she finished sincerely.

They spent the next hour talking about the baby and their hopes and dreams. As Theodora prepared to leave, Caroline took a small box from her nightstand and handed it to her.

"What's this?"

"Open it." Caroline said.

Inside was the most beautiful gold cross Theodora had ever seen. Caroline smiled at her. "It's been in my family for generations. My mother gave it to me when I got married, and I was supposed to do the same for my daughter." Her eyes searched Theodora's. "I would be proud if you would take it and carry on the tradition."

Theodora's heart was full. "Thank you so much, Caroline. I'll always treasure it."

Caroline's heart skipped a beat and she decided to take one more risk. "Call me Mom?"

Chapter 58

*T*he phone was ringing when Nicole walked in the door and she picked it up on the third ring.

"Nicole?" came the deep voice over the wire.

She was staggered. "Peter!"

"How are you?" he asked quietly.

"I'm fine," she answered, awkward and unsure of what to say.

"Nicole, Pat's left me."

Nicole felt as though all the air had been sucked from her lungs. "What?" she said, dumbfounded.

"I'm free, Nicole. We can be together. When can I see you?"

At once, the familiar churning emotions arose within her. The memories of those days and nights filled with anguish, when she'd been bereft at his absence, returned with stunning force. Was it really possible that they could be together? She was terrified of being hurt again, of exposing a wound that if reopened would never heal, but need overpowered her apprehension. She didn't know what to say.

"Nicole, are you there?"

"I'm here," she answered barely audibly.

He continued. "Nicole, we're meant to be. You don't find what we had everyday. Let's not throw it away. Do you want to live the rest of your life wondering what might have been?"

His words struck a chord. Wasn't Peter the reason she had let go of Michael? This had been her heart's desire for so long. Why was she hesitating now?

"Let me take you to dinner tonight. We can talk and make plans for the future. Don't say no."

The future. He was saying they had a future.

Suddenly she was exhilarated.

"Yes, Peter. I'll see you tonight."

At five to eight the doorbell rang.

"Peter. Come in."

"You look wonderful," he said.

"So do you," she said as they walked arm-in-arm into the living room. They sat facing each other, Peter's arm casually draped over the back of the sofa.

"So, tell me what happened," she prodded.

He shrugged.

"There's not much to tell. A few weeks ago Pat informed me she was taking the kids and going to stay with her parents, no warning, nothing. Said she was tired of the life we were living, always being in the public eye, never having any privacy. She told me I was never there for her, that my career had always come first, before her and before the kids. She was angry. I guess this has been pent up for a long time. We talked all night, and she told me that I would have to make some significant changes or the marriage was over."

"What did you say?"

"I told her I didn't know if I could make the changes she wanted."

"And she left?"

"Yes. Went up to her parents in New Hampshire. I've gone up there a couple of times to see the kids. We've done a little talking, but she's asking me to change my entire lifestyle. I don't know if I'm willing to do that."

Nicole caught the uncertainty in his words.

"What does all of this have to do with me?" she asked directly.

"I've been doing a lot of thinking. You and I, we love the same things. You're comfortable around people, you like the excitement of political life." He looked at her earnestly, "I think we'd make a great team."

Nicole studied him. For the first time, she noticed the tiny wrinkles around his eyes and mouth, how the skin around his neck was just slightly loose. She remembered the way he dealt with people, charming them with his smile, the epitome of politeness, but somehow not quite listening to their words. Always in control.

He spoke again. "As I was saying, before I turn myself inside out trying to repair a marriage that was never perfect, I wanted to see if you were willing to give us a chance again."

She cleared her throat and spoke calmly. "Let me understand. Your wife is willing to work things out provided you make some changes. You are ambivalent about the potential success of putting your marriage together and are hedging your bets by seeing if you can make things fly with me?"

Peter looked hurt. "I never was much good without a speechwriter," he joked weakly. "What I'm saying is that I'd like you by my side. With someone like you next to me, who knows the places I could go."

Suddenly she was struck by his selfishness. She supposed some women would be flattered to be placed in the role of the woman behind the man. Who was she kidding, a few minutes ago she would still have jumped at the chance. She looked at Peter and couldn't help comparing him to Michael. Michael never talked about her as if she were an asset to be acquired and he wouldn't dream of comparing her to any other woman. As a matter of fact, she realized sitting here, no matter what kind of a wife she turned out to be, she would never have to worry about Michael and another woman discussing their marriage. At that instant she knew beyond a shadow of a doubt that Peter was not the man she loved.

She looked at him. "You'll have to go those places without me, Peter."

He looked stunned. "Nicole, I swear, I won't hurt you again."

"It's no good," she interrupted him. "I'll always have warm memories."

"Don't you understand what I'm telling you? We can have more than warm memories. We can have each other."

"It's too late, Peter. That's not what I want. I don't love you, not the way I thought I did."

"What do you mean?" He came closer to her. "Nicole, this is what we've both been waiting for. We can finally be together. We can't throw this chance away."

"It's over, Peter. I'm sorry." She stood her ground and said no more.

"You're sorry?" He exploded. "Do you realize what I've given up? My whole world has been turned upside down."

"That's too bad, Peter, because mine has just come into order. Would you mind terribly if we didn't have dinner? There's someone I have to see."

He didn't know what else to do. "Do you want me to leave?" he sputtered, flabbergasted by her dismissal of him.

"Goodbye, Peter. Good luck."

After he left she grabbed her car keys and ran from the house. The half hour drive to Annapolis seemed to take forever. And then he was standing there, telling her to come in, looking slightly bewildered. His hair was tousled, and he held a thick manuscript and his reading glasses in one hand.

"Michael," she said breathlessly. "I'm so glad you're here."

He laid his work down on the coffee table, and they sat together.

"Has something happened?" There was concern in his eyes.

"Yes, something's happened." She told him everything.

"I've been so stupid, Michael. Everything I've ever wanted has been right under my nose, and I just couldn't see it." She looked into his eyes. "I love you, Michael."

He took her into his arms. "I've waited a long time to hear those words."

Chapter 59

IKARIA, GREECE

*T*he small boy's blonde ringlets bounced merrily up and down as he chased after the blue and white beach ball, his delighted laughter mingling with the soft sounds of the sea. When he finally did manage to catch it, his chubby little arms were barely able to encircle the rotund globe. Theodora laughed out loud at her son's pleasure and his determined attempts to tame the rolling orb. He was a beautiful child, the embodiment of all that was good in his mother and father, and she thanked God every day for the joy he brought. How many times she had looked at him at play or when he was sleeping and felt a love that was crushing in its power and depth, but her happiness was tempered by a deep sadness that he would never know his father. Stewart was not even a memory to their son, but a photograph, a picture to be painted, as he grew, by Theodora's stories and reminiscences. She would introduce him to the Stewart she first knew, the one she had fallen in love with. Nothing can alter a child's lifelong regret when death deprives him so early of a parent, but love covers many disappointments, and this child was loved fully and genuinely by so many.

One of those was his grandmother Caroline. This precious grandson enchanted her and she was able to express her love in a way that had been impossible with her own son. What a tragedy Stewart had never known the woman she had become.

Caroline had been sober since the day of Stewart's funeral. When

317

she left the rehabilitation center, she devoted herself to recovery. The selfish and self-pitying woman Theodora had first met slipped away; in her place was someone kind and giving, with a new outlook on the world and growing daily in confidence and purpose. She was grateful for second chances. She no longer lived life in a fog, fearful of people, fearful of her future, but faced life with peace and serenity. Caroline had put her regrets away and lived to the best of her ability in today. To their mutual surprise and delight, she and Theodora had forged a strong friendship. Theodora was thankful that her son would always have a connection to his father's family.

She scooped up the wriggling little bundle and carried him to the umbrella and chairs where Sophia sat. They hadn't been back to Ikaria since that summer, it now seemed so long ago, right before her wedding.

"He loves the beach, just like his mama." Sophia pulled him onto her lap and hugged him to her, stroking his thick blonde hair. He nestled against his great-grandmother's breast.

Theodora smiled at the picture of contentment.

"Ah, Yiayia. It feels good to be here again."

"You are healing, my little one, that is why it feels good."

It was true. She had finally left her mourning behind and was now able to embrace life again. It had been a terrible year and they had all endured enough heartache for a lifetime. She couldn't deny, though, that much good had come from it. Valuable lessons had been learned and a deep appreciation for love and joy had sprung from the ashes of their suffering. A vivid picture flashed through her mind, and she smiled as she remembered the beatific smile on her father's face when he first held his new grandson. No one tried to hide the tears at that most exquisite of gatherings, the celebration of a new life. Surrounded by three generations of family, they welcomed a fourth. It was then that she knew everything would be all right. She remembered her grandmother's words. "Life is like our circle dance," she had said. Theodora looked over at her son sleeping peacefully, his head against Sophia's shoulder. They had come full circle.